and he was real . . .

She had thought she was dreaming, when he made love to her by the *Cailleach* Stones. She could feel his wrist beneath her hands, the rough hairs and the powerful muscles corded under his skin. And his pulse, as real warm blood pounded through his veins.

That deep Scottish voice—like warm whiskey seeping into her every pore.

"Where are you?" Bella asked the empty room.

"I'm seated on your bed, lass."

"I can't see you," she whispered.

"You saw me once," he whispered back.

Bella blinked. The brief, vivid image of the Scotsman in the kilt. Big, tall, dark-haired, with eyes the color of the evening sky . . .

Maclean.

Also by Sara Mackenzie

Coming October 2006

SECRETS OF THE HIGHWAYMAN

SARA MACKENZIE

RETURN OF THE
HIGHLANDER

AVON BOOKS
An Imprint of HarperCollinsPublishers

This is a work of fiction. Names, characters, places, and incidents are products of the author's imagination or are used fictitiously and are not to be construed as real. Any resemblance to actual events, locales, organizations, or persons, living or dead, is entirely coincidental.

AVON BOOKS
An Imprint of HarperCollins*Publishers*
10 East 53rd Street
New York, New York 10022-5299

Copyright © 2006 by Kaye Dobbie
Excerpt from *Secrets of the Highwayman* copyright © 2006 by Kaye Dobbie
ISBN-13: 978-0-06-079540-5
ISBN-10: 0-06-079540-9
www.avonromance.com

First Avon Books paperback printing: August 2006

Avon Trademark Reg. U.S. Pat. Off. and in Other Countries, Marca Registrada, Hecho en U.S.A.
HarperCollins® is a registered trademark of HarperCollins Publishers Inc.

Printed in the U.S.A.

10 9 8 7 6 5 4 3 2 1

Acknowledgments

My sincere thanks to Nancy Yost and Erika Tsang for their help on this project. I truly couldn't have done it without you! And for Anne Gracie and Sandy Curtis, who were there when the panic set in.

And I'd like to thank Donald Macdonald for his kind assistance with the Gaelic words and pronunciation. For those who would like to know how to say these words aloud, there is a glossary at the back of the book. For those who would like to visit Donald's website, the address is: *www3.sympatico.ca/donaldmacdonald/*

Prologue

*He felt it first. A sensation he could remem-*ber but had not experienced in a long, long time. His fingers uncurled, feeling, stretching out. He was in a cold and silent place, with the faint echo of breathing. He felt marble, smooth and icy. It was beneath his body, an unbending slab of stone, and he was lying upon it.

He opened his eyes.

Sunlight poured through the windows on both sides of the building, golden shafts that intersected as they reached the floor. The rest of the interior was dim. Gloomy and splendidly solemn.

Cautiously, wondering if he should, he pushed down with his palms and sat up. He was in a great cathedral, the architecture soaring above him, the stained glass of the windows brilliant as they were struck by the light outside. The air was cool, scented with incense and age. Beneath him was a marble tomb, only there was no effigy on the top of it.

He *was* the effigy.

As he turned his head, gazing about him, he saw the others. They lay upon their marble tombs, still and pale, as if they had been sculptured. But they were men, living men, with only the faint lift of their chests to tell him they were still breathing.

Nothing else moved.

The Highlander swung his long legs over the edge of the tomb and stood up. He felt remarkably strong and fit for a man who had been sleeping for . . . but how long was it? He did not know. And he did not really understand why he had been awakened now, at last. He was grateful, of course he was, but a sense of unease flickered across his senses.

"Your time has come."

The voice was close by, but it seemed to echo all about him. The Highlander turned swiftly to face his foe, his kilt swinging about his powerful legs, the *claidheamh mor* at his hip ringing as he drew it from its scabbard.

There was no one there.

Now the Highlander turned, slowly, holding the blade before him. The chapel was empty, and the effigies who were men did not move.

"Who is there? Show yourself!" he demanded, with all the arrogance natural to him in his previous life.

Once he knew he would have been obeyed instantly, and in his heart and mind he still expected that immediate response. The voice came again, above him this time.

"The world has moved on. Things have changed."

The vaulted ceiling soared overhead, but it was empty.

"*You* must change, too, Highlander."

"Where are you?" he spoke through his teeth. His dark hair swung loose about his shoulders as he turned from side to side.

"Once you were too blind to see. Now you will learn what it is not to be seen."

A step behind him, the swish of cloth over stone. The Highlander turned and there, at last, was his adversary. He blinked in surprise.

It was a woman, and though he knew it was a fact that women weren't any match for a man like himself, this one increased his tension rather than eased it. And so he kept his sword between them.

She was small, her face round and sweet like an angel's, her hair as red as flames. She wore a cloak, silver fur that gleamed like ice in the sun where the light from the windows touched her. Her eyes were ocean-blue and calm, and yet when he caught her gaze there was something dreadful in it that made his breath hitch in awe.

He knew that this was no ordinary woman. This was a *Fiosaiche*. A Gaelic Sorceress.

"I can only give you one chance to make recompense. To show me you are the man I think you are. To redeem yourself and cast off the burden you carry upon your soul." She shook her head at him, her expression fierce. "So many lives lost unnecessarily, Highlander. You must right this wrong."

The Highlander's brain was turning over her words, trying to make sense of them.

"Why?" he asked, and though he would not beg, he would never beg, his voice was husky with pain and inner turmoil. "Where am I? What must I do?"

"You have been asleep in the between-worlds for

over two hundred and fifty years, neither living nor dead," said the woman with the eyes that could see into his soul.

"The between-worlds?" He cast a quick glance about him, at the chapel, the windows, the sunlight outside. The between-worlds was dark and frightening, nothing like this, he remembered that much.

"I have created this place from memories of my own past," she said with a little smile. "It is not what you think. Nothing is as you think it, Highlander."

"I am dead, then?"

"You last walked this earth as a mortal man in 1746, but you will do so again. You are going home."

The *Fiosaiche* smiled. He felt dizzy and shocked at the same time, as if he had looked upon something he should not. "Take the chance I give you, Highlander," she whispered. "Use it."

There was a flapping, a whirling of the still air in the cathedral. A large eagle brushed past him and he ducked down, suddenly afraid. The *Fiosaiche* was gone, and so was the bird, and he was once more alone with the effigies. Other men, sleeping as he had been. Only now he was awake.

The Highlander slid his broadsword back into its scabbard. There was a doorway through the thin arches that formed a path forward. He began to walk toward it, his boots ringing out on the stone floor.

He didn't understand what he was doing here. The *Fiosaiche*'s words meant nothing to him. What wrong must he right? The Highlander never admitted he was wrong, not about anything. Such admissions meant weakness and the Highlander had never been weak. He was a chief, a leader of his clan, a king to his people.

He pushed the half-open door and stepped out and suddenly the light was too bright, blinding him, and he covered his eyes with a cry of pain. When he felt able, he peered through his fingers, and realized the brilliance was gone. He looked about him at the grim, deserted hills. He took a deep breath and the air was chill and sweet.

And it smelled good.

It smelled like home.

One

Late Summer
Drumaird Cottage
Present day

"I'm waiting for Maclean."

Bella was dreaming. She knew she was dreaming, but it seemed so real. She was standing in the ruins of Castle Drumaird and there was someone with her, an old, old woman with a green plaid or arisaid wrapped over her white hair, her skull-like face peeping out. It was a hag, a creature common in Scottish myth and folklore. Bella had dreamed about her before, but she had always been on the fringes of the dream, a distant figure who watched but did not speak. This time she was center stage.

"He's been away for two hundred and fifty years, and now he's almost home. At last this day is come."

The hag leaned closer and Bella flinched. This was definitely no living creature, despite the rasp of her sour breath. No woman could neglect her skin care quite this badly.

"With him comes danger for us all, but redemption, too, if he is brave and lucky. Aye, he is coming." Her voice grew sly. "Braw, handsome Maclean. Soon, soon. . . ."

Bella was waking up.

But the hag's face was pressed up against hers and would not go away. "You must beware, Arabella Ryan," it whispered.

"Of Maclean?"

The hag breathed a laugh. "Och, no, but there is danger. The door has been breached and *she* doesno' know it yet."

"She? Who are you talking about?"

"She! The *Fiosaiche*. The door has been breached and the creatures of the between-worlds can come through. You must beware especially of the *each-uisge*, the water-horse. It will harm ye if it can."

Bella's eyes opened and she groaned. What a weird dream. Her dreams had been particularly vivid lately, but this one hadn't really seemed like a dream at all.

He is coming. . . .

Bella shuddered. She eased her toes onto the floor by her bed and whimpered. It was cold. Make that freezing. The Highland version of central heating had failed to come on again.

Moving quickly, she snatched up her sweater and pulled it over her head, wincing when her long dark hair became tangled. She slipped on her red woolen coat, and wrapped it around her, ignoring the way it stretched over her rounded hips and large boobs. She wasn't a small girl and never had been. Bella was voluptuous, a look that was very much out of fashion these days, but she had been born this way and usually it didn't bother her. Except that, recently, she had begun to feel more self-conscious about her size than ever before.

Brian's doing.

There were warm socks on the chair and she pulled those on, too, and then her sweatpants. Better, but it was still icy. Her breath was forming her own personal cloud in front of her as she made her way down the narrow, creaking stairs and into the kitchen.

At least the fire in the Aga was still alive and well. It had taken months of her landlord's patient instruction, but Bella felt as if she had finally mastered the difficulties of getting peat to burn properly.

Bella reached out her hands and felt the warmth. She sighed and drew a chair up close, enjoying the sensation of thawing out. *Much better.*

Except that now the worries that had kept her awake most of the night returned. First in line was: *Where is Brian?* They'd argued last night and he had walked out and he hadn't come back. At first she thought he was sulking at the local pub—but the local pub was in Ardloch, a two-hour trip on winding roads through the hills. Or he had gone over to Gregor's place—their landlord had a farm on the road to Ardloch and kept his sheep on the moorland around Loch Fasail—but Gregor and Brian didn't get on that well. Then she thought he might have gone back to Edinburgh to his friends' home, to soak up their sympathy. Bella knew that Hamish and Georgiana had never liked her—they made it plain enough that they considered Brian was doing her a favor by staying with her.

"Well, the three of them deserve each other. Good riddance!"

Did she really mean that? With a sigh, Bella stepped across to the small window above the sink and peered out. Her car was there, parked in front of the cottage, but not Brian's. As much as she sometimes wished Brian gone, being all alone here was unsettling. For a moment the view distracted her, the sweep down to Loch Fasail, the desolate lake; the stark beauty of the surrounding rocky hillsides with their skirts of heather and gorse. The sun was awake and shining, but there were clouds hovering, as they always were in this northwestern part of Scotland.

Loch Fasail was famous for its unpredictable weather.

She and Brian had been arguing a lot lately. She didn't like to admit it aloud, but things between them hadn't been good for a long while. Bella had hoped that living out here with no distractions would bring them together, but so far that wasn't so. Once Brian had seemed so exuberant, so much the extrovert—a big bold lion to her scholarly mouse. They were opposites attracted.

But recently the scholarly mouse had discovered that the gap between what Brian wanted her to be and what she was had widened. He was dissatisfied with Bella's weight, her appearance, her career . . . everything. And where once she might have made an effort to change herself to gain his approval—well, she'd loved him, hadn't she?—now she wasn't sure she wanted to. The love had withered into mild affection and irritation, and then . . . What *did* she feel for Brian these days? More often than not he simply made her angry. She was usually a good-natured person, not easily upset, but even Bella could only be pushed so far before she exploded. The thing was, Bella could please herself or she could please Brian, but she didn't think she could please them both.

Not any longer.

Bella looked back at her life with a sudden, painful clarity. As a child she'd been a victim of her parents' bitter marriage breakup. *Victim*, such an awful word, but a six-year-old doesn't have much say in what happens between the adults in her life. They'd ended up with joint custody, but as the years went by her English mother met another man, remarried, and made a new family, and Bella ended up with her father, a U.S. diplomat. She'd lived in London, New York, Berlin, and Paris, the great cities of the world, and none of them had been home.

Her childhood had made her self-sufficient, and despite what others saw as her air of fragility, Bella did not consider she needed looking after. She was lonely, but she'd always been alone. Despite a succession of nannies and housekeepers, Bella had only ever had herself to rely on. And her imagination.

At thirty-two years of age, she'd taught herself to harness that imagination and make a modest living from it. Bella was a writer, and she knew she was a good writer, but she also accepted that her books had a limited market. She wrote about the lesser characters of history, not the great kings and queens but those who lived and died in their shadow. People didn't flock to buy her stories of obscure historical figures, no matter how well written, as they did thrillers about serial killers. But still she loved what she did. She wouldn't change it.

Brian had seemed to understand that. He'd promised to take a six-month holiday to allow her to work on her book, to put her first for once, but she realized now that whatever he might say, his needs and wants would always take precedence over hers, and he simply could never imagine it otherwise.

As for the core of loneliness deep at her center, few people even knew it was there. Brian hadn't filled it.

Maybe no one ever would.

The Highlander was walking. It hadn't taken him long to get into his stride, that loping walk that seemed to cover miles of rough country and tire him very little. He had found the old road over the pass and followed it down into the long glen that led the way north to Loch Fasail and Castle Drumaird. He met no one.

He felt as if he were all alone in the world.

The *Fiosaiche*'s words repeated in his head. Had he really been asleep for two hundred and fifty years? It was several lifetimes. What had he done to deserve such a fate?

But instead of answers, his mind was full of shadows.

At least he had remembered his name. It was Maclean. They called him the Black Maclean, because of his hair, but he had been baptized Morven. Only his mother called him that and he had long ago ceased listening to her. Aye, he was the Black Maclean, and it was a name to be reckoned with.

He tried to remember more, his thoughts running backward from the cathedral and the *Fiosaiche*. Tunnels of blackness, and wails and screams from the souls and creatures who dwelled there. The between-worlds, the place of waiting. And then back again, and misty mountains and his heart thudding as he ran. Snatches of fighting and shouting. Running hard with his men. He had the brief and tantalizing memory of a great and bloody battle. There was a woman with hair like gold and a pale, angry face—his wife maybe? And then back even further to his home, Castle Drumaird, and the peaceful splendor of Loch Fasail. Isolated, a world of its own, where he ruled absolute.

His thoughts came to a halt as he looked about him again, suddenly uneasy. Surely there had been more folk about when he came this way before? Crofters and villagers and shepherds. And the road was different now. Hard and black, it stretched before him across the moor.

The sound came from behind him, in the distance. A low roar, quickly growing louder until it vibrated through the road beneath his feet and into his body itself. He could see it against the purple heather. A shining black monster with glowing eyes. It ran toward him faster than the fastest horse. Maclean threw himself into the bracken that grew in the dip by the road, and rolled down a slope and into a puddle.

The monster rushed past, the heat and the stink from it making him cough and choke. And then it was gone, vanishing into nothingness, and silence reigned again.

He picked himself up. He was trembling, but he stopped it and held himself proud. His kilt was damp and there was mud down one bare leg, but he was unhurt. He knew he needed to get home as soon as possible. Home to Castle Drumaird, where all would be familiar and safe. Where he could feel like himself again.

He might recall very little of his former life, but surely a mere two hundred and fifty years would not make a deal of difference? Scottish history stretched back, timeless and bloody, into the darkness of prehistory. What was two hundred and fifty years? he asked himself a little desperately. No time after all. He would return, the chief of his clan, and they would accept him as they had always done. Whatever it was the *Fiosaiche* had in mind for him could wait.

Maclean set off again, but now he walked beside the black road, and he kept his ears open.

Standing outside the cottage, Bella breathed deeply, drawing in the chill air and opening her mind to the lonely beauty about her. There was a sense of timelessness here. This part of the Highlands was particularly isolated, too far from tourist attractions for most holiday-makers and too difficult to reach for the weekenders. Even the climbers and the fishermen were all heading back to their lives in the more populated areas of the south. Brian had gone; she was alone. And yet—she closed her eyes—there was an air of expectation, a breathless sense of waiting, a feeling that anything was possible.

Bella had never felt she had a real home, not in the sense of truly *belonging* to a place. For her the pull of

Loch Faisal was irresistible. Her heart had been captured from the day she arrived. She knew she could not stay in this place forever, but she could dream, couldn't she? Pretend she'd been transported back into the distant past. Of course, on a more practical level, there was still the need to buy food and the other necessaries of modern life. Gregor sold her milk and eggs and butter from his croft, and she had a small vegetable garden to one side of the cottage—what used to be called a kaleyard—but if she wanted anything else she had to drive the two hours to Ardloch.

She looked up in surprise.

There was a pony approaching by the path around the loch. With its shaggy golden coat, it looked used to being free. Certainly this was no child's pampered pet. Bella stood and watched as it came closer. The pony drew to a halt about thirty yards away and stood completely motionless, staring back at her.

Bella frowned. Was it really a horse? There was something odd about it. The shape of the nose, the elongated body . . . a wrongness that puzzled her. The way it was observing her was almost human. It trotted closer still and she realized its eyes were green. A clear bright green.

Deep inside her, in a place she had not known existed, fear stirred. A primitive superstitious dread passed down from her ancestors.

But even as she took a step backward, she found she didn't need to run. The pony had already turned about on its sturdy legs and galloped off with its tail streaming out behind it. Bella watched it go with a relief that seemed excessive under the circumstances. Was it

Gregor's pony? Bella had not heard him speak of one, and this pony was so strange and wild. If she believed in myths like the water-horse, then she might almost think . . .

Beware especially of the each-uisge.

The dream returned to her; the hag's words rang clear in her head.

The door has been breached.

But Bella quashed them, refusing to take any of it seriously. This isolated place could make you begin to believe the unbelievable if you weren't careful. The *each-uisge* was a creature of Scottish folklore, like the hag, and it lived in lochs and deep pools, changing from a horse or a pony into a beautiful young man or woman. It lured its prey to the water and drowned the unlucky victims, before feasting on their flesh. Animal flesh, human flesh.

Bella stopped her thoughts right there. "You've seen a wild pony, that's all. Get a grip, girl." She started humming to herself, and then singing softly. It was something she did when she was emotionally charged, to calm herself down. This time she chose an old America number about a horse with no name—it seemed to do the trick.

Back in the cottage she went through her daily ritual of starting up the diesel generator in the shed out back. At least now she would have electricity. The central heating and the hot water ran on a separate oil-fueled system that was supposed to switch on automatically when the temperature dipped, but it rarely did. The hot water was supplemented by the Aga. When she and Brian first arrived, Gregor had told them that the services were unreliable, but it had been early days then and "unreliable" was part of the charm of the place.

At least she could still access modern technology; even in this isolated corner of the Scottish Highlands she wasn't entirely cut off. A telephone line gave her contact with the outside world, or she could search Google and check her e-mail. She opened her laptop and booted it up.

Bella's books were scholarly, full of carefully researched historical detail, each character painstakingly assembled. She liked to think she came to know her subjects so well that she could accurately guess what they would have ordered for breakfast. She slipped like a shadow into their lives, infusing dried-up old documents with new flesh and blood. She didn't just write about the past, she lived it.

Bella's current work-in-progress was Morven Maclean, an eighteenth century Highland chief also known as the Black Maclean. At a time when men began to question the existence of God and turn to science instead, when machines were being invented to take the place of men, in a century known for its growing enlightenment, Maclean seemed positively medieval. And, according to the legend, he was also black-hearted, vicious, unprincipled, and in league with the devil.

Not the sort of man you wanted to come knocking at your door.

In his last years, the Black Maclean ran headlong into one of the worst periods in Scottish history. The 1745 Rebellion—which dragged on into 1746—and its aftermath made grim reading. Simply put, the '45 was a brawl between Bonnie Prince Charlie, fronting a number of Scottish clans, and the Duke of Cumberland, fronting most of England as well as some of the Scots. For the losing clans it was devastating enough.

For Loch Fasail it was catastrophic.

One hundred and fifty souls were murdered, a body count that exceeded Glen Coe. Because the Loch Fasail massacre occurred as part of a larger tragedy and subsequent social upheaval, it was not famous, and since it had taken place in such an isolated spot, no one knew it had happened until some time afterward, and by then it was too late to investigate it properly. Even if the authorities had wanted to.

It was shortly after the massacre that the legend began to circulate, insinuating itself into the minds of the populace until now it could be recited by any schoolchild within a hundred miles of Loch Fasail. The Black Maclean, so the story went, had been too cowardly to fight at Culloden despite a request from Lord George Murray, one of the Scottish leaders, so when he got there he made a deal with the English to save his own skin. When he returned home to Loch Fasail he must have been in a bloody-minded mood, because he set off northward to raid his neighbors' lands. This was where the part about Maclean being in league with the devil came into it, because he had ridden upon a coal-black horse that breathed fire from its nostrils. His means of transport aside, Maclean had attacked his neighbors but had then been cut down in turn. That would have been the end of it, a bloody end to a bloody career, except the English dragoons, never good at keeping their promises, had arrived in Loch Fasail and massacred everyone as a warning to others not to take part in a rebellion against the Crown.

Extreme stuff even for those extreme times.

It could be true, of course. Some of it no doubt was, and there were similar stories in other parts of the country to back up the clan warfare and the English double-dealing. But the more Bella learned about Maclean, the more she wondered.

Black Maclean did rule his people with an iron fist, but that wasn't unusual. Living here at Loch Fasail, in this isolated area, she knew the lives of the people had not changed in the hundreds of years before Maclean was born, and neither had the chief of the Macleans' absolute control over them. The Highlands lagged behind the rest of Scotland, and this northwest corner was particularly out of step. The folk here were superstitious and suspicious, clinging to the old ways. Life was uncertain, with disease and famine the main cause of death. The chief fed them when they were hungry, gave them drink when they thirsted, and when the neighboring clans declared war the chief called his clan to him with the fiery cross, and led them into battle.

In such circumstances the chief was more important than any distant king. His power over his people was absolute and if he was the sort of person Maclean was, he ruled by terror. Except that when she began her research, Bella discovered there was nothing in the scant historical records to back up the tale of Black Maclean being a bad chief, or even a mediocre chief, up until the '45 Rebellion. Quite the opposite. He gave his people prosperity, supported them in times of famine and disease, sought ways to increase their meager crops—no concern of theirs ever seemed too small for him to take an interest in it. He actually stood head and shoulders above his contemporaries, many of whom were unbelievably callous and careless with the lives of their tenants and tacksmen. But just because Maclean saw that his clansmen had food in their bellies did not make him a New Age guy.

Still, Bella found herself admiring him in a way she had never expected to when she began this project. He was a dominant male, yes, and a brutal man from a brutal time, certainly, but there was so much more to him than what had happened after Culloden, in those dark days at the end of his life. And as for the legend . . .

Maclean seemed *better* than that.

Bella knew she wasn't being objective. And it was the fault of the Edinburgh Portrait Gallery.

Eight months ago, when she'd gone on a visit to the gallery, Bella had never heard of the Black Maclean. She and Brian were staying in Edinburgh, and the gallery was somewhere quiet, away from Hamish and Georgiana and all their pretentious friends. She'd been dawdling through the rooms when suddenly there he was.

The Black Maclean.

She still shivered when she remembered. He was hidden away in a corner, yes, but he was so *powerful*. She hadn't known who he was, but it hadn't mattered then. Feeling strangely captivated and very alive, she had stood in front of his portrait for long minutes, her eyes caressing that face, that form. She'd been like a lovestruck teenager. Later she had begun searching for information on him in the major histories of the time, reading all she could find—which wasn't much. Who was he, what had he done? The more she delved, the more excited she became.

He might be a dark and tormented soul, but *here* was a man who deserved far more space than the official tellers of history had dealt him. Bella hoped to redress that with her new book, even though the records and accounts from those times were so very sketchy. Those from Loch Fasail had all been destroyed during the massacre, so she had to rely on mentions made by outside sources. She had been using the record repositories in Edinburgh, but on her last visit to Ardloch had discovered the little library there. Not expecting much, she had been astounded to discover it held a unique collection of histories from the local area.

Bella wanted to sit down there and then and read every piece of paper the Ardloch library held in its special history collection. Unfortunately, Brian had chosen that day to have one of his sulks.

"You're obsessed with that bloody man."

"I'm researching him for the book."

"He's a coward and a murderer, but you don't want to believe that, do you?"

"It's not a proven fact."

"Not according to you. Not very professional of you, is it? I think you're suffering from some repressed psychosis, something with a long name, that makes you more interested in a man who is dead than one who is living."

"Don't be ridiculous!"

"Come on, admit it. You sit and stare at his picture as

if he's your long-lost lover. What are you thinking about? Fucking him? You certainly pay him a lot more attention than you do me."

"Brian, please. . . ."

But despite her protests, Bella had felt a stab of guilt. Maybe she *was* obsessed with Maclean. He might be arrogant and brutal and dangerous, and a murderer to boot, but she couldn't get enough of him. Maybe Brian was right, and she would like to be made love to by him. Here she was, a well-educated, sensible woman living in the twenty-first century, and all she wanted was for the big bad Maclean to step out of his portrait and throw her over his shoulder and take her upstairs.

How sad was that?

Bella sighed and glanced down at her notes. She was wasting time again. Work, she needed to get to work. She had enough material to start writing the story of Maclean's life.

She wrote down *Chapter One* and stared at the two words as if they would give her inspiration.

"Okay . . . I can lead into it gradually, begin with a brief retelling of Scottish history and Maclean's place in it. Or . . . I can begin with a bang."

Bella began typing.

Morven Maclean, born in 1716, was destined to be the last chief of the Macleans of Fasail. Dead at thirty, he must take responsibility for one of the worst civilian massacres in Scottish history.

With a sigh she backspaced and pressed the delete button.

Brian was right. Again. She didn't really believe it; or maybe she just didn't want to believe it. She didn't want to spoil her fantasy.

Bella shivered. She always felt attuned to the subjects of her books, she couldn't have written about them otherwise, but in the case of the Black Maclean the feeling was much stronger than normal. While she was appalled by the darker parts of the legend, his complexity as a man intrigued and fascinated her. She'd even hunted down a reasonable copy of the portrait of him that had first caught her attention, and now it glowered back at her from a spot above the bookshelf.

Bella's eyes drifted to it more often than she was willing to admit; it still had that spellbinding effect on her.

She looked at it now.

He was seated, a handsome man, clothed in tartan trews and a romantic white shirt with a fall of lace over his strong hands. A plaid was fastened over his left shoulder and a broad strap over his right shoulder held the broadsword—the *claidheamh mor*—in its scabbard, which rested at his hip. Dark hair was loose to his shoulders, framing a face that was rectangular and long and clean-shaven. His brows were dark, drawn in a slight frown over intense pale blue eyes.

He leaned forward toward the artist, as though something had caught his attention, his hands clasped on the arms of the chair. There was a sense that he was about to rise to his feet and stride out of the painting. Impatient, she thought, eager to get on with what he had to do. Arrogant, not willing to listen to the opinions of others. And passionate, yes, that, too. All the character traits that had worked against him and ensured his downfall, and that of his people.

The title of the portrait was: *(Reputed to be) The Black Maclean, Chief of the Macleans of Fasail, 1744. Artist unknown, in the style of Allan Ramsay.*

Reputed to be . . . well, maybe. But Bella knew it was him. Knew it beyond doubt.

Once again she found herself mesmerized, her gaze held by his. There was a savage beauty in his face, a dangerous wildness. If she had been a maiden living around Loch Fasail in the eighteenth century, she would have known instinctively that this man was a risk to her virtue and her peace of mind.

He's coming. . . .

Bella shivered again as the hag's words replayed in her head. Yes, she knew she was obsessed by him, awake and dreaming. Despite the fact that two hundred and fifty years had passed and the Black Maclean was long dead and dust, he was beginning to seem more real to her than Brian.

And wasn't that just a little dangerous?

Two

Maclean reached a village. It was a mere two dwellings and he did not recognize it; he was certain it had not stood here two hundred and fifty years ago. Glass windows were small and rare and precious, and the big bright squares of glass set in the walls of this dwelling were something he had never seen before. Warily, he noted that there were more of the monsters in front, smaller creatures these, of different colors. Several had passed him on his journey and he knew now that there were people inside them, making them work.

Maclean supposed he should have been shocked by these bizarre objects, but he wasn't. He was already assimilating them, accepting them as part of this new world he had been set free to roam. That did not mean he liked what he saw. The call of home was becoming even louder and more urgent in his head. He wanted to slam Castle Drumaird's thick doors and shut out all of this. He wanted the safety and security of home, his

home. It was still *his* and if whoever occupied it now
didn't like it, then too bad. He rested a big hand on the
handle of his *claidheamh mor*.

Maclean would fight to reclaim what belonged to him.

He could see people behind the glass walls, seated at
tables, eating and drinking. The smell of food was
strong, but it was also unfamiliar. Strangely he felt no
hunger. A man and woman strolled out of the door.
They both wore trews, even the woman, and they were
leading a dog. It wasn't like the dogs Maclean knew,
neither a beast bred to hunt nor a catcher of rats and
mice. He thought with a sneer that it was like something
a namby-pamby gentleman might pet upon his lap.

They weren't looking at him, but he expected any
moment that they would. He was a big man and he was
standing by the red monster, and they were heading
straight for it. The lapdog barked, showing its little
fangs. The man turned and gave the animal a frown,
while the woman cooed and spoke to it in a foolish
voice. "Stop it, baby," she mock-scolded, lifting it into
her arms.

The man said something to her and they laughed.
Wearing his fiercest expression, Maclean waited. They
walked right past him and climbed into the red monster.
It growled and then it moved away, out onto the black
road, leaving behind the usual heat and stink. Maclean
was frozen, staring in disbelief. They had walked right
past him. Worse than that, the woman actually walked
through him.

As if he weren't there.

Behind him more voices. Two old men, their faces

worn and lined by time. Desperate now, Maclean stepped forward, telling himself it must be a mistake.

"Dinna be afeared," he told them huskily.

The old men looked at him, looked through him, and walked to their monster, a yellow beast.

They canna see me.

A dreadful sense of loss, of sorrow, filled him. He was alive again, he had returned to the glens, but he was no more than a rattle in the reeds, a wisp of wind in the heather. A silent watching ghostie.

He lifted his head and howled out his grief and fury with a roar that echoed back to him from the hills.

And no one heard.

By afternoon Brian had still not returned. Bella wondered again if he had gone to Edinburgh and forgotten her. She had worked hard at putting him out of her mind, concentrating on her book instead. She'd mapped out a section on Culloden only to delete it again. Nothing pleased her. Nothing seemed *right*. She looked instead at Maclean's return to Castle Drumaird and what followed, but there were still so many missing facts, lost parts of the jigsaw. And Bella wanted to find them. Maclean's portrait stared back at her, daring her, urging her to discover the man behind the legend.

Her gaze slid to the window over the sink.

The sky was the pale porcelain blue color she loved. Of course, it might rain at any moment, but for now it was beautiful and she wanted to be outside to enjoy it.

Bella could never have one of those lean, prepubescent figures, she wasn't built that way. And she accepted that, although she wasn't always happy about it;

what woman was happy with her own size and shape? But lately Brian had been downright unpleasant. Bella was no petite and trim Georgiana, as he constantly reminded her, but she had plenty of traits to be proud of. It was just that Brian couldn't seem to see past her voluptuous curves. Now, every time she ordered dessert when they were together, he had that look on his face. As if he were judging her and finding her wanting.

Still, whatever her size or shape, there was absolutely nothing wrong with trying to get her body fit and healthy. And more importantly, there was a tub of chocolate peppermint ice cream in the freezer, and she'd feel less guilty about enjoying a bowl of it if she went for another walk.

Bella slipped on her pink padded jacket. Outside, the wind was chill and she felt it sting her cheeks into color as she looked up at the steep hill behind the cottage. There against that pale blue sky was the stark, vertical ruin of Castle Drumaird, a stronghold that had once overlooked the loch and all the land around it, as well as the people who lived here. The Black Maclean's people. The view from the ruins was well worth the climb.

Bella set herself upon the narrow twisting path to the top. *He* had once climbed this path, the Black Maclean. It was from here that he had set out with his men for the battlefield at Culloden, and so had begun the story that was now legend.

Two hundred and fifty years ago.

Hadn't the hag said that in her dream? *He's been away for two hundred and fifty years, and now he's almost home.* Bella stumbled, only just saving herself from falling. "Of course the hag said that," she reminded herself crossly. "She was part of *your* dream and that makes her part of you. *You* made it . . . *her* up." The hag said plenty of other things, too, none of which made much sense.

Halfway up the hillside the rain fell, a brief shower that made her dark hair curl and her trainers slosh. Bella continued up, determined now to reach the top. Her breathing was hard and painful—God, how out of shape *was* she?—but she told herself it was doing her good, and besides, the view was worth it.

She came over the crest of the hill. Broken and tumbled stone lay everywhere. Part of the keep still stood, the outer wall smooth and black and shiny from the rain. You could see how thick those walls had once been, how secure the inhabitants felt when their enemies came marching to make war upon them.

Maclean must have thought himself invincible as he gazed over his isolated kingdom. He must have truly believed he could live forever.

Bella took a breath, feeling her heartbeat begin to slow, as she, too, looked out over the glittering loch and moorland. It was empty now, deserted apart from a few of Gregor's sheep, but despite its tragic and bloody history Fasail was still beautiful. Lonely, sometimes bleak, but always beautiful.

It was strange, and she had never told Brian this, knowing he would deride her, but from the moment she'd set foot here Bella had felt as if she'd come home. After thirty-two years of wandering the world and feeling like a stranger in her father's houses, she'd finally found somewhere she belonged.

* * *

He was almost there. Home. The bewilderment and rage that pounded through him eased a little. The questions in his head ceased their endless demands. His lands were as empty as the glens he'd just walked through—where were his people?—but everything else was so extraordinary he did not want to consider the meaning of it now. He didn't dare begin to think of that. He just wanted to reach the security of his home.

Heavy rain was coming down into his eyes, and although he could barely see a yard in front of him he strode on, the powerful muscles in his legs working, his faded kilt swinging, his long dark hair plastered to his head.

Maclean passed a cottage, dim light shining out into the gloaming, smoke trickling from the chimney. It was odd that it was here, where no cottage had ever been before, but he wasn't going to waste thought on it when he was so close. So close to the place where he had been born and where he had lived and ruled. Men had feared and admired him, women had given him their bodies and their hearts. They had trusted him, followed him in the ancient unquestioning manner of a clan its chief.

And so they would again.

He reached the lip of the hill just as the rain stopped. There was a girl with a pale face and long dark hair, huddling beneath the doorway to the great hall. He wondered if she was real or a dream. And then he was looking up and up, and for a moment it was there, Castle Drumaird, soaring bleakly into the sky.

Then just as suddenly it was gone.

He blinked to clear his sight, thinking it was the rain. Only the rain. It could not be . . . his castle, his home. Broken, torn down, like some giant had swung his boot and kicked aside the pieces.

How could it be? That he had returned from the grave only to find everything he loved was gone.

Loneliness overwhelmed him as the rain lashed his face. In his quiet despair he wanted to weep, but the Maclean did not cry. He wanted to rail and shout, but he was too sick at heart to make a sound. He wanted to fall to his knees and allow death to claim him. But he was already dead, he *must* be . . . and yet he lived. The *Fiosaiche* had brought him back from death. His hands closed into fists at his sides, the rainwater dripped down his face and soaked into his clothing, and he stood in silence and faced the dreadful sight before him.

He lived, but now he had nothing to live for.

The girl was picking her way through the tumbled stones of what had been mighty Castle Drumaird. He watched her numbly, not allowing himself to hope that this time someone might see him. And, of course, she didn't. She reached a young rowan tree and grasped the slender trunk to steady herself as she jumped down into the sodden grass. It was overgrown and reached to her thighs, and she grimaced as she waded toward him.

A woman, he realized, not a girl.

Dark wet hair, a pale oval face and a lush body beneath loose, shapeless clothing. She turned her head and looked over her shoulder at the remains of the tower, and for a moment her profile was etched against the stormy sky. Despite his own grinding pain Maclean was struck by her beauty, and the cloak of tranquillity that enveloped her. She owned a still calm that Maclean in his pain ached to embrace.

The woman fastened her jacket with a shiver and moved in his direction, intending to go down the path he had just climbed up. As she passed him he smelled her scent, flowery and warm. She barely came up to his shoulder, but he was a big man. A chill gust of wind blew a lock of her long dark hair toward him . . . and through him. And then she was gone.

Maclean looked upon what had once been his beloved home and slowly, stiffly walked toward it. He did not understand what had happened here. He could only assume that during the long centuries when he lay dead, all he loved had crumbled away, leaving this sad monument to the past.

His head began to pound. There had been a battle, but not here. Brief vivid scenes of savagery. Culloden Moor? That name was familiar. The smell of campfires and food cooking, the low murmur of men and a sense of impending doom. Aye, it must be. He had fought at Culloden Moor and died there.

But with remembrances came a warning. Somewhere in his mind there was a nasty beastie, lurking, waiting to creep up on him when he wasn't looking and tear him to pieces. It was a pity he couldn't remember its name.

Maclean stayed among the ruins well into the darkness. His lands were empty and his home was gone; where else was he to go? Now and again there were flashes of long-gone faces, the call of dead voices, moments of merriment and sorrow, of everyday life. Again his head pounded, the memories making it ache, but he persisted. The night before the march to join the prince's army he had sent out the fiery cross to call his clan together, and they had feasted and drunk. He had sat at the head of the table in his chair that was more like a throne and gazed upon all that was his.

Lord George Murray has called me to join him at Culloden Moor, but dinna fear. Nothing and no one can hurt you. I will not allow it to happen.

They had believed in him, their father, their master, their king. In his arrogance he had thought himself untouchable. Only his wife-to-be, Ishbel, had reminded him in her cold and precise voice that he was not.

You are a man, Maclean, and all men can bleed and die.

Ishbel . . . aye, there was something else to be remembered about his betrothed, but instead he heard his father's voice.

Women are to be used and no' to be trusted. Do no' let them inside your heart, lad. They will destroy ye.

Maclean agreed. No woman had ever meant more to him than his broadsword and his dogs. And yet . . . Ishbel. Why did the name tease at him, as if there were something he was not seeing? Just as he had not seen it two hundred and fifty years ago.

Another rain shower came and he crouched and shivered. Why was it that although he was a ghost he could still feel? Still suffer? Still ache with sorrow?

A whiff of smoke came up from the cottage below and then the smell of cooking. Maclean lifted his head and sniffed. He was not hungry, but the homely smell brought with it a desperate need to find the company of others. To not be alone.

Slowly, stiffly, he rose to his feet and began the climb down the narrow path.

There was another monster sitting outside the cottage and despite his earlier distraction he did not think it had been there before. As Maclean stepped around it, felt the heat from beneath its hard outer shell, he heard voices from inside the cottage.

The light was still shining from the window, and he could see inside. The room was bright, and there were foodstuffs laid out upon a table. The woman he had seen earlier was preparing them by slicing them with a knife. Her dark hair had dried and lay about her back and shoulders in a mass of long, loose curls. She wore a blue robe, covering all but a V at her throat. He could see the shape of her breasts and the narrow curve of her waist where she had tied a belt of the same cloth as the robe. Her cheeks were flushed and as she leaned forward a lock of her hair fell into her eyes.

The fair-headed man standing behind her was taller, his face fleshy and ruddy as if he were jolly by nature. But from his narrowed eyes and pinched mouth Maclean knew he wasn't feeling very jolly just now. He was angry.

"This is a mistake." The man spat that last word out, and the woman flinched.

Three

This is a mistake, Brian had said.

"A mistake?" Bella repeated, tucking her hair behind her ear. There was a sick feeling in her stomach, just as there always was at the beginning of one of their arguments, but this time it was mixed with a flicker of flame.

"We should have taken a place in Edinburgh, somewhere closer to civilization."

"But we decided," she said. "We decided that this was the best place for me to write my book. You know how important it is for me to get close to my . . . my subject. And anyway, I thought you said we needed a holiday together. Just you and me."

Brian pulled a face as if she had said something particularly ridiculous. He was good at making her feel ridiculous.

The flame flared up a notch.

"Well, I've changed my mind. We only have six weeks left on the lease, and I'm sick and tired of roughing it in this hovel with nothing to do. Hamish says I can help him with his antique export business—he says I'd make an excellent front man."

"But you said you wanted a holiday! That you'd take a break from work so that we could spend time together." Not that Brian ever worked at any job for very long; he was always trying to "find" himself and so far the perfect profession had proved elusive. "You said you hated antiques."

"Did I?" Brian's voice was doubtful, as if she were making the mistake, not him.

"Brian, how can you change your mind like this?"

"I'm bored."

The silence was painful. Everything was falling apart and she couldn't seem to find the words to make it right—she didn't know if she wanted to.

"Let's pack now." He was smiling again, pretending it was just a minor hiccup. The liar. "We can be in Edinburgh by—"

"No."

The word surprised her as much as Brian, but as soon as she said it she knew it was the right one. For the first time Brian appeared uncertain, as if he might not get his way.

"No," she repeated it, and it felt even better. "I like it here. My writing is going well. I actually feel as if I'm in touch with my muse again. I'm not leaving now, Brian."

That look again, as if he could hardly believe his ears. "Your muse?" he repeated, and shook his head. Bella could hear his thoughts; he didn't have to say them aloud. *We both know you're wasting your time.*

You're just a poor little rich girl playing at being a writer. When will you face reality?

"You know how hard it's been for me over the past year," she tried again. "I hadn't been able to write since I finished *Martin's Journey*, but being here . . . it's as if . . ." she struggled to make him understand. To understand herself. "As if I've found myself again. This book is important to me, Brian. I need these six weeks."

"You can write just as well in Edinburgh," he said sulkily.

"No, I can't. There's something about this place—"

"You mean apart from the plumbing?"

Had he made a joke? For a moment Bella thought it would be all right, and then Brian reached out and clasped her hands and she knew he hadn't given in. He wouldn't give in. He never did. It was always Bella who gave in, because it was not in her nature to confront, and she hated arguments.

Lassie, that's just pathetic, said a voice in her head, and it sounded like the Black Maclean's. Or how she imagined he would sound, if he were not two and a half centuries dead.

"Come on, Bella," Brian said, smiling, earnest. "I've known you for years. Your father asked me to look after you when he died, he always said we were meant for each other. I understand you."

Her cheeks felt hot. "You don't understand me any more than he did, Brian."

Her father had never believed in her, either, although he had dutifully loved her, and left her a sizable legacy when he died.

"I need to get out of here, Bella," Brian was saying. "It's driving me mad. I want to give the antiques thing a try, and Hamish and Georgiana will put us up until we can find our own place. Someplace where I won't be ashamed to bring my friends."

"Or is it me you're ashamed of?" She cut angrily through his words.

He laughed uncomfortably, but the truth was in his eyes. Once he had found pleasure in her rather quaint, old-fashioned manner, but no more. Now he wanted someone like Georgiana, svelte and sophisticated. Out with the old, in with the new.

"We can explore the city," he was saying. "We can eat out, party. Live it up. You'll love it, Bella, really."

"I'll hate it," she said quietly, and knew it for the truth. This time she was not going to take the road of least resistance.

His mouth twisted. "I didn't want to tell you this, Bella. God knows I've tried to be supportive, to steer you in the right direction, but it's too late for subtleties now. You're turning into a selfish bore. Frankly, I don't give a damn about your silly little books, and neither does anyone else. That's why no one reads 'em. Look at you! You used to take care of yourself, but lately you just don't care. Couldn't you find something to make you look less fat? I mean, in God's name, what *is* that you're wearing?"

"Is my robe not Gucci enough for you, Brian?" she asked bitterly, and now the flames were in her eyes, because he took a step back. "And as for fat, well, this is the body I was born with. Marilyn Monroe would be called fat these days, too. And for your information, if I don't take care of myself—and I'm not saying that's true— it's because I'm unhappy. You make me unhappy."

"*I* make *you* unhappy!"

"Yes. Yes! You're a mean-spirited, egotistical bully. Go to Edinburgh. I hope you and Hamish and Georgiana will be very happy together."

He stared at her as if he had never seen her before.

"Good," he said in a flat, cold voice. "I didn't want you to come with me anyway. I'm tired of playing second fiddle to a dead man. I'll just leave you to your pathetic delusions."

He walked over to the wall and ripped down the copy of Maclean's portrait and crumpled it into a ball.

She gave a cry of distress. "For God's sake, are you really jealous of a painting?"

He didn't bother to answer her, his face filled with vicious satisfaction. "When you decide to rejoin the human race you know where to find me," he said, and flung the paper into the corner as he turned to the stairs, making certain he got the last word.

Bella listened to him opening and closing doors, and throwing his cases around up in the bedroom, and then the ominous clatter of his shoes on the stairs. Brian was leaving again and this time it was for good.

She was glad. She was, she really . . .

The front door slammed.

. . . was.

Bella felt her shoulders sag a little as the flames died. It was over. Brian was gone and she was all alone in an isolated cottage in the Highlands of Scotland.

Bella and her muse.

* * *

Maclean stood listening to the receding monster. He hadn't liked the man. He hadn't liked the way he had spoken to the woman. Maclean felt strangely indignant on her behalf, almost . . . protective. As for the wee cottage . . . Maclean looked at it with distain. He was Chief of the Macleans of Fasail, the Black Maclean, and this was no place for him.

He had drawn himself up in his pride, but now his shoulders slumped. What was the point of such arrogance if no one knew he was here? If no one could see him to obey his every word? If his people were all gone and his lands empty apart from the rain and the wind?

The Highlander stood outside in the night, gazing in through the window, his emotions twisting and turning inside him like serpents' tails. A night bird called out, the eerie sound echoing across the loch. He felt more alone than ever.

There was nowhere else for him to go. He knew it. The knowledge was a bitter bubble in his throat. But if the *Fiosaiche* had meant such a realization to humble him, then she was mistaken. Maclean did not bow to man or woman.

He almost, in his pride, turned away again, but at the last moment his gaze was drawn back to the woman. She was cutting vegetables on a board, behaving as if the argument with the man had never happened. *As if she had never driven her man away*, he corrected himself, pushing aside his earlier indignation. Betrayal, deception, mistrust. The words hammered his brain, and he knew that something very similar had happened to him, if only he could remember what it was. . . .

He breathed hard, and then stilled. She tugged at him. Was she some sort of witch? His gaze slid over her soft cheek and full mouth, and the way her lashes lay long and dark against her pale skin. Aye, maybe she was a witch, for as he stared he felt his ghostly self begin to ache for her in a manner that was all too mortal.

And then he saw a tear roll down her cheek, followed by another.

She was crying while she worked, and her lips were moving. Talking to herself? Or, could it be, singing, to try and lift her spirits? Whatever it was, it wasn't working.

She was not so hard-hearted after all, he realized. She was hurting. And alone. Maclean was stunned to think that there was a fellow creature in this strange new world who suffered.

Instinctively he stepped forward and splayed his hand against the glass, as if to touch her, to give comfort to her.

And just like that he was inside the cottage, inside the warm comfortable room, with the darkness behind him.

Four

Bella slid the vegetables into the pan. They would cook up nicely into a stir fry and . . . well, she was the sort of woman who always felt ravenously hungry when she was stressed.

She lifted her chin. Too bad what Brian would think about that. She wouldn't allow him to destroy her, even though there was a little voice in her head, the voice that belonged to her mother, telling her that what he said was true. Her mother, as thin as a whippet and perfectly turned out in her Chanel suit, could demolish her daughter's shaky self-esteem with a single glance. She was never unkind, she didn't need to be, but she couldn't hide her disappointment that her daughter wasn't as perfect as she would have liked. She left when Bella was six and now Brian was going, too.

Back to Edinburgh. Back to his own world among his own people; people who appreciated his wit and charm. Unlike her, who saw his other side. Hamish and Georgiana would sympathize with him, shaking their heads, smug in the certainty that they were right and she was a lost cause. Well, let them!

It's over.

Brian and Bella's Story had ended and now Bella had to write a new one, called Bella on Her Own. The prospect left her daunted and uncertain, but she told herself that being alone was better than listening to Brian belittle her. Loneliness was like an old friend, one she was comfortable with.

Then why wouldn't the tears stop?

The food in the cooking pan spat and a burning droplet touched her skin. Shocked, she gasped and stepped back, holding her wrist. Swearing under her breath, she turned toward the sink, ready to run cold water over the small burn.

And that was when she saw it.

The ghost.

In a split second, out of the corner of her eye, between one heartbeat and another. He must have been standing behind her so that as she turned he was to her left. He was a big man. Taller than her, taller than Brian, so tall he had to bend his head to stand beneath the low ceiling of the kitchen. He wore a plaid of mostly green and blue that was fastened about his hips and swept over one shoulder in the traditional way, and a black velvet jacket with silver buttons over a loose white shirt. Dark hair hung in wet swaths about his head, brushing his shoulders. His face was intensely masculine, domineering, and very handsome. But it was his eyes that riveted her attention. They were pale blue, the same color as this evening's sky, and they were looking straight at her.

One moment he was standing in her kitchen and the next . . .

He was gone.

Bella cried out and fell against the sink, holding herself up. Dear God, what was that? The room was empty. Her head swung back and forth—yes, definitely empty. And silent. The quiet was like a sound in itself. Rationally Bella knew she was alone, that Brian was on the road to Edinburgh, that outside her window this land was deserted and had been for centuries.

Was he a ghost? Shocked as she was, the man had looked oddly familiar . . . those pale eyes in that fiercely beautiful face. She knew him, she knew him—

Smoke was beginning to rise from the pan. Oh God, the food was burning! Bella moved, warily, toward the stove. She was loath to go anywhere near the spot where *he* had been. She edged around it, and as she took the pan off the heat she realized why he had seemed familiar.

Bella spun and stared at the wall above the bookshelf. The portrait was gone—Brian had seen to that— but she did not need to see it to know that the ghost—if that was what he was—resembled the Black Maclean. Not so elegant, perhaps, for the ghost's clothing had been damp and untidy, but essentially the same. The odd thing was . . . his eyes. The pupils were large and dark. Wild, just as Bella imagined her own to have been. As if seeing her had been just as much of a shock to him as seeing him had been to her.

Were ghosts frightened by human beings?

The idea made her giggle hysterically, and she bit her lip.

"Stop it," she whimpered. "Just stop it."

The research she had done on present-day Loch Fasail said nothing about any sightings of Maclean's ghost. Maybe the cottage was haunted? Bella knew that although Castle Drumaird had been built in the thirteenth century, her cottage was only a hundred years old. But it *had* been built with stone from the ruins. Perhaps stone could contain past memories; perhaps with the stone had come the ghost.

The thought startled her into remembering something that happened earlier, when she had gone for her walk. As she was leaving the ruins for the path down the hill she had felt something odd. A cold tingle down her backbone. An awareness. A sense of something that shouldn't be there.

She'd forgotten about it. Brian being in the cottage when she arrived back had emptied everything else from her mind. But now she could not help but ask herself: *Did Maclean follow me home?*

Had he walked a pace behind her, silent, unseen, those pale eyes fixed on her back, his breath a cold touch against her skin?

I'm waiting for Maclean.

"Oh my God." Bella turned a full circle, checking the shadows again. The trouble with being a writer was her vivid imagination; she'd frightened herself. Maybe she should call Brian's cell phone and ask him to—

But Bella stopped right there. Brian was gone; it was over. Ghost or no ghost, she was staying. Her writing was going well and leaving would be a mistake, especially when she wasn't even certain whether or not she had seen *it*. In fact, the more she tried to remember exactly what had happened, the more she doubted it was anything other than a . . .

"Hallucination."

Yes, that's all it was. She'd had that weird dream and her emotions had been in an upheaval with Brian leaving, and then she'd been writing about the Black Maclean. It was natural that she would imagine him appearing to her. . . . Well, it made a sort of sense. Ghost or no ghost, Bella wouldn't phone Brian, not after what he had said and done. She knew she was better than that.

The food was cooked. She tipped it out of the pan onto a plate and carried it over to the kitchen table and sat down. She and Brian had been eating in the other room. Brian had found a proper dining table from somewhere, and every night they'd lit candles and set out cutlery and crockery, just as he liked it. But tonight she refused to go through that charade. What was the point when she was by herself?

If she was by herself.

"Stop it!" Ghost or not, she was alone. Face it. Deal with it. Move on.

Murmuring a song by Jewel under her breath, she opened one of her notebooks, propped it up beside her, and began to read about life as it was in the Maclean stronghold of Loch Fasail in the eighteenth century.

Maclean focused his attention on the woman at the table. He hadn't imagined it, he knew he hadn't. She had seen him! Her eyes had widened, the brown of them completely surrounded by white, and she'd made a mewling sound like a kitten. Aye, she had seen something, and she had been looking directly at *him*.

Hope blossomed. She had seen him. He could work on that. If she had seen him once, she could see him again. He'd *make* her see him again!

"Lass?"

She did not look up from her book. A little frown wrinkled her brow.

"I know I can make you hear me," he muttered, moving closer. He stood, looking down at her. The gloss of her dark hair shone in the light that dangled from the ceiling like an overripe pear and hurt his eyes if he looked directly at it. So he didn't, and looked at her instead. Her robe gaped open at her throat, giving him a fine view of her plump breasts, her skin was pale as snow.

The sight of the woman stirred something in him. It was true she had the looks and body that he admired in a lassie, but it was not just lust. This was another emotion, something he had not felt in a very long time. It was the same feeling he had when he saw her crying, a softening inside him, an ache that had no name. He pushed it back, smothered it, denied it. Just as he had been doing all his life. He was a warrior, his father's son, and women were just another possession to be owned. As valuable as his livestock, but not worth as much to him as his broadsword. They served their purpose and beyond that they were invisible.

And he saw nothing ironic in the thought.

Maclean took another step closer, his kilt brushing her elbow. She continued to read, the food on her plate forgotten. He reached out a hand and touched her hair, lightly, attempting to feel the texture of it. His fingers slipped through it, touching nothing but air.

He swore.

She turned a page.

"You *will* know I am here," he said hoarsely, staring at her so intently he was certain she must feel his presence. "I promise you that, woman."

She glanced up as if something had attracted her attention. Her face had a blurred, distant look, her thoughts still with the book.

"I'm here, my pretty lassie," he said. "And aye, you're a bonny one, all right. If I were a man again, I'd see you dressed in silk skirts like the fine ladies of Edinburgh, and enjoy taking them off you."

She cleared her throat.

He held his breath.

She turned back to her book. "Strange," she murmured. "I thought I heard an insect buzzing. . . ." And she flipped over the page and kept reading. " 'The Macleans of Loch Fasail are unrelated to the southern clan of the same name who reside near Loch Linnhe. They are a branch who settled in Fasail around 1270, gaining their lands from the powerful Mackenzies, and ruling from their residence of Castle Drumaird. They lived a relatively peaceful life, apart from a continuing feud with their nearest neighbors, the Macleods of Mhairi.' "

Maclean rolled his eyes.

"Hmm, let's see, what's this? 'An Eyewitness Account of a Traveler in the Highlands, 1742.' He says here:

"I came upon a bridge in Fasail, a wondrous structure truly remarkable for the wild place in which it stood. The story I was told is as follows:

After a particularly bad winter when the stream that runs into the loch broke its banks and swept away livestock and several folk, the Black Maclean, Chief of the Macleans of Fasail, ordered that a bridge be built across it. But this was no feeble structure, cobbled together to get them through the next season or two. This bridge was built to last for generations, the piles driven deep into the rocky soil, and with hand railings for the older people to grip so they did not fall in, and a lower railing so that children did not slip through."

As he listened to the sweet rise and fall of her voice, he began to remember the bridge. The winter had been the worst he had known, so cold many had not survived it, and when the snow and ice had melted from the moors and mountains, the loch had brimmed its banks and the stream had raged like a wild thing. Maclean remembered searching for the body of a young woman, but she had been drowned too deep to be found. He had ordered his carpenters to build the bridge as soon as they were able and, wood being a rarity, had sent for sturdy hardwood to be carted to Loch Fasail. No mean task.

"So, Maclean, a railing low enough so that wee children didn't slip through." The woman tapped the page and smiled as if such a thing amused her. Or maybe pleased her. "Not so black-hearted, after all."

"'Tis a matter of practicalities," he said angrily. "Every winter children die, and children grow into men and women who work my land and fight for me against my enemies. I need them all. Why would I no' save them if I could?"

His face felt hot. Something about the woman's knowing smile made him uneasy, as if she saw things he preferred she did not. He glowered at her a moment more, but it did no good, so he went to explore the rest of the cottage. There was little to see. He noted gloomily that the rooms were poky and chilly, and halfway up the narrow stairs the lights went out. He paused, listening to the woman cursing and bumping into things in the darkness.

"Aye, now you're no' smiling," he muttered with some satisfaction, and continued on. The darkness did not affect him. It was as if, like him, it did not exist.

Upstairs there was a room with a shiny bath fixed to the floor and a thing with a lid that looked enough like the water closet he'd had built in Castle Drumaird to make him think a man might piddle in it, and another bowl, shiny like the bath, with a cake of soap in a little dish nearby. Next he found the chamber where she slept, under the slope of the roof. The height of the room was uncomfortably low, even worse than those downstairs. Maclean tried to straighten, expecting his head to pass through the ceiling, but instead it hit the wood with a dull crack.

Cursing, rubbing his skull, he spent some time examining her belongings. Female things, fripperies, he thought with disdain, and yet he was curious enough to peer into the open pots of cream. They smelled like her, sweet and fragrant. There was a bristle brush for her long dark hair with some of the strands caught in it still. Clothing of many colors lay untidily on the bed, the materials different from any he had ever seen. Did no one spin and weave anymore? In Maclean's time the women of the glen wore a plain shift with a skirt and jacket over it, and over that an arisaid, the female equivalent of the plaid.

There was a looking glass, but when he went and stood before it he had no reflection.

Frustrated, he turned to the table on the far side of the bed. It was swept clean. Even the second pillow had been removed from the bed.

The man really was gone, and it did not seem as if he were returning.

Had she driven him away as the man had seemed to be accusing her? Maclean had disliked the man, but that did not mean he should take the woman's side in this matter. A man's thoughts and feelings must always come first. Man was superior to woman, and Maclean did not believe two hundred and fifty years had changed that fundamental law.

Still . . . "The lass shouldn't be alone. She needs a man to care for her, to warm her in the night, to make children in her belly."

His voice sounded deep and unsettling in the quiet room.

Was that why she had been grieving when he looked at her through the window? Was it sorrow for the man who had left her, or because she was now alone?

Maclean realized then what the unwelcome emotion that consumed him earlier had been as he stood watching the woman cry.

Need. Want.

The woman was alone; he was alone. She suffered,

too. He could comfort her, maybe, and she could help him to understand what sort of world this was that he found himself in. Of all the people he had seen so far, only she was real to him. He wanted to be real to her.

He wanted to *be* again.

Gingerly he sat down on the bed and was surprised when he didn't sink right through it. There seemed to be rules to his invisible state after all. He could not touch flesh, or be touched by it, but now that he was inside the cottage he was bound by things like walls and ceilings and beds. He stretched out on the ocean-blue coverings, enjoying the softness, despite his legs poking off the end a good foot and a half. The now-familiar scent of the woman teased his senses.

Maclean knew there were things he must do, but his mind was weary and everything was so confusing. Right now he was nothing but a wan ghostie, but maybe through the woman he could become himself again. Aye, even though the idea of the Black Maclean being dependent on a lassie seemed ludicrous and wrong, and went against everything he had ever been taught.

He closed his eyes and smiled.

Five

The wind was cool and scented with heather and earth. It brought back the elusive memories of better times, before he was plunged into this nightmare. Briefly the past was superimposed upon the present and a single strong memory filled him. Of the land as it had been, alive with families and their animals, crops growing, smoke trickling from cottages and with it the smells of food cooking. He longed, he ached, for those vanished days, but their voices in his head were a distant echo, while all around him was emptiness.

The image faded, and Maclean knew better than to try and bring it back again. Forcing his mind to his will hurt. Agonizingly.

The woman was walking in front of him along the side of the loch, and he matched his longer steps to her smaller ones, enjoying the sight of her lush body in loose gray trews and a bright pink jacket over a tight blue vestlike top.

"Verra nice, lass," he murmured approvingly, as the wind tossed her long dark hair and her cheeks grew flushed from the exercise. "Verra nice, Bella."

That was her name—Bella. He'd seen it written on some of her papers. Bella Ryan. He liked the way it rolled off his tongue, and he found himself using it more and more instead of "woman."

At some point during the day Bella always went for a walk, sometimes two. It didn't matter if it was rain or shine, she set off with a brisk determination that made him smile. Maclean walked, too, slowing for her as she panted her way up the hillsides and slipped and slithered her way down again. He found himself reaching out to help her over the more difficult bits, forgetting his hand would pass through her, and always irritated when it did.

Today they were walking along the loch, but yesterday she had taken him up to the castle ruins. He still didn't understand what had happened to bring about his home's destruction, but he decided that the catastrophe must have occurred long after his time. Maclean drew comfort from the knowledge that on his death his people had been safe and their future secure; he was a good chief and he had prepared for such an event.

On his death? Aye, there was a question. Just how had he died?

Only once had he tried to recall his last moments, though it made his head ache and pound like there was a wee man tossing a caber inside his skull. When he persisted he had heard the faint sounds of fighting. Culloden Moor again? But it was not so much the battle that sickened his stomach. It was what he *felt*. A sense of guilt and betrayal so keen it cut into his flesh like a blade. And the bone-deep pain of being in the wrong place at the wrong time and knowing he was going to die for it.

But full understanding slipped through his fingers like something dark and foul, and he could not grasp it properly. He could not catch hold of it. Even as he tried, shadows fluttered at the edges of his sight, closing in, threatening him with an unspeakable something.

Gasping, frightened, Maclean had pulled back at that moment. Maybe it was better not to push, he decided, as the caber-tosser rested and his heart stopped racing. Let the questions bide their time, let the answers come to him when they were ready.

Things have changed. The *Fiosaiche* had said that to him when she woke him. He had not understood it then. He did now. She had also said he must change, too, and this he still did not understand. *So many lives lost unnecessarily, Highlander. You must right the wrong.* What did that mean? What lives, what wrong? He supposed he had to be patient, but Maclean had never been a patient man. While he lived he had striven hard to complete the tasks needed to be done each day, and still found time to enjoy himself into the night. Maclean was not used to *waiting* for anything.

A bird cried shrilly high above him, and Maclean looked up. For a moment he thought he saw a golden eagle, far into the sky, but it was no more than a speck. Bella had paused for a rest, sitting herself down on a stone wall by some flowering heather. The wall ran by the old stones that stood two upright and one crosswise, forming a low doorway that led to nowhere. The stones had been here when the Macleans came, and no one dared interfere with them. They were Goddess Stones, *Cailleach* Stones. He wasn't surprised to see them still here, weathered but unchanged.

Maclean remembered when he was a lad and he had run up and down these hills. Then when he was a man he had come here to teach the young men of the clan how to use a sword and to fight, to school them in the intricacies and brutality of battle. He had . . . had . . .

Maclean sighed. He saw the image for a moment, himself as a man, and then it was gone, as though a door had slammed on his mind. Resentment simmered inside him, both for the sorceress with her bewildering instructions and for Bella because he could not make her see him again.

"What am I doing following this bloody woman about? I am the Chief of the Macleans of Fasail! Dinna ye know, woman, that your job is to cook a man's meals and ease his lust and bear his children? Men make the decisions, men make the rules and the laws. It is men who matter. Aye, it should be the other way around. *Ye* should be following *me*."

Just then Bella sighed and rested her chin upon her hand. She looked sad today, her shoulders rounded, her full mouth turned down. Maclean imagined her thinking of the man she had driven out and wishing she had held her tongue. Well, she had only herself to blame, he told himself self-righteously, even while he secretly would have liked to pound the man senseless for the words he had used with her. But that was because he himself never used cruelty in his dealings with women. A strong man had no need of it when correcting a gentle creature like Bella.

Aye, and she was gentle. Sweet and calm and gentle, like midsummer in Loch Fasail.

He reached out his hand, as if to brush her soft cheek with his finger, but stopped himself. She would not feel him; he was as invisible to her as the air they breathed. They were bound together, she not knowing he was here, and he fated to watch her and follow her about like a shadow.

"Is this my future? Is this the life I've been given by the *Fiosaiche*? A life that is no life at all!"

"Stop feeling sorry for yourself."

It was as if her words were addressed to him.

Startled, Maclean opened his eyes to find that Bella had climbed to her feet. Her sadness still lingered, but she had straightened her shoulders and her mouth was set as stubbornly as her chin. Maybe she was not so fragile after all, Maclean thought. He remembered when he had seen her through the window in her cottage, her eyes flashing as she faced the man. Aye, there was real strength there. He felt pride in her, as if she belonged to him.

Maclean smiled as she took a deep breath and set off at a march, back toward the cottage. And then he remembered what she had said. "Why should I no' feel sorry for myself?" he belatedly shouted after her.

He had reason, hadn't he? Just for a moment Maclean was tempted to turn and walk in the opposite direction, into the country of the Macleods of Mhairi, his enemies. Anything was better than being tied to a bloody woman! He chafed against such bonds, longing for escape, longing for action.

The ground vibrated beneath him and a heartbeat later he heard the hoofbeats. Alert, he turned, every muscle rigid, his hand already on the handle of his *claidheamh mor*.

A horseman, his blood-red cloak sailing behind him, came galloping his horse down from the slopes above the loch. But he wasn't looking at Maclean. His sights were fixed on Bella.

Sweet Bella, who, even with her hidden strength, would be no match for an armed man.

Maclean roared, wrenching his broadsword from its scabbard and taking off at a run toward the approaching rider. He was a big man, but he was powerful and strong, and as he ran now he was filled with purpose. He must reach the rider before he caught up with Bella. The man had not acknowledged his shout, his gaze still fixed ahead on Bella where she had stopped to test the shallows at the edge of the loch with her fingertips.

"Run, woman, run!"

She looked around. Did she hear him? The horse?

Maclean had no time to ponder it, or the startled expression on her pale face. His breath burned in his chest, the weight of the sword in his hand was as nothing and, although he stretched the muscles in his legs and gained even greater speed, the world around him slowed. As he approached diagonally to intercept the man, he could clearly see the foam on the horse's flanks, the grim determination on the rider's face, the cut across his cheek, and the battle madness in his eyes. There was only one way to stop a man with the scent of blood in his nostrils.

Behind him he heard Bella scream, and the shrill sound spurred him on.

Maclean flung himself into the path of the horse and rider, raising his sword with both hands and swinging it down, aiming to cut the man in half.

The blade passed through without resistance.

Maclean struck the ground hard. Briefly he lay, dazed, struggling for breath, and then he rolled over and lifted his head. The sun blinded him and, cursing, he shoved himself to his feet, heart pounding, expecting to see Bella trampled. Dead.

She was standing stock-still, her mouth hanging open. "Oh God," she whispered. "Oh *God*."

For a moment, a wonderful and terrifying moment, he thought she could see him. But then he realized she couldn't. She was looking to one side, up the slope where the horseman had come from before he . . . vanished.

Bella blinked, hard, her hands in tight fists.

Maclean stumbled a few steps, turning to look all around him. The blood throbbed in his ears. The rider really was gone . . . if he had ever existed. Was he a ghost? Or was he something like Maclean, who had been awoken from a long sleep by the *Fiosaiche* and released from the between-worlds? In which case, what game was she playing?

"Bloody hell!" Maclean returned his broadsword to its scabbard with an angry ring of metal and wiped the sweat from his palms. And that was another thing. If he was a ghost, then why was he puffing and panting, with his heart thudding fit to burst open his chest?

Maclean cursed some more, when all he really

wanted to do was grab hold of Bella and shake her. Hard. And hold her. Tight.

He started off after her, his long legs eating up the distance in no time. He was more than a little annoyed that he had just saved the woman in a very heroic manner and she didn't even know it. As soon as he was close enough he began his tirade.

"When I say run, then ye will run! Do ye hear me, woman? Bella!"

As his heartbeat quieted he became aware of her voice. What was she saying? Something about him causing her to feel like a natural woman?

Bloody hell, she was singing! In a tremulous voice, her eyes still big and scared, she was singing to soothe herself.

Maclean groaned. She had done that before, in the cottage, when the man had left her, and then again when she had seen him. What sort of woman sang songs in her darkest moments?

"Singing willna save ye. You've no more sense than ye were born with," he said huffily, trying to hold on to his anger. But just like that it was gone. He even found his mouth twitching, trying to smile, and with a sigh he let it. She was safe, that was what mattered. The rider had returned to wherever he came from, and although Maclean knew he should consider what new threats awaited him, instead he found himself thinking of Bella. He'd grown so used to having her near that without her he'd feel desolate.

It was a strong word, but Maclean knew he wasn't exaggerating. Bella had become his companion and in his loneliness and confusion he relied on her. He needed her.

Maclean walked beside her, bending his head to listen to her singing. Her voice had steadied, she seemed calmer and the words were easy enough, though very silly in his opinion. "Oh Baby"? What the bloody hell did that mean? Tentatively he began to sing along with her, his uncertainty dropping away. He hadn't sung much when he was alive; it was not fitting for a Highland chief to break into song as he went about his tasks. But now he found he was enjoying hearing their mingled voices, the high note of Bella and the husky baritone of Maclean. Aye, they were well matched.

Even if she didn't know it.

Six

Bella didn't know what to do or think. First the Highlander in her kitchen and now that man on the horse, riding toward her. His face . . . He'd wanted to kill her, she'd known it with a cold, hard dread. And then, a moment later, nothing. The loch was still as glass, the air was sweet and chill, and the silence absolute. Bella could tell herself she was imagining it, that the past few days had scrambled her brain, that her synapses had gotten crossed.

But she knew what she'd seen; she just wasn't sure what to do about it.

And there was something else. Just after the man on the horse disappeared into thin air there had been a movement on top of one of the shallow hills that surrounded the loch, where the road ran across from Gregor's croft. Something pale brown and shaggy and elongated had been standing there. She hadn't seen it for long, but long enough to know it was the pony with the strange green eyes.

When Gregor came to see her later in the day, bringing her milk, eggs, and butter, and asking her about some missing sheep he'd had grazing by the loch, she didn't know whether to mention her experiences or not.

"You've seen no one about?" he asked, concerned for his sheep. "No strangers?"

Yes, a ghost in the kitchen and another one riding a horse.

"Well . . . no."

"Where's Brian?"

Bella looked away from Gregor's keen gaze. "Brian's having a holiday. Sort of."

Gregor nodded. "Verra well." He gave her a dour smile. "If sheep went missing in the old days it was the way of the people to blame the *each-uisge*. There were other monsters, too, like your Nessie in Loch Ness, and creatures in other lochs that are not so famous. The waters of Scotland have always held their secrets. Only nowadays we dinna believe in such things."

Bella frowned. "Strange you should say that, Gregor. I did see a horse by the loch. Well, a pony. Twice. I thought it might have belonged to you."

Gregor shook his head. "I have no horse, Bella. Mabbe it was from over Mhairi."

"Maybe."

"I'll ask about. See if there's one missing. What did it look like?"

"Odd."

He gave her another dour smile. "Next you'll be telling me you're seeing ghosts, Bella."

She grimaced and knew she couldn't talk to Gregor. Whatever was happening to her, it was up to her to sort it out for herself.

When Gregor had gone, Bella stood and gazed across the reflections in Loch Fasail and over to the gray bulk of the mountains that sheltered Ardloch on the coast. The long twilights seemed to go on forever, so that there was very little darkness. It felt like another world, a dreamlike place where anything was possible. On nights like this Bella had no difficulty in believing the Highland tales of ghosties and ghouls and monsters in the lochs.

Brian had swum in the loch once and rushed out, white-faced, saying something had tugged his foot. She had laughed at him, but he'd been adamant it wasn't his imagination.

"This place is haunted. That massacre you're writing about, there must be restless spirits all around us. That's why no one else wanted to stay here. That's why it was so cheap."

"It's not haunted," she'd mocked, "and if it is I don't care. I want to live here forever."

"I *do* want to live here forever," she said now to the silence. "Despite the spirits and the *each-uisge*. Please, can I stay?"

And it was strange, but when she looked up there was a big bird, a majestic eagle, soaring above her. Considering her request.

The sweat popped out on Maclean's brow. Could ghosts sweat? Well, they must be able to, because he was.

He tried again, concentrating fiercely on the tea mug Bella had left on the desk the night before, and his fingers shook as he tried to close them about the hard shiny surface. For a heartbeat he felt it . . . and then his fingers slipped through.

Maclean sat, head bowed, feeling confused and depressed.

Since the rider had appeared and tried to hurt Bella, Maclean had felt a change in himself. A tingling in his fingertips. He'd hoped it meant he was regaining his sense of touch, but although several times he had almost caused the mug to move, it seemed he still had a long way to go.

He was worried, too.

What if something else happened to Bella? How could he protect her properly if he was barely anything more than a puff of air? He needed to regain his full faculties as soon as possible. When he was alive, there hadn't been much about warfare and battle he did not know. He had been protecting his people since he was a boy—it was one thing he was very proud of—and watching over Bella would be no hardship.

Indeed not.

Sometimes he wondered whether the real reason he wanted to feel again, to be a man again, was to protect Bella or because he wanted to hold her in his arms and *feel* her womanly curves. Both, maybe. It was true that the sight of her burned into him. He admitted it. For a man who could not feel hunger, Maclean was ravenous with lust. If this was two hundred and fifty years ago, he'd have taken her into his four-poster bed by now. He let himself picture them lying on the fine feather mattress with the bedcurtains pulled all around them and her soft pale skin flushed by his attentions. Muted, safe, intimate—just the two of them.

But that was a randy dream—there was no possibility of taking her to his bed. Whether he liked it or not, Maclean could only watch and listen, and every hour that passed increased his awareness of her.

Last night he had watched her sleep.

When Bella slept she had such a peaceful expression on her face and her body grew soft and relaxed as her breathing slowed. Maclean did not sleep himself. Like other functions of the living, this was denied him, so instead he watched her with an intensity that was almost envy.

"Maclean?"

With a jolt he had leaned closer in the darkness of Bella's bedroom.

"Maclean."

Bella was calling his name in her dreams.

All the hairs on his skin had stood straight up. She was dreaming of *him*.

"I'm here," he'd whispered, peering into her face. "Och, Bella, ye are so beautiful." He bent forward and kissed the air above her cheek.

"Maclean . . ." She'd turned over and snuggled into her quilt, a smile curving her mouth.

Maclean's eyes stung with tears. He had not cried since he was a wee lad, but he was in danger of it now.

Because, if he lived in her dreams, did that mean he existed, somewhere in the shadowy realm of sleep?

Did that make him *real*?

At that moment Bella came into the room, her hair

still tangled from sleep, her face fresh and beautiful, all of her so delicious. He badly wanted to stand up and swing her into his arms and take her straight back upstairs to bed.

"Not real enough, unfortunately," he muttered dejectedly, and reaching out his hand tried to grasp the mug once more.

Bella couldn't stop smiling as she began to make herself some toast. Last night she had a wonderful dream. She paused, butter knife in one hand, toast in the other, and closed her eyes to remember.

Maclean had been standing in the shadows, watching her.

"You're not real," she told him firmly.

"I'm caught between life and death, neither one thing nor the other. But I am a man. I want ye like a man wants a woman."

How could he do that? Make her heart beat stronger like that? Just with his voice and his words?

And then the scene had changed. They were lying in the soft fragrant grass by the Cailleach *Stones, beneath a night sky full of strange moving colors—green and blue and yellow, surging and shivering. She was watching the sky over Maclean's broad, strong shoulder, because his body was on top of hers. Heavy, powerful and very masculine. His legs between hers were moving with a rough friction, and his hands on her hips, his fingers strong and callused, were probably bruising her skin with a grip more used to a sword hilt than a woman's tender flesh.*

But the thing was, she was loving every moment of it.

Her mouth clung to his and she heard herself moan. Her Highlander was not gentle, but he wanted her. And she wanted him to stay just where he was now—inside her. She could feel every inch of him. He was big and silken, elegantly stroking her inner flesh, making her senses quiver and ache. Another moment and she would shatter. . . .

He lifted his head and his eyes were full of tenderness.

"I like to watch ye while ye sleep."

The surroundings had altered again. Now Bella was back in her bedroom and Maclean was leaning over her, his face darker than the night. Bella's eyes opened and she thought: Is this a dream or am I awake? *Although she knew it could not be the latter, such things were not possible.*

"Och, Bella, ye are so beautiful." His voice was husky, deep, and it stirred her very soul. *And then he bent and kissed her cheek, his lips as gentle as a moth's wing. "Sleep now, sleep now. . . ."*

And Bella drifted away on the warmth of his breath.

Now Maclean's husky voice played over in her head and she smiled again, knowing she was being silly. Very silly. In reality Maclean had been a black-hearted villain and here she was making him into a romantic hero, but she couldn't help it. She wished she could dream about him every night. It certainly lifted her spirits, not to mention her libido.

"Och, Maclean," she murmured.

The mug on her desk suddenly flew out over the edge and crashed to the floor.

Bella stared, wide-eyed.

And then the phone rang and nearly sent her through the roof.

It was Georgiana in Edinburgh.

"Bella, there you are," she said in her brittle voice. "I thought I should let you know that Brian is staying here with us."

"He told me."

"Oh. I didn't know what he'd told you. He was in a bit of a state when he arrived here. Actually, I thought *you* might ring him."

Did Georgiana expect her to apologize for upsetting Brian? Bella knew she wasn't going to do that, not ever again. The silence seemed to unnerve Georgiana and when she spoke now there was a catch to her voice.

"I don't pretend to know what happened between you two, Bella, and I don't want to, but I did wonder . . . you wouldn't consider coming down to Edinburgh for a few days, would you? Just over the weekend. You and Brian could talk, sort things out. I'd make sure you had time alone. I'm certain you're just as keen to see him as he is to see you."

"I don't think that's a good idea." Bella's heart was bumping and she felt slightly sick. "Brian said everything he wanted to say to me before he left. I think you'll find he doesn't want to see me."

"Bella, I'm sure—"

"I'm working, Georgiana. If Brian wants to talk, he knows where I am."

Georgiana gave a loud sigh, as if she thought Bella was being childish. Perhaps Brian was right to covet Georgiana, perhaps they were made for each other.

"All right. If that's what you want, I'll tell him. Goodbye, Bella."

The call disconnected. Bella pulled a face at it. Her good mood was spoiled now. She glanced at the mug on the floor. Maybe there was a very slight earth tremor? Bella glanced about her, but nothing else seemed to have moved. Her gaze fell on a stack of her heaviest books. She had put the replica of Maclean's portrait under there to flatten out the creases after Brian had crumpled it. She removed it now and held it up to inspect it. Not too bad, she thought. Almost as good as new.

Her good mood restored, Bella replaced it on the wall above her desk, so that she could look up and see it as she worked. Her fingers lingered on the paper.

Och, Bella, ye are so beautiful.

If only dreams could come true.

Seven

Maclean was in a good mood, too. He had gotten the mug to sail off the desk very satisfactorily; it had caught Bella's attention nicely. And now she had a picture of him she had placed upon the wall. He grinned in pleased amazement. It was the portrait he'd had painted in 1744, though Bella's copy was far smaller and of poorer quality than the original, but it was definitely the same painting. Maclean remembered how the wee artist shook in his boots while it amused Maclean to play the savage bloodthirsty Highlander.

"Boo," he'd longed to say, just to see the wee man wet himself, but he was the chief so he showed some restraint. But the artist had his revenge by making Maclean look as if he were about to reach out of the canvas and throttle someone.

And now he was on Bella's wall.

Maclean was flattered that after two hundred and fifty years dead he could still occupy a woman's thoughts so fully. What he didn't understand was the why of it; what connection she had to his current predicament.

Bella had settled in front of the machine and was munching on a piece of toast while she flicked through her pieces of paper. Maclean came up behind her and stood waiting for her to begin talking to herself. Every morning Bella sat at the machine that clacked beneath her busy fingers and made words and sentences appear upon a square flat surface that rested upright in front of her. The words themselves danced like fireflies before his eyes, so he didn't try to read them. It wasn't that he couldn't read—he had been educated well. As was the way with his memory that gave up insignificant details so easily and yet refused him the important ones, he could remember his first tutor. An enlightened man, he taught the young Maclean that there was a world that extended far beyond his borders. He introduced him to poetry and prose and ideas, but his father called such things a waste of time and the tutor had left, and another, far more "suitable," was found.

Maclean found he enjoyed watching Bella's face and the thoughts that flitted over it—her eyes changed with every emotion so that he did not need to guess what she was feeling or thinking. In any case she was one of those women who frequently spoke aloud to herself, even when she was alone, or maybe because of it. Maclean found a guilty pleasure in closing his eyes and pretending she was speaking to him.

"Why can't I get it right?" she said with a sigh, and pressed the button that took away all the words again. She did that a lot.

He leaned forward, eager to answer. "What have you done now, woman?"

"I've never had this much trouble before."

"Why do you no' find a priest or a scribe? In my day, women found a man to do their writing for them."

"It's not as if this is my first book."

"So you are a scribe yourself?" He was impressed. He had known of women who were well taught, but not many came to Fasail. Bella seemed exceptional. "Do you write down the works of learned men? Is that what you're doing, lass?"

"My last book sold . . . well, at least five thousand copies."

Maclean heard the ironic smile in her voice but did not understand it. "Five thousand? That's an awful lot of books."

"Then why is this story so hard to tell? Am I being true to history? Or am I writing it the way I want it to be? My fantasy Scottish warrior." She groaned and buried her face in her hands.

He peered down at her, frowning in his attempt to see into her mind. But she was off again, lurching forward to begin her furious tapping, the words lighting up the screen. If he had been a living man they would have butted heads, but as it was she passed right through him, leaving him with an odd dizzy feeling and the lingering scent of her perfume.

" 'Tis a beautiful morning," he said, glancing longingly at the window. "We could go for a walk?"

She sighed. "Work, Bella, work."

Work? Did she call her tapping on the machine work? He smiled indulgently. Women's work was cleaning and cooking and raising babies. And pleasing a man. Maclean thought Bella could please him very well. She was perfect, her skin creamy and smooth, her curves lush and womanly. Any guilt he might have felt watching her wash and dress was soon overcome by the pleasure it gave him. But there was something odd about the speed with which she covered herself. Almost as if she knew he was there, or . . . was it possible she was ashamed of her beauty?

He pondered on it now, turning the question over in his head. Was physical attractiveness something to be kept hidden in this new world?

He could not accept it.

Unless . . . Did Bella not know she was beautiful? Had someone convinced her she was ugly—not fit to be seen? This seemed a far more likely explanation for Bella's strange behavior. Words could be cruel. They could continue to cause pain and suffering long after the person who had spoken them was gone.

Maclean's own father had a vicious temper, and would strike out at those around him with words that slashed and cut and maimed as efficiently as a sword. The memory came out of the void in his mind.

His mother's face, tear-streaked and unhappy, the bruise growing on her cheek, and Maclean, his voice quavering, "She dinna mean it, Father, please, forgive her," and his father, raging, "I'll no' put up with ye taking sides against me, laddie! She has betrayed me, betrayed us both. There can be no forgiveness. Tell him, woman! Tell him how you meant to abandon your child!"

And his mother, bleak, wooden. "I did plan to leave Loch Fasail, Morven. I didna want to abandon you and

I would not have done so, only . . . your father would never let me take you with me. He would kill me first. Now it does not matter. My lover is dead."

Her lips wobbled. Tears spilled from her eyes.

But he did not see her anguish, he was not old enough to understand her conflict. Only one thing had relevance for him.

"You meant to leave me?"

Maclean could still remember the incredible sense of betrayal as his mother's silence confirmed the worst he could imagine.

From that moment on, Maclean was his father's son, turning his back on his mother as she had turned hers on him. And now that he was a grown man, he did not feel as if he knew her at all. Women were a mystery to him.

Maclean frowned.

Women are no' important. A man must look to his lands, his clan and his enemies. Women are nothing but a distraction.

There was his father's voice, ringing in his head. Maclean knew it was a fundamental truth that distractions could kill a man.

The ironical thing was that now he had nothing to do *but* be distracted by a woman.

He glanced down at Bella, and the familiar warmth spread through his ghostly body. She had dressed in a white overshirt today, so tight he was amazed that she had got it on. He'd noticed before that some of her clothes seemed to stretch out as she tugged them over her head or hips, and then reshape themselves lovingly to her curves.

One strand of her long dark hair had fallen out of its pins, caressing her cheek. Maclean clenched his hands into fists to stop himself from trying to brush it back, knowing it would spoil the illusion that he was a real man.

Would his father be pleased with him now? If he knew his warrior son's one ambition was to take a woman's lock of hair between his finger and thumb and experience the feel of it? The scent of it? No, Maclean knew his father would not be pleased about that.

He wondered abruptly if his brutal father ever felt love for a woman, for his wife? As he stood, breathing in Bella's scent, it occurred to Maclean that part of his father's savage bitterness toward women may well have been because of his own hurt and betrayal. In his own way, he had loved Maclean's mother, and her planning on leaving him for another man had curdled that love and blackened his heart forever.

It did not excuse his treatment of her—the blows, the curses—but it made sense. Maclean's father had blamed all women for the faults of one. And he had taught Maclean to feel the same, and to protect himself from the hurt that loving could cause. But at what cost?

Distractedly, he glanced at the screen as the lit letters flashed upon it. And froze. The letters were no longer dancing in front of his eyes like fireflies. He could read them!

Intrigued, Maclean shuffled closer, ignoring the disconcerting way in which parts of Bella's body merged with his. He read the first line aloud. "Morven Maclean was named for his grandfather—"

His name was on the screen. She was writing about him! Maclean gave her a bewildered look. Why would she be writing a book about *him*? It was not as if he were a king or a prince—he could understand if she was writing about Charles Stuart or King George, but Maclean? What had he ever done, that Bella would want to write it down in a book? Though important to him, his life was private, his alone, and the idea of it being scrutinized by others made him very uncomfortable.

"You've written that I was called Morven after my grandfather," he said irritably. "That's wrong."

She couldn't hear him.

He gave an impatient sigh and tried again. "You see, Morven was a sea warrior from the old days. He had the strength of many men and he performed heroic feats and was thought to be invincible against his enemies. My mother was fanciful and thought the name would make me a better man, and in those days my father loved her enough to let her have her way."

Bella kept clacking.

Maclean restrained his frustration and moved closer to the machine, reading the new words as they appeared there.

"No, no, lass, I wasna an only child! I had a sister, but she died when she was a wee thing. Her name was . . . was . . . Bloody hell!" His memory failed him again.

Maclean's unease and impatience only grew as he read through Bella's version of his childhood. He couldn't turn the pages of her book to peruse them at his own pace, nor could he push the buttons that removed or added the words. He tried, but his fingers slipped through into nothingness. All he could do was stand and peer over her shoulder, and try not to grind his teeth.

He was angry, aye, but even angry as he was, she had the ability to distract him. First her perfume tickled his nose, and then he found himself fascinated by her hair and how the darkness of it was lit by strands that had been touched by the summer sun. If he was a man of flesh and blood he would stoop and nuzzle her neck, tasting her skin, before slipping his hands around her waist and lifting them to stroke the underside of her breasts in that tight white cloth.

Perhaps she felt his invisible gaze, because she folded her arms over her breasts. Maclean smiled and concentrated harder, imagining himself lifting her tight white shirt and revealing her skin inch by inch, and then using his tongue to explore and tease her until she . . .

"Where is that draft coming from?"

She was looking around, a frown wrinkling her brow.

"I'm no draft!" Maclean said in disgust.

Bella shivered again. "There's something wrong with this house," she muttered. Then, reluctantly, as if she didn't really want to believe it: "Maclean?"

Just then the talking box began to sing its song. Again.

As usual, Bella rushed to answer it. Only this time she jumped up and walked right through him.

"Bloody hell, woman, dinna do that!"

She started and looked back over her shoulder, her eyes wide, and for a moment he thought for sure she had heard him. Or seen him. Heart beating hard, he waited, but she was already grabbing up the box and holding it to her ear.

"Hello?"

Maclean sat down on the chair she had just vacated and tried to think. Bella was writing about him in her book; he was fairly certain the whole book was about him. Why else would she have his portrait on her wall? Why else would she be here, in Fasail, where he used to live? When he first arrived he hadn't thought much about the significance of her being here, but this changed things. This meant that it wasn't just chance. He had attached himself to Bella because it was meant to be. The *Fiosaiche* had chosen this moment to bring them together, and they were both playing a part in her plan.

But if that was so, then why couldn't he show himself to Bella in the flesh?

"Yes, of course it'll be ready on deadline." Bella was still speaking into the box. She gave a little laugh, but she was pretending. Her eyes had a worried expression. "I didn't realize you were so keen on this one, Elaine. You said you couldn't even promise you'd take it on until you had read—" She paused, a frown wrinkling her brow. "Oh, I see. Is that . . . good?" The frown cleared and she smiled, a proper smile this time, wide and beautiful.

Caught up in that smile, forgetting his own problems, Maclean leaned forward. The chair creaked ominously.

Bella stopped smiling. Her gaze was fixed on the chair.

Maclean held his breath and moved again. The chair gave another creak.

Bella's eyes widened. "Yes, yes, I see," she was saying, but it was obvious she wasn't really concentrating. "Thanks for calling, Elaine."

* * *

Bella finished the call from her agent. Her empty chair had creaked and when she looked at it she could have sworn it . . . it *moved*.

She squeezed her eyes shut and opened them again. Nothing. The chair was perfectly still. The room was completely empty. What did she expect? Maclean sitting there writing her book for her?

But she didn't laugh. She'd remembered that when the phone rang and she'd gone to answer it she had felt a small, intense electric shock. That was the only way she could describe it. As if she had passed through some living . . . force.

Bella narrowed her eyes and gave the room another minute inspection. However much she might fantasize about Maclean, it was really just that, a fantasy. He wasn't real. Then why did she have this intense awareness of someone else sharing her cottage? Was it the man on the horse with his hate-filled face? Bella shuddered. She'd much rather have Maclean; black-hearted villain or not, he was the man for her.

"Maybe you can help me with the book," she said aloud, wildly, to try and jolt herself out of the creepiness of the situation. "Do you hear me, Maclean? Come on, give me some clues. What were you feeling as you marched to Culloden? What went through your mind? *An Interview with a Dead Highland Chief.* Mmm, I wonder if *Reading England* would want to review that."

At least it made her laugh.

The smile stayed. That was what her agent had rung to tell her. Bella's last book had just been reviewed on the prestigious television show *Reading England.* A five-star review. It was unheard-of. And since then it had sold out and the publisher was reprinting.

It was unbelievable. Her books never sold out, they never went into reprint. Not once in twelve long years of writing had this ever happened to her.

"Five stars," she whispered, and laughed.

Not that the book didn't deserve it. *Martin's Journey* was the story of an obscure village in England whose inhabitants had struggled to survive the Black Plague in the fourteenth century. Bella had thoroughly researched the villagers who had lived and died there, putting together the story with a combination of parish and other existing records—the priest had written a heartrending account. Several villagers had stood out as heroes, but Martin in particular. She had written his story with verve and poignancy, lifting him from seven centuries of obscurity and giving him the respect she felt he deserved.

And now everyone was reading about him.

"Maybe this time," she whispered. She'd been waiting for the rest of the world to catch on to her work. The minor figures of history who fascinated her had a strong appeal, but until now no one but her agent and publisher had seemed to recognize that. *Martin's Journey* deserved to be a bestseller, but even moderate sales would help to get *The Black Maclean* onto bookshelves around the country.

Her heart sank as she realized she had just faithfully promised to deliver the book on deadline when she was already way behind schedule. Why hadn't she used Elaine's good mood to her advantage and insisted she needed more time?

The kettle began to boil, and Bella tipped the steaming water into her cup and jiggled the tea bag. Another thought occurred to her that was not so amusing.

"I wonder if Brian knows about the five-star review."

Dear God, she hoped not. With luck, Brian was too busy with Hamish's antiques, and her brief brush with fame would be over by the time he knew about it. He would still be livid that after all these years she actually had some recognition and he wasn't here to bask in it.

And Bella wasn't the least bit sorry he wasn't here. She could just imagine it: He'd be pestering her to get a complete makeover. She'd end up not recognizing herself. Bella Ryan, the new and glamorous version.

Only it would still be the old her underneath, looking out.

Her tea was ready, and she took out the bag and added milk and sugar. She glanced through the window at the sunshine outside. The loch was awash with gentle light, more of Gregor's sheep cropped the moorland grass, and an eagle soared in the cloudless blue.

She had another four weeks on the lease of the cottage. Where would she go then? To Edinburgh and Brian? No, that was over, whatever Georgiana believed. Perhaps it was better not to think too far ahead. Get the book finished first and then deal with what came after.

Bella sipped her tea and forced herself not to turn and look over her shoulder. *There's no one there, there's no one there . . .*

Maybe if she repeated it to herself often enough she might believe it.

Eight

Bella had been working all day, shuffling through her pieces of paper, reading her books and staring at her machine. Whatever the voice on the other end of the talking box had said to her, it had driven her into a frenzy. She muttered to herself, she sang, she crumpled sheets of paper and pelted them across the room— one of them went right through him—and she drank lots and lots of her cups of tea.

Cat's piss, he called it.

Tea was the fashionable drink he'd seen everywhere when he was visiting Edinburgh and Inverness, but he had never developed a taste for it himself. Whiskey and wine and coffee, they were drinks he enjoyed, aye, and in that order.

Maclean didn't like the way she was carrying on—it made him feel queasy. Instead he wandered about the cottage, pretending to take great interest in the stones from which it was made. They looked awfully like the stones from Castle Drumaird. . . .

"Thieves," he snarled.

After that he inspected the shiny white box which kept the foods inside it cold—the way the light always came on when Bella opened the door fascinated him, and he longed to be able to open it himself. He felt restless, agitated, and frustrated. She knew he was here. She might deny it to herself, but he could tell she was more aware of him now than she had been before.

But it wasn't enough. He wanted to touch her, hold her. He wanted to be a man to her.

As twilight turned to shadows outside, Maclean couldn't help himself. He came once more to peer over Bella's shoulder.

As if she knew the instant he was back, Bella said feverishly, "I know, Culloden Moor! I should start the book there. That's when things started to go wrong."

"I fought," Maclean retorted. "I fought bravely. Write that down on your wee machine."

"The legend says he didn't fight. He went home again."

"I did not!"

"He made a deal with the English, promising not to fight if he was granted free passage home to Loch Fasail and his people remained unmolested."

"No!" Maclean shouted it, furious, and swung out his hand. His fingertips struck the mug on Bella's desk.

Bella's china mug rattled. She eyed it warily. "The fourteenth of April, 1746, and Maclean and his men arrive at Culloden Moor. A Monday night. They line up with the rest of the prince's exhausted army for their confrontation with the English. They wait until eleven o'clock Tuesday morning, but the Duke of Cumberland doesn't appear, so they stand down again until Wednesday the sixteenth."

Bella paused, but there wasn't a sound. Maybe she'd imagined the mug jumping about. She'd been up all night, after all. "Um . . ." She cleared her throat. "I could write that Maclean was no fool and what he had seen was enough for him to make up his mind. He went searching for Lord George Murray, one of the more experienced commanders of the Jacobite army, and when he couldn't find him he sent a letter to his quarters in Culloden House. Where's the copy I made . . . ?"

She shuffled more papers around until she found what she was looking for. "It says:

I have come here at your request, my lord, and now I find that my men will be at a great disadvantage in the front line. They are brave and strong fighters, but they have only broadswords and claymores and will be cut to pieces by the English fire before they can engage the enemy. I ask your permission to move them back."

Maclean's head hurt. Her words were conjuring memories. Brief painful flashes, as if he were once more facing the wrath of the English muskets, though nothing that made any sense.

"The battle plan had been prepared by John O'Sullivan, and he was a poor choice. The Jacobite line was spread too wide, and Maclean had been ordered to the right wing, which was the closest to the English army. He knew they'd be torn to pieces by roundshot and grapeshot long before the order was given to advance.

What Maclean didn't know was that Lord George Murray had already argued that it would be better to move the battle to softer ground, where the English couldn't make use of their cavalry. He knew the Highlanders did better when their enemy was less comfortable, less prepared. The men's wild looks and wild screams were perfect for the sort of blitz attacks that put so many bigger armies to flight. But on Culloden Moor the ground was flat, and most of the Jacobite army was exhausted from their long retreat from England. The Jacobite leaders were quarreling among themselves, and many of the clansmen had been forced to fight against their own inclination by their chiefs, dragged from their beds, threatened with eviction or worse. The English were well seasoned and well armed and outnumbered them. Maclean knew that if he fought, he and his men would die before they'd taken one step forward.

"And then he got the message he'd been waiting for. One sentence, in a different hand, is scrawled across the bottom of Maclean's note. *Tell him denied. O'Sullivan.* The note to Lord George Murray reached the incompetent O'Sullivan instead, and the denial must have been passed on verbally to Maclean by some subordinate.

"How you must have hated that," she murmured, as if Maclean were standing in front of her. "Being told by O'Sullivan to stay put despite what you knew would happen. Being ignored by Lord George Murray, when it was his request that brought you all this way. Certain death, Maclean. You didn't want that, you refused to accept it." She sat up straighter. "Maybe that could explain what you did next."

Death? Maclean had managed to move the mug, but that seemed paltry compared to the agony in his head. Was it at Culloden that he had died? Was this the great battle that he knew he had been a part of? Had his men also died in the cold and the mud? Were those the lives he was responsible for losing? But it didn't seem to fit; it didn't seem right.

"That's it, isn't it? It wasn't cowardice that drove you to the English camp that night. You wanted to save your men, save your people from the repercussions you knew would eventually come. You made a bargain not to fight if you were allowed safe passage—"

The mug shook.

Bella stared at it, fascinated and frightened, but with a growing sense of dizzy excitement. *Was* it Maclean? Was he here, listening to her, and communicating with her in the only way he could?

"I'm not judging you," she tried, sitting tense upon her chair. "You were a man of your times, and you were no follower of Bonnie Prince Charlie. I understand your real loyalty, your real duty, was to your own. Freeing Scotland from English rule sounded like a nice idea and perhaps you'd been seduced into it for a time, but now your eyes were opened. You . . . eh . . . made a bargain with the—"

The mug skittered several inches along the desktop, tilting dangerously. Bella put her fingers over it, to keep it from falling, and then pulled her hand back with a gasp. She'd felt a shock, the same sort of zing she'd gotten when she jumped up to answer the phone yesterday.

"Are you saying that you didn't make a bargain with the English?" she said tentatively.

The mug was still and silent.

Bella took a deep breath. "Okay. You didn't make any bargains, you just . . . um, left, and led your men home again to—"

The mug shook ominously. Bella gasped and jumped up, backing away. The skeptical side of her brain was telling her she needed treatment, immediately, but the other side, the side that believed in the unbelievable, was urging her on.

"Then what?" she cried out to the empty room. "I don't understand what you're trying to tell me. Look, I have this . . . this . . ." Frantically she scrabbled among her papers and found what she was searching for. "It's a memoir, written by one of the Macdonalds, who left the same night. He remembered you, Maclean. He and his men walked with yours for miles. He says . . . where is it . . . here! He says, *Their chief said he thought the whole affair was sheer bloody madness and he wanted no further part in it.* You didn't fight at Culloden. You made the best decision for your men and took them home."

Maclean ground his teeth. He'd remembered something vital and now the bloody woman wouldn't listen to him. She might be right, he might have gone home anyway, he was far too pragmatic to let his men be slaughtered for a dream, but he knew now he hadn't deserted. Lord George Murray had come to him, late, and they had talked. "Go home," he'd said, his handsome face grim. "I'm sorry, Morven, that I ever drew you into this mess."

"I remember it," he said to Bella, shaken, triumphant. "I *remember* it!"

"It was a long way across the mountains and the glens," Bella murmured wistfully, almost as if she'd been there.

Aye, it was a long way. His head hurt, but he pushed through the throbbing ache and found he was drawing up more memories. Like water from a deep, deep well. Memories of walking, of exhaustion and desperation, of cheering his men with talk of Loch Fasail and the welcome awaiting them there from their wives and children. Not his wife and children, of course. Not Ishbel. . . . Once he had hoped, but by the time of Culloden he knew with a bleak certainty that such happiness could never be for him.

He frowned. He had clenched his hands down at his sides. There was something else, something more, something dreadful. . . .

"Tell me, woman," he said hoarsely. "What comes next? Tell me the worst, Bella."

But she was still twittering on about Culloden. "You would not fight the English if it meant the death of your clansmen. You put your men, your people, first. I think that was admirable."

She meant it. He felt a rush of warmth and gratitude at her words. Any other woman would have run screaming by now, but here she was, still talking to the ghostie. His Bella was brave, no doubt about it. A true Highland chief's woman.

"That's why what happened next is so incomprehensible." Her voice dropped. "It was your fault, Maclean. You brought it on yourself."

His ears pricked; his heart began to beat with slow hard thuds.

"Brought what on myself, woman? What are ye blathering about? I always protected my people," but his voice was dull, filled with dread.

The *Fiosaiche* spoke in his head: *So many lives lost unnecessarily, Highlander. You must right the wrong.*

Maclean had always thought himself brave, but now he knew that wasn't so. He was a coward. The truth awaited him, the truth he'd struggled to remember since he first awoke, and now he didn't want it. He didn't want to hear. Sick and shaking, he turned and stumbled from the room, barely noticing as he pulled open the door and slammed it shut behind him.

Outside, it was raining, a miserable drizzle that soaked Maclean after a dozen steps. It took a dozen more before he saw the *Fiosaiche* standing waiting for him on the path.

He knew then that his memory had not done her justice. The fiery locks of her hair, the silver fur-lined cloak, the terrible stare of her deep blue eyes.

But he took a step closer, refusing to let her see his fear. He even set his feet apart and rested his hand upon his sword, looking down at her and putting a smile on his lips. Just as he would face any enemy. She was a woman, that was all, a small, insignificant woman. . . .

"You must go back, Highlander," she said, and for all her slight stature, her voice rang out.

"Och, must I, now," he retorted. The rain dripped into his eyes, but he noticed it didn't seem to touch her. She was utterly dry.

"The woman is your doorway to life."

"She canna see me!" he burst out, his frustration evident.

"Not yet."

Ah, Jesus, the awfulness of her eyes. . . . He could barely keep his gaze on hers. There were *things* behind the blue. Serpents, monsters, writhing in a black sea, and an endless dark labyrinth that was horrifyingly familiar. He knew that place. He'd been there. The between-worlds, neither heaven nor hell, where lost souls wandered. Where *he* had wandered until the *Fiosaiche* had chosen him and taken him to the cathedral.

"Why me?" Maclean's knees were trembling so badly he had to lock them to stay upright.

The *Fiosaiche* smiled and it was worse, because there was no human kindness in that smile, nothing human at all.

"Because I have chosen you, Highlander. I have given you this chance to be the man you were always meant to be. I have indulged myself by taking you under my wing." Her smile was gone in an instant. Her eyes shone silver as she stared into his. "It has taken years to find the right moment, the right time for you to redeem yourself. The right woman to stand at your side. Do not fail me, Maclean. Do not fail *her*."

He opened his mouth, closed it again.

The things in her eyes, the shiny lithe bodies twisting and splashing through the dark sea, churned the water white. Monsters, water-horses, creatures that fed on the flesh of Scotsmen.

"You will be sorry if you do."

And then, just like the last time, she was gone. Soaring up in the shape of a golden eagle, her wingtip stirring his hair as she passed by. He gasped, and she flew into the sky, and in a moment was far above him, vanished through the clouds.

Maclean realized then that he was no longer upright, he had fallen to his knees on the ground. He picked himself up, staggering as if his strength had left him.

He must have struck a stone when he went to his knees because there was a gash and it was bleeding. He touched it with his fingertip and stared at the red blood. Only a living man could bleed. Did that mean he was a living man, or on his way to becoming one?

The *Fiosaiche*'s voice filled his head once more: *Do not fail me, Maclean. Do not fail her.*

"I will not fail," he said with gritted teeth. "Bella, I will not—"

His head spun, sick and dizzy, and the horrible black shadows flapped at the edges. But he would not back down. Not this time. He grasped at the memory and held on, clutching it tightly though it slithered and squirmed, and dragging it out into the light.

So that at last he could look upon it and remember.

Ishbel.

Confusion and doubt rocked him. But she was to be his wife! Ishbel Macleod, daughter of Auchry Macleod, his neighbor. He had taken her hostage when she was sixteen, and held her for Auchry's good behavior, to stop his thieving and raiding over the border. Whatever other morals Auchry lacked, he loved his daughter, and her presence at Castle Drumaid had curbed the worst of his behavior.

Maclean blinked and her face filled his mind, unlined and pure, a young girl's face. She had worn flowers in her hair, amusing him and secretly thawing his cold heart a little with her naïve charm. He had kept a proper distance from her, but as time went on an idea took shape in his mind, and when she turned seventeen he decided he would marry her, to peacefully join the lands of Macleod and Maclean.

It seemed like a good idea at the time.

Her face came to him again, but it was very different from before. Gone was the sweet young girl; this Ishbel's mouth drooped and there was hatred in her eyes . . . aye, hatred for him and the life she did not want to share with him.

"I'll not let my future wife tell me what to do." He heard his own voice, so grim, so final. *"You've turned me weak and soft, an' I'll have no more of it!"*

Then, like a spring tide, Ishbel came pouring into him.

"You dinna see me as a flesh-and-blood person, do ye? You canna accept that I may be worth more than you're willing to give me. I am to be your wife, but I mean less to you than your broadsword. I dinna want to be another like your mother."

Maclean tried to shake it out, but now that the voice had found him it would not go away. It cried out at him from two hundred and fifty years in the past.

"Let me go, Maclean. You dinna want me. Give me this chance of happiness. You dinna care for me, you care for no one but yoursel'. Let me go back to where I belong!"

Maclean's heart was thudding in his chest. He took a shaken breath, forcing the air through the constriction in his throat. The ache in his head was half blinding him.

"Dinna betray me, Ishbel, or I will make ye sorry!"

"It is I who will make ye sorry, Maclean!" Ishbel screamed. *"Ye and all those ye love will pay dearly!"*

There was a sound behind him, but Maclean, confused, still trapped in the past, was slow to turn. When he did, he found that the shadows had turned to night, and he could not see properly. Something was moving swiftly far down toward the loch. An animal, maybe a small horse.

He shook his head; it was nothing. He was looking for distractions because he knew very well what he had to do next.

With a shaken breath, Maclean limped toward the cottage and peered through the kitchen window. Bella was there inside, looking pale and frightened. He'd done that.

He put his hand to the glass, just as he did that first time, but nothing happened. He tried again, closing his eyes, wishing himself inside, in the warmth, with Bella. But again nothing happened. He shivered as a chill breeze whipped around him. There was no easy way back, not this time. He had moved on from being a ghost, and although he was still not a man, he was getting closer.

Maclean went to the door and reached for the doorknob.

The first time his fingers went through it, the sensation a little like plunging them into cool liquid. Frustrated, he wanted to roar at the sky and stamp around. How the bloody hell was he supposed to be the man he should always have been if he couldn't get inside the cottage?

Maclean reached out for the doorknob again, but just as his fingers closed on it, an image of Bella's pale, frightened face flashed into his mind. He needed to protect her, he needed to be with her, but more than that he needed not to fail her.

His hand closed on the metal doorknob, and it turned. The door opened. And for the first time since he'd come home, Maclean understood how he might escape his current predicament. Bella was the key. Every step forward he made as a man was connected to his feelings and attitude toward her. Although he wasn't quite sure yet what he was doing right, it was a start.

Bella looked up as the door opened and her eyes were enormous.

"Maclean?" she whispered.

"Aye," he said, although he knew she could not hear him. Not yet.

"Oh, Maclean," she said, and she sounded so frightened and so sad his heart almost stopped. "I want to clear your name, I really do. If the legend is wrong, then I'll do my best to find out what *really* happened, but you have to help me."

And then Bella's machine made a noise, the words flickered and blurred. There was a smell like burning, and she gasped and pushed frantically at the buttons, just as everything went black.

Nine

The screen was black and there was not a sound in the room. After so much violent emotion, it seemed like an anticlimax.

Bella was staring at the machine in rigid silence, as if she couldn't believe it, and then she picked up a book from the pile beside her and flung it at the wall, straight at his picture. It landed with a crash and bounced onto the shelf beneath before plummeting to the floor, taking several other books with it. His portrait fluttered by one corner, but did not fall.

Ah, now he understood! Bella's accursed writing machine was dead and she thought it was his fault.

Maclean gave an evil chuckle. "Och, Bella, you have a wee temper there," he scolded gleefully.

He was truly delighted the fiendish thing had broken; if she couldn't write on it, then she couldn't tell those lies. It was a reprieve for him, a little bit of time to consider what was happening.

But Bella hadn't finished yet. She flung another book, and then another. The portrait hung doggedly by its corner and would not be dislodged. Maclean watched her expectantly, his lips twitching, but the fire had gone out of her. She dropped her head into her arms and began to sob so hard the whole desk shook.

His smile vanished. Despite his anger and his pain, the sight of her brought so low made him ache inside. It was a very long time since he had been moved by a woman's tears; those softer feelings had rarely escaped the locks and chains he kept upon them. Women were a distraction and love made fools of men. But for once Maclean ignored his head and acted on what his heart was telling him.

He reached out his big, scarred hand and rested it gently on Bella's shoulder.

"Come, now, lass," he murmured, "things are no' so bad."

He could feel her. Her skin, soft and warm, the pulse of her body in her blood, the bones beneath the skin, the movement of muscles as she sat up with a gasping cry and looked wildly about her.

Her face was white and streaked with tears, her eyes were red-rimmed, the pupils huge and black with fear. But she was brave, his Bella. Where other lassies would have run screaming, she stayed put.

"Who's there?" she said, her voice shaking.

He was standing behind her, but now he stepped back, away from her. Withdrawing into himself. *He had touched her. . . .* And she had felt him.

She was still looking all around, anxious little glances. And then she gave a sigh and pushed her long hair out of her face and wiped her teary cheeks with her fingers. "You know, I don't care if you are here, Maclean. Do your worst!"

She waited, Maclean waited, nothing happened. Then she looked at the broken writing machine and sighed again. "I'm going crazy," she said. "When did I last sleep? I need to *sleep*."

She stood up. "Maclean?" she whispered again, but when no one answered her, she shook her head and moved toward the door.

He was standing immediately in her path. This time he didn't step aside. He waited. Hoping . . . longing. . . . Bella walked right through him and up the stairs to bed, flicking off the light as she went.

Maclean was alone in the dark room. He had touched her and she had felt him, and yet a moment later he had been a ghost again.

What had made the difference?

He thought back, trying to remember what he had felt as he reached out his hand, but all he could see were images of the past. Some were from his own unreliable memory and some were pictures put there by Bella's words. They were jumbled in his head, confusing and frightening, and he couldn't tell truth from lies. But still he knew. Something very bad had happened in his past, and although he had just taken a step backward, he could not escape it for much longer.

Bella stood at the window staring out at the loch, her arms clutched about her, ignoring the chill floor beneath the soles of her bare feet. Odd things were happening. The sense that she wasn't alone had heightened, and then the mug moving by itself and the door opening and closing. She'd felt certain Maclean was with her; she'd even spoken to him. But now . . . doubts were creeping in.

What about the hand? Did you imagine the hand?

No, she didn't imagine that. She'd felt a hand on her shoulder, a big warm hand. Maclean's hand. It was beyond creepy, but at the same time there had been a sense that the hand was trying to comfort her—she'd just gone into meltdown, after all.

The Maclean in the legend would never offer comfort to a woman. But then, she'd never completely accepted the legend.

Outside, the loch was a stretch of silver, an echo of the moonlight above. There was a splash in the water, and a ripple ran all the way to the shore. Bella frowned, trying to see what it was. A bird landing, probably, or a fish surfacing for a final snack before bed. Loch Fasail was deep and cold, and there were stories about what lay in the depths of such places. She remembered Brian insisting something had tugged at his foot as he was swimming, and how she had laughed at him.

It didn't seem very funny now.

The splash came again, bigger, and for a heartbeat a dark shape was silhouetted against the water's surface. There was a low keening sound. A stag, she told herself, even though she knew it was nothing like the call of a stag. Some of Gregor's sheep were cropping the moorland grass. The sound came again, and in unison they turned and fled, their woolly rumps vanishing over the crest of the hill.

Bella snapped the curtains shut.

When had she last slept a straight eight hours? She was exhausted. Maybe that was what the hand on her shoulder had been—not Maclean, just sheer exhaustion.

Bella went to bed.

Maclean was so deep into his thoughts that it was almost like sleeping. Like dreaming. The peats in the Aga settled as they burned to ash, but he didn't notice. His dreaming self was down by the loch, and it was as if he had never left.

He was walking, his kilt swinging, the sun upon his head. Women stared at him admiringly and men lowered their eyes with respect, for he was the Black Maclean. He smiled, feeling his heart swell. This was where he belonged. *This* was his rightful place. Not in a world where giant machines tried to run over him and people ate their meals from boxes and bags behind walls of glass and women wrote lies about him on machines.

He noticed then that Bella was up ahead of him, sitting on the stone wall in a sea of purple heather. She had her back to him and her hair hung long and dark to her waist, the ends of it moving gently in the soft breeze. As he drew closer she must have heard him, for she looked over her shoulder at him. Skin like cream, eyes dark and deep and a full, kissable mouth above a stubborn chin.

Och, Bella.

"I knew you'd come," she said, and smiled.

He circled her until he stood before her, knee-deep in the heather, gazing down as she looked up. "You dinna belong here," he told her sternly, but his lips were trying to smile back.

"But I do. I'm researching you," she said.

Maclean wasn't sure what that meant, but he shrugged as if he didn't care. "Everyone on my land belongs to me. Mabbe that's what you want—to be mine."

"You can't own people."

"I do. They are mine and I am theirs, like a father his children."

"A father would care for his children, he wouldn't let them die."

Maclean's frown grew darker. "I dinna remember—"

"Try and remember. That's why you're here, isn't it?"

"I take no instruction from women," he said coldly.

She blinked at him, long dark lashes sweeping over her watchful gaze. "Why not?" she demanded. "What makes you better than them?"

Maclean laughed at her simplicity, but she did not smile in return; she was deadly serious.

"You have a lot to learn, Bella Ryan."

Bella smiled then, but it was a pitying smile, as though he were the one in need of help. "So do you, Maclean."

"Maclean?"

The voice was old. He looked up, dragging his gaze from the fascination of Bella's face, and suddenly she was gone and he found himself confronted by an ancient hag. White hair straggling about her stooped shoulders, a face so wrinkled and creased it was hardly a face at all, apart from the milky eyes.

"The *Fiosaiche* said ye would come," the creature cackled.

"What are you?" he whispered, unable to disguise his horror at the sight of her.

"Och, Morven," she sighed, "ye see these stones?" She gestured to the *Cailleach* Stones. "This is a doorway into the between-worlds, and I am its keeper. The door is open and I dinna have the strength to close it. My powers are fading and I can only come to you in dreams, to warn you—"

"Warn me about what?"

"Long ago your people passed through this door, into the between-worlds and then on to the world of the dead."

"They died together?"

"Aye, murdered, cut down most foully. They cried to me as they passed because you were not among them. They asked me why you had abandoned them at such a time, but I had no answer."

Maclean groaned.

"But there was one of them who did not weep. Be warned, Maclean. She has tricked me with her sweet face, tricked me into . . ."

Her voice was fading.

"What did you say, hag?" he shouted. "Warn me against what?"

". . . Ishbel . . ."

The old woman was gone.

Ishbel? Maclean felt a slow, heavy dread take hold of him. Ishbel—it seemed she was everywhere.

Bella stirred in her sleep. She had been sitting on the old stone wall by the loch, talking to Maclean, when suddenly he was gone and the old woman appeared. It was the hag in her green arisaid. Now the hag leaned over her and peered into her face. She was so old it was impossible she was really alive. Her fingers, thin and hooked as claws, closed on Bella's wrist and held on with surprising strength.

"Ye must remember what I tell ye, girl."

"What do you want?"

"Listen."

Her eyes were milky white and Bella found herself staring into them and unable to look away.

"I warned ye once against the *each-uisge*."

"I—I think I saw it."

"Aye, mabbe ye did. The door is open and the *each-uisge* comes and goes as it pleases. It will try and take your life."

"But . . . why?"

"It does no' matter why. Listen to me, lass. Ye must watch for when the *each-uisge* is changing its form. That is when it is vulnerable. That is when it can be captured. Ye must have the magic bridle at hand."

"M-magic bridle?" This was absurd.

The hag was nodding slowly, and now she smiled with no teeth. "Dinna worry, I will see to it that you have such a thing before the time comes. Slip the bridle on, but remember, the creature will no' be easily restrained, and if it knows what ye are about, then it will kill you."

"I know this is a dream. I want to wake up now."

"Aye, just a dream," the hag agreed gently, "but ye must remember it nonetheless. There is a monster in the loch and it belongs to the *each-uisge*. Have ye seen the loch monster, girl?"

"I think so. . . . Last night something frightened the sheep."

"Aye, he comes through the door from the between-worlds, and he's always hungry. Dinna go too close to the water in the darkness, Arabella Ryan."

"I don't—"

The hag looked up suddenly and her eyes narrowed. She swept her green arisaid about her head, peering from the folds and shadows in a way that made Bella think that whatever the hag was looking at was very nasty.

She muttered something in Gaelic.

Bella tried to turn, but found she couldn't. Then the sound of movement behind her, a splashing in the shallows of the loch and a wet, dragging sound as something heavy approached across the stony beach.

"I want to wake up now."

The hag's eyes gleamed in the shadows of her arisaid, and now Bella could see an image within them. It was the loch monster, its skin scaled and dripping, with a head similar to that of a stag without the antlers, and yet long-necked like the pictures she had seen of the Loch Ness Monster. The smell of it hung in the air around them, like rotting fish. As Bella stared into the hag's eyes, she felt something fall onto her shoulder, something cold and slimy. Reaching up with a trembling hand, she felt it.

Water weed from the depths of the loch.

A cold, sour breath huffed against the flesh of Bella's nape, and the hag began to chant in Gaelic, softly and fiercely.

That was when Bella began to scream.

Maclean woke with a start, still shivering from his waking dream. He was alone in the dark kitchen and above him he heard Bella cry out. He didn't remember climbing the narrow stairs, but the next moment he was in her bedchamber, standing over her.

"Bella?"

"I want to wake up!"

"Bella, quiet yourself, 'tis but a dream."

He saw at once that this was true. Her face was tear-streaked, her long dark lashes clubbed together, her hair tangled about her. She was wearing her bedclothes, loose trousers of a sunset-pink and a long-sleeved shirt of yellow. The shirt was twisted about her and had been pulled up, disclosing the underside of one plump breast. Her trousers had slid down to rest on her rounded hips, and there was a stretch of curved belly, soft and pale and extremely tempting.

Maclean was holding his breath, all sensible thought vanished from his mind, leaving only a hot and desperate yearning.

Bella gasped again, twisting on her bed, and the shirt rose even higher. Her breast was half exposed now, the dark pink nipple contrasting with her lush creamy skin.

Maclean felt the yearning within him grow almost painful. He stretched out his hand toward her, tentative, wondering if a miracle might happen and that he might feel.

Because he wanted to. More than anything in a very long time, he wanted to feel the marvelous softness of her skin, bury his face against her and breathe in her scent, her warmth, her tranquillity. He needed her and it looked to him as if she needed him.

His shaking fingertips touched flesh. He bit back a

groan. So soft, so smooth, so warm. Not daring to think in case it ended, he began to explore the curve of her breast, fingers shaking more than ever, holding his breath, afraid that the slightest sound might make it all stop.

Were women's bodies always this beautiful? he asked himself feverishly, as he ran his fingers over her nipple and felt it tighten and harden. He wanted to close his eyes and savor the sensation, but he dared not linger. In another moment he could be a wraith again, feeling nothing, hovering between life and death and not really inhabiting either.

She had calmed down, the nightmare passing, and now she made a little sound and turned her face away, presenting him with the curve of her jaw and ear and the delicate line of her neck. He touched her breast again, stroking the warm fullness, dizzy with the knowledge that he could feel again. And that she could feel him. *Dinna stop*, he thought. *Dinna let it stop. I promise to go back to my hell without a fight if you dinna let it stop just yet. . . .*

His fingers glided down over her ribs to the rounded swell of her belly, and he cupped his palm over her hip. She shifted slightly, but not to move away. In her sleep she was pressing closer. Braver now, he trailed his fingers down to the edge of her trousers, where they rode low across her midriff. The cord was untied, making them loose, and when he slid his hand beneath there was no resistance.

Bella opened her legs, as if to invite him to touch. She murmured in her sleep. He let his hand follow its path down, through the warm soft hair that covered her mound, down into the slick, womanly folds.

His heart was pounding. The muscles and sinews of his body were taut, as though he were readying himself for battle. His breath was hurting his chest and his throat as he struggled to calm himself. It was so good. As he stroked her, felt the heat of her, he knew he had never felt anything so good, nor anything he had wanted so much.

She arched her back, pushing against his hand. Her own hands moved aimlessly across the rumpled quilt and sheets, and her lips parted as she murmured something, a word.

"Maclean."

"Bella," he whispered, his body alive and tingling and no longer a useless imitation of a man.

Asleep, she had shed the doubts and uncertainties that seemed to plague her waking self. She was all woman, beautiful and warm and passionate, and as he gently pressed his fingers into the core of her, she surged against him, seeking to bring herself to her peak. She moaned softly, then louder as he flicked his thumb against that tight, eager nub. She reached out and her fingers wrapped around his forearm, gripping him tightly, holding him just where she wanted him.

He laughed in delight, watching her, enjoying her. His own body was rigid with lust, but he didn't care about that. For so long he had not felt, and now he had no need to sate himself to experience the ultimate pleasure. Watching her was enough.

She was rubbing herself against him, gasping a little as the sensation built, the moisture on his hand telling him she was almost done. And then at last she peaked, crying out so wildly that he laughed again, pleased and admiring.

Here was a woman not afraid to enjoy herself! This was the real Bella, hot and sensual, unashamed of her body. *His* Bella, a woman to spend a lifetime with.

Suddenly Maclean realized she had gone very still.

Her fingers, still wrapped about his forearm, had relaxed and loosened. Now they tightened again, convulsively, and with a shriek she leapt away from him to the other end of the bed. He heard a thud as she fell off and hit the floor.

His body was aching with incompletion, but he did not mind. Observing her, pleasing her, had been enough for him for now, and such a thing did not even seem strange to him. He watched, amused, as her tousled hair appeared over the top of the mattress, and then two big eyes. He wondered what she would do when she saw him, and waited, his breath held.

She blinked, slowly, looking about the room. Looking at him, then past him, then through him.

Disappointment ravaged him, compounding the ache he was already suffering. She couldn't see him. He reached out but didn't dare to touch her again. He couldn't face the anguish if his hand passed through her.

Bella stood up, swaying a little, and pushed her hair out of her eyes. The bedclothing hugged her curves and he felt his body stir again. He wanted her, but what was the point of trying to ease his body on a woman who didn't know he was there? What if he fell right through her as if she were water?

He wanted to feel the warmth of her, her soft living flesh beneath him, her mouth against his. He wanted her eyes looking into his eyes. He wanted her to need him as much as he needed her.

"Dear God," she murmured. She reached and with shaking hands flicked on the light by the bed. Nothing happened. So she searched around, fumbling and cursing, and lit a candle. Then she sat down on the side of the bed and put her head in her hands.

Maclean looked at the dejected curve of her spine. He wanted to comfort her, but it was not something he excelled at—comforting women hadn't been part of his position as chief of the clan. But he was no longer a chief, and Bella needed kindness and understanding. . . . Once again he went with his instincts.

"I didna mean to hurt you," Maclean said in his deep, slightly husky voice.

And Bella froze.

Ten

His voice! *She jumped up again and spun* around. Nothing. The room was the same, messy and empty of all but shadows. There was an ache low in her belly and her head was spinning, and she kept remembering the hand on her body, touching, urging her, until she had climaxed harder and stronger than she could remember doing for a very long time.

If ever.

She had thought she was dreaming, like before, when he had made love to her by the *Cailleach* Stones. It was only after the climax that she realized it wasn't a dream after all. The man was real. She could feel his wrist beneath her hands, the rough hairs and the powerful muscles corded under his skin, the bones within. And his pulse, as real warm blood pounded through his veins.

He was here and he was real.

Except, when she peered over the side of the mattress, he wasn't here after all. There was no one here, and certainly a man wouldn't have had time to rush from the room and down the stairs, not without her seeing him, hearing him. . . .

But she *had* heard him.

That deep Scottish voice—like warm whiskey seeping into her every pore. A shiver that had nothing to do with fear zigzagged through her body, and she was acutely aware of the lingering ache between her thighs.

"Where are you?" she asked the empty room. Because he was here! She knew it. Felt it. And deep down she had known it for a while.

"I'm seated on your bed, lass."

Her gaze found the source of the voice. Nothing. Except . . . She squinted. There was an indentation on the side of the mattress, and now that she looked more closely she could see it was a very large indentation for a very large . . . ghost?

"I can't see you," she whispered.

"You saw me once," he whispered back.

Bella blinked. The night in the kitchen after Brian had left, the brief but vivid image of the Scotsman in the kilt. Big, tall, dark-haired, with pale eyes the color of the evening sky. *Maclean.* It had been his hand, his fingers, inside her just now, knowing just what she liked, just where to stroke.

She didn't know whether to laugh in amazement or cry with embarrassment.

"Why are you here?" Her voice was sharp.

The dent moved, flattened out, and then she heard the floor creaking from the approach of a heavy weight.

Suddenly she was frightened. He was much bigger than her, and he was invisible.

"Stay away!" she cried. "Don't come near me."

The creaking stopped, and she heard him sigh. "Verra well," he said. "I dinna know why I'm here. I canna answer you."

"You're . . . dead?"

"I dinna think so."

"But you must be!"

He laughed, that soft husky sound that caught her low in the belly and intensified the ache. "I'm far from dead at the moment, believe me."

"Who are you?" But she knew; she'd known all along.

There was a pause, and Bella waited, and then he spoke again. "I am the Maclean."

Even though she'd known what he was going to say, the name made Bella dizzy. She thought about lying down on the bed, but she didn't dare in case he saw it as an invitation. This was the Maclean, the Black Maclean, the man she had been fantasizing about ever since she saw his portrait.

"Then you must be dead," she said as matter-of-factly as she could, "because the Maclean died over two hundred years ago."

"Two hundred and fifty," came the dry reply.

Suddenly it was too much for her.

"Go away," she whispered. "I . . . I need to dress. Can you wait downstairs?"

Another sigh. "Aye. I willna go verra far," he said, and she had the feeling he was mocking her. The heavy footsteps moved toward the door, and then it closed very quietly, all by itself, and he was gone.

*   *   *

Bella sat down and tried to order her thoughts. She had known there was a ghost in her cottage, but there was a difference between knowing and *knowing*.

But *was* he a ghost? A man who said he wasn't dead, whom she'd only seen once but who'd made his presence felt by moving objects, touching her, speaking to her.

Did that make him real?

He'd felt real a moment ago, when he'd sent her into blissful orbit.

Bella took a deep breath, and then another. She had heard, somewhere, that sometimes the spirits of the dead walked the earth because they did not realize they were dead. They needed someone to explain it to them, guide them gently on their path to wherever they were meant to be, and then they would just . . . vanish.

She felt a stab of disappointment. She didn't want him to go away. She had an eighteenth century Highland chief in her cottage. They had been together in bed. . . . She squeezed her eyes tight shut. Oh God, this was the man Brian had accused her of having steamy thoughts about, and she had, but Bella knew she wasn't ready for that kind of relationship with a . . . a ghost. And what if he now expected her to be his sexual plaything? It was true, he *had* left the room when she asked him to, so perhaps he could be trusted. Come to think of it, he had been very polite. Thoughtful, even. A gentleman.

Except he wasn't, not according to the legend.

She mustn't be lulled into trusting him; this wasn't the time to let her emotions overrule cold good sense.

Grabbing up a sweater, she pulled it over her pajama top, and some baggy trousers over the bottoms, then tugged on some warm socks. It seemed a bit silly to cover herself up now, when he had seen so much of her, but it gave her confidence.

Wondering if she was completely insane, Bella picked up the candle and made her way cautiously down the stairs.

The kitchen was empty.

Bella wasn't deceived. He was there, she could feel his presence like warm breath against her skin. Nervously, she edged into the room. "Maclean?"

"Lass."

His voice came from right behind her and she jumped and backed away, trying to steady her breathing. Her gaze flicked about, but there was nothing to see but shadows.

"I saw you . . . I think I saw you once. Are you wearing a kilt and a black jacket?"

"Aye, a plaid and a velvet jacket, and I have my *claidheamh mor* at my side. I am like the painting you have a likeness of, only without the trews."

"The tr-trews, of course." She flicked a glance at the painting. "You sound very tall."

"Aye, I'm tall. Six foot and four inches. I canna stand straight in your wee house."

He was complaining about the height of her ceilings? Bella cleared her throat. It was bizarre; she was talking to someone who wasn't here, and yet she could see him in her mind. Tall, stooping beneath the ceiling, his dark hair falling forward, his pale eyes fixed on her. Maclean was here in her cottage, and tonight he'd made her feel so wonderfully alive she could still feel the aftershocks.

"Why are you here?" Her voice shook, but she hoped he didn't know why. *Please don't let him be able to read my mind.*

"Here?"

"In this cottage."

"I dinna know."

"Are you sure you're not dead? Maybe you are and you don't know it. Maybe you need to accept it and then go on your journey."

He made a scornful sound, and she felt her face flush.

"I was taken by the *Fiosaiche* and I have been sleeping in the between-worlds for two hundred and fifty years. Now I am awakened and my task is before me, but I dinna know what it is except that I am to become the man I should always have been. To fail means I must return to the between-worlds, and believe me that is not a place anyone would wish to go."

Bella sat down and tried to make sense of this. Between-worlds? Where had she heard this recently? It sounded crazy, but then the whole thing was insane. "What is the *Fiosaiche*? I've heard that name."

"She who decides our fate when we die. The *Fiosaiche* has powerful magic. She can send a soul to the world of the dead or punish them in the between-worlds, or she can return you to the mortal world, as she did with me."

"You mean a sort of witch? A sorceress?"

"Aye."

"So the between-worlds is something between life and death?"

"Aye, a place of punishment and waiting."

"Do you mean purgatory?"

"It is no' called that." He sounded impatient. "Many souls are gathered there to hear their ultimate fate, but there are other creatures, too. The ancient ones who walked this land before man, and monsters and beings we know only through fable and legend. The between-worlds is their home."

Bella remembered then where she'd heard of the between-worlds—the hag in her dream. "Is there a—a doorway into it?" she asked cautiously.

"Aye, but it is closed."

"Are you sure?"

Maclean didn't answer, but whether because he was considering her question or because he found it simply too foolish, Bella was uncertain.

"You say you have a task to perform, that you have to 'become the man you should always have been,' and the *Fiosaiche* hasn't told you how you're going to achieve this?" Bella frowned, concentrating on the moment in case she ran screaming out the door. "Her planning isn't great, is it?"

That laughter again, so sexy it made her shiver. He was standing beside her. She wondered if she reached out her hands whether she would feel him, big and solid. She clenched them tighter in her lap.

"Did the *Fiosaiche* send you here?"

"I had nowhere else to go but home," he said bleakly. "I dinna imagine it would be destroyed and everything gone. I thought I would come home and live here again, become the man I used to be."

Bella wondered what he would have done if there had been someone resident in his castle. Throw them out? Run his sword through them? Perhaps it was best not to ask. This man was possibly both brutal and violent, and she must not forget that and lower her guard. She was dealing with an eighteenth century Highlander, a barbarian with a surface veneer of sophistication, and according to legend that veneer was very thin. She needed to be extremely careful.

"So what are you going to do?"

"Do?" he asked, although it was more like a demand.

"Yes, *do*. You have no home, so you've taken up residence in my cottage. I think I have a right to know your plans. What are you going to do?"

"Wait."

"I see." Bella looked up to where she thought he was. "But I live here. I'm finding it a little difficult coming to terms with the fact that you're here with me and I can't see you."

She heard the smile in his voice. "I will sing if you like, so that you won't be frightened and you will always know where I am."

"I'm not frightened," Bella said levelly, although she was.

It occurred to her that it might be difficult to get any work done with a singing ghost. Bad enough that she sang to herself, but if Maclean did it, too . . .

"But . . . won't you get bored? What do you do all the time?"

"I watch you," he said, "and I walk with you."

She went cold. "I don't understand."

"You are the only one who can see me, hear me, feel me. No one else can. I want to stay here with you."

Bella had a ghostly stalker. "My lease runs out in

four weeks, but apart from that I don't think I want you to stay here."

"These are my lands. *You* are the interloper, Bella."

Oh God, he knew her name. Goose bumps rose on her skin; she rubbed her arms vigorously. "How long have you been here?"

"I was born in 1716 and I—"

"*This* time, I mean."

"Since your man left you."

"I knew you were here, I *knew* it. The mug moving—that was you, wasn't it?"

"Aye. No' that it was easy, mind!"

"You've never touched me before, though."

"I've tried," he said promptly. "This is the first time you've felt me."

Bella swallowed, refusing to let her imagination distract her with memories of his warm fingers.

"You've walked right through me many times," he added with a note of complaint.

That explained the zings she'd been getting.

"You couldn't talk before, you couldn't touch before. What's happening?"

"I dinna know exactly, but I think it has something to do with you, Bella. The *Fiosaiche* is giving me back these things, rewarding me, whenever I please her. I'm just no' sure what I am doing right and what I am doing wrong." He sounded petulant, as if he wasn't used to being subordinate to another.

"So it's possible you may soon become a man again?" Bella asked curiously, trying not to imagine how she must look, talking to an empty room.

"I will be myself again," he said proudly, "the Black Maclean, Chief of the Fasail Macleans."

"Except there are no Fasail Macleans left."

She was sorry for her words; his sigh was the saddest sound she had ever heard. Bella's soft heart fought with her good sense, and she clenched her hands again so that she didn't reach out to comfort him.

"You are making a book about me," he said with quiet pride, but there was an edge in his voice that spoke of desperation. "I can help you with that."

"Oh? I know quite a lot already—"

He snorted. "I have read the lies you write on your machine. Mabbe you dinna want the truth, is that it?"

Now she had made him angry. Bella edged away, but when he spoke again his voice was soft and persuasive rather than the ranting of a bully.

"You said you wanted to know what happened, Bella. I can tell you what I remember, and mabbe together we can learn the truth."

Bella was aware of her growing sense of excitement. What other historian could say she had a direct link to her subject? Maclean could tell her so much, things no one else knew. Always assuming it *was* the truth, of course, she reminded herself. But even so . . . this was a unique opportunity.

Maclean didn't wait for her answer. "I had a sister," he said loudly. "She died when she was wee. You said in your book that I was my parents' only child, but I had a sister, though I canna remember her name."

"You have trouble with your memory, then?"

"Aye, it has holes in it. I remember unimportant things, but the rest is . . . difficult."

Convenient, said her cool common sense. Was he saying he did not remember what he had done two hundred and fifty years ago? "Tell me something unimportant, then," Bella dared him, and held her breath.

Maclean gave it some thought. "The tutor I brought to Loch Fasail to teach the children was my kin—a cousin of my father's cousin. He dressed in clothes more suited to an Edinburgh dandy, and he wore a wig. When he arrived to begin his work he had so much luggage the children believed he must be a king, and ran about screaming with excitement."

Bella smiled at the image.

"But it wasna just his clothes that were above his station, his ideas were verra grand as well. He thought I was a fool, and that he could order my people about and encourage them to go against me, all for his own benefit. It seems he had some misguided notion that Fasail was his by blood right, when the truth was I only invited him because I was asked to by his father. He was no' a good man. When I heard all he had done, I came for him and dragged him out of his house. He was cursing me, and using words I had certainly ne'er heard a schoolmaster use. I threw him in the loch."

"Could he swim?"

"The place I threw him in was shallow enough. He was spluttering and splashing, and when he climbed out he looked like a slippery eel, his lace sleeves all dirty and his high heels full o' muck. He packed up all his trunks and off he went home to Edinburgh."

The picture he conjured, and the satisfaction in his voice, were a little shocking, but to Bella it was just like the Black Maclean she had always imagined.

Bold and larger than life, dangerous and arrogant, dispensing his own brand of justice upon the hapless schoolmaster.

"You like that," he murmured in that husky, sexy voice. "I thought ye would."

"I must be going mad," Bella rubbed her hands over her arms again, but now the goose bumps weren't from fear. "You're offering to help me write my book?"

"Aye, I am."

"And you won't hold back, even on the bits that put you in a bad light?"

"I swear to you I willna hold back, Bella, but there are things I do not remember."

An idea was forming in Bella's mind, a way of testing the truth of Maclean's convenient memory.

"I give you my word I will do my best," he said.

He was making her an offer too good to refuse, and it gave her an excuse to say yes. She nodded. "All right. You can stay here. As I said, my lease runs out in four weeks, though perhaps I can ask about extending it. But if you stay, you have to let me know where you are, and you can't go sneaking around when I'm getting dressed or sleeping. I agree it was very . . . nice, just now, but I didn't ask you to do that and I don't think you should touch without consulting me."

"It was verra nice," he murmured thickly.

"Tomorrow," she said hastily, "I'm going into Ardloch. I have to shop and see about my laptop. You can come with me if you like," she added blithely, hoping again he couldn't read her mind.

"Walk, do ye mean?"

"No, drive in the car."

He shuffled. "Ah."

Clearly he was nervous about the car, and who could blame him? It must have been quite a culture shock to wake up two hundred and fifty years into the future.

"Maybe you're wrong, Maclean. Maybe someone else can see you. If you come into Ardloch we might be able to find out."

"Aye." He was tempted, just as she hoped. "Verra well, I'll come in the . . . car."

"Do you want something to, eh, eat? To drink? A cup of tea, perhaps?"

"Cat's piss," he muttered with disgust. "I wouldn't mind a dram of whiskey, but I canna seem to eat or drink anything."

"Oh. Do you sleep?"

"No, but sometimes I dream."

Bella was suddenly reminded again of the nightmare she had been having before Maclean woke her up. The hag in the green arisaid and the *each-uisge*, and the magic bridle, and the hideous loch monster panting behind her. Dear God, what next?

"Okay." She pulled herself together and managed a smile. "You dream down here and I'll go and . . . ah, dream upstairs."

She moved past him to the door, but he touched her hand. Big warm fingers, slightly callused, brushed over her skin. If she closed her eyes she could see him standing there looking down at her, big and handsome and barely tamed.

"Thank you," he said quietly.

As Bella made her way upstairs, she had the feeling he had not said that to many people. Maybe it was even a first.

Eleven

To Maclean's relief, Ardloch was still thirty miles across the hills, but to get there meant driving on a single winding road with passing points. He would much rather have walked.

They hadn't left as early as Bella would have liked. Gregor had sent a man to hammer and swear at the machine that worked the heating and the hot water. Maclean knew Bella was worrying he might speak, so he said and did nothing. At least it answered the question as to whether others could see him—they couldn't.

The man was there for a long time, and then Bella gave him tea, and bread with thin slices of meat inside it, and ate some herself. It wasn't until he was gone that they were able to set out at last for Ardloch.

Now Maclean sat in the car beside her, stiff as a poker. Being inside such a thing was much more frightening than he had imagined it would be, but he didn't want her to know how he was feeling, despite the fact she could not see him. The Black Maclean was afraid of nothing; he had a reputation to maintain.

"Are you all right?" She seemed to know anyway.

"Perfectly."

The road rushed toward them through the glass wall, and the rocks and gorse and heather skimmed by so fast they were a blur. His eyes ached from trying to make sense of it, and in the end he shut them tightly and prayed for it to end.

Two hundred and fifty years ago, Ardloch had been a small fishing village on the coast that held a cattle market every month—a gathering point for fishermen and crofters, shepherds and thieves to come and buy and sell their wares, meet up and get drunk and eye any women less than eighty years old for the position of future wife or lover. Try as he might, he could not imagine it as other than a smoky cluster of dirty stone cottages with sagging peat roofs, smelling of fish, with animals running wild in the streets.

He wondered what Bella hoped to achieve in such a place. If she showed her laptop, as she called it, to the people of Ardloch they would laugh in her face. Or burn her for a witch.

She was a sort of a witch. Not like the *Fiosaiche*. Bella was *his* witch. He had thought on her long into the night, remembering how she had responded to his touch, and wondering if he would ever have the chance to do it again. She had enjoyed it, he knew she had, but she was frightened of him. How could he blame her for that? And yet it frustrated him. He was the Maclean and he was used to obedience. Bella had been prepared to send him away last night, and although he had no intention of going, he had felt a sense of anger and helplessness previously quite alien to him.

She was a woman and he was the Maclean, yet she held the upper hand. He had to coerce her by agreeing to help her with her accursed book, the last thing he wanted to do. Of course, he could have used physical force, but Maclean could not bring himself to do that. He had never used force on a woman before.

What about Ishbel? Dinna ye force her to your will by taking her hostage?

He shivered.

There was something wrong; he sensed it. In his dream last night the hideous old woman who claimed to be the doorkeeper to the between-worlds said the door was open. And later, during their conversation in the kitchen, Bella had asked him whether he was certain the door was closed and he hadn't answered her. Because he just wasn't sure.

If it was open, what did that mean? It would certainly explain the origin of the rider who had tried to attack Bella, but it did not explain why he had done so. What else was waiting on the other side?

"We're here."

Her voice startled him into opening his eyes, and at first he was too surprised to answer. *This* was Ardloch? Before him was a sprawl of houses against the blue waters of the bay. Ardloch had changed a great deal since he was last here. As they drove down into the center of the town, he could see that the buildings were strongly made with square lines and glass windows, and the streets were paved in gray and there were motorcars everywhere.

"It must be market day."

"They still have a market here?" He was comforted to know that at least some things hadn't changed.

"Yes. I'll just find a place to park."

Bella slowed to dodge around something she called a van, and passed a shop that sold bread. The warm, mouthwatering smell of it caught Maclean's attention briefly, but he couldn't concentrate. Ardloch had changed in other ways as well. It was bigger and busier. There were people in the streets, and they were dressed similarly to Bella, though some of them far more outlandishly.

There were strangers in his country.

Or maybe it was Maclean who was the stranger.

Bella had found her place to park and now she angled her car into it, turning the wheel as she inched her way back and forth until she was satisfied. Maclean felt his heart beating hard and did not breathe until she was done. She turned and smiled encouragingly at the place she presumed he was, as if she knew how he must be feeling. Maclean had discovered since they set out this morning that Bella had made up her mind to accept his presence completely and not argue over what was possible and what was not.

He just wished she'd stop treating him as if he were coming down with something, just because he was invisible.

"Now, I thought that I'd take the laptop into the electronics shop to be repaired, and then we can go to the museum. What do you think?" Her voice was high, as if she were even more nervous than before.

"Verra well," he replied cautiously.

She nodded, went to get out, and then hesitated and looked back over her shoulder. "Maclean, I'll open your door, okay? In case anyone notices if you do it by yourself. And I won't be able to speak to you when we're with other people. It wouldn't look good, you know. And you shouldn't speak, either, just in case they can hear you. You'll frighten them. Just stay close to me and we'll be all right."

Orders from a woman! But this was Bella, he reminded himself, and he didn't mind so much. "Verra well," Maclean repeated stiffly.

She opened her car door to climb out.

The noise flooded in, unfamiliar and distracting. He could hear the engines of other cars and some sort of loud music—was it music?—from an open doorway across the narrow street. A bell was ringing persistently from another shop doorway, and a group of children with an adult at their head walked in line, their clothing all the same.

Bella came around to his door and opened it, pretending to look for something in the passenger side of the car. Hastily Maclean climbed out and she slammed it, and then she did something with her key that made the car beep. Finally, with a warning glance in his direction, she set off.

As he walked close by Bella's side, peering at the faces he passed, he realized with a sense of relief that they weren't really strangers. These faces were the same as, or similar to, the faces he had known two hundred and fifty years ago. Scottish faces, Gaelic faces, Highland faces.

There were a few that startled him, faces of different

colors, but Maclean had read of countries far away, and the possibility that people from these countries had traveled to Ardloch was not beyond his ken.

A woman was walking toward them talking into a small black box like Bella's, but this one had no cord attached. Maclean stared at her, completely bemused. The woman knocked against his arm and bounced back, a look of shocked surprise on her face. She turned and glared at Bella as if it were her fault, and hurried off.

"Maclean," Bella hissed anxiously.

He was stunned. The woman had felt him. He was still invisible, but now he was solid and real, something he had definitely not been a few days ago. Was he becoming a mortal man again? Whatever he was doing, the *Fiosaiche* was pleased with him. He knew it had something to do with Bella. If only he could pinpoint exactly what it was. . . .

Bella spoke again, sounding panicky. "Maclean? Are you there?" Several people glanced at her questioningly as they walked by.

Maclean shook himself out of his stupor and reached out a hand and clamped it around her arm.

She jumped.

He leaned in close, his front pressed to her back, and bent his head so that his lips were against the sweet shell of her ear. "I'm here."

"Oh. Yes."

She sounded dazed, standing perfectly still, as if afraid to move. Or maybe, like Maclean, she was just enjoying the moment.

"I feel like I know ye, Bella," he went on quietly. "Ye are no stranger to me."

"Yes, I feel like that, too, Maclean," she admitted reluctantly. "It's very odd."

Passersby stepped around them and the noise went on, but Maclean did not see or hear—he and Bella had made a special place amid the chaos—and besides, her body felt so good against his. He slid his arms about her waist, beneath her pink jacket, and enjoyed that, too. The top of her head came to his chin, just, and her bottom nestled very nicely against his groin.

Aye, verra nicely indeed.

"You are a fine woman, do ye know that, Bella?"

Bella wondered if this was really happening. Here she was, standing in the middle of busy Ardloch High Street being groped by a ghostly Highlander, and he was obviously very happy to see her.

"Maclean!" she hissed. "I didn't think ghosts could . . . could . . ."

He chuckled and made goose bumps up and down her arms. "Neither did I. Proves I'm not a ghost."

An old man in a kilt wandered past and gave her a curious smirk. Bella blushed, realizing how odd she must appear, and gave Maclean a little jab in the midriff with her elbow. He huffed in her ear and let her go.

"Stop it," she said loudly as she stepped away, and then froze.

What on earth was she doing? Apart from the series of uneasy looks she was getting from the people around her, she had just jabbed Maclean in the stomach. The Black Maclean, the black-hearted villain of legend who was in league with the devil. He could kill her . . . couldn't he?

And then she heard his laugh, so soft she had to

strain to hear it. She amused him. He wasn't angry with her, his male pride wasn't hurt, he didn't feel the need to strike out at her or threaten her. He had laughed at her, but it was a friendly teasing laugh, and she realized with surprise that Maclean liked her.

Just as she liked him.

It made her feel even guiltier for what she had planned for him in the museum. The plan had seemed to make perfect sense last night. He had told her he couldn't remember his past, so this would be a sort of test, to see if he was telling her the truth. Now she was wondering if it was such a great idea after all.

The electronics shop, as Bella called it, was like a cave, full of machines with moving pictures on large and small screens or boxes with flashing lights and loud, jarring sounds. Maclean squinted his eyes and wished he could do the same with his ears. How could the people in here put up with such a din? And yet they seemed immune to it, even enjoyed it, if he went by the blissful looks on their faces. Maclean shook his head in amazement as he followed Bella to an alcove at the back, where there was a counter and behind it a man in a shirt the color of mud. She handed over her writing machine.

"I don't know what happened," she said, and proceeded to blather on, making herself sound more foolish with each passing minute.

Maclean wondered what was wrong with her; this wasn't the Bella he had come to know.

The man was frowning. A man? More of a lad, really, barely old enough to shave. And he didn't like the way the lad was looking at Bella, with his lip curled, as if she were just a silly woman and a waste of his precious time. Maclean wanted to shout at him that this was Bella and he'd best treat her with respect if he knew what was good for him.

"Could it be something simple, like a fuse?"

The lad gave a scornful laugh.

Bella's cheeks colored, but she bit her lip as she watched the lad fiddle with the machine, taking bits off it and peering inside.

"Hmm," he said, and then he darted a sly glance at her breasts.

Maclean went still, his own eyes narrowing.

"Hard drive . . . motherboard . . . drivers . . ."

The conversation passed over Maclean's head, but from the disappointed look on Bella's face he guessed the problem was worse than she had thought. And all the while he was showing off, the lad was looking at her chest.

Maclean bristled, the hairs standing up on his body like a dog's. If he could have growled, he would have.

"I need to save my documents," Bella said anxiously, leaning forward over the counter as if to snatch back her machine. "I didn't have a chance to make a copy. It all happened so quickly."

The lad's gaze dropped to her breasts again—he wasn't even trying to hide what he was doing now—before his attention returned to the machine. "You should always make a copy," he said, and yawned. His eyes dropped again, longer this time.

Bella stepped back and wrapped her jacket tightly about her chest and folded her arms. Maclean realized she felt threatened, embarrassed by the lad's obvious interest. "I know," she was saying. "I just . . . I was so caught up in what I was doing that I forgot. Copying documents wasn't uppermost in my mind."

"There's no excuse," he said sanctimoniously.

Maclean had had enough. He gritted his teeth. He'd have that laddie by the scruff and give him a thrashing he'd long remember. His hand dropped to the handle of his *claidheamh mor* and he imagined swinging it in an arc, removing the lad's sneer and his head. There would be satisfaction in that, aye, but he could see it might not be a sensible thing to do while he was invisible. And Bella would be upset.

"I know," she was blathering again, "I'm sorry. Can you just save what's on there? I understand if the laptop is past it, but I really need the documents."

He made a face, enjoying his power over her. "I can't promise anything."

"But you'll try, yes?"

His eyes slid down again, and Maclean thought he was going to explode.

"I'll try. Leave your number with the girl at the front and I'll give you a ring when I've finished. Probably be two weeks. We have a waiting list, you know."

Bella nodded, thanked him again, and turned toward the front of the shop. The laddie gave her a long look from the back. Maclean stepped around the counter and in close, without touching him. He leaned toward his ear, until he could smell the overripe body beneath the lad's clothes.

"Ye'll no' look at her again without the proper respect, or I'll make my home in your wee shop. Do ye hear me?"

The lad heard him.

It suddenly occurred to Maclean that whenever he stood up for Bella in his thoughts or actions he became more mortal and less of a ghostie. Something to keep in mind for the future, but just now he was otherwise occupied.

The lad was looking as if he might faint, his face white, with the freckles standing out like grains of sand. He *was* only a lad, Maclean reminded himself, probably at the age when all he thought about was lassies, and Bella was very much the sort of girl that men dreamed of at night. But even a randy lad needed to learn respect.

"Who's there?" he gasped, swinging around wildly.

"Never you mind," Maclean whispered, stepping away, out of reach. "Just make sure ye do what she asked ye to do an' I'll no' return. Otherwise . . ." He reached close again, and gave the boy a clip behind the head, not hard enough to hurt him seriously, but enough to send him stumbling against the wall.

"Oooh God!" He cowered, covering his head with his arms.

"Do ye promise?"

"I promise, I promise, just leave me alone."

Her transaction completed, Bella had left the shop, and Maclean, satisfied with his own result, hastened after her.

A shower of rain had come through Ardloch while they were inside, making the paving shine, and there were less cars and people about. Maclean sniffed the salt of the ocean and smiled.

Bella was still holding her jacket tight about her, and as Maclean watched, she zipped it up to her neck and then dug her fists into the pockets. It hung down to midthigh, covering her, so that it was difficult to know how curved and gorgeous she was underneath it. Maclean frowned as he watched her, remembering how he had thought once before that Bella was ashamed of her body. The lad had been admiring her—not so subtly, it was true—but instead of getting angry, Bella seemed to think his glances were some kind of judgment on her, and not a favorable one.

Maclean tried to peer into her face, but her head was bowed, her hair falling about it, and there was a crease between her dark brows. Aye, Bella wasn't happy.

Maclean slipped his hand around her arm, curving his fingers about her elbow in a firm, strong grip. Her head swung up, startled, and for a moment he let himself pretend that she could see him, that her eyes were looking into his rather than slightly past his nose.

"You're a lush beauty, Bella Ryan. You have a body any man would be happy to die dreaming of. You canna blame the lad for looking at what he will never have, even if he is a randy wee bastard. Dinna let him make you feel uncomfortable, you are far too fine for him. You should hold your head up and be proud."

For a moment she stared, shocked by his words, and then laughter bubbled to her lips and made her cheeks glow and her dark eyes shine. She put her hand to her mouth and her shoulders shook. Maclean wondered why she found his words so humorous, but with her eyes sparkling and her face flushed she was so delicious that he wasn't insulted one bit. In fact he joined in with a guffaw of his own.

"Maclean," she managed at last, "you're nothing like the legend."

"Och, well, I think that must be a good thing," he replied cautiously.

"Yes." Bella bit her lip and sobered. "I know you're trying to help, but it's just . . ." She glanced at him sideways. "Women have come a long way since you were around, Maclean. We demand to be treated as equals, we have our own lives and aren't dependent on men. We're not objects, not things to be owned or checked out . . . eh, inspected, like cattle in a market stall. You think it's okay that . . . that *boy* in there admires my . . . my assets, as long as he isn't too obvious about it. Well, it makes me angry when I'm being judged solely by the size of my breasts."

Maclean cleared his throat. He had noticed the size of her breasts from the first moment he saw her, and the sight of them still made him dizzy with lust. But he didn't think he should tell Bella that when she was looking so fierce.

"Why are men like that, Maclean? Like . . . like animals."

"Aye, em, well, that's a difficult question. Mabbe it's because men's brains are closer to those of beasts, Bella. Wolves only think about eating and sleeping and . . . em, female wolves, don't they? Why should a man be any different?"

"I see. So women have evolved and men are just slower at it." Bella smiled and nodded. "Good point. Are you a beast, Maclean?"

Jesus, she wasn't one to skip around a thing. Maclean decided that if she was being direct, then it was only fair he should be, too.

"Aye, sometimes I am verra much a beast, and sometimes I lock my beast away in his cage, but he's always there. I can never be entirely free of him and I dinna think I would want to. He's what keeps me alive."

She nodded, and her beautiful face was somber. "So I should beware? Thank you, Maclean."

He cleared his throat again. "Where do we go to now, lass?"

Bella gave a sideways glance in his direction. "We'd better get on to the museum now, and then I need to stop in at the library."

There was something in her manner that made him suspicious. Bella was up to something and she wasn't very good at hiding it. "What *is* a museum, woman?" he asked brusquely.

"Well"—Bella wouldn't look toward him at all now—"there are different museums. Clothing museums, train museums, toy museums. This is a folk museum, which preserves Ardloch's past; places like this help us to understand days gone by." Bella tucked her hair nervously behind her ear. "I seem to remember seeing your name in there, Maclean."

Was that what was wrong with her? Was she thinking he'd make a commotion? Was she testing him in some way?

Maclean felt his heart sink. He didn't want Bella to know how desperate he was. Her opinion of him mattered, and he didn't want her to think him a lesser man.

"Lead the way, lass," he said, with as much bravado as he could manage.

Twelve

Just as Bella remembered, the Ardloch
Folk Museum was well presented. Sadly, places like
this were often nothing more than a repository for junk,
but the Ardloch museum was well thought out and there
was an attempt to give it relevance to the people of the
area, while at the same time catering to any tourist who
might wander in.

The front of the museum was built as a "black
house," a replica of the simple home of a Scottish rural
working family. The single living space had been di-
vided by partitions into rooms, each one telling its own
story of hope and struggle, with placards describing life
in the nineteenth century.

Bella paused in a room where the mannequins in
their Highland costume looked almost real in the shad-
ows. There was a brief retelling of Culloden and the
Clearances, as well as stories of the rise and fall of the
Scottish coastal herring industry, and the emigration of
Scots to other parts of the world.

That was when Bella realized she had lost Maclean. She decided not to make a fool of herself by calling out his name and waving her arms. She'd set up this test for him and now he'd disappeared—in a manner of speaking. Never mind, he was here somewhere and in a moment he'd probably scare her witless, putting his arms about her and pulling her back against his big hard body, his breath hot and shivery in her ear. The man had definite sex appeal—last night had proven that—but she mustn't encourage him. She'd just tried to explain to him how insulted she'd been by the behavior of the boy in the electronics shop, and now she was dreaming of Maclean's hands on her.

The two things were very different, she knew that, but she wasn't sure if Maclean did.

She was part of the present and he belonged to the past. She couldn't rely on him, she couldn't begin to think of him as permanent in her life. He might vanish again tomorrow if the sorceress came for him and . . .

"Oh God." Bella stopped her thoughts right there and wondered for the hundredth time whether she was insane. And for the hundredth time she decided she wasn't. This was really happening to her. Maclean was here, with her, and whatever the reason for it, she was glad.

And that was the scariest thing of all.

A family, mother and father and two children, had begun to make their way through the cottage. The children's shrill voices echoed beneath the low, dank ceiling. "Yuk, I wouldn't like to live in here!" "It smells!"

Bella smiled. It *was* rather dark and smelly, but most houses in the past were. The modern citizen didn't realize how lucky she was with plumbing and sewerage and air-conditioning, not to mention toilets and showers and deodorant. In Black Maclean's day, life had been precarious enough without worrying if you were on the nose—though as far as she could tell, Maclean didn't smell.

There was a small display on Highland superstitions and folklore, and she cast a doubtful look at an artist's impression of the Loch Ness Monster. It looked a bit like the thing in her dream, with its wet skin and scales. Bella shuddered. Her dreams were beginning to worry her: First the hag had foretold Maclean's arrival and then she'd mentioned the *Fiosaiche* and the between-worlds. She had read about people suddenly developing the power to see into the future, but those cases didn't seem to apply to her. . . .

Her heartbeat sped up.

An arrow was pointing toward a glass case in a nook with a sign: THE LEGEND OF THE BLACK MACLEAN.

Bella moved unwillingly in that direction.

A large cardboard replica of a Highland warrior stood, all hairy and fierce, a sword in one hand and a targe—a Highland wooden shield—in the other. When she'd first seen it, Bella had laughed aloud because it was nothing like the Maclean of her imaginings. Now her heart quickened again as she leaned toward the glass case and began to read the so-called legend.

THE BLACK MACLEAN
ONE OF SCOTLAND'S
MOST SHAMEFUL STORIES

Morven Maclean of Fasail, called the Black Maclean, set off for Culloden with his men. Unfortunately, Maclean was too cowardly to fight, made a deal with the English and soon returned.

Another arrow pointed onward, to a second placard on the other side of the warrior, above a plaster mock-up of Castle Drumaird. Bella took a step, just as the door behind her slammed shut, trapping her in the small room.

"Bastards."

The boiling fury in his voice made her jump, but Bella managed not to cry out. There wasn't much space in here, and she could feel him beside her, the heat and rage of his body like a physical force. If she closed her eyes she could visualize him in his kilt and black velvet jacket, his hair loose to his shoulders and his eyes pale and piercing.

Bella had convinced herself she would be able to tell if Maclean was lying. She needed to jolt the truth out of him. What sort of man was she dealing with? Was her belief in him real, or just part of her fantasy? Now she wondered whether she was safe.

Maclean knocked against the cardboard warrior, making him rock on his base as if he were spoiling for a fight. "This is no' me!"

"I know, Maclean. You look nothing like—"

"I dinna run away!"

"Maclean—"

"I saved my men from dying at Culloden Moor for a cause I could see was lost. Lord George came to me that night, before the battle."

"Are you sure?"

"*I remember it.* He dinna get my message, but he

came anyway. He was unhappy with O'Sullivan and the prince, and he told me I should go. He said he was sorry he had called me out on such a fool's errand."

"He did?" For a moment she was stunned.

"I dinna run away from the English, and I dinna make a deal with them."

She tried to think how she could prove it. How did you prove the honesty of a man? And she knew she couldn't, not with dusty documents and old letters. A man's worth was in his voice, his words, his strength of character. . . .

"What is this?" he whispered, his arm brushing her shoulder as he turned to the replica of Castle Drumaird and the second part of the legend.

"Maclean—" she began, but it was too late.

THE BLACK MACLEAN
SHOWS HIS TRUE COLORS

On his return to Fasail, and despite his people's pleadings for him not to, the Black Maclean mounted his black devil of a horse and went off to steal from his neighbors, the upright Macleods of Mhairi. Maclean was struck a death blow by Auchry Macleod, and died unmissed and un-mourned. The English had followed Maclean home, and being no more honorable than he, they rode into Maclean's lands and slaughtered every last man, woman and child. Maclean's body was never found, and it was popularly assumed that the Macleods had cut him to pieces and tossed him to the four winds.

A fitting ending for an unsavory character from Scotland's bloody past.

The Black Maclean.

His breathing was thick. She moved closer still, felt his kilt brush against her legs, and searched with her hand until she found his fingers. They were clenched around the handle of something . . . oh God, his broadsword. Was he going to attack the display? She slid her hand into his and squeezed, hard, to get his attention.

"Maclean, listen to me," Bella said, drawing on her dwindling courage. This had seemed like such a good idea! "You got home safe and sound, and then you marched northwards, into Mhairi. Why did you do that? Did you take on the Macleods through sheer bloody-mindedness? I know that the Macleans and the Macleods fought, and this time the Macleans lost. You were killed. Your men were killed. There was no one left to protect your people at Fasail—the old folk, the women and children—when the English dragoons came riding in."

"The Macleods killed me? I died under Auchry's blade? But Auchry was a coward and a worm! He would never dare raise his sword to the Black Maclean!" And then the rest of what she had said registered with him. "English dragoons? The red army was at Loch Fasail?"

"Yes. I'm sorry. They killed everyone, Maclean. And they burned Castle Drumaird and every other building to the ground. Nothing was left standing. That's why Loch Fasail is empty today. It's been empty for two hundred and fifty years."

Maclean's hand had turned cold, his fingers losing their strength.

He couldn't seem to breathe.

Nothing was left standing.

Bella's words repeated in his head. Numb, he tried to take it in. His lands deserted, his people murdered. He'd thought that whatever had emptied his lands must have taken place many years after his time. And Bella was saying it was his fault? No, it couldn't be so. He didn't believe it.

"News filtered through to the authorities, eventually. In the muddle and confusion after the defeat at Culloden the killings went unreported. The Macleods of Mhairi knew and when they were questioned about it long afterwards they blamed you. Said you had come boasting about your deal with the English, so full of yourself, wanting to celebrate by stealing their cattle and their women. You fought each other in a vicious battle, and this time you lost. You were already dead when the dragoons came to destroy Fasail."

He tried to see himself as the villain in Bella's book, boasting about his bargain with the red army, knowingly betraying all he believed in, but he could not, he *would* not.

"Why are you saying this, woman?" he cried in frustration. "Is it to torment me? There is more to the story, there must be. You have but skimmed the surface. My people died, and I was not there to protect them, but if ye think I would do such a thing without a just reason, then you wrong me. You wrong me!"

There were voices in his head, like a great wind howling. His people dying, slaughtered as the English dragoons rode through them like scythes through long grass. And he wasn't there to stop them. He wasn't there to save them. According to Bella, he was exchanging death blows with the Macleods over a few mangy cattle.

"The 'upright Macleods of Mhairi,'" he sneered. "They were thieves—Auchry was the worst of them. He struck me no death blow! He would have been too busy hiding in some wee hole in the ground. Only Ishbel was worth something, and even she . . ." His fingers held hers so hard it hurt. "Ishbel Macleod, she's at the heart of this thing."

"Ishbel?" The name was new to Bella.

"Auchry's daughter. I took her hostage for his good behavior, to stop *his* stealing from *me*." Then, when she was silent, "'Tis no' unusual to take hostages. I did no' hurt her. I wished to marry her."

"And did you?" she asked quietly.

"No."

That was all, just the one word, but Bella must have felt the weight of secrets behind it. He could hear the questions forming in her mind. Behind them the door began to open. Maclean reached back and held it closed. His voice was a harsh croak: "Bella, ye must believe me."

But of course she kept on. Searching for her version of the truth.

"Did you make a deal with the English at Culloden,

only to have them break their word and follow you home to Fasail?"

"Bloody hell, woman, is it likely I'd let those bastards into Fasail?" he roared. "And if I did, if I knew they were coming, then I would no' have run away. I never ran away from a fight in my life!" Behind them the door rattled but he pressed harder against it, keeping out whoever wanted to get in.

He sounded so sincere, so passionate. Bella wanted to believe him, she really did. "Most so-called legends are hearsay and lies spread by enemies. That's why I am writing my book, so that I can tell everyone what *really* happened. The English dragoons always denied their part in it, although the garrison at Fort William was famous for its brutality. But then again, maybe the massacre wasn't official—there were plenty of renegade bands around with little regard for the lives of—"

"Bella." Maclean's voice sounded strained. "I made no deal with the English, and they dinna follow me back to Loch Fasail. Ye must believe me. I command it!"

He stumbled against her, his fingers bruising hers. Big, hardened fingers used to fighting; a warrior's hand. Bella gasped, clinging to him, praying he had enough self-control not to lose it.

"You can't command something like that, Maclean. If I believe you, then it's because *I* choose to, not because you order me to. Tell me about Ishbel."

"I've tried to remember more, but remembering hurts."

"Unpleasant memories can be painful, I understand that."

"No." He groaned. "It *hurts* like a hammer in my head, like my brain is being boiled in oil."

"Oh." She swallowed, and even in his own pain he could see she was upset. Did the past have such an effect upon her, or was it just *his* past? Bella wanted him to be perfect, and he wasn't. She wanted him to be a hero, and if what she was saying about him was true, then he was far from that.

"You were a chief who cared for his people, who was willing to walk away from a fight to save his men's lives. You could have been a great man, and then you blew it. You're famous, Maclean, but for all the wrong reasons."

"This piece of paper"—he crashed his hand against the glass display—"says I was dead by the time the red army came into Fasail. I wasna there to protect them." His voice sounded wretched. "I didna even know that was what had happened. I left Fasail in good order. I was a good chief, and I believed that when I died all was well!"

He was in painful earnest. Despite the damning words of the Black Maclean legend, Bella believed him. She had made her choice. Whatever happened two hundred and fifty years ago at Loch Fasail was done without his knowledge.

A familiar excitement arced through her. History had wronged Maclean, and Bella must put it right. This was what she was good at, what she had been born to do.

"You will remember," she said, trying to soothe him. "Why else would you be here? And maybe when you do it will explain why the sorceress brought you back."

"Learn from my mistakes, you mean?" he said bitterly. "Oh, aye, there's something, I know it, but mabbe I dinna want to learn from it. Mabbe I'd do the same thing again."

That didn't sound good. He knew something, or sensed it, and whatever it was it made him uncomfortable with himself.

Behind her the door rattled again.

"I am no' the man this legend speaks of," Maclean whispered furiously. "I am not!"

"Maclean—"

"They have turned me into a monster! A beast to frighten wee children!"

"Please, Maclean—"

"And you believe them. I see it in your face, Bella Ryan. You brought me here to shame me and to prove yourself right. Deny it if ye can!"

And of course she couldn't.

The door was flung open and he was gone. Bella started to follow him, opening her mouth to try and comfort him, and was startled by the sound of a giggle. A child was waiting to one side of the door, gazing at her with round blue eyes.

"You're talking to yourself," the child announced, and giggled again. Then, turning and running back toward his family, "That lady's talking to herself!"

Bella groaned. That was all she needed, someone to tell the museum authorities that she was a dangerous nutcase.

The sun was shining outside, as it often did after a late summer shower. It would probably rain again soon, but for now the air was fresh and warm and she felt as if she could see the grass growing.

"Maclean?" she hissed, glancing around her. He had come this way, so where was he? "Maclean!"

But there was no answer.

Thirteen

Maclean walked with long furious strides. He didn't know where he was going, and he didn't care. It wasn't true! And yet his heart ached. He knew that he had done something. Something terrible. He needed to face it, the *Fiosaiche* probably wanted him to face it, but at the same time he was afraid to do so. Bella was saying he was to blame. The empty land, the broken castle, the disappearance of his people. Bella believed it was all his fault, and now she would write it down so that others would believe that, too.

Self-doubt and disgust ravaged him. Surely a man who had played a part in such an atrocity was not entitled to a second chance? Then why had the *Fiosaiche* brought him back?

As a punishment? To taunt him with the knowledge? Maybe he was doomed to this half life for the *next* two hundred and fifty years. Better if he had never awoken.

And yet deep in his heart he knew he needed to

know the truth, to face it, no matter how horrifying it might be.

Ishbel.

Why did her name return to him again and again, like a curse?

He had to know.

Maclean's head ached and he shook it like a maddened bull. The waves of pain brought pictures, and as he concentrated the pictures gradually grew brighter, clearer. The past was being replayed for him, but in silence, as if he were watching it from a distance.

A mere spectator.

Let her go, son. Trembling tones; his mother spoke. *Let her have the chance of happiness that I ne'er did. Let her find a man who is no' blighted like ye are, whose heart has no' turned to stone. Morven, 'tis no' wrong to want to be loved. Let Ishbel go home to her father and make a life for hersel' there.*

And then Maclean, in a roar: *Let her go! After all I've given her? She is to be my wife, we made a vow. Who are you to know of such things, you who betrayed my father and broke his heart? No, I will not let Ishbel go! I'd rather see her dead.*

Maclean saw himself returning from Culloden Moor, only to find that, just as she had promised she would, Ishbel had left him. She had run off with Iain Og, the son of his piper, a lad who was lowly and unimportant in comparison to Maclean. That she had chosen him was an insult, but more than that, Maclean felt a pain so extreme, so intense he wanted to break every bone in Ishbel's body. This was a blow to his pride as a husband and a man and a chief. It was understandable, and yet . . .

Looking at his reaction from this distance, Maclean was puzzled. There was more, something he wasn't remembering. But already the pictures in his head had moved on. He heard his voice echoing through Castle Drumaird. . . .

I will go after her and bring her back and no one will stop me!

Maclean fell to his knees on a stretch of wet grass surrounded by a narrow garden. A bell was chiming the hour, and a car sped past on the road beyond the museum. Maclean neither saw nor heard. He was spinning back into his own past. And he was no longer at a safe distance, he was right *there*.

Living it.

Women. There were dozens of them. They had come to Castle Drumaird to plead with him not to follow Ishbel. They were crowding into the great hall, strangely silent, their faces wan. Maclean sat in his great chair, watching them suspiciously. There was his mother, her familiar face with hollowed cheeks and lined brow, her hair swept up untidily beneath the fold of her yellow arisaid. She seemed tentative, more anxious than usual. Maclean had seen little of her since his father died, not that he had seen much of her beforehand, but somehow he had thought that when his father was gone she might have taken a step back into his life rather than withdrawing even further from him.

But then why would she? They were strangers, or near enough, and there were memories between them that neither wished to revisit. Her betrayal during his boyhood resonated with him still and he knew he could never forgive her. And yet . . . he needed her now. He wanted her approval.

Unaccustomed tears prickled his eyes, frightening him, hardening him, and he set his jaw. He would not tell her of the sacrifice he had made in order to stop Ishbel from hating him, and how she had betrayed him anyway. He would not tell her of the vow he had made, and ask her where he had gone so wrong.

His father would have said it was just punishment for allowing the softness inside him to escape the chains and locks he should have kept upon it. He had been weak, that was the simple explanation for all of this. He had been weak in the worst possible way—with a woman.

His mother came closer, the other women huddled behind her, and for a strange, ecstatic moment Maclean wanted to believe she had come to offer him comfort, to sympathize with his plight. She alone must understand how he was feeling. But then she began to speak and he realized she hadn't come for him, she had come as the spokeswoman for Ishbel and all the other women. He was the enemy, it seemed, and she had set herself firmly on the other side.

"Our menfolk have barely come home from Culloden Moor, Morven, and we do no' yet know what will happen to us because of the Rebellion. There are whispers that the English have sent ships to our coast carrying men who are ready to burn out traitors. Ye should be traveling to Inverness to ask pardon. Ye should be vowing your allegiance to King George. But now ye wish to take us with ye into further danger. I say no, Morven."

Her voice wavered but she stood tall, as though his glowering did not give her pause.

Even as disappointed anger simmered within him, Maclean realized he was not surprised she was so respected that she would be chosen as the one to speak to him. His father had always treated her with scorn, but Maclean knew many of the others had never accepted his bitter and damning comments, and now that his father was dead she had grown in stature.

Sometimes he thought she was the true heart of Loch Fasail, but he never told her so. It was not his way. Maclean did not speak of his feelings. He had been taught not to.

And now here she was, standing before him, standing against him, and in her eyes was the same expression she wore when she had looked at his father.

"Ishbel vowed to pay ye back. She swore it, we all heard her. Dinna go after her. There is something ominous about this matter. For your own sake, Morven, dinna go after Ishbel. Dinna do this thing. I know matters have no' always been well between us, but listen to me. Stay home, and keep us safe."

He wanted to believe she had his welfare at heart, but his doubt was stronger. He had believed in Ishbel, and look what had happened! He would not put himself into such a vulnerable position again.

"My intended wife has run off with a boy when she could have had a man. She has insulted me. Should I just shrug and say 'tis acceptable?"

"Morven, let her go. She's not worth the having."

"That's not the point!" he roared.

She blinked, and for a moment he thought she might realize, might somehow see inside him to his aching heart. "Shedding more blood is not the answer."

"I'd shed Macleods' blood any day," he retorted.

"If ye go after her there will be death. Ishbel will no' return willingly. She will fight ye, she will resist ye."

"She is a woman," Maclean sneered. "What can she do to me?"

His mother's eyes grew cold, and he knew she was again remembering other times, other words and another man.

I am not my father! he wanted to shout, but he bit his tongue. Because if he had been his father Ishbel would never have dared to run away with Iain Og.

"Look into your heart, Morven," she said, and her voice had lost its tenderness. "I canna believe there is not some spark of life there yet, some small coal of warmth and compassion. Let Ishbel go. If you follow her and force her to your will, then you are not my son."

He didn't answer her. He told himself that her words meant nothing to him. Seeing the implacable set of him, the women began to beg. They even wept. But still he refused to be swayed, and eventually he rose to his feet and said the last words he ever spoke to them.

"What sort of Highland chief listens to the bleating of womenfolk? What sort of a man would I be if I allowed Ishbel to go free after such an insult simply because my mother begged me to?"

And then he walked away.

* * *

Maclean sat on the damp grass and saw in his mind's eye those women's faces. All dead. All gone. His mother's pale eyes awash with tears as she pleaded for him to listen. For this once, to listen to her. As if she were his equal. As if her age and experience made her so. As if she had never preferred her lover over him, just like Ishbel nearly thirty years later.

The cold wet grass soaked into his kilt, but Maclean didn't feel it or care. The pain inside him made such trifling things unimportant. When Bella had said that he was to blame, she'd been right. Fundamentally he was. He and his men had set off after Ishbel to bring her back, and at some point after that the English must have come to Fasail and slaughtered his people, and he hadn't been there to fight for them.

They had ridden into his lands unopposed while his men lay dead or dying at Mhairi. *That* was the great battle he remembered, the one between his men and Ishbel's father—Macleans and Macleods, dying in the heather. And while they fought over a fickle woman, Loch Fasail had lain unprotected.

Maclean frowned, sitting up straighter.

How had the Macleods killed his men so easily? Maclean knew he was superior in numbers and skill. Despite their weariness his men should easily have subdued Auchry Macleod and his clan.

Maclean sighed. He was clutching at straws. History blamed *him* for the bloodshed at Fasail, not the English. Whoever it was who held the sword, it was Maclean who was the monster, the coward, the black-hearted beastie.

And what of Ishbel? Had she survived the encounter

between Maclean and the Macleods? He tried to picture her in that final battle. Was she there, somewhere, watching on? Did she weep when she saw her would-be-husband die? Maclean knew he had killed Iain Og; he did not remember the details, but he knew.

But try as he might, Maclean could see no image of Ishbel, pale and weeping, as Maclean fought Macleod. All he felt was the guilt and horror that had beset him once before, that sense of dread when he found himself in a place where he should never have been. And now he knew why he felt like that. The women of Fasail had begged him to stay and he'd refused. They were right and he was wrong. And at the very end he'd known it.

Maclean pressed his face into his hands.

"I killed you once, Maclean. I can do it again."

Ishbel!

Maclean sprang to his feet, drawing his broadsword in one fluid motion and turning to face the woman he had once wished to marry. Her whisper came from behind him, so close that she must be standing at his back, breathing on his nape. She could touch him, if she wanted to. If she had a dirk, she could kill him.

But there was no one there.

Confused, Maclean turned again, his sword in front of him, his gaze sweeping over the bright flowers and the damp grass, knowing that no mortal woman could move so swiftly.

"Speak!" he demanded. "Are you invisible like me, Ishbel?"

Nothing, not a sound.

And then something caught his eye. A woman, at some distance, her golden hair gleaming in the fading summer light. She was wearing trews in a red and green pattern and a dark jacket. She turned, a brief glance over her shoulder. He could not see her face. And then she was gone.

Maclean's skin crawled and he found himself seized by a new fear.

Had the *Fiosaiche* brought Ishbel into the mortal world, too? And if so, then why? What could Ishbel want from him?

Apart from his death.

Fourteen

Bella spent a useful couple of hours in the Ardloch library. The small section dedicated to Maclean was little more than a rehashing of the legend, but Bella knew that if she could discover the source of that legend she would be on her way to understanding who had the most to gain from besmirching Maclean's name and reputation.

And now there was new information she needed to follow up on: Ishbel Macleod, Maclean's hostage and the woman he had planned to wed.

After a quick search in the Ardloch collection, she chose a couple of histories of the Macleod clan, one of them a poorly produced document on the local Mhairi branch and the other a far more professional effort on the part of the Macleods of Skye. Hoping they might contain something about Ishbel Macleod, Bella borrowed these two books. She couldn't help worrying about Maclean and where he might have gotten to.

What if he was lost or in trouble? What if he had vanished altogether? What if he was looking for her and couldn't find her? When the niggling worry couldn't be ignored any longer, Bella collected her books and left.

Outside, there'd been another rain shower and the sun was lower. There was a bite in the air and she zipped up her pink jacket. As she strode along the street, she could see many of the shops were closed, and the shoppers and workers had gone home to their families and their television soaps. By the time Bella did her shopping at the little supermarket outside of town and drove home to Drumaird Cottage, it would be twilight, although the northern twilight could last until eleven at night at this time of year.

Assuming she could find Maclean, of course.

Bella wondered whether she would have to wait here until he turned up, or if she should just go home and hope he would find his own way back. It wasn't as if she could go to the local police station and report him as missing.

Missing. Highlander, six feet four inches tall, wearing traditional Scottish dress, two hundred and fifty years old, invisible.

Yeah, right.

The car was where she had left it, but no longer surrounded by others; it now sat alone. Bella found herself glancing over her shoulder as she released the locks. The soft beep sounded very loud. Footsteps approached her from behind, and before she could turn, she heard the voice that in so short a time had already grown familiar.

"I was waiting for you, Bella."

He was still angry.

"I was working, Maclean."

He gave that scornful snort, as if the idea of her working were somehow laughable. Her own anger ignited. Perhaps if she'd thought about it she'd have realized his bad mood was because of what he'd read in the museum, and his prejudice was due to the period he was born into and the position he held, but she was remembering Brian and how he was always quick to criticize, and to treat her work as less relevant than anything he did.

"Excuse me? Do you think I'm here just to chauffeur you about? You might have been important once, Maclean, but as far as everyone here is concerned, you're dead and gone. I have a book to write, that's how I make my living. This is the twenty-first century and women stand on their own two feet. We don't need men to look after us, we don't *want* men to look after us. We make our own lives and we expect to be treated with the same respect as men because of it. If you don't like that, then I suggest you move out into the heather and sleep there with the sheep."

"I dinna sleep anyway," he said quietly.

"Well, whatever it is you do!"

There was a silence. She could hear herself breathing hard. It was so annoying that she couldn't see his expression and read what he was thinking, although she could probably guess. It was unlikely Maclean had ever been spoken to like that before. His people probably approached him with their eyes lowered and prostrated themselves before him until he gave them permission to stand.

"I have nowhere else to go," he said woodenly.

"Is that my problem?"

She sounded cruel, and she was lying. She *did* think it was her problem; Maclean had landed on *her* doorstep. But he needed to understand that this was now and if she helped him it was because she wanted to and not because he ordered her to.

"You dinna trust me," he said bleakly.

"I don't know you, Maclean. But I'm trying."

He took a heavy breath. "Verra well. I'll try and remember what you said. Men and women are equal. Sheep, too?"

"Don't be fatuous."

"Like you, Bella, I'm trying."

He didn't sound arrogant or pompous. He sounded like a man coming to terms with something he'd rather not have to think about. Bella opened the car door and climbed in, and waited while the other door opened and closed, too. She felt Maclean settling himself in the passenger seat, the car rocking slightly from his weight.

She said briskly, "I have to stop at the little supermarket on the way out of town. The place where I buy food and . . . and things. It'll still be open."

He said nothing, and when they arrived at the cash and carry he declined to come inside with her. Sulking, probably, Bella thought as she rushed through the aisles, grabbing what she needed, and hurried out again. Oh well, she was used to men who sulked, and if he thought he could outlast her, then he was wrong. Soon they were leaving Ardloch behind and heading back on the narrow road to Loch Fasail.

"Did you find what you wanted in the library?"

He was trying to make conversation. Maclean had

surprised her again. Bella smiled in his direction, pleased he was not like Brian. "I have some books to look at, yes, but I don't have high hopes. You were an enigma, Maclean, and when your people died they took the truth with them. I was hoping to find some sort of written account from around the time the . . . it happened, but no luck so far. There don't seem to have been any witnesses."

He grunted.

They lapsed into silence. Bella allowed her thoughts to touch on her current financial situation. She hadn't been joking when she told Maclean she had to finish this book. Her royalties weren't huge, but at least the money was all hers, not her father's, and these days she was determined to live within her means without dipping into his legacy. Brian didn't have the same moral doubts, but maybe that was because his tastes were more expensive than hers. She'd never questioned his actions. "Our money" she'd called it, in the days when love was blind.

She glanced sideways at her invisible companion.

"Are you feeling better?"

Maclean shifted in his seat. "Better?"

"You were upset in the museum."

"You mean am I feeling better that my people were all murdered by the English and it was my fault—according to legend?"

"I suppose I do mean that. Have you remembered anything more?"

"I went after Ishbel, aye, I've remembered that. She ran off with my piper's son. What man would not after her? I followed her to Mhairi." He sounded stiff and self-righteous.

Maclean chased Ishbel to Mhairi and left his people unprotected? What did that say about his feelings for Ishbel?

Bella eased around a hairpin bend, the road dropping away into the shadows below them. "Did you love her, Maclean?" Bella had no right to be jealous, but she found herself awaiting his answer with held breath.

"No," he growled.

Bella refused to feel relieved. "Well, whatever the case, you went after Ishbel and . . . Look, I'm not saying that if you'd been there you could have saved them all, but—"

"Unless it was my own black-hearted plan for the English to come and kill everyone," he said wryly, but there was deep pain simmering below his level voice, and Bella felt it.

"I don't believe that," she said quietly. "You cared too much, Maclean. You were too good a chief. You wanted to save lives, not give them up for . . . well, for what?"

Her believing in him seemed to please him.

"Thank you, Bella." He shifted restlessly in his seat. "Do you think we can stop a moment? I feel . . . my stomach is all in knots. I think it's the car that does it, I'm no' used to it yet."

"Oh." She glanced at him uneasily. A ghost that suffered from car sickness? She slowed and pulled over into the next passing place, although there was no other traffic on the road. For a moment they sat in silence, then the passenger door was thrown open and Maclean was gone.

Bella climbed out of the car after him.

The shadows were long, the sun just butting the horizon between two monolithic hills, and everything looked as if it had been dipped in gold. She blinked and for a heartbeat she thought she saw him, the dark shape of him, moving against the light. She set off after him at a run.

"Maclean!"

The edge of the road fell away quickly and there was a sort of promontory jutting out here, overlooking the narrow glen below, turning it into a scenic lookout, with a low railing to prevent accidents. She stopped, breathing quickly. Where was he? Anxiously she called his name again.

"I'm here." His voice was so close it startled her.

"What are you doing? You're frightening me."

His hand brushed her arm. "I dinna mean to. I felt queasy, but it's passed. I dinna like your car, Bella."

"I'm sorry."

"I canna forget the lies I read in that wee cottage, that museum."

"We'll find out the truth, Maclean. Trust me, I've done it before."

His breathing sounded thick. "Trust ye?"

"Yes. I can help you, Maclean."

She felt his fingers beneath her chin, lifting her face up as if he were searching it. He laughed softly, recklessly.

"There's no guile in you, Bella. Your sweet face is so honest and clear. So, aye, I'll trust ye," he said, just before his lips closed on hers. They were warm and a little rough, and heat filled her instantly, making her head spin. She felt herself responding.

"Mmm"—his voice was low and husky— "ye taste good."

He tasted good, too. In a moment she'd be lost, and she didn't want that. Bella tried to clear her thoughts, to put some distance between them. She stepped back, holding out her hands. "No. I don't think this is a good idea."

"Bella," he groaned, "you want me, I can feel it. Why will ye not let us enjoy each other while we can?"

"Because I don't want to be hurt."

"I would ne'er hurt you!" he said indignantly.

"That's easy to say."

"I say it because it's true!" He spun away, his steps crunching on the gravel. He was moving against the setting sun and . . . Bella squinted her eyes. She really could see his silhouette. Big and dark, with broad shoulders and the kilt swinging from his hips. It was him.

"Maclean," she cried, "I can see you!"

"You can what?" he demanded crossly.

"I can see you against the sun. Your silhouette."

He turned and faced her. He was a featureless, colorless shadow bathed in gold, but it was more than he had been before. Maclean was there, in front of her, looking back at her.

"*I can see you*," she breathed.

He laughed. He threw back his head and laughed, and in it there was joy mixed with such despair that tears sprang to her eyes.

He walked toward her, the dark shape of him getting larger, until she tilted her head to look into his face. He wasn't really opaque to look at, she realized, she could still see the vague shapes of the hills through him, as though through a dark mist. But when she reached out and pressed her hand to his chest he was as solid to touch as any living man.

He caught her fingers and held them gently in his big hand.

"Mabbe it is because my memory is returning."

"Maybe."

"Or mabbe it is you, beautiful Bella."

He was gazing down at her, and for a moment she thought she saw his eyes, pale blue, in the dark shadow of his face. Bella shuddered. She was afraid, afraid of what he was, of being tangled up in something far beyond her understanding, and afraid of the way she was so powerfully attracted to him. Danger swirled around him, and if she wasn't careful she'd be drawn in and swallowed whole.

"What is it?" he said in such a tender voice that her heart ached. "Are you cold, Bella?"

"Yes." She was a coward, but she couldn't say what was really in her mind and her heart. Not yet.

And then she gave a gasp of laughter, because Maclean, the monster of legend, the black-hearted warrior who killed with one swing of his mighty *claidheamh mor*, had wrapped his arms around her and was holding her close to his own body.

Keeping her warm.

Fifteen

*The remainder of the journey home was un-*eventful. Bella was weary and hardly spoke; she needed all her concentration to negotiate the narrow and winding road in the increasing darkness. Beside her Maclean was also silent, deep in his own thoughts. Finally they reached the cottage, the headlights sweeping over the front of it and reflecting back from the kitchen window.

Inside, she felt the chill. No heating, despite this morning's effort, and the Aga had gone out. Rather than start up the generator, Bella found a few candles to light. She glanced at the spot on her desk where her laptop had been and sighed. She was relying on that smart-ass at the electronics shop to save her work for her.

She should have stood up for herself. Maclean was right. She should have told him to stop eyeing her boobs and show some respect to a woman old enough to be his . . . older sister? Instead she'd huddled into her jacket and herself, letting him intimidate her. Bella lifted her chin. Time to turn over a new leaf. From now on she wouldn't take crap from anybody, no matter who they were.

Maclean was still outside, so Bella rid herself of her jacket, hung it on the hook by the door, and climbed the stairs to slip on a comfortable pair of jeans and an old favorite sweater. Both were baggy and faded, but who cared? She needed comfort clothing. Brian had never understood that. He thought she was a slob when it came to fashion, but Bella could never relax in the sort of clothing Georgiana wore. Or Brian, for that matter. When they had decided to come and live here in the Highlands he had busily gone out and bought all the gear he thought a laird would lounge in.

Bella had thought it ridiculous then and she still did. Who cared what she wore? No one could see her. And Maclean . . . well, he probably thought what she had on was haute couture for the twenty-first century.

Beautiful Bella.

Bella smiled, remembering his arms around her, his warm sexy voice. He was attracted to her, he liked her, he thought she was beautiful. Maclean might be only half man, but he was a definite improvement on Brian.

When she came downstairs she saw to her surprise that Maclean had stacked peats in the stove and used some slivers of wood as kindling, and already there was a wave of warmth coming from it. He'd also set the kettle on the hot plate on top and placed her mug—complete with tea bag—nearby.

"Oh," she said, pleased surprise in her voice. "Thank you."

Of course, he had spent the last two weeks watching everything she did, and Maclean was no fool. She wasn't astonished by the fact that he had quickly learned how to do these things, but she was surprised that he had been so thoughtful. This was a man who had probably never lifted a hand to help a woman in his life—not in the kitchen, anyway. Clearly her becoming ticked off had borne fruit, and she appreciated the effort he was making for her.

"I am no' so good at cooking," he said with an offhandedness that didn't deceive her. This was a big deal for Maclean.

"Never mind, I'm not very hungry. Perhaps I'll just have some soup."

Maclean hovered as she prepared it. "I dinna feel hunger or thirst; I exist without either."

"That's a shame, because I bought you some wine at the supermarket. They didn't have any whiskey, but the wine looked nice. It's Australian."

"Australian?"

"Oh." She gave him a sideways look. "Maybe they hadn't heard of Australia when you were here before. It's way down in the south, an island continent, kangaroos and kookaburras and . . . and . . ." She cleared her throat as his silence grew.

After a moment he said tentatively, "Can you see me still, Bella?"

She shook her head. "No, not now. It was only when you were standing against the sun. I saw the shape of you like a dark mist, and perhaps . . . your eyes."

He didn't answer her and she heard him move away, wandering aimlessly about the room, picking up objects and putting them down again. She finished heating her soup, and then carried it to the table. After a moment she heard him sit down opposite her.

"Maclean," she said, "I wish you wouldn't watch me. It's unsettling."

"I like to watch you."

"I feel self-conscious."

"Aye, I know," he teased.

Bella set down her spoon. "I'm aware that this is all new and strange to you, but—"

"If you were in my time," he went on, "I'd have watched you, too."

"Why would you have done that?"

"I canna help it," he said in surprise. "Everything about you draws me to you."

"Everything?" she asked, suddenly breathless.

"Aye. Your eyes are so dark and expressive, they tell me all that you are feeling, even when you're trying to hide it. And when you're pleased with yourself, your mouth tilts up at the edges, just a wee bit, just enough to make me want to kiss you."

"You want to kiss me, Maclean?"

"Aye." His voice dropped into the low husky tone that gave her goose bumps. "And when your hair is falling around you, like now, I want to twist it up in my fingers and rub it against my skin. You smell of blossom, so sweet and delicious, I canna get enough of it. Did you know that, Bella? I want to taste you. I want to hold your breasts in my hands and stroke them until you canna think anymore, until you ache for me, ache for my body atop yours. Until you open your legs to me and want me inside you as much as I want to be there."

Bella's fingers were shaking. "You talk of men and women being equal, being the same, but that is not so in my world, Bella. Except in bed. If you and I were in bed, then it would no' matter what century we were in."

She told her heart to stop flipping over and over. Maclean was trapped here in this cottage with her; it was only natural he would be thinking about her a lot, even obsessing about her. She mustn't read too much into what he was saying. But apart from that caveat, the honest appreciation in his voice overcame any insult or embarrassment Bella might have felt. This man was from an age when plain speaking was far more fashionable than it was today and political correctness was unheard-of. He truly made her feel beautiful, and Bella refused to blush or simper; she gave herself permission to enjoy this moment to the full.

She took a breath and tried for a matter-of-fact tone. "Do you think about sex a lot, Maclean?"

"Sex?"

"You know, men and women," oh God, she *was* blushing, "doing it. Having it off. Bonking. Making love."

He was laughing at her. "Aye, all the time," he said at last. "Don't you?"

"Of course not."

"You say it as if there's something wrong with 'bonking,'" he retorted. "Mabbe you just haven't had a man who knows what he's doing."

It was Bella's turn to snort. "You're very sure of yourself."

Maclean did not answer her, and somehow that made it even more infuriating.

"I suppose," she said curiously, taking a sip of her soup, "you've had lots of women."

"There were many," he agreed thoughtfully, as if it weren't a thing that had occupied his mind before. "Once when I was in Edinburgh I went to a whorehouse by the Lawnmarket. There were French tarts there, and they were verra good, but . . . there is something about a willing woman I much prefer. When she wants *me* and no one else will do, aye, that stirs my blood in a way I canna explain."

It sounded as if Maclean had just had a revelation, but Bella refused to be distracted.

"Was Ishbel willing, Maclean?"

The chair creaked and Maclean cleared his throat. "I didna touch Ishbel."

"What, no bundling? Isn't that what it's called, when a couple have a trial marriage before it's official?"

"There was no love between Ishbel and I. She was young and timid and looked at me as if I were an animal rather than a lusty man. She said the marriage bed was unseemly. Mind you, that was before she ran off into the arms of Iain Og, my piper's son."

"Ishbel doesn't sound like the sort of woman you should ever have considered marrying. What were you thinking, Maclean?"

She could almost see him draw himself up indignantly. "Our marriage would have helped bring peace to our two clans, and Ishbel would have had the Macleod lands at Mhairi when her father died. Auchry was in favor of it, too. He wanted to see his grandchildren rule over my lands as much as his. Just because a girl dinna like the look o' me, dinna mean I should put her feelings first."

Of course, Bella knew marriage in the eighteenth century had nothing to do with love. It was all about power and money and blood ties. Unless you were a peasant, but even then a girl might choose an ugly man who could give her the best loaf of bread and the best feather mattress over a handsome one who had barely two shillings to rub together. Though not always. Sometimes love did still conquer all, and Ishbel must have truly believed that when she fled with Iain Og . . . or she must truly have loathed Maclean.

Had he been he cruel to her? Bella thought that perhaps he could be cruel. Maclean the chief, the tyrant, could not afford to worry about trampling on the feelings of others. And yet he had lit the fire for her and made her tea. Still she mustn't allow that to get in the way of the truth.

"How long did you take Ishbel hostage?"

"A year. At first she was content, but then she became restless. She wanted to go home before I made the march to Culloden Moor, but I told her she could no' go. My mother spoke for her, but I would no' listen, I had my mind set on it. I thought Ishbel was resolved to the matter, but when I came back she was gone, and Iain Og with her."

Ishbel must have been desperate. Didn't she realize Maclean would go after her? Or had she hoped his mother would persuade him against it? Bella tried to be sympathetic and fair-minded, but she couldn't help but think Maclean deserved better.

"What of this . . . this Brian?" Maclean demanded. "Were you and he well matched?"

"I . . . sometimes," she answered. "At first. I met him through my father. My father was an American diplomat, a man who traveled the world. My mother was born in England, but I've lived in Europe and America, we seemed to be always moving. I never really felt as if I belonged anywhere."

Until I came here to Loch Fasail, she thought.

"My mother divorced my father when I was quite young—they never got along. She is very fashionable, very stylish. She married again, and I never see her. I was a disappointment to her. She wanted a daughter in her own image, and I wasn't. I lived with my father, when I wasn't at boarding school. He treated me like an invalid, because I preferred to bury my head in a book, and later on to write books, rather than socialize with him. He didn't understand me at all. He married a couple more times, but there were no more children. When he died five years ago he left me plenty of money— enough to pay the bills while I kept writing—and a broad hint that I couldn't do much better than spend my life with Brian. Brian is the son of one of his friends, and my father likes to tie up any loose ends, and to him I was always a loose end."

"Are you wed to this Brian?"

He had answered her questions, so it seemed only fair that she should now answer his. "No, I've never been married. Brian is gone now and I don't expect him to come back. He says he's bored with me."

Maclean snorted. The chair was pushed back and his big hand was on her face, cupping her cheek. "The man's a fool," he muttered, and then . . . dear God, his mouth was on hers.

Warm and strong.

There was nothing subtle in it, he kissed like he did everything else, with confidence and enthusiasm. Bella closed her eyes, finding that staring at nothing was disconcerting. His fingers slid up into her hair, holding her still so that he could plunder her mouth as he willed.

No wonder a timid girl like Ishbel had feared him. He was fire and flame, and by the time he drew away from her, Bella's heart was pounding and she was struggling to breathe. But she wasn't frightened. Maclean, the bold, strong warrior, was someone she responded to as she never had to Brian. The Bella who never felt comfortable with herself around Brian changed and grew and gained confidence when Maclean touched her. It was a marvelous feeling.

But this wasn't the moment to tell Maclean.

"I thought we said you wouldn't touch me unless I asked!"

"Dinna you like it?" he demanded, surprised.

"That's not the point."

"Aye, it is the point."

"Maclean—"

"Aye, all right, then! You're nagging me, woman, and I'm weary of it. To bed with you, you've circles under your eyes."

She considered refusing, but then decided it was a waste of breath arguing when she was tired anyway. With a shrug of her shoulders Bella wished him goodnight. She was halfway up the stairs when he spoke again.

"Your name," he said suddenly. "Bella. Is it a pet name?"

Puzzled, Bella looked over her shoulder. And blinked. He was standing in the doorway below her, the light behind him, and she could see him. A dark shadow with blurred edges. He had one hand against the door-jamb, his head lowered because he was too tall to stand beneath the lintel. Her heart quickened.

"What is it?" he asked sharply. He was reaching for something and when he straightened again he had a weapon in his hand.

"What are you going to do with that?" she demanded, pointing.

Maclean looked down at the broadsword and then up again as quickly. "You can see me!" he bellowed.

"Just against the light. Yes, I can see you, Maclean. Put the sword down."

He lifted it up, admiring the weight of it, swinging it in a brief controlled arc in the narrow space in front of the stairs. " 'Tis a fine weapon."

"I don't think you'll be needing it, Maclean."

He gave a scornful laugh, as if she didn't know what she was talking about. "When you were walking by the loch the other day this sword saved your life, woman."

Saved her life? For a moment an image of the hag and its scaly companion flashed into her mind.

"There was a man riding a horse, or the ghost o' one, I'm no' sure. He rode at you, but I struck him down with my *claidheamh mor* before he could harm you."

She knew she was staring at him, she couldn't help it. "You saw him?"

"Aye, I cut him down, but then he was gone. Has such a thing happened to you before?"

"Never. Not until you came. I thought I must have imagined it, but he was so real. And then . . ." The pale brown pony, watching from the hilltop.

"Mabbe the door isn't closed as it should be," Maclean murmured. "The between-worlds is a dangerous place, Bella."

"Is that where that man came from, the between-worlds?"

" 'Tis something I must find out. Dinna fear, though, woman, from now on I will stay verra close."

She smiled.

The dark shape of him seemed suddenly alert. There was a tension in the air that had nothing to do with talk of ghosts and everything to do with physical attraction.

"You asked about my name," Bella said, a little breathlessly. "It is a—a pet name. My real name is Arabella. Arabella Ryan."

"Arabella." She heard the smile in his voice as he said it, rolling the *r*, turning it into a thing of beauty. "Do you want me to tuck you in, Arabella Ryan?"

She bit her lip, composing her expression. "No, thank you, Maclean."

He laughed, and for a moment she was certain she could see his face through the dark mist, wild and handsome and dangerously appealing.

Bella did the only sensible thing under the circumstances.

She fled upstairs.

Sixteen

Maclean stared at the glow in the Aga. It had been a mistake kissing Bella Ryan. Even a ghost-man such as himself could feel desire. Lust. It throbbed in his blood, in his sinews and muscles, until his whole body burned. Two hundred and fifty years without a woman was a long time for a man like Maclean, but there was more to it than that. Bella was the sort of woman he had always dreamed of in his secret heart, that soft part of him he kept locked away from his father's sharp eyes. He had kept those emotions hidden for so long he had forgotten they existed, until he was compelled to be kind to Ishbel. And look where that had gotten him.

And now here was Bella, who wasn't afraid of him, who burned beneath his hands and mouth like a bright flame. What he had said to her tonight was true—he wanted her, but he was beginning to think he did not deserve her.

He remembered the terrible gaze of the *Fiosaiche* with a shudder. The images in her eyes. And the unsettling possibility that Ishbel was loose in the present with vengeance on her mind. Such things had nothing to do with sweet Bella, and although she had been generous enough to help him in his quest so far, it would be wrong of him to put her in the path of danger. Bella belonged to this world and Maclean wasn't at all certain where he belonged.

There was a strange ache in his belly and he rubbed at it as he stood in the shadows. It felt oddly familiar, but he couldn't work out what it was. He grimaced as his stomach made a loud rumble and the ache intensified. He found himself thinking of roasting beef over a crackling fire, of salmon, and fresh baked bannocks, and whiskey that warmed him from the inside out.

And that's when he realized he was *hungry*.

Upstairs, Bella was curled under her quilt and blankets, only the top of her dark head showing. Maclean felt other parts of him ache, remembering the swell of her breast beneath the tight nightshirt, and the warmth of her woman's body as she arched against his hand. He wanted to crawl into her bed and wrap his arms about her and show her what she had been missing with her ruddy-faced Brian. She had kissed him tonight as if she wanted him as much as he wanted her, but he knew he mustn't force her. Aye, she had a heat and passion to match his, but she had told him she did not want him to touch her and he had agreed to abide by that, and Maclean was a man who did not break his word lightly.

Maclean gave the bed a shake, to try and wake her,

but she didn't move. Glancing around, he could see the pile of books on the bedside table. Was she researching the past so energetically for the sake of her book? Or was it possible she cared about him?

His stomach grumbled.

Impatiently, Maclean shook the bed again. Bella moaned, ducking her head even farther under the covers. "Go away," she said, her voice muffled. "I don't want your magic bridle."

"Bella?"

"Maclean? What's wrong?"

"Bella, I'm hungry."

There was a pause, and then she lifted her head and squinted in his general direction. Her hair was messy and her face was crumpled with sleep. Maclean thought she was gorgeous, and he was enjoying the sight of her when his stomach gave an extra-large rumble.

Bella laughed. "You *are* hungry. Is this another good sign?"

"Mabbe I am becoming a whole man again."

"Maybe you are."

"Will you cook me something to eat?"

Bella pushed her hair out of her eyes. Maclean was asking her to cook for him? She had the feeling that he would consider cooking to be a woman's work. She hoped he wasn't expecting her to take over the role of his personal servant—that would never do—but neither could she let him starve.

"I'll cook for you this time, and I'll teach you to cook, Maclean, so that you can look after yourself. In this world men need to learn to cook and clean and wash, unless they can pay someone else to do it. And you are currently unemployed. All right?"

He was silent as if mulling over what she had said. "Aye, all right," he sighed. "It seems verra strange, but if that is how men behave now, then I will learn to cook, Bella."

She threw the covers back and swung her legs out of the bed. The floor was cold and she flinched, quickly huddling into her robe and slippers. Maclean thumped after her down the stairs and into the kitchen, where it was much warmer. Bella set about preparing scrambled eggs on toast, and then Maclean set about eating them.

Watching the food vanish from the plate into nothing was very disconcerting, so she tried not to watch.

"I'll need more," he said, a few minutes after she gave him a second helping.

Bella turned to stare over her shoulder. "More?"

"Aye, I'm as hungry as a stag in the winter, Bella."

He sounded so mournful that she set about frying some sausages and bacon, with tomato and mushrooms, and toast. He ate that, too, so she heated up some soup and rolls. He finished that off with a slice of carrot cake with lemon icing, and the bottle of Australian wine.

"At the rate you're eating, Maclean," she said, peering into the cupboard, "there'll be nothing left in a couple of days. Not that I mind. It must mean you're returning to normal. Maybe you're making up for two hundred and fifty years of hunger."

Maclean gave a sigh of repletion. "It does feel good."

"I'm glad." She smiled. It *was* a good sign, this

hunger of Maclean's. Did this mean that very soon he would be completely visible again? She imagined having the Maclean in the portrait on the wall striding about the cottage. He was so domineering and handsome—altogether rather overwhelming. Before he arrived she had already been attracted to the image of him, so when he was whole again would she lose it completely, or would she be able to hang on to her self-control?

There was a thought. Maclean as her lover. Waking up in the morning with Maclean, and going to bed at night with his arms about her. The images made her feel hot all over.

"Well"—she took a breath, and tried to distract herself by glancing about at the mess—"I think I'll leave this and go back to bed . . . eh, sleep."

"Goodnight, Bella."

She hesitated in the doorway. "I was reading one of the books I found in the library today. It's a history of the Macleods of Mhairi, cobbled together by someone who's related to them. It isn't very well written, but it made me realize something I should have known. The origin of the Black Maclean legend must have been Auchry Macleod. There's no other explanation."

"Ishbel's father?"

"Yes. When the authorities eventually got around to investigating the massacre, it was him they spoke to. *He* seems to be the starting point in all of this. Didn't he like you very much, Maclean?"

"He was a sly weasel of a man," he said coldly. "It doesna surprise me he would do something underhanded to hurt me when I was dead and couldn't accuse him of the lie. That would be Auchry's way."

"He must have been very fond of his daughter if he'd forgive her for abandoning her useful marriage to you and running off with Iain. I would have thought most fathers in your day would have given the girl a sound beating and dragged her back to her future husband."

"Auchry was always weak when it came to Ishbel. Once she got home she would turn her sweet smile on him and he'd do anything she asked."

"So do you think he . . . killed you?" *Cut your body into pieces and threw it to the four winds.* She shuddered at such barbarity.

"No, not Auchry."

Bella waited. It sounded as if he had more to tell her, but when he remained silent, she said lightly, "Then it doesn't surprise me that Ishbel's father would use your death to blacken your memory. If he could turn you into such a villain that she had no option but to leave, then there's no stain on her character, or his."

Maclean pondered a moment. "Aye, you're right. Blackening my name would suit him. But I dinna understand how he overcame me and my men. He was a thief, a man to sneak up in the dark and rob his neighbors, no' a soldier."

"He wouldn't have gone to Loch Fasail afterwards, then?"

"Even Auchry would hesitate when it came to the murder of innocent women and children, even if they were Maclean women and children. No, there is more to it, Bella."

"Then I'll have to dig further." Again she hesitated. She had a feeling that Maclean was remembering something, but he was keeping it to himself. Bella wished he would tell her, but she could hardly force it out of him; she didn't think Maclean was a man who could be forced to do anything against his will. He would open up to her when he was good and ready.

"Goodnight, Maclean."

"Goodnight, Arabella."

Bella closed the door. She was tired and longing for her bed, but still she took a moment to stand in the cold hallway and think of Maclean. To try and make sense of what was happening to her. And to wonder why, in the midst of all this craziness, she was so happy.

"Take care, Bella." She whispered the warning. "Remember, he could vanish again as quickly as he appeared."

It was better to shield herself from being hurt, she had learned that much from Brian. She would be a fool to trust Maclean implicitly. The unfortunate thing was, she wanted to. Despite all her precautions he had slipped beneath her guard, and was dangerously close to making a captive of her heart.

When Bella woke it was to the smell of cooking. Surprised, she made her way downstairs, realizing she had slept far longer than usual. The flush of dawn had come and gone, and now there was a soft misty rain falling over the loch. When she opened the door into the kitchen she was immediately enveloped by a haze of smoke and steam and the smell of meat sizzling.

Maclean was busy playing chef.

"There you are!" he said when she came through the door. "I couldna wait any longer, woman. My belly was pressing against my backbone."

Bella cast an eye over the scene and decided he didn't need any immediate help. She sat down at the table, trying not to notice how pans and pots were moved by his invisible hands.

"You really are becoming a man again, Maclean. The *Fiosaiche* must be very pleased with you."

"I want to please her. And you, Bella. I want to be a man again, so that I can please you."

Bella cleared her throat, an image of Maclean and herself flashing into her mind with hot, sharp clarity.

He seemed to read her thoughts because he chuckled, and for a moment, just a moment, she could see a man-shaped cloud. Not black, like his silhouette against bright light, but bluish and green. Perhaps the color of his plaid? A pan crashed into the sink, he cursed, and now she could definitely see him. All of him. Enveloped in a fuzzy white mist.

"Maclean," she breathed, afraid that saying it aloud might make it go away. "I can see you . . . I think. I can see something."

He froze. As she stared he moved toward her, becoming bigger, and then part of the hazy shape reached out and she felt Maclean's fingers wrap about her wrist. Staring down, she could see the vague outline of his arm and hand, but no detail; he was very poorly defined.

"I can see you," she said. "Not clearly yet, but I can see you."

His fingers trembled. "I really am becoming a man again," he said, his voice hoarse with emotion.

Behind him a pot boiled over with a violent splutter.

With a curse he turned back to the mess he was making. But nothing was damaged and a moment later he had served up two plates of bacon and eggs with half-burnt toast. Bella thanked him, finding it touching that he had not just cooked for himself, but had gone to the trouble of thinking of her, too.

"This cooking business is simple," Maclean announced around a mouthful of food. "I dinna know why women fuss about it so."

Bella narrowed her eyes at him. "So you're an expert now, are you, Maclean?"

"I'm a man."

"Your point being?"

"A man is naturally better at everything, apart from bearing babies."

Bella itched to throw something at him. Instead she said, "You're medieval, Maclean. A medieval despot. A feudal lord."

He munched a moment in silence. "Do you know, Bella, I've been to the homes of some of the nobles of Scotland, and I tell you that just because they dress in lace and wear wigs and have people to wait on them doesna make them good landlords and chiefs. 'Tis my opinion that the more money a man has, the more he wants. He forgets his people and the reason he was born to be a leader of them, and thinks only of having as much fine furniture and gold plate about him as he can get hold of, and wearing as many jewels on his fingers as he can bear."

"Hmm, very Calvinist of you, Maclean." But he impressed her with his thoughts, and the depth of frank feeling behind them.

"I never wanted to prance about Edinburgh in high heels," he retorted crossly. "I liked it fine here in Fasail.

This was my place and my people, and I was born to protect them from harm." He stopped. After a moment he pushed his plate away, food still on it. "Aye, and look what a mess I made of it," he said bitterly.

Bella spoke gently. "Maclean, when you returned from Culloden and Ishbel was gone, did you ever have any doubts about going after her?"

"No," he said stiffly.

Bella leaned forward. "Why not? I mean, if you didn't love her and she was desperate to go, and you were certain of your authority over her father, what did it matter if she left? Was the land that important to you that you'd forgo your own happiness and hers for the sake of it?"

"*I am the Maclean.* Do you think my people would respect me if I allowed my future wife to run off with a scrawny wee laddie?"

His voice dripped ice and an arrogance that chilled her blood. He didn't sound like the Maclean she had come to know. He sounded like the man in the legend, and capable of anything.

Bella swallowed, refusing to be intimidated. "I don't know, Maclean. Perhaps in hindsight your people would have preferred to forgo the respect and keep their lives. What value do you place on their 'respect' for you after all?"

"I am a man, and I have my pride, woman!" He shouted it, making her jump and the plates rattle. "You canna put a price on a man's pride!"

"Pride!" Bella's own voice rose several decibels. She hesitated, not because she was shouting at a Highlander who did not exist, but because she was shouting. Bella didn't shout. She brooded. She stayed silent and mulled over the injustices in her life, and thought of all the things she wished she had said at the time. Now Maclean, with his blustering bullheadedness, was infecting her with that same need to express herself. Loudly.

"What has your pride done for you, Maclean? Look at yourself. You should have humbled your pride that day, not chewed upon it like a sour bone."

"What would a woman know about pride?" he roared back, and now the whole kitchen shook. "Women have no pride. They are devious sluts, their tongues saying one thing when they mean the opposite, their smiles luring an honest man into making a fool of himself and believing in them, when all the time they are plotting to run off with another. Ishbel didna deserve to be happy!"

He stopped, breathing hard, his bitter betrayal a heavy weight between them.

Bella felt sick with the new suspicion engulfing her. "So it *was* love that sent you to fetch Ishbel back," she insisted. "You loved her and she betrayed you and you couldn't forgive her. Couldn't forgive the fact that she chose another man over you, the great Maclean. You went after her, full of jealous fury, and killed that man. My God, did you love her that much, Maclean?"

"I've told you," he growled, "I didna love her at all! But she was *my* future wife. A man doesna let his wife run off if he has any pride. He fetches her back, and that is what I went to do."

Abruptly Bella stood up. "Let me get this right, Maclean. You are the Chief of the Macleans of Fasail, and they mean everything to you. In fact, you decided not to fight at Culloden because you realized your men would die, and you thought more of them than any lost cause. I understand that. Where was your pride then? If you were as puffed up with it as you've just led me to think, then you would have fought, whatever the consequences, because to fail to do so would lower you in the eyes of your betters."

"M'betters!" he snorted. "I am my own man, I make up my own mind, and I dinna bow and scrape to anyone."

"Exactly! You put the interests of your people before anyone else. *You* did that. So why did you go after Ishbel? Fetching her back was of no advantage to you, surely? An unwilling wife and all that. Unless you were afraid of what her father would do once your hostage to his good behavior was free?" Bella paused. "But no, you've already said you did not fear Auchry, you despised him. So why did you do it, Maclean? There has to be a better reason than you've given me so far. Why?"

He stood up, his chair crashing backward onto the floor and catching the handle of a pan and a plate as it went. Maclean's roar of anger drowned out the ensuing din.

"Because I was tired of listening to the bleating of women!"

Bella stared back at him, or where she thought he was—he seemed to have vanished altogether again now. "What women? Ishbel?"

"The women of Loch Fasail, my mother, all begging me not to go, all wringing their hands at me. They didna understand, none of them."

"The women didn't want you to go," Bella said

slowly, finally understanding. "But you didn't listen to them, did you? It was beneath you to listen to women."

So Maclean had chased after Ishbel, and that was when everything had gone wrong. If he had listened to them like the clever and reasonable man she knew he was capable of being, if he had been a truly great and wise man, then history would have been changed. The massacre would still probably have occurred—they did not know the details yet—but Maclean and his men would have been there to fight, not lying dead at Auchry Macleod's feet.

And suddenly Bella realized that Maclean knew it, too. The guilt was eating him alive, but he'd never admit it. He had far too much *pride* to lose.

"Maybe you were right," she said quietly. "Maybe you can't change. Maybe all of this is a waste of the *Fiosaiche*'s time."

He didn't reply, but then, she hadn't expected him to.

Seventeen

Bella's pink waterproof jacket was hanging on the hook by the door and she snatched it up as she went out. "I'm going for a walk," she said, and slammed the door. Behind her, in the cottage, there was another appalling crash, but with rigid shoulders she ignored it and set off, her thighs soon burning with the effort to get away from Maclean, as far away and as quickly as possible.

"Insufferable," she grumbled, wiping the tears from her cheeks. The rain sparkled in her hair and the air smelled of damp earth and vegetation. "He's not my problem," she reminded herself. "I don't have to worry about him."

She had enough worries of her own. She had a book deadline to meet and no laptop, a rented cottage whose lease was about to run out and nowhere to live, and a boyfriend who had left her for the bright lights of Edinburgh. Suddenly she felt overwhelmed by the pointlessness of her own life. The five-star review on *Reading England* should have been a high point, and it had been for about five minutes. Bella loved writing about the past, but since Maclean had come into her life she realized that writing about it wasn't enough. She was living vicariously, through the lives of others.

It was time she found a life of her own.

The path up to the ruined castle was slippery, but she was so deep in her thoughts she hardly noticed. And then suddenly there she was, at the top, with the world spread out before her. Bella took some deep breaths and tried to visualize this place as it must have been. People all living here together as a clan, a family of one hundred and fifty souls. And their father and ruler, the man they looked to for wisdom and protection, was Morven Maclean.

I bow and scrape to no man!

Arrogant, chauvinist, medieval. Yes, he was all that. But he was also intelligent and frank and honorable in a way she found completely captivating. He was like no man she had ever met in her life. Maclean was a giant in any century, standing head and shoulders above the rest, and he should have been remembered for that rather than for being . . .

A monster.

Maclean felt his legs shaking as he struggled up the hill toward Castle Drumaird. He looked up, squinting against the rain, and was reminded of the first time he had climbed this hill after the *Fiosaiche* brought him back to life. A similar despair swept over him now.

With a curse, he shook the water from his face. He

could see Bella standing on the brow of the hill. Apart from her long dark hair whipping around her, she was very still against the gray and cloudy sky. For a breath he stopped, staring at her. Bella against the storm was spellbinding. There was a strength in her raised chin and straight back that made him ache with pride and longing.

Why could he not have met someone like Bella two hundred and fifty years ago? *She* would never have run off with a puling lad and made a fool of him. She would never have been afraid of his kisses and his bed. When he came home from Culloden Moor she would have been there, waiting for him, loving him. She would have matched him well, and he would have been a better man for having her at his side.

And now it was too late.

He began to walk again, his legs trembling worse than ever. After their argument in the kitchen he had begun to feel strangely feeble, as if all of the strength he had so recently gained were trickling out of him. He was a water bladder with a hole in it. When he had tried to pick up the pieces of the plate he had smashed, he found his fingers slipped through them and he could not grasp them. He could not even *feel* them.

The *Fiosaiche* was angry with him. He was a stubborn fool and to teach him a lesson she was undoing all she had done. Soon he would be sent back to the dark labyrinths of the between-worlds, a lost soul forever wandering.

Horrified, Maclean had followed after Bella.

He needed to see her again, before he vanished forever. To touch her skin and kiss her lips, to tell her she was his bonny woman and he regretted so much that he could not stay.

"Bella!" There was a deep well of grief in his voice. He watched her eyes snap open as she turned her head to seek him out. The wind snarled and gusted about them. Suddenly he was so cold.

He was turning back into a ghostie. His brief second chance was fading and very soon he would be gone.

"Bella!"

It already felt as if it were too late.

"Maclean?" Bella was crying out his name. "Where are you? I can't see you."

"I'm invisible again," he said, and his voice sounded weaker, less certain, fading away. He took the final few steps so that he could reach out a hand to brush her cheek. He could feel her skin, soft and warm, only just, but he could still feel her. He let his held breath go in relief and focused on that sensation, knowing that this would have to last him forever. . . .

"Maclean!" she stretched out her arms, finding him. Her hands caught his jacket, then slid awkwardly around his waist, pulling him nearer, until their bodies were pressed as close as they could be. "Maclean, you mustn't let it happen. Don't go." She sounded frightened.

"I dinna want to go," he mumbled, and rested his face against her hair, his whole being concentrated on seeing her, feeling her, smelling her, listening to her voice.

If the *Fiosaiche* returned for him and he was cast back into that nightmare place, then at least he would have these memories to sustain him.

"Maclean," Bella moaned, and she was weeping, her tears making a damp patch on his shirt.

And suddenly he couldn't bear for her to be so sad for his sake. "Bella," he whispered, "Bella, dinna grieve for me. I'll be fine. And if I see you in my dreams, then I willna mind so much."

"You're giving up!" she shouted. "Don't you dare give up."

"I'm no' giving up. . . ."

Even as he spoke the words, he began to feel stronger.

"I'm no' giving up!"

Some of the lost feeling in his hands was returning, and despite the wind and the rain he was not quite so cold. Maclean turned his face and kissed her temple, and then tipped up her chin and kissed her lips. Her mouth opened to his. Her loving warmth filled him, held him in a way he had never been held before. Maclean knew that he didn't want to leave Bella, and yet deep in his heart he had a dark dread that this might be what was required of him.

Sacrifice.

The word echoed in his head even as he kissed her, clasping her in his arms, hot with his need for her.

Bella pulled away from him, gasping, her cheeks flushed and her lips red and swollen. Maclean groaned and again pressed his face to her hair, breathing in the scent of her. He felt like a stallion, insatiable, wild and desperate to mate. Maybe, like being hungry, this was just another part of his becoming a man again. Except there was more to it than that. This woman meant more to him than simply a willing female to rut with. If she was, then he would have taken her already, but he didn't want to frighten her with the strength of his passion, he didn't want to make her his if she wasn't ready for him to do so.

It was important that when they came together it was something both of them wanted.

Maclean rested his hands upon her shoulders and felt himself trembling with the effort it took to step back, away from her, and finally let her free. Bella swayed a little, gazing up at him, her dark eyes blurred with desire.

"Maclean?" she whispered.

"I have no' the right to touch you, Bella, unless ye wish me to."

Her lashes dropped over her eyes, and she took a shaken breath. "I know I asked you not to, and you've abided by that, Maclean. But I've changed my mind. I'm tired of doing things to please other people. I want to please myself. I *want* you to touch me," she said, and looked directly at him.

His laugh was mixed with a half groan. "I dinna know what will happen to me from one moment to the next. I am a wraith. I canna protect you as I wish."

"I don't need you to protect me," she said sharply, then gentled it with, "although that you want to protect me sounds very comforting."

He caught her hand in his, his fingers closing painfully. "I am a Highland chief, Bella. That I offer to protect you is no' an insult or a comfort, it is simply what I am. It is all I have to give now, and I offer it to you."

Tears filled her eyes.

"Are you sure ye want me, Arabella?" he murmured against her ear, his warm breath making her shiver.

"I'm sure."

"Come, then," said Maclean, his voice full of passion and promise. "Come with me."

Maclean's big warm hand enveloped hers as he led her toward the ruins of what had once been his castle. The bleak walls rose above them, and Bella looked nervously at the places where the stones had fallen away. The arched door was over eight feet thick, and although now it led nowhere, it still gave them shelter from the wind and rain.

"Where are we going?" she asked as he stopped beneath the arch.

"This is my home, Bella."

"Maclean . . ."

When she'd agreed to this, Bella had been thinking of her own warm bed, not a gloomy ruin on a hilltop in the rain. Surely even her passion for Maclean would cool under these conditions?

And then he kissed her, his mouth hot and open, his tongue seeking hers, and she was no longer sure. Fire coursed through her. Her hands slid beneath his jacket, around his waist, feeling the soft linen of his shirt and the hard power of the body beneath. He eased her back against the stone and leaned into her. She should have felt crushed, trapped, but she felt so warm and safe, with his big body a bulwark against the weather and the world. She felt like weeping with joy.

He kept kissing her. He was not rough, but he wasn't gentle, either. He wanted her and he showed it, and his honesty encouraged Bella to show it, too.

He pulled apart her jacket and reaching for the hem of her sweater, pulling it up. She was wearing a bra, and for a moment that confused him. Bella showed him how to unhook it, and soon it was loosened and her breasts spilled free.

He groaned.

She felt dizzy as he stroked her, his mouth wet and hot against her flesh, his fingers tugging at her nipples. Bella knew how uncertain their relationship was, and awful as the thought seemed, it also set her free of any inhibitions. She lifted his face to hers and kissed him back, deeply.

Maclean reached between her legs, his fingers rubbing through the cloth of her baggy jeans, feeling the shape of her, making her arch against him as pleasure washed through her. She ran her hands over his thighs, feeling the thick strength of them beneath the wool of his kilt. His fingers tangled in her hair, and he stooped and claimed her mouth again, tumbling to his knees in front of her and pulling her down with him.

"Bella," he murmured, "my wild beauty."

Bella *did* feel wild and beautiful. Maclean had the gift of letting her see herself through his eyes. He wanted her, he desired her, there was no pretense in him. It was wonderfully refreshing and freeing. Bella could be herself.

She clung to his shoulders and he caught her around the hips, and turned them both so that he was resting against the stone archway, and she was sitting across his lap. Bella kept her eyes closed—it was too disconcerting to see nothing when she could feel the broad masculine strength of his body beneath hers as she straddled his thighs. His open mouth found her breasts, suckling, making her whimper with delight.

And then her hands found his erection, stroking him through the cloth of his kilt, and Maclean stopped as if he'd been shot.

"Bella." His voice was a rasp, somewhere between pain and pleasure.

She hitched the woolen cloth up over his heavily muscled thighs until she could touch him.

There was nothing ghostlike about this.

He groaned his pleasure, arching up into her hands, completely without artifice. He liked what she was doing and he showed her. She stroked him more boldly, reaching down to the root of his shaft, running her hands over the hard slope of his belly. He swooped forward and nipped her neck, just above her collar, then lathed it with his tongue to make it better.

Bella grabbed handfuls of his linen shirt and held on, head thrown back, her chest heaving as he proceeded to lick down to her breasts, cupping them in his palms and holding them pressed together so that he could adore both nipples, side by side.

Her body clenched.

She was going to come before he was even inside her.

He must have known it, because he laughed, deep in his throat. And he slid his fingers between her thighs again and pressed hard on her clitoris before rubbing his thumb over it.

He caught her as she fell back, her body shuddering with orgasm, her breath heaving in her chest.

"Aye, we're a fine match," he growled, "you and me, Bella."

She felt his hair against her cheek, his hands tugging at her waistband, and then her jeans were open and he was pulling them down her thighs and away, turning her and lifting her as if she weighed nothing to him.

Just as she was beginning to regain her breath and her senses, he settled himself beneath her once more and, with barely a pause, slid the tip of his cock inside her slick entrance.

"I'm big," he gasped, "so tell me if it hurts, aye?"

"Oh . . . yes, of course."

He rested his large hands on her hips and adjusted her slightly, pushing himself up inside her with a smooth determination that left her helpless. She felt him stretching her but not unbearably; the fullness was pleasant and, when he adjusted her hips again so that he could move against her with friction, achingly good.

"You like that?" he said, his mouth against hers.

She held her palms on either side of his face and kissed him with all the intensity and passion she was capable of.

Above them in the ruined castle the wind howled and moaned, but Maclean's body was hot and Bella was oblivious to anything but the ecstasy building between them.

He held her hips steady and thrust up, deep inside her, and she shattered. A moment later so did he. Her head fell forward against his shoulder, her body lying limp against his chest. Maclean cradled her in his arms, and they lay together, sheltered from the weather, beyond speech or thought. Except for one.

This feels so right.

Eighteen

A rattle of stones as someone jumped from the lower part of the ruins. A whisper of clothing as someone brushed through the thick grass nearby. The sounds caught Maclean by surprise. In an instant he was on his feet, Bella pushed to safety behind the bulk of his body, and reaching for his *claidheamh mor*. She tumbled off him, still limp and replete, but the rasp of the metal blade sliding from the scabbard made her cry out in fright.

Maclean glanced at Bella to be certain she was all right, before he turned once more to face any possible danger.

"Show yoursel'!" he demanded.

The rain had stopped and so had the wind. A mist was creeping in, covering the hilltop and its scattering of stones with opaque fingers of white. It meant Maclean and Bella couldn't be so easily seen, but it also meant Maclean couldn't see whoever was out there. Watching them.

Something appeared briefly in the mist, a red and green plaid, and a wisp of long golden hair. An echo of laughter, fading. Maclean felt his heart thudding so hard it made him feel sick. He knew that laughter.

Another rattle of stone, this time in the direction of the path, and a hissing curse as someone slipped. And then running steps, fading into silence. He waited, watching, listening, until he was certain that whoever had been up here with them was gone.

Maclean tried to tell himself that he had been mistaken. How could Ishbel be here? And how could she have been in Ardloch yesterday? She had been a sweet girl, maybe somewhat manipulative like her father, but she had changed before he left for Culloden, grown sullen and secretive, with a bitter edge. And now she was back and she was no longer Ishbel.

She was something else.

"Maclean?"

At the sound of Bella's voice he turned and two things happened. He felt a wave of happiness and relief, that she was here with him. And he felt a terrible fear that Ishbel would take her away from him. Was she capable of it? Aye, the creature that was Ishbel was capable of anything.

"I'm here," he called back.

She was still standing in the archway, and although she had returned her clothing to order and zipped up her jacket, her hair was tangled and her eyes wide. There was a loving mark on her pale throat where he had been too enthusiastic.

"What was it?" she whispered, looking past him into

the mist, then back again. Her eyes fixed upon the broadsword, and he could tell she was frightened at the violence it represented. Quickly he sheathed the blade as he closed the distance between them.

He bent his head until his face was level with hers, brushing her cheek with the backs of his fingers. "You're safe with me, Bella," he said softly. "My oath on it."

She swallowed, her eyes searching his as if she were looking for the lie. And then she seemed to slump, her face relaxing into a smile. "I can see you again, Maclean."

"I guessed mabbe you could," he said, and grinned back. His gaze dropped down, over her body. She'd covered herself up, but he remembered the sight of all those lush, voluptuous curves, and he felt himself growing hard again.

Was this part of the *Fiosaiche*'s plan? That he and Bella should be bound together by passion and desire? That his feelings for her would make a better man of him?

In truth, right now Maclean didn't care.

He caught her hand in his, and found to his surprise that her fingers were cold and trembling. When he looked at her face more closely, he discovered her nose was pink and her teeth were chattering. Maclean cursed softly and wrapped his arms around her, bringing her in tight against his body.

"What am I thinking?" he said gruffly. "You're cold and I'm keeping you here blathering. This time we'll use the bed."

Bella gave a muffled chuckle, her face pressed to his chest. "Maybe that would be best," she teased.

Maclean led her back toward the cottage, glancing about him in a manner that to Bella would look casual but wasn't. There was something not right here in Loch Fasail. He felt it in the air, a heavy oppressiveness, as if a storm were building. He must be ready for whatever came. This time, Maclean swore to himself, he would not make the mistake of leaving what belonged to him undefended.

Bella sat on the edge of the bed in the twilit room, trying not to wake Maclean, watching him as he slept. She couldn't help looking at him. Maclean was almost entirely visible. Maybe a very slight fuzziness about the edges, but otherwise . . .

He was perfect.

She pushed her hair over one shoulder and grimaced as the movement caused her muscles to protest. Maclean was not a man to stop when he was roused. Not that she'd wanted him to; far from it. She'd been more than willing to meet him halfway. In fact she'd surprised herself with just how uninhibited she could be, given half a chance. It had never been like this with Brian; the very thought of making love with him as she had with Maclean made her cringe in embarrassment.

Brian would be horrified by such lack of cool finesse.

Bella had relished every moment of it.

Maclean moved, and in the half-light she let her gaze drift over him. He was taking up most of her bed, one leg dangling off the side, the other sticking well off the end of the mattress. His arms were flung outward, his chest bare, the covers twisted about his hips but not hiding much. His face was turned to one side, his hair spread behind him.

There were few words she could think of that described him adequately. Desirable was one, magnificent was another, heart-stopping, spellbinding . . . frightening. He had changed her, or perhaps he had simply set her free. She trusted him. She could say and do anything with him and not feel as though he would judge her for it. Bella had never had that experience with a man before.

He was like no other man she had ever come across, and although her life had been sheltered, Bella did not think there was another Maclean out there somewhere. He was as unique in the twenty-first century as he had been in the eighteenth century.

No wonder the *Fiosaiche* wanted to save him.

"You're looking at me again, Arabella," he teased, and opened one eye to peer at her. "What time is it?"

"Late. Nearly dark. Are you hungry?"

He made a growling noise and pounced on her, making her shriek as he rubbed his face against her neck.

"Stop it, Maclean, you have whiskers!"

"I know. Isn't it wonderful, Bella?"

She laughed and rubbed her knuckles over his jaw, feeling the rough scratch of the shadow that was getting darker by the minute. He really was returning to manhood, in every way. She leaned forward and licked the tip of her tongue over his chin, and then began to nibble his lips, little kisses that turned into longer, hotter ones.

He caught her to him, sliding his palms up under the skirt she was wearing and murmuring his appreciation at her lack of underwear. He caressed her with bold, knowing fingers and her kisses grew drugged and burning.

She slid her thigh over him, poising herself above his erection and sinking down. "So good," she whispered, pleased that she could say her secret thoughts aloud for him to hear.

"Aye," he groaned, lying still and letting her do the work.

She used his chest for leverage, feeling the broad expanse beneath her fingers, the rough hair and powerful muscles. He caught her hips in his palms, thrusting into her body eagerly, meeting her passion with a passion of his own. The climax took them by surprise, Bella's gaze tangling with his, caught and held in that moment of intense pleasure.

"We are well matched, me and you," Maclean said, tucking her against his side. He had spoken the words before, but she didn't mind. It was true.

The room was dark now, just the faintest light in the sky outside the window.

He stroked her hip and she waited, because it seemed to her that he had something more to say.

"You were right, Bella. I should have listened to the women. To my mother. When I was a wee lad she planned to run away. Leave me and my father for another man. My father found out and the man . . . died. I canna say who or what was to blame, but after that my mother didna try and run away again. But he never forgave her. I didna forgive her, either. I never trusted myself to love her again, nor any woman. My father's bitterness infected me. He was no' an easy man, I know, but he loved her . . . in his way."

"So Ishbel—"

"I gave more of myself to Ishbel than any other woman since my mother turned her back on me. Ishbel was afraid of me and what a man does with a woman, and her fear worked on me. I promised her that if she and I wed I wouldna take her in that way until she was ready. I tried to be kind and gentle with her, everything my father abhorred, but still she left me. Abandoned me like my mother for another man . . . no, a boy! I had given her everything, I had bared my heart and soul, and she'd paid me back with lies and deceit. I knew then that nothing else would do for me but to force her back to Loch Fasail and show her I was no' such a weakling as she imagined. But I know now it wasna to show *her*, not really. It was to show mysel'."

"She hurt you, Maclean—"

"I was in a rage. My father was in my head. It seemed to me then that he must be right when he told me a man's rage must be hot and his heart cold, and because I had gone against his words I had become a weak fool. I was angry with mysel' and my father and Ishbel. And I was angry with my mother when she came to me, for not understanding my feelings."

He ended on a rush, breathless, hurting. Bella considered what he had said. It made sense. A man like Maclean, brought up by a brutal and angry father in his image, and at the same time he was his mother's son, longing for something more. For the first time, with Ishbel, he had dared to show the part of himself that longed for love, for a normal happy life, but he chose the wrong woman. It must have seemed like a divine lesson. Maclean would have determined to return immediately to his father's ways and punish Ishbel. The hurt little boy inside him overruled the older, wiser man.

Bella sighed. "I see it all now," she said. "And you promised not to touch Ishbel?" she added, feeling her face coloring that this part of all he had said should be so important to her. "You never . . . um . . ."

"Never." He said it grimly.

Bella sat up, her face shadowy above him, but he could see the soft gleam in her eyes. "I know it is very wrong of me, Maclean, but I can't help feeling glad about that."

He smiled, and reached up to rub his thumb back and forth over her lips. "Neither can I."

"Do you think you'd take another chance, with another woman?"

She was holding her breath, dreading the answer. Bella knew all about hurt feelings and the effort involved in exposing your most vulnerable emotions. One could only do it so many times before it just didn't seem worth the pain.

"Aye," he said, his voice low and husky. "I wouldna have said so once, but now . . . I think I would, if I found the right one."

"And . . . do you think you will? Find the right one, I mean?"

He slid his palm to her cheek and drew her slowly, inexorably down to him.

"Aye," he whispered, just before his mouth closed on hers.

Nineteen

Water dripped down the walls, oozing to a floor that was thick with slime. Screams echoed through the dark tunnels, fading into silence. Something scuttled in the gloom, claws scraping on the wet stone. This was the between-worlds, the place of waiting, the place where the flotsam and jetsam of the universe gathered.

The *Fiosaiche* strode through the unlit tunnels. Her silver cloak swept about her, and the floating strands of her auburn hair were like flames licking the shadows. The creatures she passed cringed, moaning and wailing and hiding their eyes. She paid them no heed and rejected her urge to pity. For those who dwelt in this place deserved to be here, and their fate would be decided. Eventually.

The tunnel narrowed and the roof dropped lower. The sorceress clicked her tongue and stooped, ignoring the blank-faced souls huddled in niches along the way.

They cowered, sensing that here was something to fear more than the darkness, here was a being powerful enough to change history and stop time. But if it crossed their minds that she might help them escape their own fates, then one glance of her terrible gaze convinced them she had not come for them.

The soul sought by the *Fiosaiche* was up ahead.

The tunnel widened and broadened and suddenly opened out into an enormous cavern. Inky black water lapped a silver shore and stretched endlessly into the half-darkness. As she stared across the underworld sea, something roared, its snakelike body writhing and twisting and making the ebony water boil, before it sank back into the depths.

Sea serpents, loch monsters, water-horses. Once they had been feared and revered, now they were treated as myth and legend. Mankind no longer wished to believe such creatures existed, but they did, and this was their true lair. Centuries ago doors had led from this world to the mortal world, and although now they were closed, they could still be opened. If you knew how.

The *Fiosaiche* strode on along the silver beach toward the woman seated on a rock, one of many littering the sand. Behind her, out in the dark sea, the monsters continued to roar and splash. As if they sensed the presence of one stronger than themselves.

Ishbel Macleod looked up.

Her golden hair was matted, her green eyes narrowed and vicious, her once-fine clothing ragged. She looked like a prisoner who had been locked in a castle dungeon for too many years to remember, but it hadn't dimmed the fire inside her. If anything, the hatred burned stronger than ever.

There was no remorse in Ishbel for what she had done.

The *Fiosaiche* stopped and for a time stared at her while Ishbel attempted to meet her eyes without flinching, and then she smiled. Ishbel cried out like an animal and ducked her head, letting her hair fall over her face. Out in the ebony sea the monsters called again, closer now, drawn by the scent of fresh meat.

Ishbel shuddered. "They are hungry," she said in a voice ravaged by suffering. "Every night they come out seeking food. Every night they tear me to pieces and feed on me. But they do not kill me, they canna kill me. I become whole again, and then the next night they come again, and so it goes. Pain and torment, over and over. This is your doing, witch."

"No, this is your doing, Ishbel."

Ishbel gave a little smile through her tangled hair. "The only way I can bear it is knowing Maclean suffers, too."

"You are so predictable," the *Fiosaiche* said.

Ishbel screeched, spitting, and sprang from her rock to land at the *Fiosaiche*'s feet. "Free me, free me, and I will show you what I can do!"

The sorceress waited until she was quiet again. "I admit that when I came here the possibility of you being free was on my mind, Ishbel."

Ishbel stiffened, as if she could hardly believe her ears, staring up blank-faced. "You really mean to set me free after all these centuries of torment?" A cunning expression slipped over Ishbel's face. "I will try and be good," she said in a little voice.

"You misunderstand me," the *Fiosaiche* said sternly. "I came to see if you were still here. There have been whispers that you have made your own way to freedom, impossible as that seems. You have been seen in the mortal world."

"Who told you that, witch?"

"I have my spies."

A sea monster roared close by, sending a spray of black water onto the sand. Ishbel glanced toward it anxiously, but when she turned again to the sorceress her expression was carefully empty of anything but hatred.

"Well, as you can see I am still here, still waiting for you to come and release me, *Fiosaiche*. What must I do to redeem myself?"

"Show genuine remorse, Ishbel," and the sorceress's voice was almost tender as she held out her hand. "I will know when I touch you if you are honest with me, and if you are not . . ."

"You ask too much," Ishbel said thickly, drawing away from the hand, eyeing it uneasily. "Take me to your masters, the Lords of the Universe. Let me talk to them. I think you are exceeding your power, witch. I think it is you who needs to be questioned, not me."

"The Lords would not waste their time on something as insignificant as you. Poor Ishbel. Do you really want to stay here and suffer? Don't you want to move on to the world of the dead, where you can sleep at last?"

Ishbel shook her head stubbornly, and once more her eyes flicked sideways to the black sea and its inhabitants.

"Why can't you let your hatred go?"

Ishbel pushed herself to her feet, staggering, and

then she straightened and stood proud despite her ravaged looks. "I want to be set free, aye, but only so that I can find Maclean and feast on his soul. I thought he was in the labyrinths, but I canna find him. I have searched for many years now and he is not here. What have you done with him, witch? Taken him to one of your secret hiding places, where you keep your favorites? Do the Lords know about that?"

"Be silent!"

But Ishbel was past caution. "I want to see Maclean here in my place, damned to be food for the loch monsters forever. I want to tear out his soul and destroy any chance he has to find peace in death. That is what I want, witch. Can ye give me that?"

The *Fiosaiche* fixed her with that terrible stare. "You have made your choice, Ishbel."

She turned and began to walk back along the silver sand.

There was a roar from the ebony sea, and then something monstrous heaved itself onto the beach.

"And Ishbel," the *Fiosaiche* called over her shoulder, "you're right, Maclean is not in the labyrinths. He is gone. I have given him the chance to become a mortal man again. He is beyond your reach."

Ishbel screamed with pure rage, but the sound was cut off abruptly. There was a splash as the water creature returned to its home, taking its prey with it.

Twenty

Bella drove slowly, the car rattling over the potholes. The rain had made the ground slippery, too, and she had to be careful on the turns, despite the fact that her mind wasn't really on her driving. She had been to see Gregor at his farm, to ask about extending the lease on Drumaird Cottage. Now that Maclean was here, she wanted to stay longer, to be with him in the place they both loved. But instead of giving her the permission she had hoped for, Gregor told Bella some news that shocked her.

Gregor was building a road around the side of Loch Fasail, to make it more accessible to tourists, but that wasn't the worst of it. He was also constructing a dozen holiday cottages along the loch shore. The project was not in the public domain as yet, and Gregor's cousin expected there to be objections when it was—conservationists and nature-lovers would protest vigorously—but he hoped to overcome them. The road would mean easier fishing for those less inclined to carry their gear over miles of rough terrain, and it would mean easier access to some of the hills and rock climbs to the north. The cottages would mean strangers invading the peace and quiet, treating it like another disposable holiday destination. The isolated beauty of Loch Fasail would be gone.

But Gregor needed the money.

"In the circumstances I dinna think I should re-lease Drumaird Cottage." Gregor had given her a sympathetic look.

"But I'm extending my lease; surely that's different?" Bella had insisted.

"Well, I'm no' sure when the work will begin. I tell you what, Ms. Ryan, I'll find out exactly next time I talk with the bulldozer driver. That's the best I can do, I'm sorry."

A bulldozer! Bella could hardly bear to think about it. A road around the loch, and cars traveling where now there was only silence or the lonely call of a bird. Loch Fasail would be ruined completely.

"Ye haven't seen those sheep?" Gregor called out, as she went to leave. "They still haven't turned up, and now there's a couple more I canna find."

"No, I'm sorry." She paused, her hand on the car door. "I did hear something splashing in the loch the other night, though. Do you think they might have fallen in?"

He gave her a strange look. "Something splashing?"

"Yes. Something in the loch." Bella was remembering the night she looked from her window and saw the shadow on the water. The sheep had been afraid, and if they were missing, then maybe it was with good reason.

"Have you seen the wild pony again?" He gave her a

sly look. "I can give you a hint, Ms. Ryan. If you check the pony's mane and find a strand of water weed, then you know that what you are facing is no ordinary animal. It is certain to be an *each-uisge*."

Bella had forced a wry smile in return. "Thanks for the advice, Gregor, I'll remember it."

She now drove slowly back toward Drumaird Cottage, and wondered how she was going to tell Maclean that Loch Fasail would soon be ruined forever. He would be very upset. It was the nearest thing he had to a home, and she suspected he had visions of living here, alone with his memories. What would he do when he heard about the road? What would happen to him, an eighteenth century Highlander trapped in the twenty-first century?

The car reached a crest and there before her was Loch Fasail and, on the far side, the smoke from the cottage and above it the stark ruins of Castle Drumaird. The early mist had risen and the day was clear and the water of the loch sparkling. Beautiful. For a second she imagined it all torn, with the soil scraped bare and giant machines roaring and shuddering as they went about their work.

She was sunk in gloom when something caught her eye.

Near the *Cailleach* Stones, a movement, a flicker of color.

For a second her heart raced, her hands clenching on the wheel as she remembered the hag who had spoken to her in her dreams, and her pet loch monster. But the next moment the shadows shifted and she saw that it was in fact a red deer, half hidden by one of the upright stones and the gorse bushes, and no doubt feeding on some tender shoots. Bella laughed in relief.

No wonder Gregor had told her to take care! He probably took one look at her and thought she shouldn't be out on her own.

There was a splash in the loch, a fish jumping, and the deer bounded off over the moorland grasses. Bella watched it go, sitting in the stationary car and letting her thoughts drift.

Of course, they returned to Maclean. He was a flesh-and-blood man now, or soon would be. He had told her that the *Fiosaiche* was causing this to happen, that with every step he made in the right direction she was rewarding him. But it was Bella who was showing him the way, Bella who must discover what really happened that terrible day here at Loch Fasail.

She felt the fire of the true historian burning inside her. She'd hunt down the truth and find it. Two hundred and fifty years of subterfuge and lies had built up a thick and thorny barricade, and she needed to cut her way through, to expose what really happened.

Even if she had to use Maclean's broadsword to do it.

Maclean slept on. He had never been so tired. Each time he tried to wake and pull himself out of this warm and pleasant fugue, he was sucked down into it again. It was as if his body were making up for all the days and nights he had wandered this cottage unable to rest. It was the same with his sudden feelings of hunger and his desperate need to eat, and his insatiable urge to "bonk" Bella, as she called it. Now all he wanted to do was sleep.

And dream.

He was underground. Not in the awful labyrinths of the between-worlds, but in a great cave with an ocean of ink stretching as far as the eye could see. The shore was empty, deserted. Maclean stood, puzzled, wondering what the point of such a place was and what he was doing here. Deep in his thoughts it was a moment before he felt the slight vibration under his feet and saw the shape approaching him from farther down the beach.

It was a small horse, its coat golden brown and shaggy, the long length of its tail and mane flaring out as it ran, and its hooves striking the sand with musical precision.

Maclean stood and watched, spellbound by the strange sight. He knew there was something not quite real about the creature, the proportions were wrong. It resembled a mystical beast from a fairy tale or a Gaelic legend rather than a flesh-and-blood horse.

Maclean . . . Maclean . . .

The horse began to change, its shape altering, the mane into hair, the forelegs into arms, the long equine face foreshortening into the smaller face of a woman. For a brief moment the two were both visible, one image upon the other, and then the horse was gone and the woman remained. He knew then that she was an *each-uisge*. The most fearsome mystic monster in the Highlands, and the most deadly. It fed on man-flesh and knew no pity, using its powers to tempt its victims close enough to carry them away into the lochs or the deep pools, and there to feast on them in peace.

And it was Ishbel.

She sauntered toward him in her red and green trews, a darker green jacket nipped to her slender waist and her golden hair loose about her shoulders.

"Maclean, at last I have ye."

As she came he sensed movement to his side, in the inky ocean, and a great creature began to rise out of it, dripping water from its scaly hide. With a bulbous body and long, snakelike neck, it floundered toward him as if it were not used to being in the shallows.

Ishbel began to croon to it, and the monster lifted its head, listening to her. It swayed and its large eyes half closed, dreamy, enchanted by Ishbel's voice. She laughed at the expression on Maclean's face.

"The witch thinks I am afraid of these creatures, but 'tis not so. I have tamed this one, and I am his mistress."

"You are in good company, then," he said evenly, as if he were humoring a child.

"The witch is not so clever as she thinks. I have fooled her. I have fooled the hag who guards the door to the between-worlds, too. *Please help me, please, please.*" She laughed at her own cunning. "She let me out and now she canna stop me from passing through her door whenever I wish it. I am too strong for them all."

"You were ever boastful, wee Ishbel."

She cast him a look of hatred. "The witch says she has freed you, given you a chance to become a mortal man again, but I knew that already. I have been beyond the door and I have seen you. I canna let you go free, Maclean. You dinna deserve to be in the sunshine while I spend my years down here in the darkness."

"Ishbel—"

"You lied to me, Maclean. *I willna hurt you, I promise, I promise.*" She mocked his words to her from long ago. "But ye did hurt me, ye slew Iain before my verra eyes and took all my happiness away."

"Ishbel, I am sorry for—"

But she would not listen to him. She cried out, raising her hands, and the monster howled. It heaved itself toward the beach, the ground shuddering beneath its great weight.

Maclean tried to back away, but his feet wouldn't move, and when he looked down he realized they were stuck fast into the sand. He tugged at them furiously, while Ishbel laughed and the monster drew closer. Now he smelled the fishy stink of it, felt the violent excitement in its clumsy movements.

"He is hungry," Ishbel whispered.

I am asleep, Maclean thought. *This canna be.*

"He likes to strip the flesh from your bones and suck each one clean."

Wake up!

"But I have told him to leave your heart for me, Maclean. I want that for my own."

The monster's breath puffed hot into his face as it lunged.

And Maclean's eyes opened with a jolt.

In that instant of waking he wondered where he was, but then his grasping hands found Bella's bed and he realized his face was pressed into her soft pillows. He was lying on his belly, sprawled across the mattress and some of him off it.

"A dream," he murmured to himself, and gave a relieved laugh, tempered by scorn for his own quaking flesh. But the uneasiness the dream had caused in him was slow in disappearing. The bedchamber felt unfamiliar, unsafe. And that was when he knew.

Something had lured his vulnerable sleeping self to the between-worlds and then attached itself to him.

Something had followed him back.

Maclean . . . Maclean . . .

Ishbel. Her voice was the same as it had been a moment before, only now it was calling him from the bottom of the bed. Maclean shook himself and rolled over, trying to chase away the numbing effects of his long sleep. But he was bound by that strange heaviness, as if his feet were still stuck in the sand.

Maclean . . . I have come for you. . . .

The bedchamber was full of mist. He could hardly see a hand's breadth in front of him. He knew this couldn't be so, but the more he tried to deny it, the thicker the mist grew. Whatever stood at the bottom of the bed calling to him was well hidden.

Something touched his leg. A nudge. And then again, only this time he felt sharp teeth nipping at his skin. He cried out, using his great strength to drag himself back out of harm's way, and reaching down for his *claidheamh mor* on the floor by the mattress. His fingers searched, scrabbling upon the wooden boards, but he couldn't find it.

Movement stirred the mist. He could hear *it* breathing with hard little spurts of air.

His heart began to beat in a thick heavy rhythm.

The long pale equine snout poked through the mist,

and he saw a green eye, wicked and watchful, before the *each-uisge* vanished once more.

"Ishbel."

The thing laughed with Ishbel's laugh. "Maclean," it whispered, "dinna expect the *Fiosaiche* to save you this time. I am verra powerful now. I made the hag show me how to creep into your dreams and I have followed you back through the door, into the mortal world. Into *your* world, Maclean."

Maclean's head swum dizzily, but then his fingers touched the scabbard of his broadsword and he swung it up, drawing the blade with a savage ring of metal.

"Ye canna kill me with that, Maclean," it hissed. "But I can kill you."

"I'm no' afraid of you, Ishbel."

"Mabbe not, but you're afraid for *her*, aren't ye? For your woman, Arabella Ryan."

"No!" the word burst from him before he could stop it.

He jumped up, wild with horror, lifting his sword to strike . . . and found himself face to face with Bella. With a gasping scream, she stumbled back, floundered as her feet tangled in the sheet that trailed on the floor, and began to fall. Instinctively Maclean reached out with his free arm and caught her as she fell, rolling over on the bed with her, pinning her beneath him.

They stared at each other, she clearly not knowing what to expect and he still reeling from his experience with the *each-uisge*.

"I was dreaming," he said, knowing that was only half the truth. "I thought you were someone else. I'm sorry, Arabella, I'm so sorry."

With trembling fingers he smoothed a dark lock of

hair away from her cheek. He had almost hurt Bella. Ishbel had entered his dreams, just as she said, and was playing games with his mind, using Maclean as her weapon. He had believed her to be real; she had wanted him to believe it. Maclean shuddered to think what might have happened if he had struck Ishbel the death blow and killed Bella instead.

"You slept so long I was worried."

She had forgiven him already, he could see it in her dark eyes. He wanted to shake her and warn her against himself, but he couldn't bear to do it. If the door to the between-worlds had been opened and Ishbel was on the loose, if even dreams were not safe from her interference, then Maclean was the only protection Bella had.

"Och, I've never been so tired in my life," he said, making his voice ordinary, forcing a smile.

"Is that a good thing, do you think?"

"Aye, I think it is."

She was soft and warm and sweet. The feel of her underneath him was already having its effect, his desire for her soaring, but he kept it under control. He glanced up and around the bedchamber, searching the corners, but there was nothing. Everything was ordinary, and there was no sense of anything amiss, no feeling of danger. Ishbel had retreated again. Maclean trusted his instincts and relaxed.

"Maclean?"

Her eyes had widened and she was staring up at him nervously.

He grinned, and moved against her, his cock hard against her soft belly. He slid his thigh neatly between hers and reached down to unfasten the waist of her trews.

"*That* doesn't feel like tired, Maclean."

"Hush, woman, I'm busy," he mock-growled, and she giggled as he slid her clothing down over her hips, tugging it over her legs and out of the way. She was wearing a tiny scrap of black cloth, which he inspected with interest, before disposing of that, too. "Ah, that's better."

Bella made a little sound as he stroked her, his big fingers gentle but sure. He settled himself between her thighs and eased himself inside with a grateful sigh.

"Och, Bella, this is heaven," he groaned.

Afterward, he held her in his arms, half dozing again, until she thumped him on the shoulder to wake him up. "Wha'?" he demanded. "Are you never satisfied, woman?"

Bella smiled. "Well, there wasn't much foreplay, but I have to admit I didn't mind."

"Foreplay, is it? I'll give you foreplay—"

With a shriek, she jumped up and ran to the door. Her hair was down, she was bare from the waist, only her long shirt protecting her modesty. She stood there, panting, laughing at him.

"I can see you," she gasped. "You're more visible even than an hour ago, Maclean. The fuzzy edges are gone."

"Are they?" He stood up, bumping his head on the sloping roof and rubbing the spot ruefully.

"I can see the hairs on your chest, Maclean, and farther down, too. You're rather a hairy man, aren't you?"

"Can you see my cock?"

"Maclean!"

He laughed, and she watched him through her lashes, clearly enjoying the sight. Her gaze ran over the contours of his body, the long lines of his back and legs, the curve of his buttocks. Maclean smiled. Bella liked the sight of him just as much as he liked the sight of her, though she was too coy to tell him so.

He raised his arms above his head, palms flat on the ceiling with his elbows bent. He was too big for this cottage.

"Who were you dreaming about?" she asked him quietly, and tucked her hair behind her ears.

"A water-horse," he said dryly, reaching down to rub his leg.

"Oh." She looked thoughtful. "There's been a pony around the loch. Gregor was teasing me, saying it might be an *each-uisge*. Some of his sheep have gone missing."

He felt his chest tighten with anxiety, but somehow kept the smile on his face. "What have you been doing while I slept all this time?"

If she noticed he'd changed the subject she didn't say. "Working on my book. I've been writing longhand—until my laptop is ready, I have no choice. Actually, I found something, that's what I came up to tell you. I borrowed two books about the Macleods from the library. The one on the local area and the other about the Macleods on Skye. It isn't a proper history, just a hodge-podge of stories told by different people. I've found a woman in it called Tamsin Macleod."

He said nothing, watching her. He wanted to look at his leg, to see if Ishbel really had bitten him. Except he didn't intend to let Bella know what he was up to—no need to frighten her just yet.

"Tamsin was ninety-three in 1830 when she told her life story to a visiting historian. He was traveling the Highlands recording people's memories, and he wrote down Tamsin's very carefully, because of course she was a living treasure by then."

"Oh, aye." He sat down and glanced at his ankle. There was nothing there, no teeth marks. He felt himself relax a little as he realized the dream-Ishbel could not herself inflict physical damage—only cause others to do so.

Bella took a breath, holding on to her patience with difficulty. "Yes, Maclean, but the exciting thing is her name was actually Tamsin Maclean. Unlike most Scottish women, she preferred to use her married name of Macleod and forget she had been born a Maclean."

He finally felt a stirring of interest. "Tamsin Maclean?"

"Yes, and according to the few pages she gets in the book, she was from Loch Fasail. That would make her nine years old at the time of the massacre."

"But the book doesna say she was here at that time, only that she came from Loch Fasail?"

"Yes, the book deals with her life on Skye, the traditions, the history, and so on. But"—she held up her finger—"there is reference to the original document written by the historian. It still exists, and it's in a private collection in Inverness. I can go there and look at it. It may tell me more."

"Do you really think it will help?"

"It's worth a try, don't you think?"

"Aye."

"You haven't remembered, have you? What happened here, to your people?"

"I followed Ishbel and Iain Og," he sighed. Ishbel was right, he had sworn not to hurt her if they married, to wait until she was ready to receive him into her bed, but when she ran away he had forgotten his gentle promises. "I dinna remember how I died, not exactly," he said grimly. "And no, I dinna know how the English came to Fasail and killed my people. I dinna think I ever did, Bella."

"Then I will go to Inverness and find out what I can."

"Go?"

"Just a night or two, not long."

"I'll come with you," he said firmly.

Bella opened her mouth as if to argue, then closed it again, but Maclean knew she hadn't given in. She didn't trust him to behave himself out in the world and she was just biding her time, hoping to convince him to her point of view later on. But Maclean had no intention of letting her go off alone to Inverness, not after what he had seen. The Tamsin Macleod thing might be a trap, to lure her away from him. Ishbel wanted to hurt him and she knew that the best way to do that was to take from him something he loved.

Like Bella.

Twenty-one

The water was hot and soapy, and after all their hard work in getting enough of it to half fill the bath, Bella and Maclean were determined to enjoy it.

Earlier Bella had asked, "How long is it since you had a bath, Maclean?"

"Two hundred and fifty years. Do you think I'm about due for one, then?"

Bella smiled. "I think you are."

"Will you share it with me?"

"Is there room?" she asked dubiously.

"Aye, there's room."

The water splashed onto the floor more times than Bella could count. Maclean didn't care if he made a mess, and he got her into a state where she didn't care, either.

As she clung to his soapy biceps, her thighs resting over his hips, slipping against him in the warm water, her body felt so attuned to his body that they might have been one. He reached up, stroking her breasts, tugging at the hard nipples, and she groaned, grinding herself down on him. He sat up, sloshing more water, and cupped her bottom, turning her over so that it was now she underneath and he on top.

He pushed deep inside her and she felt her body coiling itself for another cataclysmic orgasm. His mouth closed on hers, and she was drowning in him, unable to think, only to feel. He stroked her again, inside, and she arched against him, clinging and moaning, as she came.

After a long time she opened her eyes.

Maclean was smiling at her, his hair wet and slicked back from his forehead, his body more out of the bath than in. There was sudsy water everywhere, probably dripping through the ceiling into the rooms downstairs. Bella cupped her hand to his cheek and shook her head at him.

"You've spoiled me for any other man, Maclean."

His face grew serious. "Good," he said. "I dinna want *you* to run away from me, Bella."

"Ah, but you know I never would run away. Empty threats, Maclean."

"My threats are ne'er empty," he retorted, but he was smiling.

"Perhaps you will be the one who runs away. Once you've discovered what happened to your people and why you are here, you might leave me."

"I might have no choice," he said softly.

"Then we should make the most of the time we have?" Bella asked, forcing herself to smile.

"Live every moment as if there will be no more."

"Is that an old Gaelic saying, Maclean?"

He chuckled. "No, I read it on the box from which you eat your muesli."

She laughed, hugging him in the cooling water, and trying not to think sad thoughts. He was right, they should live every moment as if it were their last, no regrets, no worrying over things that may never happen. Maclean had helped her to understand just how important it was to squeeze as much as possible out of each day, and although Bella liked to think she would have learned this for herself eventually, he had made it happen sooner.

She was also learning to find peace in being herself, and that meant accepting her rocky childhood. She had made mistakes, her parents and Brian had made mistakes, but they mustn't be allowed to weigh her down and hold her back. Look what had happened to Maclean! His mistrust of women, his childhood pain, had caused him to make a fatally wrong decision, the price of which was still being paid two hundred and fifty years later.

But at least he could see that now, and Bella knew she had played her part in helping him to do so.

They worked well together.

The acknowledgment was bittersweet.

The telephone was ringing when they cleaned up and went downstairs at last. It was Elaine, wanting Bella to come to London as soon as possible so that she could arrange for her to make some appearances in the larger bookstores. Bella should have been elated, but instead her heart sank.

"Oh. No, I can't make it now. I have to go down to Inverness to research something for the book I'm writing. You want me to make the deadline, don't you? I know I should make the most of the opportunity. I know you worked hard to . . . Look, I'll just have to pass. I'm very sorry. No, I can't let you speak to Brian, he's away. What has he got to do with this anyway, Elaine? I'm quite capable of making my own decisions."

Maclean was watching her face. Bella was agitated and anxious enough without him reading her every emotion, and she turned her back and hunched over the phone, speaking in a lower tone. When she ended the call a short time later, she wiped her palms on her jeans.

"What is it?" he asked.

"That was my agent. She wants me to go down to London and show myself, talk about my books."

Maclean frowned. "Your book-writing is important to you, Bella. You should go. You need to go."

"Not right now. I need to research your book, Maclean, I *need* to stay here."

"But—"

"I hate appearing in public. I always have. I still cringe when I remember when I was a child, being scrutinized by my father's friends. The looks they gave each other when they saw my mother in her Chanel suits, and me in old jeans and sweats. They laughed at me then and they'll laugh at me now—"

She stopped abruptly, shocked at herself. After all her positive and affirming thoughts! But the words had just burst out of her. And they were the truth; they had been simmering below the surface for years. Maybe it was time to voice what she felt.

Maclean smiled, and when he spoke there was nothing patronizing in his voice, only the honest truth as he saw it. "Och, Bella, they will fall in love with you. How could they help it?"

She took a breath. How did he do that? Send her thoughts spinning. "I wish Brian could hear you. He'd be trying to bully me into doing all sorts of things I don't want to, dressing up like a literary princess. Turning me into someone else. That's why Elaine wanted to talk to him; she knew she could get him to do the persuading for her."

"The bastard," he said mildly.

This time Bella gave a startled laugh, and some of her nervous emotion dissipated.

"There is no law that I know of that says you must go to London if you dinna want to. And if you do go, there is no law that says you must pretend to be someone else. You are Arabella Ryan, beautiful and clever, tranquil and gentle as Loch Fasail on a summer's day. But I see beneath your surface, and there's strength there, and fire, and a stubborn determination to get to the truth no matter how much it hurts. That takes courage, Bella, and when I look at you I am amazed, for I fear I am no' that strong. So, no, Bella, dinna play at being someone else. Be yoursel'."

"Maclean . . ."

She wanted him to come with her, but she would not say it because it was impossible. Besides, she would consider asking him a weakness, and she did not want him to think her weak.

"Remember what I say," he said quietly, holding her gaze with his.

"Of course."

"Sometimes ye may be afeared, but fear is something to grasp on to. It quickens the blood and sharpens the wits. When a Highlander goes into battle he knows these things. Dinna let fear overwhelm you, though, Bella, and make you weak. Keep it chained, use it, and dinna let it use you."

"Do you think the bookstore owners will mind if I arrive to sign my books swinging a broadsword?"

He eyed her smiling lips with a frown.

"I appreciate your help," she said quickly.

He shrugged in a grumpy way that made her want to smile again. Not at him, not exactly, but because she was suddenly so happy.

"Oh, I forgot. . . ." Her smile faded. "I was thinking about your land, Maclean. After your people were gone, the land would have been seized by the Crown, and yet Gregor owns it now. His last name is Macleod."

Maclean said nothing but he looked wretched.

"It may mean nothing. Macleods are common enough around here, but I suppose there's a possibility Auchry bought the land, or was given it, after you died."

His land, taken by his enemy. Maclean wanted to smash something, but he knew it would be pointless and his violence would frighten Bella. She was doing her best for him and he should be grateful, but some days he just did not want to hear any more awful news.

"What about Ishbel?" Bella was not willing to let go. "Did she die that day with you? And if she didn't, then where did she go and what did she do?"

Maclean knew where she was now. She had come through the door from the between-worlds, and she was watching and waiting for her chance to do him as much injury as she could. It was his fervent wish that Bella would never have to know what Ishbel had become, that he could deal with her without dragging Bella into it.

"It'll help to have my laptop back," she was saying, and then she gave him a beautiful smile. "I forgot to tell you, there was a message on the phone to say that my laptop is fixed already. I want to go into Ardloch this afternoon to pick it up."

Maclean considered her words. He would have liked to go with her, to watch over her, but there was something else he must do, something important, and it was best done while Bella was away from the cottage.

"You will be home before dark, Arabella?" he said seriously.

"I expect so."

"Dinna linger."

Bella stilled, trying to read his expression. "What is it?"

"I have something I want you to do when you get home, that is all."

She looked puzzled, but when he didn't answer she shrugged off his intensity. "While I'm in Ardloch I'll ask at the library about the private collection with Tamsin's manuscript in it. With luck I'll be able to ring the collector and we can drive down to Inverness as soon as possible and take a look. Are you sure you want to come?" she added. "If you thought Ardloch was busy, then you'll find Inverness in summer far, far worse."

"Och, I'll be fine." He waved a hand as if it were the easiest thing in the world for an eighteenth century

Scotsman to make his way in twenty-first century society.

But Bella was no fool, and she gave him a considering look. "Okay, then, but I think we'll need to buy you some new clothes when we get there. I doubt anyone'll let you into their home looking so dangerous. A nice dark suit, Maclean, that should make you less threatening."

Dangerous? Was that how she saw him?

"I have no money."

"I'll pay."

Maclean opened his mouth to tell her no, she wouldn't, but her eyes narrowed. Saying no would give her a reason to go without him, and he couldn't have that.

"Verra well," he grumbled. He just hoped she didn't turn him into one of those namby-pamby gentlemen he had seen in Edinburgh, with their high heels and floppy lace sleeves and long curling wigs. He'd rather go naked.

"Dinna worry, Maclean," she said softly, swaying toward him, her eyes glowing with amused triumph. "I will no' let ye be made a fool of. You're far too handsome for tha'."

He closed his own eyes as her hands stroked his face. "I dinna speak like that, if that is what ye are inferring," he said with cool haughtiness.

"No, when you speak you make my toes curl." Her breath was warm against his lips, and Maclean knew if he opened his eyes she would be close enough to kiss.

He smiled. "I like the way you speak, too," he murmured.

"Do you?" she asked, surprised. "My accent is a mixture. Too many places, too many schools, when I was young. I'm a cross-breed, Maclean. Londoner with a touch of French and German, and a hefty dollop of New York."

"You make my toes curl, too, Bella."

He opened his eyes and she was close. She blinked and smiled, and he realized she had been thinking sad thoughts and was trying to disguise it. She was remembering, probably, that he may not be here forever, and that one day she would be alone again. Maclean opened his mouth to tell her that it may never happen, or if it did, then at least they had these moments to remember, but she leaned forward and kissed him.

And it didn't seem worth stopping her, when it was what he wanted, too.

Bella looped the strap of her laptop case over her shoulder with a puzzled frown. The young man behind the repair counter in the electronics shop had been so shocked to see her standing in front of him when he looked up that his face had turned red and then white. As he swung his head jerkily from side to side, searching the area all around her, she thought for a moment he was going to faint.

"You rang to say the laptop was fixed?" she reminded him coolly. Bella had been prepared to confront him if he tried the same tricks again, determined not to let him intimidate her this time. Maclean was right, he was nothing but a randy boy. She needed to let him know what she disliked about his behavior; she needed to speak up for herself.

He stammered some sort of reply, and when he reached down and swung the laptop onto the counter before her, his hands were shaking. "I worked as fast as I could," he said, his eyes fixed on hers unblinkingly, as if he were afraid of looking any lower.

"I'm sure you did." Damn it! Now she was being kind. Why couldn't she be tough and abrasive?

He looked relieved, and brought out the worksheet to point out what he'd done and that it had been necessary to send for some parts. "We don't keep a large stock in the store," he said as she leaned over to read his writing. He glanced down, swallowed, and began to sweat. "I couldn't work any faster," he said. "Just tell him I did my best."

"Tell who?" she asked suspiciously, straightening up, but she was beginning to have an inkling.

"Nothing, I didn't mean . . . Look, here are two copies of the work I retrieved. You didn't lose anything."

Bella found herself feeling almost sorry for him, though she knew he didn't deserve it.

"I've given you a discount, too."

Maclean was behind this. Bella opened her mouth to ask questions, and then closed it again. How could she phrase them? *Oh, by the way, did a six-foot-four invisible Highlander pass this way?* And anyway, the laptop was fixed now. She was annoyed, yes, because she had been prepared to stand up for herself and Maclean hadn't given her the opportunity. Didn't he realize that threatening someone just because you didn't like the way they looked at you wasn't allowed nowadays? But that was the thing, he didn't. Where Maclean came from, it was perfectly natural for him to take charge and enforce his will. Bella knew she'd have to explain matters to him before he got himself arrested.

After she thanked the shaking wreck that was the repairman, and who seemed extremely eager to see her gone, Bella made her way to the Ardloch library. They didn't have the number of the private collector, but rang through to someone who did. Armed with name and address and telephone number, Bella contemplated what else she should do.

There was a possibility that she could track down what had happened to the land at Loch Fasail after 1746, when it had reverted to the Crown, but the Ardloch library would be unlikely to hold such records.

Apart from that, and more importantly, she needed food. Maclean was eating her pantry bare. He seemed to have developed a love of the chocolate peppermint ice cream she herself craved. She had been having a few nice fantasies in which she dripped the melted mixture onto his skin and licked it off, but so far she hadn't quite found the courage to follow them through.

She shivered.

Suddenly all she wanted to do was get back to Loch Fasail and the cottage. And to Maclean.

The stark truth made her catch her breath. She had fallen in love with him. With a man who died in the eighteenth century and who may vanish again at any moment. And really she only had herself to blame.

Twenty-two

Maclean stood by the wall near the Cailleach Stones and looked about him. Aye, this was where he had been in his dream. This was where the hag had spoken to him.

They were murdered, cut down most foully. They cried to me as they passed because you were not among them. They asked me why you had abandoned them at such a time, but I had no answer. But there was one of them who did not weep. . . .

Maclean set his jaw. He was tempted to lock away the pain as he had been taught to do, but lately he had learned that if he was to be a complete man again, then he must face that pain, admit to his mistakes, and try to resolve them.

Last night he had gone out into the darkness and gazed at the sky and called for the *Fiosaiche*. Maclean wanted to ask her what Ishbel was doing here, and how she had slipped through the door into the world of the living. But the sorceress had not come. She had not visited him since the day she ordered him to return to the cottage and face his past.

If the *Fiosaiche* would not help him, then there was only one person who might be able to. Someone else who straddled the between-worlds and the mortal world.

The hag.

The air was very still, dragonflies zipping about him, barely brushing the surface of the loch as they hunted. A fish splashed, capturing one of them, and sank back below the surface with the iridescent wings spilling from its mouth. The sour smell of broken weeds and crushed grass rose from where he stood waiting. It was almost eerily quiet.

Maclean closed his eyes and tried to reach that state between waking and sleeping, the place where dreams resided.

At first it was difficult. He felt his mind drifting, back into his childhood.

Dinna hurt her! He heard his own voice, childish and strained. His mother was holding her cheek, tears in her eyes, staring up at his father. But she wasn't so much frightened and bowed by the blow as defiant. Her voice was measured.

Ye may not like what I say, but I will continue to say it.

Maclean was reminded of Bella. She had that same quality of steel beneath the soft sweetness of her exterior—she just didn't know it. But once she had learned how to use it, she would be formidable—a woman others would look up to and admire.

"Och, Maclean."

The voice was faint and weak. Shocked, his eyes sprang open and he spun around.

The hag was standing behind him, a green arisaid tucked over her stringy white hair. Her eyes were blue and milky, as though she could no longer see, and yet she was looking directly at him.

"Maclean," she whispered. "Why have ye come? The *each-uisge* is on the loose, the land reeks of danger. None of us are safe."

"I have come for your help."

"The *Fiosaiche* doesna want you to have help, Morven Maclean. We must abide by her wishes." She gave a toothless smile. "The *Fiosaiche* has her reasons. We must trust in her and hope for the best."

"You said that my people passed through this door into the between-worlds?"

"Aye, they did, a long twisting line of them, wailing and crying and calling your name."

"But one of them wasn't crying."

"Ishbel Macleod. She was there with them. She died here, too, Maclean."

Ishbel died here? He did not know what to think, but he didn't have time to speculate on why Ishbel should have been with his people when the massacre occurred. Other matters were more pressing.

"Ishbel is here now. I have seen her. She is the *each-uisge*."

Her face grew even more skull-like within the folds of the green arisaid. "Aye, I know. We all have a choice in such matters and she has taken the dark road. Over the centuries she has thrived on her misery and turned it to wickedness. She tricked me into teaching her things. . . ." Her wavering voice was bleak. "When the *Fiosaiche* discovers it, I will be punished."

"Then I am sorry for you. Ishbel has threatened Bella."

The hag swayed toward him, but she was growing misty around the edges.

"She is coming to me in my dreams, old woman. I dinna trust myself to sleep in case I do Bella harm. This is your fault. You must help me."

The hag nodded sadly. "I am weak, but I will do my best to make a spell to protect the cottage and keep Ishbel out, for a little while."

"I thank you."

"Your Bella will be safe while she stays within," the hag went on, her voice tremulous. "But I canna do more than that. I am no' as strong as Ishbel. This battle is yours and ye must fight for your woman if you love her. Do ye love her, Morven Maclean?"

She was watching him closely.

Once, Maclean would never have admitted to such an emotion. Love was not something a Highland chief allowed himself to feel, unless it was for his horse and his dogs. But the days of denying himself were gone, and Maclean straightened his back as he spoke.

"Aye, I love her."

"That is good." She sighed, as if she were remembering something in her own past, and Maclean wondered if the hag had ever been a mortal woman herself, and if so, what had happened to her. Was being the keeper of the door a reward or a punishment?

"I canna stay any longer," she was saying, "but if ye need me, then call to me and I will try to help ye if I can."

And she was gone, the breeze stirring the grass, the dappled shadows teasing him with an echo of her arisaid.

"Did the laddie stare at your chest, Bella?"

Maclean was asking her the question in stern tones, his gaze fixed on her face.

Bella shook her head, narrowing her eyes suspiciously. "No, he didn't. He could hardly look at me. He fixed the laptop, and he saved my work, and that's more than I expected him to do the other day."

Maclean nodded, as if it were just as *he* had expected.

"What did you do to him, Maclean?"

He looked blank. "I dinna know what you mean, woman. How could I do anything to him? I was invisible, remember."

"I know. I just . . ."

There was something, but before she could get to the bottom of it Maclean stood up and peered from the window at the calm twilight and said, "Come outside for a wee while." He was holding his hand out to her, and, bemused, Bella stretched her own hand toward him, letting his fingers close hard on hers.

Once outside on the flat area before the cottage, Maclean unstrapped his *claidheamh mor* from his body and drew the blade from the scabbard. For a moment he held it before him, both hands wrapped around the handle, testing its weight. He looked at Bella, who was watching him warily, and then lowered the sword and moved toward her, reaching to turn her about.

"Maclean?" she said a little anxiously, peering over

her shoulder to see his face. "You're looking grim. Should I be afraid?"

"*Whist*, just trust me, woman," he soothed.

He positioned himself close behind her, his arms supporting hers, and clamped her hands, with his atop them, about the handle of his broadsword. He swung it a couple of times, gently, smoothly, his strength guiding her.

"Oh." Bella smiled.

Maclean brought the blade down from shoulder height in a slashing movement, first on one side and then the other, as if he were threshing wheat.

"This is easy!"

"Oh, aye?" Another smooth swing of the blade, and then he let her take some of the weight.

The sword sagged immediately, and would have struck the ground if he hadn't taken the weight again with his own powerful muscles and held it steady.

Maclean sighed. "Your arms are puny, Bella."

"I'm a writer, not a fighter," she protested breathlessly. "I never expected to wield something pointy that weighs as much as me."

"Sometimes even writers must learn to fight."

He sounded serious despite his attempts to make a joke of it, and Bella turned her head and gave him a long look. "What's the matter?" she said quietly.

"My sword is too heavy for you," he retorted, and bent and quickly kissed her lips, before disengaging himself from her and striding inside the cottage. Through the window he could see Bella staring after him, her brow furrowed as she tried to understand what was going on. Maclean sighed. And she would. This woman could find her way out of a maze in the dark with her hands bound, her mind was so sharp and clever, and Maclean knew she'd eventually wheedle from him the threat that was Ishbel.

But Maclean also knew that he was going to try very hard not to tell her. Not yet. Ishbel was for him to deal with, although he wasn't quite sure how one dealt with an *each-uisge*, a creature that straddled two worlds and could move so freely between them. But he would find a way.

That didn't mean he wanted Bella to be completely helpless while he played the big man, because if something happened to him, if he wasn't able to be here, then she needed to know how to protect herself with something other than her clever mind. She needed to be able to wield a weapon.

No matter how puny her muscles were compared to his.

"Ah!" With a smile he closed the door to the cupboard he had been rummaging in and strode back outside with his prize.

When she saw what he had, Bella blinked at him and laughed.

"Tell me you're kidding, Maclean."

Even when he put the broom in her hands and proceeded to show her how to hold it and use it in lieu of the sword, she was still smiling.

"I will find you a proper weapon you can use," he promised, "but in the meantime this will have to do. You can deliver a painful blow with anything if you are determined enough, and your enemy would no' be expecting a woman like you to fight."

"A woman like me?" she asked carefully, as if she were expecting him to say something nasty.

"Sweet and gentle and clever, Bella. Ye dinna look like a warrior, so you will surprise your enemy all the more when you strike."

"My enemy? Just who is my enemy, Maclean?"

"Well, there is Brian, for one."

She laughed, as he knew she would.

"Let me do this for you, Bella," he insisted. "I canna do much, I know, but I can do this."

Bella still looked inclined to refuse to cooperate, but he pressed the broom into her hands with determination and she sighed and resigned herself. He knew she was humoring him, but he still managed to teach her a few basic moves, mainly in self-protection rather than aggression, and explained what she could expect from an experienced swordsman. Or woman.

"I think mabbe you should go for the eyes," he said, remembering the wicked green of the *each-uisge*'s eyes in the mist, and the sharp white teeth.

"Go for the eyes," Bella repeated, jabbing into the air with the broom handle.

"Again."

She jabbed again.

"No, no, ye must really mean it!"

More vigorously this time.

"Good. Now you've taken out her . . . his eyes and he canna see where you are."

Bella wiped a hand over her brow, and he could smell the fine warm scent of her. "Okay. My enemy is blinded by my expertise with a broom. Now what?"

Maclean looked at her, standing with his hands on

his hips, his feet apart, his expression thoughtful. His voice was measured, as if he were imparting tremendous wisdom. "Now you must turn and run away as fast as you can."

Bella burst into laughter. He couldn't help but smile back at the sound, even though he knew this was deadly serious. Bella couldn't imagine anyone in the world wishing her any real harm, but she hadn't lived as he had or been in the places he had been. Maclean was prepared to do all in his power to prevent her from being hurt, he would give his life for hers, but he was almost a mortal man now, while Ishbel was a creature of magic. His strength and skill alone may not be enough to defeat her when the time came.

At least the cottage was safe—he hoped the hag had seen to that with a combination of her spell and the stones from Castle Drumaird.

Bella had stopped laughing, but her face was flushed and her eyes sparkling. She looked so delicious that Maclean decided to finish his teaching for the day, and instead swung Bella up into his arms and turned to carry her back inside.

He expected her to struggle and protest and tell him that women in these times didn't want men carrying them about because they had two legs of their own. But she didn't. She snuggled up against his chest, her head on his shoulder, more than happy exactly where she was.

"You're carrying me," she whispered. As if it were the most amazing experience she had ever had. "Maclean, you're carrying me."

"Aye, I am." He raised an eyebrow. "Do you want me to stop?"

"No, don't stop. It's wonderful." She looked up at him. "You're wonderful."

Maclean smiled. "I will be. Just let me get you upstairs, Arabella Ryan."

Twenty-three

The drive down to Inverness was slow—there was no direct route from Loch Fasail—but after they reached Ardloch, Bella took the coast road and the views were enough to keep Maclean from worrying too much about other vehicles on the narrow roads. Now that he was visible, Bella could see why he felt carsick on their last journey to Ardloch. He was so big that he was squeezed into his seat like a sardine in a tin, and because she had not realized it she had not thought to make adjustments for his height and size. This time she was able to ensure he was far more comfortable.

They stopped for lunch at Ullapool, with its white houses facing the water, and Maclean could watch the passenger ferry arriving across the Minch from Stornoway on the Isle of Lewis, while Bella was able to have a mochachino, so they were both happy. After that she took the faster route eastward, directly to Inverness.

"The Forsythes live to the southwest of the city, in a

place called Auchtachan. When I rang Mrs. Forsythe said she will be at home but her husband is away, traveling overseas. He makes his living buying and selling historic documents. But she says it's all right for us to come and see the original manuscript—I think I persuaded her we aren't going to steal it. She's given me directions to the house, and there's a hotel we can stay in not far away from them, but I want to drive on to Inverness first and buy you some clothes."

He grunted, which she took as a sign of acquiescence, and went back to staring at the passing scenery. The mountains were gray rock and scree, with barely a blade of grass in sight.

"It seems so empty," he said at last. "Are there no people anymore? I canna remember it being so bare."

"It is empty. The landscapes up here can be very harsh, Maclean, you don't need me to tell you that. Maybe people were willing to struggle on in your day, but these days they feel they deserve more from life than just surviving."

"Why?" Maclean demanded. "I canna believe my people would want to live in a dirty, smoky place like Edinburgh rather than Loch Fasail. At least you can breathe there!"

"But that's exactly what happened. In the nineteenth century Highlanders were dispossessed, their land taken over by sheep because the chiefs could make more money that way, or they simply could no longer survive on the small patches they were reduced to living on. Rents were high, and then there was a potato famine—"

"Potato famine? I have heard of potatoes, but they were still uncommon in my day."

"They became more common, a fallback when there was nothing else to eat. And then a disease struck the potatoes and rotted them in the ground, and because the people had come to rely on them so greatly, they starved. There was the herring fishing on the coast, and a lot of people were employed with that, but then it collapsed when there weren't enough fish left to catch and process."

He was frowning, clearly wanting to argue with her and yet fearing what she said was true.

"The Highlanders had no choice but to move south, to industrial cities like Glasgow and Edinburgh, and look for work in the mills and factories. Some of them emigrated, either by choice or else they were loaded aboard ships without any say in it, and sailed away to other countries like Canada and Australia and America, to make new lives. I'm very sorry, Maclean, but *your* Scotland has been gone for almost as long as you have."

Bella glanced again at his profile, stern and aloof, and knew with an aching heart that although his emotions were held in check, he was grieving for the past.

"I don't believe life at Loch Fasail was ever easy, was it?" she said gently. "You were such a good chief, Maclean, that you kept your people alive and well when others failed. But even you, or your descendants, would have found it difficult to continue on as conditions deteriorated. It's possible that Loch Fasail wouldn't have been populated today even if the massacre hadn't happened."

He turned to look at her and his expression was deadly serious. "If I had been here to protect them, I would have found a way to get my people through the hard times, Bella. I would no' have let them starve or die from sickness."

"You may not have been able to help it, Maclean," she whispered, tears in her eyes.

He shook his head angrily. "No, you're wrong. I could have kept them safe, and though mabbe some of them might have left in the years between then and now, I dinna believe Loch Fasail would be empty as it is. People would have stayed and lived on. *My* people."

Bella knew she shouldn't believe in him, not when Scottish history so obviously told a different story, but she did. She did believe he really could have made a difference through the sheer force of his powerful will.

Perhaps that was part of the reason for his success as a chief and as a man. Bella knew that, like the Clan Maclean, she would have followed the Black Maclean anywhere.

Inverness was unrecognizable, although now and again Maclean thought he saw a stretch of the river or a curve of landscape that stirred in him an elusive memory from the past. Bella parked the car and led him firmly through the pedestrians who turned to gawk, to a shop that she said sold clothing, while Maclean tried to pretend he was above such curiosity, his back stiff and his face aloof.

The place they entered had a sign upon the window that read OUTFITTERS FOR THE COMPLETE GENTLEMAN. It was wee, and there was very little light. The people who worked here spoke in hushed voices, as if it were a church, and they would not meet his eyes, which he did not know whether to be glad of or to worry about. After Bella had explained their business, they were led through to the back, which was far bigger, with clothing everywhere and in varying stages of completion.

Maclean was outfitted with long black trews and a shirt not unlike the one he already owned and a black jacket that clung to his shoulders without a crease. There were shoes, too, black and shiny. Bella knelt down to help him tie them, and he took the opportunity to whisper in her ear that he preferred his plaid.

He earned an exasperated look and a sigh.

"Excuse me, sir." One of the laddies who worked in the shop was holding Maclean's black velvet jacket. "I wondered if you'd tell me where this garment was made, sir. The workmanship is very interesting indeed."

Maclean, fearing he meant to steal it, snatched the jacket from him. Bella gave him a sharp look and turned to the laddie with a smile, blathering about Maclean having been overseas and only lately returned and the jacket being made in foreign parts. Maclean himself said nothing.

"You are a frustrating man," she murmured when they were alone again. Then she turned him to the long mirror and, smiling, said, "But a very impressive one, Maclean."

The dark trousers and jacket made him look bigger, somehow. Although he had shaved this morning, there was already a dark shadow on his jaw, making him look like a wild reiver, while his pale eyes stared challengingly back.

"Very nice, sir," one of the laddies was simpering. "Do you no' agree?"

He frowned and opened his mouth to tell him what he thought of such arse-licking, just as Bella hastened into the fray. "He looks perfect, thank you so much."

Then she went about the business of paying with the piece of plastic, as she called it. As he watched her standing there in her baggy jeans and woolen coat, Maclean had made a decision of his own, and found one of the laddies to ask his own question. He had his answer, and a short time later they were out on the street.

Although he was no longer in his plaid, Maclean noticed that people still stared at him. He reached down for the comforting grip of his *claidheamh mor* and then remembered he wasn't wearing it. Bella had told him he had to leave it at home, but he had insisted on bringing it, so she had made him leave it in the trunk of the car.

"If you carry it around Inverness, we'll be arrested," she informed him sternly when he tried to argue.

"Arrested?" he snorted, but he knew what the word meant. "Verra well, woman, I'll leave it in the car. For now," he muttered, as she turned away, but Bella chose to ignore him.

"I've something else I wish to do," he said now, firmly.

Bella gave him a nervous glance. "Oh?"

"There is another shop I wish to visit."

"Oh?"

His mouth twitched. "The name of it is Siren, and it is in Bridge Street."

Bella's eyes widened. "Oh no, you don't, Maclean!"

"Oh, aye, Bella. I have suffered at your hands, and 'tis your turn now."

"Maclean, places like this Siren only cater to skinny teenagers. Believe me, I know." And when he gave her a blank look, "Wee girls, Maclean! I'm not made for those slinky numbers. You don't understand."

"No, Bella, you dinna understand. I am no' asking you, I am telling you."

She opened her mouth and he could see the words waiting there to pour out, and then she met his eyes and closed it again. With a shrug, she turned and led the way, but he sensed a new emotion in her, a painful acceptance. Aye, it was as he had always thought: She believed herself unattractive, she had been told so by Brian and maybe her mother, and although Bella was strong, the words had lodged deep.

Like a thorn.

If he did one last thing before the *Fiosaiche* decided his fate, it would be to make Bella realize just how beautiful a woman she was.

Twenty-four

Siren was far more friendly-looking and better lit than the Outfitters for the Complete Gentleman, and there was music. Evidently women were allowed to enjoy themselves while they chose their clothing. Maclean pulled her into the doorway, his grip tightening on her hand as he felt her resistance.

"Maclean," she hissed, "I really, really don't want to do this."

"Lass!" he called, ignoring her, and the woman behind the counter looked up. She was tall and skinny, with dark makeup around her tired eyes, eyes which widened in amazement at the sight of him.

"Ah, yes, can I help you?"

"I need something for Bella."

The woman's eyes slid to Bella, who was trying to hide behind him. "Anything in particular?" she asked in amusement.

Maclean hesitated, then turned and gave Bella a stern

look. "Stay here," he said, and walked over to the counter, carefully avoiding racks of bright clothing as he went. And then he bent and murmured his request in the woman's receptive ear, too softly for Bella to hear above the plaintive wail of the music.

Bella stood and watched him, listening to Chris Isaak sing about falling in love, and wondering whether Maclean would chase her if she ran. The shop assistant was enthralled, it was obvious. Maclean cast his spell on everyone who met him, or saw him, and Bella was the worst of the lot.

She was being pathetic and she knew it, but she couldn't help it. So much for the new leaf being turned over! Her heart was stuttering in her chest as she remembered every embarrassing moment she had ever had with Brian. All the posh shops he had dragged her into, all the clothes he had tried to make her wear that made her look so unattractive and so unlike herself, and it was always *her* fault that the skirts were too tight or the blouses pinched, never the fact that they were the wrong shape or size.

"If you lose a couple of pounds, you'll look better," he'd say to her, as if it were nothing.

"I'm not made that way, Brian."

"You just don't try, Bella."

And now Maclean was going to do the same thing to her, he was going to humiliate and belittle her, not in words but by his actions, and it would be all the worse because he thought he was helping. No, she wouldn't let him.

Bella decided she would have to run, just as Maclean turned around and pinned her with a look. All the fight went out of her. This would be humiliating enough without struggling with him in the street. Better just to get it over with.

The shop assistant was peeping around him, smiling. "I'll make it painless," she promised.

Maclean quirked an eyebrow.

Bella huffed to hide her anxiety and followed the woman toward the back of the shop.

"Lucky you," she whispered. "He's gorgeous! And sweet as well. Where did you find him? Maybe he has a brother."

Bella choked. "No, I'm sorry, there's only one."

The woman sighed, but rallied as she pulled out some dresses from various spots along the wall. Bella eyed them nervously.

"Don't worry," she said, sensing Bella's anxiety, "they'll fit, and look good, too. You'll be stunning."

But Bella could not help feeling breathless as she entered the changing room and began trying on the clothing.

The first garment was black, a wraparound skirt with a halter top, and although nice enough, it made Bella uncomfortable. What if one of those knots came undone and the whole thing fell down? Still, it looked much nicer than she had expected. The second garment was a silky dress in a rose-pink color, and as soon as she put it on, she knew it was the one. It did something amazing to her. The bodice was low-cut, exposing lots of pale flesh, but not in a way that made her worried something might fall out, and the skirt clung and yet flattered her lush curves, flaring out just below her knees. Bella stood and looked at herself in the mirror in delight.

She was beautiful, and suddenly she looked at herself *as* herself and knew it.

"All right back here?" The sales assistant was there, smiling, her glance taking in Bella's transformation. "Wow! He was right, your gorgeous friend. Do you have shoes for this? I've just taken delivery of some strappy sandals. Want to try some on?"

Bella agreed, and chose a black pair, not too high, but high enough to flatter her legs. She felt dizzy with pleasure.

"What did he say?" she asked as the woman grinned back at her in the mirror. "My . . . my friend, what did he say to you?"

"He told me to find something that would make you realize you were as beautiful as he said you were."

"Oh."

"Not that you need much help," the woman went on. "You look like Elizabeth Taylor in her Cleopatra days. Nicely curved. A couple of centuries ago you'd have been hailed as a goddess. A pity fashion these days decrees one has to be half starved."

When the woman left, Bella took a deep breath, slipped off the dress, and instead of avoiding her reflection, as she usually did, she looked at herself, really looked.

And she was still beautiful.

The transformation had come from within herself, but she also knew that something had sparked it off. Maclean. His appreciation of her, his desire for her, had given her this new perspective. He had given her back her love for herself.

Bella smiled and her reflection smiled back.

"Never again," she swore then, "will I think less of myself because of someone else's opinion."

"Bella?" It was Maclean outside, impatiently waiting.

"I'm nearly finished," she called. Hurriedly she dressed in her own clothes again and, with a secretive smile at him, headed to the counter.

The woman grinned. "Enjoy yourselves."

Maclean slid his arm around Bella and gave her a squeeze. "Aye, we will."

Bella paid, and they left.

"I didna see it," Maclean complained.

"You will," she promised, and laughed.

He smiled back. "What is it, Bella?"

"Nothing, only . . . I'm happy, Maclean."

"Aye," he said indulgently, "and so you should be. You were made to be happy, Arabella."

And he meant it, she could see it in his eyes.

The woman in Siren was right: He was gorgeous. Bella only wished she could keep him forever.

Maclean was glad to be gone from Inverness and back inside the car. It was late afternoon now, and they were supposed to arrive at the Forsythe house for their dinner, but first they had to find a place to stay. Auchtachan had a hotel with comfortable rooms, according to Mistress Forsythe, and Bella found it, parked, and they went to book in.

"Are you here to make a film?" the girl behind the desk asked, her eyes never leaving Maclean.

"Film?" he demanded haughtily.

"Just visiting," Bella assured her, hurrying to fill out the forms and snatching up the key.

The staircase creaked on the way up and Maclean followed her, thinking the hotel looked old and dingy and could have been around when he was alive the last time. Only it would have been new then. He had noticed as they drove from Inverness that there were more buildings down here than there had been farther north. People lived in boxes, packed together, as if they were afraid of being on their own or afraid in their own land.

It made him feel like he couldn't breathe.

Their room was large and clean, but as usual Maclean found the ceiling too low, so he sat down in a chair by the window and glowered at Bella while she hung up a few items of clothing.

Castle Drumaird had been built for a man of his size. All his family were tall. He missed the place, he missed his own people and his own land, and his own life. He ached with the knowledge that all of that was destroyed when he died, and he chafed at the realization that he could have stopped it.

A gentle hand pressed upon his shoulder and Bella asked, "What is it, Maclean? You look as if you've eaten something that disagreed with you."

He cleared his throat. "I'm sorry, Bella, I dinna mean to be glum, but I'm sick for my home," he said. "This time is so different, everything is so different. I dinna belong here."

She smoothed his cheek with her fingers, feeling the roughness of his whiskers. "Wouldn't you get used to it? I know everything is strange now, but you seem to be more comfortable already. In a year or two no one would ever guess you hadn't been here all your life."

"Mabbe if I lived at Loch Fasail, then I could bear it. It wouldna be so foreign to me then. But here, it's as if I'm caught between two worlds, Bella, and I dinna like it. There's no sense of belonging."

She said nothing, but he could tell that she was upset. It had not been his intention to make Bella sad, too, and now he drew her down onto his lap, shifting uncomfortably from the restriction of his new set of clothes—the suit, as Bella called it.

"You've been brought here for a reason," she said quietly. "Perhaps when you know what it is, then everything else will make more sense."

He opened his mouth to reply, just as a great noise rushed overhead. Maclean flew out of his chair, gazing up, expecting any moment that the ceiling would fall in and they would be crushed.

"Maclean!" Bella was tugging at his arm, trying not to laugh. "Maclean, it was an airplane."

He narrowed his eyes at her, furious with himself and everything else. How could a man protect those he loved in a world like this, where things flew in the sky? As Bella calmed him, explaining as best she could, he pretended to listen, while all the while he knew in his heart that he would never be happy here.

He was like a castaway, washed up on a strange shore. He might try and fit in, he might genuinely marvel at modern life, he might pretend he was happy, but every moment of every day he would be dreaming of his home. And all that he had left behind.

*　　*　　*

Bella smoothed the skirt over her hips, examining herself in the mirror. This was the second time she had put on the dress since its purchase. The first time Maclean had asked her to take it off again, so that he could make love to her. She felt beautiful, he thought she was beautiful, and he showed her so, constantly. It was a dream come true.

Bella tucked her hair behind her ear and caught up her jacket. Maclean was standing, peering broodily out of the window. Checking for airplanes? Bella thought with a smile, but she didn't ask it aloud. Poor Maclean, he wasn't at all happy with modern technology. As the Chief of the Macleans of Fasail he had controlled everything; nothing had slipped by his watchful eyes. Here he was in control of nothing.

I'm sick for my home.

His words had lodged in her chest like a hard little lump.

Would he leave her if he had the chance? Of course he would—he must! Maclean belonged to the past. It was where he was comfortable, where he was born to be. She could not ask him to stay here, not when he was so obviously unhappy. If a chance came for him to go back, to return as a living man, then she would insist he take it. Whatever the cost to herself.

But, guiltily, she could not help but wonder if perhaps he would not have that chance. He might be stuck here forever, and although he would not like that, she would be with him.

"When can we read Tamsin Macleod's words?"

Maclean had turned and was watching her from the shadows. In his dark suit he looked even more dangerously handsome than he had in the plaid. Bella had hoped the modern dress might make him fit in, but it didn't. He was so striking and unusual that she knew he would be noticed wherever he went, whatever the century.

"I'm hoping to persuade Mrs. Forsythe to show us the document before dinner. Then we can eat and leave afterwards without being rude."

"You dinna know these people, then?"

"Not personally, no, although I have heard of their collection. I am not a great believer in private collections myself. I think history should be for everyone, in a public place, for the public. It belongs to us all. My father wanted to possess things, to own them. Houses, land, cars, women. . . . I'm not like that."

He smiled at her passionate outburst. "Your eyes are flashing, Arabella. I wish I could show you Castle Drumaird as it was. I'd take you up onto the tower and we could stand in the weather and look out over my lands and you could instruct me on how I should no' possess so much, me being just one man."

"Would I like that, do you think?" she asked, a little wistfully.

"Aye, I think ye would. I have a bedchamber with a roaring fire and a comfy bed with a feather mattress and many soft pillows, and there are curtains of green silk to pull around us to keep us warm. There's a bath, too, big enough for two, and servants to carry the water up to fill it to the verra top. Some mornings, though, I go down to the loch and bathe there in the cold water with the fishes."

"God, you *are* medieval." Laughing, she reached for

his hand. "Come on, let's go down to the car. The sooner we discover what Tamsin has to say, the sooner we can go home to Loch Fasail."

His big hand closed on hers and she hoped he didn't feel her trembling, and realize just how hard it was becoming for her to pretend it would be okay to see him go.

Twenty-five

*Mrs. Forsythe had that English upper-*middle-class reserve that Bella knew well from her own family. Good manners and politeness were everything and real feelings were scrupulously hidden. It was Mr. Forsythe who was the collector, not her, and she reminded them of it so many times after they arrived, Bella was certain Mr. Forsythe's wife was not entirely pleased with his line of business.

Mrs. Forsythe was bored, alone here at home, and Bella's plan to see the Tamsin Macleod document before dinner was thwarted when she insisted they take drinks first and chat.

"Of course I've heard of *Martin's Journey*," Mrs. Forsythe said, her eyes watchful behind their fashionable glasses. Her hair looked as if it had been recently cut and set, and she had the smooth, well-turned-out look that Bella was familiar seeing with Georgiana, although Mrs. Forsythe was older by at least twenty years.

"I've been pleased with the publicity," Bella said politely.

"I haven't read it yet, but I've ordered a copy. The bookstore was sold out, but I am told they are re-printing."

Bella made a sound that could have been approval at the reprint or commiseration at the wait.

"And you have another book on the way, Ms. Ryan? I've always wanted to write a book, but I've never found the time." Behind her glasses, Mrs. Forsythe's eyes were rather sharp and beady, and suddenly Bella didn't like her very much.

"I'm working on a new book, yes," Bella said, ignoring the rest.

"And you, Mr. Maclean." Mrs. Forsythe turned to him with her curious smile. "What do you do?"

"Em . . . I am Bella's . . . em—"

"Mr. Maclean helps me in my research," Bella said smoothly. "To be honest, I wouldn't be able to write the book without him."

"Oh, I see, another historian." Mrs. Forsythe's smile grew forced, and she was obviously bored by the subject. "I rang my husband, by the way. He's in Moscow bidding for some scrap of paper which was found in a tomb." She shuddered delicately. "He says you are welcome to look at the Tamsin Macleod document, but he would be very grateful if you mentioned him in the book."

"Of course."

Mrs. Forsythe gave a satisfied nod, and Bella wondered if the mention had been her husband's idea or hers.

Despite her sudden dislike of Mrs. Forsythe, the meal was pleasant enough and Bella found she was enjoying it. She had worried at first that Maclean might give himself away, not because he was a fool but because he was a man who had never had to watch what he did or said, and was not used to it. But when he didn't seem to be about to declare himself the Chief of the Macleans of Fasail over the soup, she relaxed and let herself trust him.

Mrs. Forsythe was an experienced hostess, and Maclean was not averse to having his ego stroked. He fit into the surroundings—the meal being served by a discreet servant and the best wine poured into the best glasses—better than Bella, who had grown up in such situations but always found them stilted and uncomfortable. Maclean constantly surprised her. As he answered Mrs. Forsythe's questions on the eighteenth century— he had told her he specialized in that period of Scottish history—Bella realized again that this was no primitive Highland cattle thief. If he had been, then she might have felt as if she were his caretaker, but she didn't. Maclean was educated and clever, a leader of others, and he was certainly her equal in this century and any other.

"Well, I suppose you want to see the document now?" Mrs. Forsythe said at last, and rose from the table. She smiled at Maclean; she seemed to have taken quite a shine to him. "This way."

Maclean followed, his hand resting naturally on the small of Bella's back. His palm was warm and strong, and Bella felt desire curl in her stomach.

"We have security, of course," Mrs. Forsythe called

over her shoulder as she led the way to the room where the collection was kept. "My husband insists on it. Sometimes I think he cares more about these pieces of paper than he does about me." She laughed, to show she was joking, but Bella thought that perhaps the subject had been a matter of dissension between them. "Of course, his collection is very valuable, so he's right to take precautions. Some collectors are not as scrupulous as he is. They will pay just about anything to get their hands on what they want, and they don't seem to mind how it is obtained."

Mrs. Forsythe punched in a code at the door, and the lock clicked open. Inside, the room was enclosed, with no windows, rather like a museum. The various pieces of the collection were on display in glass cases, and the only light in the room was artificial because, as Mrs. Forsythe explained, natural light faded the delicate paper and ink.

Maclean gave Bella a look of skeptical amazement and she could tell what he was thinking: A few scraps of old paper with bad spelling and they are treated like precious jewels? The people who wrote these diaries and letters would be surprised to see the reverence with which they were kept. For Maclean their importance was negligible compared to the truly important matters, like food and warmth for his people, things which would mean the difference between life and death.

Perhaps Maclean was right, and the modern idea of what was and was not important was skewed, but still Bella could not help the rush of excitement she felt as she looked upon the stained and wrinkled sheets of paper that told the story of Tamsin Macleod née Maclean.

Mrs. Forsythe unlocked the case and handed Bella a pair of gloves to wear while she handled the document, to protect it from the oils from her fingers. "If you like, you can sit over there at the table to examine it," she suggested.

"Thank you. It may take me a little time to decipher the writing and make notes. It is rather faded. At least it's not written in Gaelic," she added.

"I know Gaelic," Maclean reminded her. "I was verra well educated. Private tutors, you know."

He was mimicking the way Mrs. Forsythe spoke, and Bella hoped she didn't notice.

Mrs. Forsythe carried the document to the table and, after hovering a moment while Bella and Maclean made themselves comfortable in the leather chairs, gave some excuse and left them to it.

Bella peered at the faded and stained script, a little crease between her brows as she puzzled out the archaic spelling. Then, with a tight little smile in Maclean's direction, she began to read it aloud.

"My name is Tamsin Macleod and I was born in Fasail in 1737 in the time of Morven Maclean. My father was a tacksman for the Black Maclean, and my mother weaved wool into plaids and arisaids, while keeping an eye on me and my brothers and sisters. We lived well, better than many others, for the Black Maclean was a better chief than many others. I know it is not the done thing to say so now, and I do not usually speak out among the people I have made my life with, but I am old and I don't think anyone will deny me my opinions.

"She talks about her husband, who is dead, and her loneliness without him. She says that her children and their children welcome her, but they have their own lives and times have changed so much that she misses the old ways like an ache in her very bones."

"I know how she feels," Maclean muttered.

"Ah, here's something. . . ."

"I came to the Clan Macleod at a time of great suffering, and not at all willingly. The man who saved my life was the father of my husband, but at the time I hated him. I hated them all. I did not speak for a year after I left Loch Fasail.

"The man who saved my life . . . what do you think that means?" Bella looked up when he didn't answer.

Maclean was seated opposite her, his hands gripping the arms of the chair, his jaw rigid. She reached out to cover his fingers with hers, but he made no sign that he felt her, or even knew she was there.

Shocked, she realized then that he was in the past. Tamsin's words were a key that had unlocked the door in his mind. He didn't need to hear them all, he didn't need to be told what she had suffered.

Maclean was seeing it for himself.

Maclean shivered. The temperature had dropped, and when he looked across at Bella she was gone. The room was gone. He wasn't at the Forsythes' house anymore.

He was at Loch Fasail, two hundred and fifty years in the past.

It was the noise that struck him first.

The screaming and shouting, the roaring blast of fire as everything around him was set alight. Consumed. People staggered past him through the smoke. A pig bolted, almost knocking him over. Maclean fell against the wall of a cottage, coughing and trying to get his bearings, and that was when he saw the child.

Tangled red hair and a white face, bloodied across one cheek. The little girl was standing in the midst of it, shocked. Screams erupted from inside the cottage and she flinched. And then a man came riding out of the swirling smoke. Maclean recognized him. It was the same man who had tried to ride down Bella, the man he had fought and who had subsequently vanished. The rider's sword was swinging, and he was just as intent on murder as Maclean remembered. The child turned and ran, and disappeared into the smoke.

"That is Tamsin," a voice said behind him.

Shocked, he turned. The *Fiosaiche* stood there, her silver cloak flapping in the wind, her red hair brighter than the fires about them.

"Why have you brought me here?" he cried in his pain and fury.

Her eyes fixed on his, as terrible as he remembered. "Because it is time for you to know, and to properly know you must see."

A couple more men rode by in the dragoons' uniform of red coats and buff breeches.

"Is it true, then?" he asked her, his voice husky with pain. "Did the English follow me home to Loch Fasail?"

She didn't answer him. Around them women scattered, unprotected without their menfolk, although some stood and fought their foes. He saw faces he

knew, one of them swinging her husband's broadsword
at her attacker, using a strength of which he would not
have believed her capable. The man grinned as if he
found her desperate fury amusing.

"Och, ma bonny lass," he mocked, "ye are making
me shake in ma boots. Dinna ye know your great chief
is dead? He died like a dog on Macleod land and we
sliced him to pieces. He canna protect you now."

Tears ran down the woman's sooty cheeks, but she
held her ground. "Murdering Macleods," she hissed. "Ye
have killed the Black Maclean and ye will pay for it!"

But the man just laughed. He wouldn't pay for it, not
ever, and he knew it.

Maclean's people hadn't been massacred by the
hated English alone, but by the Macleods as well.
Maybe Bella was right, and Auchry Macleod had seen a
chance to take what was not his. Maybe his greed had
overcome his cowardice.

"I canna abide it," he whispered. "Take me back."

"You *must* abide it," the *Fiosaiche* replied fiercely.
"You played your part in this terrible thing, Maclean.
Feel their pain, feel your guilt. *Never* forget it."

Farm animals scattered wildly, adding to the chaos,
while the men he hadn't taken with him to Mhairi, the
old and infirm, fought and died. And the children . . .
Maclean cried out, looking about him, seeing the faces
confused and dazed. His heart felt as if it were being
torn from his chest.

"I should have been here," he said. "I should have
been here!"

He was caught up in the nightmare, but they couldn't
see him, couldn't hear him, couldn't feel him. He was

useless. A ghost. Some of them were even calling out his name, as if hoping he would be able to protect them from beyond the grave, and it brought him to the brink of absolute despair.

An old man lay dying upon the ground with a terrible wound to his chest, and he gazed up at Maclean as he ran past. Something flickered in his eyes, a recognition, and he smiled. "M'lord," he whispered, "God bless ye." The next moment those eyes had dulled in death.

Cursing, his face hot with tears, Maclean struggled on. He no longer looked back at the sorceress or expected her to help him. She was here simply for her pound's worth of flesh, and he understood that. He deserved to suffer, just as his people had suffered.

Maclean turned, coughing as the thick smoke rolled toward him from the burning buildings.

There was something moving in it.

At that moment the smoke parted, and he saw the horse standing upon the rise. Maclean backed up a step and looked to its rider. Her booted feet were in the stirrups, her trews molding to her shapely legs. Her hair was like pale spun gold and her green eyes were burning with a fierce hatred.

"Ishbel?"

But just like the others, she couldn't see him. This was Ishbel as she had been in 1746, not the creature she had become.

"Maclean," she shouted toward the carnage, and her voice shook with her grief and her fury. "Tell me, do ye feel their pain? Do ye feel their suffering? Good! I want you to. I want you to suffer even in death. *This* is your punishment for what ye did to me."

Ishbel did this?

He should have known it; in a way, he *had* known it.

Ishbel raised her dagger and shook it to the sky, the tears streaming down her cheeks. "I have soaked my hands in Maclean blood this day!"

Maclean staggered. Ishbel had been part of the massacre, and then Auchry had lied for her sake. Begun the legend that was still believed today, so that his beloved sweet Ishbel could escape censure, and no one would argue when he brought his sheep to graze upon Loch Fasail land. Finally Maclean understood.

And it gave him no satisfaction.

Maclean started toward her, wanting to drag her from her horse and break her to pieces. But even as he came forward, the smoke thickened and she was gone, and when he spun about, so was the vision of the massacre of his people.

"It is not over yet," the *Fiosaiche* said, and for once there was a trace of compassion in her voice. "There is more, Maclean. You must remember the day you died."

He tried to take a step, but he was falling, falling further back through time. He felt his body jolt, and he straightened and reluctantly opened his eyes.

Maclean was seated upon his horse, at the head of his men, facing Auchry Macleod of Mhairi. He could feel the animal beneath him, the chill wind on his face, the smell of fear and sweat, the aching tiredness of his own body. And his raging pain and pride. Like a knot inside him, it twisted, urging him on, telling him he had no choice but to teach Ishbel, teach them all, that he was every bit a man like his father.

He wanted to tell himself no, he wanted to turn

around and go home, but he wasn't able to do anything. He was Maclean, and yet he wasn't. The *Fiosaiche* was forcing him to be an observer only. His mouth opened and the words that came out were the ones he had spoken long ago.

"I have come for Ishbel," he said, and his hands tightened on the reins.

And there, behind Auchry, was Ishbel, smiling a strange little smile, and at her side gangly Iain Og, his eyes reddened by the cold and maybe sleeplessness. The boy was looking upon his own death and he knew it.

The *Fiosaiche*'s voice was in Maclean's head. "Remember. Savor the pain. Learn the lesson. It is the only way. . . ."

He was back in the airless, windowless room where the Forsythes kept their collection, with Bella's worried face before him and the hum of the air conditioner in his ears.

"I know what happened," he said in a voice that sounded like a stranger's. "And I wish to God I did not."

Twenty-six

Brian put down his cell phone, his hands shaking so much he nearly dropped it. Elaine, Bella's agent, had just called him. She'd been trying to ring Bella, but no one was picking up. Elaine didn't seem to know that Brian and Bella had split up, or if she did, she wasn't about to let on. Instead she launched into a diatribe about Bella's book *Martin's Journey*, and how it had sold out and was about to go into another reprint. Elaine finished the call with details of the publicity Bella had turned down, begging Brian to talk some sense into her. In ten minutes he knew everything about *Reading England* and all the chances Bella was letting slip through her fingers.

Bella's book was a bestseller.

He couldn't believe it.

Brian had been avoiding anything to do with writing since he left the cottage, and now he learned that Bella had finally done what he never thought she could.

He had walked out on her after all this time, and *now*

she had a bestseller. He sat down heavily on the antique chair in Georgiana's gleaming entrance hall.

Anger built in him, a hot, self-righteous fury, with Bella and the way she'd treated him. She hadn't once tried to call him and apologize. It had been he who had gone back to the cottage to see her, to try and talk some sense into her.

He'd arrived to find the place empty, but there were plenty of signs that someone had been there recently. The smashed plates and smell of burning worried him, and he'd only waited a minute or two before deciding to climb the path to the castle ruins. She was probably up there. She was always up there, moping around, dreaming about Maclean. Brian had come to loathe the man. If he wasn't already dead, Brian would have wished death on him.

At first he couldn't believe his eyes. The mist had come down over the castle ruins, and the whole scene was just as cold and bleak as he remembered, but as he stood peering toward the gateway, he'd seen movement. He couldn't take it in at first. He'd kept watching, thinking it must be a hallucination. Bare skin and entwined limbs, an erotic living sculpture. Bella and her man were so caught up in their lust they didn't even know he was there. Shameless. Sickening.

He'd been utterly shocked. Bella? This woman who was acting so wildly and primitively was his Bella? More embarrassingly, he'd been turned on. He'd never seen her like that, wanton, her hair loose about her, and giving as good as she got. She was like one of those pagan fertility goddesses he'd looked at in the museums she was always dragging him into.

Brian had begun to back away, but the man had heard him and jumped up, calling out aggressively. Until then Brian had been tossing up the idea of confronting him, but now he thought better of it. God Almighty, the bastard even had a weapon, some sort of sword! Brian had run off, back to the car, and left before they could catch him. He'd glanced in his rearview mirror for miles, worried he might be followed.

But he couldn't forget what he'd seen, and he'd been mulling over his hurt and anger ever since. The memory stayed with him. It was like the car crashes he sometimes came across when he was driving on the motorway, when he couldn't seem to help looking despite knowing he might catch a glimpse of something he'd rather not see. The memory of his visit to Bella was like that, and he replayed it over and over.

The question he found himself asking the most was: *Why didn't she ever behave like that when she was with me?*

That she hadn't just made her betrayal all the worse.

After all the sacrifices he'd made for her, all the times he'd tried to help her and turn her into something better. She'd never appreciated him or his efforts. She hadn't understood that if it hadn't been for him, she'd never have been able to keep going. If it hadn't been for him, she'd never have become a bestselling author.

And now that Bella *was* a bestselling author, who on earth was going to be there to help her choose the right clothes and get her into some sort of shape to face the media?

Brian shuddered as he had a vision of Bella appearing on television in her blue robe and slippers, with those extra pounds on show for all the world to see. He'd just die of embarrassment.

There was only one thing to do.

He'd have to forgive her and take her back. She'd be so grateful she'd soon give her new man the elbow, if that's what he was. Thinking about it now, Brian began to doubt it was anything more than a fling. The brute probably came calling at the cottage looking for a handout, decided Bella was easy pickings, took what he wanted, and was now long gone. When Brian turned up at her door, she'd fall on him in tears and beg him to help her.

Pleased with the ego-soothing scenario he'd created, Brian smiled to himself. Yes, she'd be so very grateful when he agreed, a little grudgingly, to help her. He wouldn't forgive her straightaway, oh no, he'd make her earn it. And he'd drop a few hints about what he'd seen up in the ruins, nothing concrete, just enough to keep her guessing and worrying that he might leave her again.

Perhaps he should travel up there tonight? There was so much to do if he was to get her into shape, and they'd need to head south to London as soon as possible if they weren't to miss out on the opportunities Elaine had created for them.

But Brian decided he didn't want to look too eager. Tomorrow would be soon enough, and he could take some champagne with him. Yes, champagne would be a nice touch, something good but not too expensive.

To celebrate Bella's success, and their reconciliation.

Twenty-seven

"You have what you wanted, then?" Mrs. Forsythe asked curiously.

Maclean knew he looked haggard and Bella pale, but he tried to be polite in return for the woman's kindness. It was not her fault that his pigheadedness and pain had set in motion the events that destroyed his clan and emptied his lands. Ishbel might have been complicit in the massacre, but his pursuit of her and the murder of Iain Og had begun it.

"Thank you, we do."

"Good." She led the way out, pausing as she passed a small table with a grubby cloth on it. She clicked her tongue. "I thought I asked for that to be disposed of," she murmured, picking it up with a grimace. "My husband has contacts all over the place," she explained, "and sometimes they bring him objects they think he might be interested in. Someone came this morning and left this, but really I don't want it in the house. The old woman who brought it was very . . . odd. I told the maid to throw it away."

Maclean glanced at the bundle curiously. "What is it?"

"I'm not exactly sure. Some bits of old leather wrapped up in a piece of old woolen cloth. I can't imagine what it was used for. To hang someone, perhaps," she said, and laughed nervously, as if it weren't really a joke. "Would you like to see, Mr. Maclean?"

Maclean took the ragged piece of cloth, feeling the grease and grime of centuries clinging to it, and began to unwrap it very carefully to expose what lay within. Leather strips, like rope, knotted and frayed and very old.

Mrs. Forsythe made an expression of disgust, but Bella moved closer and Maclean could feel the tension in her body.

"What is it?" she whispered.

Maclean stirred the leather strips with his finger. There was a dull jangling sound. Some of what he had thought of as knots were actually thin circular pieces of discolored metal, silver maybe, and there was a long, narrower rod of metal. "Something for a small beast, I think. A pony, mabbe."

Bella's breathing was loud at his side.

"That's a bit," she said in wonder. "It's a bridle, Maclean."

"Good heavens!" Mrs. Forsythe was completely unimpressed. "Well, my husband doesn't collect horse tack."

Maclean frowned, leaning closer to the bridle. "It's verra grubby and I can hardly see, but there seem to be engravings on the metal pieces." He pointed with his finger. "A shape, a woman mabbe, holding the harness?"

"It's very old," Bella added, her voice strangely distant.

"Yes, I can see that. Old and very smelly. I do not want it, Ms. Ryan." She gave Maclean an oddly shy look. "Do you want it, Mr. Maclean? Please, feel free."

Maclean hesitated. He was aware that Bella had grown very still and was even paler than before. She must have sat with him all the time he was in the past. How long had that been? Had he said anything, done anything? He hadn't been able to ask because Mrs. Forsythe had come into the room almost as soon as he awoke, but Bella was •clearly upset and probably frightened.

"We dinna need—" he began, meaning to refuse.

"Thank you." Bella was forcing a smile at Mrs. Forsythe. "I'll try and clean it up and look at it more closely. If it is important or valuable, then I'll certainly return it to you and your husband, Mrs. Forsythe."

"If you must," the woman sighed, "but really, I don't want it."

Bella reached out as if to touch the harness, and then drew back, folding her fingers tight into a fist. She was afraid of it, thought Maclean. Or she was afraid of him.

They were back in the car on their way to the hotel. Bella, who hadn't been able to wait to leave so that she could talk to Maclean about what he had seen, was silent.

At least the old document had revealed what had happened to Tamsin. The girl had been caught up in the massacre, although she barely remembered it by the time her story was being written down. She had been found, frightened and bleeding, some way from the main site of the killings by one of the Macleod clansmen. He had recently lost a daughter of his own to illness and, thinking to please his wife, had taken her home with him. Tamsin hardly spoke a word for a year, but after that she seemed to recover. In time she married the son of the household and moved house to the Isle of Skye.

Bella could imagine how it felt to be the only survivor of the massacre of Loch Fasail, and she understood why Tamsin had kept quiet about it. Perhaps her host family had warned her to hold her tongue.

And then there was the bridle. *The magic bridle*, the hag's voice sounded in Bella's head. As soon as Maclean had begun to unwrap it, she had felt dizzy with an excitement and awe she had never felt before when confronted with even the most precious of objects. It was as if on some deep level of consciousness she knew it was important, and she must have it.

Bella had never been superstitious, had never believed in signs, but she was shaken by the power of what was happening. Her dream and reality had collided. But what on earth was she meant to do next?

Slip the bridle on, but remember, the creature will no' be easily restrained, and if it knows what ye are about, then it will kill you.

The voice sounded in her head like an echo, quite clear and precise, and utterly impossible.

"Bloody hell." She sounded just like Maclean.

Perhaps that was why he turned to look at her strangely. "Bella? What is wrong?"

"I think I must be tired." She didn't want to explain to him, she wanted to think about it first, try and understand what was happening to her.

"Aye, it has been a day to remember."

"Maclean—"

"Wait until we are in our room and I will tell you. I will tell you everything."

When they were finally back in the room, Maclean poured himself a dram of whiskey from the tiny bottle in the bar fridge, and crouched to examine all the other bottles and crinkly packets of nuts and chocolate bars—the man was fascinated with refrigerators. Then he straightened and drank the whiskey down in one gulp, and stood a moment, gathering up his words, while Bella sat quietly and watched him.

"I did go after Ishbel," he said at last. "I went to fetch her back from her father's lands. I believed I had justice on my side and that Auchry would agree with me and hand her over. I wasna afraid of him; if anything, he was afraid of me. But in my blind hurt I had underestimated what a weak treacherous weasel of a man he was. When I reached the borders of Auchry's land, he rode out to speak with me."

"Was Ishbel there?"

"Aye, she was there, and Iain Og."

Auchry was listening to his complaints, nodding in agreement, and all but crawling up his arse. Maclean could hear his own voice, so much like his father's, and it made him feel sick with shame. His eyes flicked to Ishbel, standing behind Auchry, but he could read no fear in her face. She didn't believe that she would be sent back to Loch Fasail. She had it all planned, Maclean realized now in despair.

Ishbel lifted her arm. It was a signal.

The crest of the hill behind her came alive as dragoons surged over it and down the other side in a tide of red. They had been there all along, watching and waiting for her to call them forth.

"They are from Fort William," she said, still smiling. "They are looking for rebels, Maclean. How fortunate for us that you are here. Now they will leave my father alone. A fair trade, don't you think? You for him?"

Maclean's men roared their fury, the sound echoing around them, but he stayed them, holding up his hand. "Wait!" he shouted. He still didn't believe she would truly do it, that such a thing could happen to him.

Ishbel was screaming, turning toward Auchry's men and the dragoons, who had reached them now and were lined up to the rear. "He is a rebel, a traitor to the Crown!" Her voice rose. "Kill him!"

It was chaos, the noise of the men and Ishbel's screaming. Maclean couldn't think. He looked to Auchry to tell her to stop it, to behave herself, but he didn't. The older man urged his horse back, and Maclean knew then he had given up his right to lead. Like the weak bastard he was, he had handed the privilege over to Ishbel.

Sickness washed over Maclean. He was outnumbered, and the dragoons were well armed. He had blundered into something he could never escape.

"I am betrayed!" he roared, and surged forward, drawing his broadsword. His men followed, tearing up the ground with their running feet, their voices so loud he felt deafened. He was about to die and it was too late to do anything about it.

He struck down one man, then another, but there were always more of them. The dragoons rode among his men, slicing with their swords, inflicting terrible injuries. Maclean looked up, wiping the blood and sweat from his eyes. His shoulder was cut, but the pain wasn't too bad and he could still use it. He could see Ishbel some yards away, clinging onto Iain Og and trying to pull him away from the fighting, to safety with her.

She doesna deserve happiness. Maclean burned with her betrayal. He pushed forward, fighting like a madman, making a path to Ishbel and her lover. Iain Og saw him coming and pulled away from Ishbel, standing like a proper man, pride overcoming the terror on his young face.

It wasn't much of a fight. Maclean killed him with one blow.

But he felt no sense of achievement, just a sickness deep in the pit of his stomach. It was wrong, all wrong.

Ishbel was screaming again, but now she was saying, "Vengeance! I want vengeance! Kill him, kill him, kill him. . . ."

Maclean felt the hot breath of a horse at his back, sensed the blade before it swung down upon him. The dragoon struck again, and again.

* * *

"And afterwards? What happened after you were . . . dead?"

It was Bella's voice, drawing him back into the room, and he wanted to cling to it, and her. What he had seen and felt that day was an insanity he never wanted to repeat, and if he could, he knew he would undo it, whatever the cost to himself.

He found his voice. "When you were reading Tamsin's diary I was shown what happened at Loch Fasail. I had killed Iain Og, and Ishbel wanted her vengeance. My death wasna enough for her. She rode on to Loch Fasail with her men and the English dragoons, and massacred my people. She has that burden upon her soul. But *I* must take the blame. I know that. If I had stayed at home, it would no' have happened; if I had listened to the women, I would no' have gone. I didna love her, I never loved her, and I had no right to force her into the same unhappiness as my mother. You have taught me that, Bella."

Bella's eyes filled with tears.

"I died at Mhairi with the sound of Ishbel's curses in my ears and then my body was cut to pieces, just as the legend says, and cast to the four winds. I didna even have a proper grave. Not that it matters. I was already on my way to the between-worlds."

"You remember that?" she whispered.

He nodded slowly, watching her. "Ye want to know what that was like, don't ye, Bella? Mabbe it is not something a mortal woman should hear."

"But I want to hear. This is about you and I want to know. I need to understand."

He thought a moment, his gaze turned inward.

"I remember the pain. The sword . . . and then there

was darkness. A great long tunnel of it. The cold darkness of the between-worlds. I was stumbling along and I couldna see where I was going, so I pressed my hands along the walls and felt my way. The stone was wet and slippery, and there was a dreadful silence. As if I wasna alone but whatever was in there with me was holding its breath—"

"Maclean!" He looked at her sharply, but she shook her head, forcing back the horror. "No, please, go on. Tell me."

"There were things in the darkness." He shuddered. "I couldna see them, but I knew they were there. Things with claws and teeth. I tried to turn back once, but then there were more of them, nipping at my feet, turning me again the way they wanted me to go. But the tunnel just went on and on, and there was no way out."

He stopped, and for a long moment he was silent, perhaps collecting his thoughts, perhaps reminding himself that he was safe now.

"What happened then, Maclean?"

She heard him take a deep breath.

"I'd given up. I dinna know how long I was there, days, months, years. I stood in the dark with those things about me and I longed for nothingness. This wasna death, there was no peaceful sleep, this was a place of punishment and suffering, and it was cold and dark and far more terrible than I'd ever imagined. That was when she came, the *Fiosaiche*. She had a light with her, a glowing circle of flame that floated before her, and her voice was as soft as lamb's wool and her wings as strong as an eagle's, and her gaze on mine was more terrifying than anything I had ever faced when I was alive."

Bella imagined it, Maclean hunched beneath the roof of the nightmare tunnel and the sorceress before him in all her fearsome glory.

"What did she do?"

"She said . . . she said that my time would come and when it did I must redeem myself and cast the burden from my soul. She said that too many lives had been lost because of me and it wasna supposed to be so. She would not have it so. And then the tunnel was gone and . . . and there was nothing. I slept. I slept on through the centuries until she came to wake me again, two hundred and fifty years later."

Bella felt excitement stir in her. "You shouldn't have died like that. It was a mistake. You were meant for greater things, Maclean, but you messed up."

He stared at her. "I see that now, but the seeing isn't enough. I need to make things right, I need to change them, but how can I do that when the world I knew is gone?"

"I—I don't know."

He spun away, and Bella watched him go. He was right. How could anything be changed now? He might accept his part in those terrible long-ago events and ask forgiveness, but for Maclean it would not be enough. He wanted to go back physically and change history. He wanted to do it *right* this time.

But could history really be rewritten? Could the *Fiosaiche* be that powerful?

As a historian, Bella found that idea extremely disturbing.

Twenty-eight

Brian did not see the woman at first, she just suddenly *was*, standing by the road with her thumb stuck out. She stepped forward as he came closer and he slowed, worried he might knock her over. That was when he saw the clothing she was wearing.

It was odd, to say the least.

Faded tartan pants that clung to her slim legs and a dark green jacket with gold buttons. Her yellow hair was loose about her shoulders, and she was breathtakingly beautiful, in a fey sort of way. He wondered if she was going to some fancy dress party, or maybe she was one of those New Age travelers.

Despite his urgency to get to Bella, Brian found himself almost compelled to stop his car to pick her up.

The woman sauntered toward the car, smiling at him, and he lowered his window. She leaned forward, her long hair framing her face. "Where are you headed?" Brian asked.

"Loch Fasail."

Her eyes were an enchanting green with gold flecks, dazzling, like the sun on water. After a moment Brian realized he was smiling at her like an idiot and hadn't answered.

"Loch Fasail? That's where I'm going! Well, Drumaird Cottage, anyway. I didn't think anyone lived around there anymore. Is it Gregor's farm you want?"

"I dinna know a Gregor." A secretive look had come into her eyes now.

Brian hesitated—there was something about her—something strange. Perhaps he should just drive on. . . .

"My family lived there," the girl said, so soft he had to strain to hear her. "A long time ago. I wanted to see it again."

Brian relaxed. She was reliving her past, maybe some extra-special summer spent at the loch with her family. Nothing wrong in that. He might as well give her a lift; no one else would be coming this way today. Anyway, it would be nice to have some company for the last part of the journey, to take his mind off what lay ahead.

"Get in."

The girl skipped around to the passenger side of the car and stood waiting. Brian smiled. A real little lady despite her weird clothes. He reached over and unlatched the door and pushed it open. She slid into the seat and carefully pulled the door shut behind her.

"Okay?" he asked her, easing his car back onto the road.

"Aye."

"I'm Brian. What's your name, then?"

She glanced at him in that secretive way. "Ishbel."

"How do you do, Ishbel?"

"You're wrong, you know," she said, and now she was staring ahead through the windscreen.

"Wrong?"

There was a musty smell. From her clothing, perhaps? It reminded him of something.

"There *is* someone who lives at Loch Fasail."

"Who's that, then?"

"Maclean."

Brian gave her a look. "Maclean?"

"Aye. He lives there."

Maclean . . . could that be the man that Bella was with? It had been difficult to make him out through the mist, and Brian knew he had been too shocked and angry to really take in the details of who and what he was seeing. He glanced at the girl again, but she was sitting very still, her hands clenched in her lap. Her hair hung down, shielding her profile, and there was something dark tangled in it. Was she afraid of him, or was it the car? Brian was a careful driver, so he doubted it was the speed they were traveling.

"What does this Maclean look like?"

"He's a big man, braw, with dark hair."

"He wears a kilt?"

"Aye."

"Is this Maclean a relative of yours? Or an old boyfriend?" he added with an arch grin.

She laughed and her long fair hair tumbled about her, and he realized the dark object was a piece of water weed. At the same time he knew what the musty smell was—stale water. Her clothing smelled of the loch.

"Och, no, mister, Maclean's ma intended husband!"

Better and better! Brian laughed back in honest delight. He couldn't wait to tell Bella that her lover was almost a married man, and to this little beauty, too.

"I'm coming to claim him," Ishbel added quietly.

"Good." Brian speeded up, just a little. "I'm glad to hear it."

Drumaird Cottage was empty when they reached it, but Brian knew where Bella hid the key. He unlocked the front door and peered inside, but he could tell Bella and her new friend Maclean were out. The place felt cold and deserted.

A pity. He had been looking forward to the confrontation. Ishbel enticing Maclean away with her, Bella weeping and wailing, and Brian there to pick up the pieces. Perfect timing, really.

"Do you want a cup of coffee or something?" He turned, expecting Ishbel to be behind him, but she was still standing outside, a few yards beyond the doorway. The sun was shining and he couldn't see her expression; she was standing against the light, her shadow cast long before her.

In that moment his previous unease returned. Her shadow struck him as odd, wrong, mismatched. Such a large shape couldn't possibly belong to so slight a woman.

He blinked and the effect was gone. "Do you want to come in?"

"I canna. I am no' allowed."

"Not allowed?" he said with an arrogant laugh. "They're not here, you can come in if you like. I'm asking you to. I don't know where they've gone, they might take hours."

"Och, ne'er mind," she said sweetly. "I have a way to pass the time."

Her smile, her eyes. He was drawn. Almost against his will, Brian's feet propelled him toward her and out of the cottage.

Her shadow wavered, shimmering in a way that turned his blood cold. He peered closer, thinking it was his eyesight, thinking he must be imagining things, and that was when he realized her face was changing, growing longer, and . . . and her body was enlarging, elongating, taking the form of something else.

"Ne'er mind," she said again, her voice deepening and echoing all around him. "We have things to do before they return."

Twenty-nine

They slept late and the journey home seemed longer than it had the day before. Bella was edgy, deep in her own thoughts, not herself at all. Maclean supposed that he had given her much to think of, and left her alone. They drove mostly in silence until it was time to stop and take a break.

Maclean had insisted on dressing in his plaid and jacket, packing the suit carefully away in the trunk of the car, so when they stopped for a break he was once again the center of attention and speculation. After a couple of lassies asked him for his autograph, Bella lifted an eyebrow at him as if to say, *Told you so*.

The weather had grown cooler, reminding them that summer was over, and a misty rain hung low over the mountains, hiding them for much of the time.

Bella shivered, huddling into her red woolen coat, her long hair tucked inside the collar. Maclean reached over and tugged the silky locks free, combing the tangles with his fingers. "That's better," he murmured.

She cuddled in against him and he slid his arm about her, hugging her body to his.

"What will happen now?" she said, speaking at last of what was worrying her.

"I dinna know. Mabbe the *Fiosaiche* will come and tell me that."

"Perhaps I will finally get to meet her." But Bella did not seem to relish the thought.

His spine tingled. It was not Bella meeting the sorceress that worried him so much as Bella meeting Ishbel. *She* would not want him to have a second chance at life and happiness. He knew that Ishbel would do anything to hurt him; she had told him so.

"Maclean?"

He turned and Bella was watching him, her dark hair teased by the wind, her cheeks stung to pink by the cold. His heart warmed just looking at her—aye, she was his woman. But at the same time something brushed his skin. The icy breath of the mountains, pausing briefly beside him to whisper a warning, before rushing on to the south.

I will no' let you touch her, Ishbel, he called after it. *I will not!*

"We'd better get going." Bella stretched up to press her lips to his jaw. "Aren't your legs cold, Maclean? Not to mention other parts beneath your kilt."

"Not at all," he said with surprise, and then with a lecherous smile, "I can show you if you like."

"Maybe later."

He bent his head and kissed her properly.

"I will take that as a promise."

* * *

He felt it as they left Ardloch and turned east, toward Loch Fasail. A strong sense of unease that deepened, and darkened. By the time they passed Gregor's croft it had become a weight upon his head and shoulders, like a heavy stone, pressing him down. And he knew that there was something very wrong.

Maclean began to fidget, wishing he had not let Bella talk him into leaving his *claidheamh mor* in the trunk. The rain had continued all the way home, making the road slippery and visibility difficult. Good weather for hiding for an ambush, bad weather for fighting in the open, he noted out of habit. As they drove on to the crest of the road that gave the first view of the loch, he kept looking, trying to pierce the rain on the moorland, but everything was gray and forbidding. And then the ruins of Castle Drumaird rose above the surrounding land, and the loch was like a silver mirror with someone's steamy breath upon it.

His keen gaze was drawn back to the castle ruins, and he caught a flash of color. Red, maybe. But then the rain came in heavier, shielding whatever it was he had seen. He leaned forward, eyes narrowed, while the windshield wipers slid back and forth.

"Maclean?" Bella was watching him anxiously. "What is it?"

"I dinna know," he answered honestly. "Slow the car down as you get to the last rise. Aye, that's it, slowly, now, so that I can see. . . ."

They crested the final small hill and stopped. Everything appeared calm and untouched. Nothing was changed. And yet Maclean knew there was something wrong. He felt the threat to him, to Bella, like the point of a dirk at his throat.

"I don't see anything," she began, and then sat up straighter. "Wait! Is that Brian's car behind the cottage? What on earth can he want?" She sounded more irritable than anxious now.

Maclean frowned. Was that what he was feeling? Brian's anger, like a dark cloud upon his home? Was this nothing more than a jealous lover's petulance?

He wanted to believe it.

Bella was already driving forward again, moving along the track that led to the cottage. Birds, disturbed by the noise of the engine, took off silently from the loch's surface, while some of Gregor's sheep bundled out of the gorse bushes and ran up the rock-strewn hill, their fleeces wet and grubby.

They pulled up outside the cottage, but neither of them moved from the car. The kitchen window was blank and the cottage appeared deserted. There was no welcoming smoke from the chimney; no one opened the door.

"If Brian was here, he would have lit the fire and made himself at home. And why has he parked at the back? He never does that. It's as if he's trying to hide. Brian just wouldn't do that. He'd want to be seen."

"Mabbe you should wait here and I will look," Maclean suggested evenly, but Bella was already opening her door and getting out of the car.

"He doesn't know you," she reminded him. "He won't know who you are. It'd be better if I speak to him first."

"Bella." He said it sharply.

She turned, frowning, surprised by his tone.

"Open the trunk so that I can get my broadsword. Just in case, aye? I promise you I willna touch Brian with it."

She hesitated, clearly not wanting to.

"I give you my oath," he said softly. "I need my weapon, Bella."

Maybe she sensed it, too, the darkness that hung over the land, for she glanced about her quickly, and then with a nod she went to unlock the trunk. Maclean removed his sword and buckled it about his hips. The grubby piece of cloth was there, too, wrapped around the bridle, and without thinking he lifted it out, carrying it with him.

Bella was at the door.

"It isn't locked. I know I locked it when we left. I always do. Habit." She gave a nervous smile.

Maclean nodded, but his face was grim. He stepped in front of her and pushed the door open. Just as he had expected, the kitchen was empty. He glanced to the sink, to the Aga, but there was no sign that anyone had been here.

He heard Bella's footsteps, and before he could stop her she was hurrying through to the back door. He caught up with her and placed his hand over hers and drew the bolt himself. Sure enough, it was Brian's car parked there, the front half of it deep in a briar bush, as if he had lost control at the last moment. Several of the thorny branches had been smashed, and one of the front lights on his car was broken, the plastic casing scattered in the ridges of mud caused by the churning of the wheels.

"I don't understand," Bella said dully.

Maclean felt the fear swell in his throat, making it hard to breathe. He caught Bella's arm, pulling her back inside the cottage and closing and rebolting the door. At once he felt better. Safer. Keeping her close, he made his way back to the kitchen, checking each room as he passed.

Nothing.

He knew with a sense of relief that they were safe in here. He hoped the hag's spell would stop any evil from entering the cottage, and as long as they stayed within it they would be protected, too. However, as Bella turned to climb the stairs he caught her hand and drew her back. Better to be cautious.

"Wait," he said, touching her face, holding her attention.

"Maclean, what is it?"

"I am the one with the weapon," he reminded her.

"I have my broom," she retorted, but her eyes were wide and frightened.

He smiled, to ease her fears, and slowly climbed the narrow staircase. The rooms here, too, were empty, and he could not see that anything had been touched. Turning back to the head of the stairs, he looked down at Bella, who was waiting below.

"There is nothing."

He made her stay in the kitchen while he searched the shed outside and looked about close to the house. Brian's car was open and he even checked the trunk. Nothing. Brian had vanished.

"I have to find him," Bella said when he returned to her side. "I can't sit here knowing he's around somewhere. He'll make a scene, call me names. I just want to face him. I just want it to be over, Maclean."

"Would he go out for a walk?"

"Brian?" she sounded doubtful, and then shrugged. "Maybe he went up to the castle to keep watch for us. Maybe he's on his way down to the cottage right now."

"Aye, mabbe."

"I'll go and see—"

"*I'll* go and see. You wait here. It is safe in the cottage, but ye must no' leave it, do ye understand me?"

She shook her head. "No, I don't understand you. Tell me what's going on."

"I dinna know exactly," he said quietly, not releasing her gaze, "but I know the scent of evil. I smell it now."

"Evil?" Bella's confused thoughts flashed across her face, but she was quick-witted. "Maclean, could something come through the door from the between-worlds? Could something escape?"

She seemed to be thinking of something in particular, but he didn't have time to question her. Brian might be dead already, but Maclean could not huddle in here if there was a chance to save him, no matter what he thought of him as a man.

"Mabbe."

"Mabbe? Maclean, I need a proper answer!"

"Then it is aye, something could come through the door from the between-worlds. I think that door has been opened, and I think that Ishbel has opened it. She is here, Bella, and she will do anything she can to make me suffer."

Bella stepped closer and wrapped her arms tight about him. "Maclean, please be careful!"

He hugged her briefly, and then lifted her face and bent to tenderly kiss her lips. "I will. But you must stay here where it is safe. Aye?"

His urgency got through to her at last.

"Aye . . . eh, yes."

With an unsmiling nod, Maclean left her. Closing the door firmly behind him, he looked up and saw her white face at the window, watching him.

"Be safe, Bella," he whispered. And then he turned up the path that led to Castle Drumaird.

Thirty

"*Hmmm-mmm.*" *Bella tried to remember* the words from Coldplay's latest, but they escaped her. She peered anxiously out of the kitchen window. She hadn't moved for so long that her body was stiff and cramped, a headache developing behind her eyes.

The weather was getting worse. The rain had stopped, but now a white mist was drifting across the landscape. In places it was so thick that it was impenetrable, although every now and then it would lift to show a stretch of green moorland or the still gray waters of the loch.

Just then, her heart beating fast, she saw something moving, only to realize in the next instant that it was one of Gregor's sheep.

Bella gave a nervous laugh. Maclean's talk of evil and doors to other worlds had disturbed her. She wanted to dismiss such stuff as superstitious nonsense, but she couldn't. Maclean was a man who had died and come back to life, who spoke of labyrinths and sorceresses. He was not like her, he was not like anyone else she had ever known. He had seen things, done things she could never hope to. Things she did not want to.

She shivered and, turning, saw the cold Aga. At least that was something she could do, she thought, as she busied herself replacing the ashes with more peats. It would take a while for the cottage to warm up, but by the time Maclean returned—with Brian—it should be cozier in here.

Just right for one of Brian's nasty little speeches.

Bella felt anger begin a slow burn inside her. *He can't hurt me now*, she reminded herself. *Because I don't care anymore what he thinks of me.* Brian would never change, but Bella had.

Where was Maclean?

Anxiously, Bella turned again to stare from the window, only to stop when she noticed the folded piece of cloth on her desk. Maclean must have brought it in with him, because she hadn't touched it. She hadn't been able to bring herself to do so.

Cautiously she approached it. There was a powerful force emanating from it, and she wasn't sure yet whether it was good or otherwise. Her fingers tingled as she reached out and flipped open the cloth. The tatty leather strips were still curled inside, the metal disks dull with age and dirt.

The magic bridle?

It was ludicrous. But even as Bella told herself such things did not . . . could not exist, she knew they did. This bridle might look innocent and harmless, but it wasn't. It was as if she could feel the thing stirring.

Waking. As if she could sense it, like a wave of warmth, enveloping her. *I'm here*, it was saying. *Look at me.*

Bella reached out and rested her hand on the bridle. She caught her breath. It *was* warm. The metal pieces in particular. They seemed almost to hum. There was some polish in the kitchen cupboard, and Bella went to fetch it. Tipping a few drops onto a soft cloth, she gently rubbed the very edge of one of the metal pieces. Only a couple of rubs were needed and she could see the bright silver shining through the grime.

Carefully she cleaned more. They were engraved, as Maclean had said. Bella peered closer, turning the silver to the light. A woman holding the bridle, a woman in a shawl or arisaid. Bella swallowed, and inspected another of the silver disks. This one showed a pony that appeared very much like the strange creature she had seen by the loch. The next, when she cleaned it, represented the woman and the pony, and the bridle was being lifted over the creature's head.

Bella was cleaning the final piece of silver—it seemed to show the pony in some sort of bother—when she heard a voice calling.

It was coming from the direction of the mist-covered loch. A drifting, mournful sound.

Bella, help me. . . .

Maclean stood among the ruins of Castle Drumaird. He had been calling, but no one had answered, and now he wasn't sure what to do. Brian might not be expecting another man to appear, and if he was suspicious he might not answer. It was difficult to see if anyone was hiding up here. The mist played games with him, tangling about his legs, blinding his eyes, so he proceeded with care, his broadsword by his side, searching the area as best he could.

He was worried about Bella. He believed she was safe in the cottage, but still he didn't like to be away from her for too long. There was a niggling sense of urgency inside his head and it was growing. He had just decided that Brian, unless he was lying dead or injured, could not have come this way, and that he should now return to the cottage and Bella, when he heard it.

A man's voice; Brian's voice. Calling for Bella to help him.

It was coming from the direction of the loch, near the *Cailleach* Stones.

Maclean froze, because he knew. He knew she would respond. Bella would not stay inside, in safety, when a man needed her help. Especially a man she knew well.

She would go to him.

And that was exactly what Ishbel wanted.

Life surged through him. With a desperate shout he headed for the path and began to run down it. His foot slipped on the wet earth, and then it was as if the very ground beneath him buckled and moved, throwing him from one side to the other. He lost his balance and could not regain it. Maclean found himself sliding and then falling, tumbling over and over on the muddy ground. Ishbel's laughter sounded in his head. He tried to save himself, reaching out to grasp at the tufts of grass, but they came away in his fingers. Then the side of his head struck the jagged edge of a rock.

Pain engulfed him. It numbed his thoughts and he couldn't remember what he had been doing. He lay, stunned, breathing heavily, and sliding in and out of consciousness.

Sleep, Maclean, sleep. Ye dinna need to go anywhere. Close your eyes, Maclean, and sleep.

Ishbel!

He tried to fight her, but the urgency in his head was muffled, distant.

Bella. I need to find Bella.

He didn't know how much time had passed, but gradually his own voice became clearer and louder.

Maclean knew he had to get up. He had to get to his feet and walk. He began to urge his arms and legs to bend, to move. He crawled a few yards, and then he stumbled upright, staggering and almost falling again on the steep slope. He groaned aloud at the jarring pain in his head, and then doubled over to be sick. Cursing, he wiped his mouth and spat before forcing himself upright once more.

His eyes wouldn't focus properly, and every step was agony as he began the journey down the remainder of the castle path. At last he reached the cottage. As he pushed against the unlocked door, crashing it against the wall, he immediately became aware of the warmth inside the empty kitchen. Bella had lit the Aga.

"Bella!" he shouted, hoping that he was wrong and she was here, upstairs, maybe. He forced his hurting body to climb the stairs, leaning his back to the wall, using it for support, knocking down framed pictures as he went. Glass broke and crunched underfoot, but he hardly noticed. He was calling out her name with increasing desperation, but he knew it was no use.

His Bella was gone.

*   *   *

Bella picked up her pace. The ground around the loch was mushy and the misty air was cold and clammy against her skin. She felt stifled, claustrophobic, and each step was an effort, but she couldn't go back.

Brian's voice had come from the direction of the old stones, the *Cailleach* Stones. Or at least she thought so. It was difficult to tell in the mist, where sounds were blunted or distorted, but she hoped she was heading in the right direction.

"Brian!" she called, but her voice didn't seem to travel very far.

Bella didn't let herself think about what might be happening to Brian, whether he was hurt, dying, drowning. It only made her feel sick and frightened and she needed to be calm and clear-headed. She needed to think and prepare.

"I should have waited for Maclean," she admitted to herself, but it was too late now. She'd been closer than Maclean, and Brian had called for her. She had to find him and help him. Anyway, it was Maclean who was in danger from Ishbel, not her. She should never have let him go out alone—

Abruptly one of the two upright *Cailleach* Stones rose before her. It was gone again as suddenly, but that glimpse through the mist was enough to reassure her she was where she thought she was. Confidently Bella stepped forward . . . straight into a patch of nettles.

She jumped back, but it was too late. Bella sucked in her breath with pain. The nettle leaves had stung her bare ankles, exposed between her socks and jeans, and with a curse she bent to rub at the painful lumps beginning to form on her burning skin.

"Bella."

Startled, she looked up, the nettle stings forgotten. It was Brian. He was sitting on the stone wall where she often sat, his hands folded in his lap, his head lowered. He was watching her with dull eyes and his skin was sickly white.

Her first thought was that he was injured in some way.

"Brian?" She straightened and took a step toward him, stretching out her hand. "Are you hurt?"

He didn't answer her, and for some reason she didn't want to touch him. She dropped her hand back to her side and stood frowning at him.

"Brian? What are you doing out here?"

Slowly, jerkily, he lifted his head.

"Brian?" Bella could feel something happening. The misty air was more oppressive, thicker, as if it were coming viscous. "Why won't you answer me?"

But he was looking beyond her. Behind her. His pupils grew larger until almost all of his iris was black, and he made a little whimpering sound in his throat.

She heard the sound behind her then. Hard spurting breaths as something heavy dragged itself over the ground, coming nearer.

Bella remembered the dream, the hag and her warning, and the monster reflected in her eyes. But this was no dream, this was real, and she could not turn. She could not look.

Brian's mouth opened and closed, but no sound came from it.

There was a smell, rank and fishy, and Bella heard water dripping. She cried out, or tried to. Whatever was behind her nudged her shoulder, and she felt a dull ache of pain as it caught her up in its jaws, holding her, securing her.

Her shoulder went numb.

Terror and shock rushed over her like a wave, deadening her senses and her mind, but she thought she heard a woman singing. Sweet, mesmerizing, the sound tugged her toward it. Not her body, her body was beyond movement, but something inside her. Her soul, maybe. The singing was drawing on her soul.

Bella felt her unresponsive body being lifted, carried, and then the loch was before her. The monster that had her slid into the water, away from the shallows and into the deeper parts. The icy loch closed over her legs, her chest. Somehow she lifted her head as the water reached her mouth, and called out the one word that meant everything to her, and then the cold water spilled into her mouth and nose, and there was no more air.

She sank down, down, where darkness embraced her.

And she ceased to be.

Maclean ran all the way to the *Cailleach* Stones.

He was still dizzy and sick from the blow to his head, but he forced away the weakness as he had been taught to do. The warrior within him took over the man, and he pushed himself onward. *I will no' fail her, I will no' fail her.* His legs pumped out the message as he ran. His heart beat the words over and over again through his blood. The scabbard of his *claidheamh mor* swung against his bare leg, and he kept his hand on the handle. Sweat dripped down his face and made wet patches on his shirt. And still he ran.

The mist was lifting rapidly now, as if its job were done. It was even starting to rain again, soft and constant. Peering ahead through eyes that refused to focus, he could see the broken wall and the *Cailleach* Stones. There was a man sitting there, in Bella's spot.

He knew it wasn't her, but Maclean's heart still thumped violently. Brian! Hope increased his flagging speed, and he pounded through the weeds and grass that surrounded the place where once the old ones had worshiped the goddess, before the priests and the preachers came and brought with them a scorn for all things magical.

When Maclean reached Brian he was so out of breath it took him precious moments to gasp out the words.

"Where's Bella?"

Brian didn't move; he didn't even look up. Maclean grasped his arms and shook him, but Brian dangled from his hands like a dead thing. He wrenched up the man's chin so that he could peer into his face. It was empty, as if his mind had left him. With a groan he let Brian go and turned around, searching the area, but there was nothing.

Bella was gone.

With a roar he jerked his broadsword free of its scabbard and swung it at the wild undergrowth, slicing the heads off dandelions and nettles. Violence gripped him, the need to find an outlet for his terrible pain, and as he slashed his blade he was not really seeing what he was doing. It wasn't until he stopped, chest heaving, that he realized he had uncovered something previously hidden beneath the long grass and weeds.

Maclean went down on one knee for a closer look.

Wool, stained and dirty, and part of the skin of a sheep. A carcass. The insides of it were gone, torn out and eaten, but the head remained. It was Gregor's missing sheep, or one of them, and something had rent it to pieces.

The same something that had taken Bella?

Maclean knelt on the wet ground and lifted his head, gazing up into the sky and letting the rain fall into his eyes. "Sorceress," he whispered through his aching throat, "help me. I canna find Bella. She went outside the cottage and I canna find her."

But the *Fiosaiche* was silent.

Maclean groaned and hung his head. Bella, beautiful Bella, in the hands of the *each-uisge*. Despair overwhelmed him. He felt it pressing on him, taking away his will to live.

"She said your name."

The voice came from the stone wall. It took a moment for Maclean to understand it was Brian who was speaking, and then he could only turn slowly, painfully. Brian still had his head bowed, but the voice had definitely come from him.

"What did ye say?"

This time Brian lifted his head, awkwardly, as if it were very heavy. His throat bobbed as he swallowed, forcing the words out as if they hurt. "You're Maclean, aren't you? Maclean, from Bella's book. I don't understand it, but I know it's true."

"Aye, I am Maclean."

"Bella, she called out your name as it took her. That thing. It took her into the loch. And I couldn't help her. I couldn't move a muscle."

Tears filled his eyes and his lips wobbled.

"I couldn't save her," Brian mumbled again.

Maclean climbed to his feet. He felt numb inside at the picture conjured by Brian's words. Bella had called out to him for help, she had called out for *him*, and he hadn't been here. Just like the last time.

"She's in the loch?" he said, his voice husky with the awful pain. "I must swim and find her."

"I think there is another way," Brian said, before Maclean could take more than a step. "Ishbel, she was singing to that—that *thing*, then she went through the stones."

Maclean stared at the *Cailleach* Stones. Gray and weathered, they had stood here for eons. The door into the between-worlds. But it was closed, and he knew he could not open it alone.

"Help me," he whispered. "You said to call on you for help and now I do. Help me, doorkeeper. Cast a spell, use your powers again."

"No, Maclean." Suddenly she was here, the hag, her face a wan oval within her green arisaid. A pale shadow of her former self, but she was here. "I canna cast a spell," she sighed, her milky eyes drowning in tears. "I am too weak, and besides, the *Fiosaiche* will no' allow it. You must go through the door alone and seek Bella in the labyrinths, where Ishbel has taken her. Go now, before it is too late."

"How?" he cried. "How do I open the door?"

She began to speak, Gaelic words of great age and

magical power. The *Cailleach* Stones shimmered and hummed, and there was a growing darkness at their edges. As Maclean stared, the space made by the two upright stones and the single cross stone flickered and blurred. And then there was a terrible rending sound and light began to pour from within the stones, light of a color and intensity he had never seen before.

"The door to the between-worlds is open." He could hear the hag's voice as if from a distance. "Go now. . . ."

Maclean stepped forward, into the strange light, and suddenly there before him was a narrow staircase made of shadows, and it led down. As far as the eye could see.

Thirty-one

There was something heavy resting on her legs. Bella lay on her stomach, cheek pressed against the damp cold ground, her eyes closed, trying to think what it could be. Her feet felt quite numb, as if the blood circulation had been cut off. She tried to wriggle her toes, but couldn't manage it.

Maybe my legs have been amputated in an accident and I'm lying by the side of the road bleeding to death.

The awful thought came from nowhere, but it was enough to startle her into movement.

Bella pushed herself up with her hands, and at the same time whatever was lying across her legs moved with a thunderous roar, splashing water over her. She screamed, rolling away, eyes wide.

She was lying on a beach and it was twilight.

The thing roared again, and she turned her head and saw it, long neck and humped body, propelling itself out into the waters of a black sea.

She had to run. She had to get away before it came back again.

Whimpering, Bella tried to rise, but her legs were still numb and she couldn't do more than drag herself a few feet. Maybe she'd lost the use of her legs forever, maybe she'd never be able to walk again, maybe . . . The sudden onset of pins and needles lay those fears to rest. She gritted her teeth and sat up, rubbing her unresponsive flesh to try and ease the pain, as she tried to understand what had happened to her.

I am dead.

Was this the between-worlds?

But it didn't look like the place Maclean had described, Bella thought, looking about her. She was in a cavern, an enormous cavern. The black sea washed the shores of a long curving beach, and there were cliffs at the far end and a fall of rocks close by. How had she come to be here, and what did it mean?

Pain jabbed her legs with a thousand needles and she rubbed at them frantically, tears burning her eyes. Her shoulder hurt, too, and when she tried to see what was wrong with it, she discovered her favorite red coat was torn and there was dried blood on the sweater beneath.

The monster had taken her into the loch.

With a shudder she remembered it all now.

It had taken her down into the water and she had believed herself dead. But now—she felt her clothes in amazement—she wasn't even wet, apart from lying on the damp sand. Was none of it real, not even Maclean?

"Maclean," she whispered.

"He's no' here," a voice said from a little distance away.

Bella's head snapped up. "Who's there?"

A woman slid down from her perch upon one of the rocks and stood on the sand, watching her. She wore trews in a red and green tartan with a jacket of a darker green. Her hair was long and fair, and her face pale and beautiful.

And Bella felt chilled to the bone by the sight of her.

"I am Ishbel," she said, sauntering closer. "We have met before."

"Have we? I don't remember it. What is this place?"

"This is my home. Do ye no' like it, Arabella Ryan? This is the place Maclean condemned me to, and that"—she pointed out into the black sea— "is the company I keep."

"Maclean did not condemn you to this," Bella replied sharply. "You did it to yourself."

Ishbel came closer, her green eyes unblinking. "I asked him to let me go. I begged him to give me my freedom so that I could find happiness. He would not. He came after me and killed my love. So I returned to Loch Fasail and destroyed all within it, and then I went to Castle Drumaird to kill his mother. She was no' so easy to kill. The building was afire and I followed her into the heart of it, up the stairs. She cursed me for killing her son, and when I stabbed her with my dagger, she clung to me so fast I could no' free myself. She took me down into the flames with her."

Dear God. Bella longed to cry out against the awfulness of what she said, but she knew that was what Ishbel wanted. To shock her; to weaken her.

"You died at Loch Fasail? Why do you blame Maclean for it, then? It was your choice." Somehow she succeeded in sounding almost nonchalant.

Ishbel looked puzzled, just for an instant. "No, it was *his* choice, he brought all this about, and now he will pay for my misery."

"He's already paid for it."

"Not enough. He has not suffered enough."

"He has in the *Fiosaiche*'s opinion."

Ishbel frowned. "Your tongue is insolent. I will have my creature bite it out."

Bella felt dizzy with horror, but that was what Ishbel wanted and she refused to let her have the pleasure. Maclean's voice came to her, *Dinna let fear overwhelm you, Bella, and make you weak. Keep it chained, use it, and dinna let it use you.*

She made herself reply evenly, "Your creature didn't kill me last time. Maybe it isn't as obedient as you think."

"I ordered him not to kill you," Ishbel said testily. "Not yet."

Bella had regained the feeling in her legs, and now she got shakily to her feet. If she had to fight for her life, she'd prefer to be standing. Maybe she could run to safety? But, looking about her, there didn't seem to be anywhere to run. The beach was very long and the loch monster would catch her, and that would only amuse Ishbel.

If it comes for me I won't run, she told herself.

Something out in the black waters howled and splashed.

I'll try *not to run*, she amended.

"You say this is your home?" Bella asked, hoping her voice didn't tremble as much as the rest of her.

Ishbel smiled. "This is the between-worlds, Bella, where the souls of those who are neither dead nor living dwell. We are waiting here for the *Fiosaiche* to decide what becomes of us. She rules here . . . or thinks she does," Ishbel added slyly.

Bella dug her hands into her pockets, to warm them, to stop them from shaking.

"She wants me to say I am sorry," Ishbel mimicked viciously, "to show remorse."

"Perhaps you should," Bella said, as if her mind were on something else.

"But I am not sorry."

Bella believed it. Ishbel wasn't human, she had lost whatever it was that made her so. She was as cold and vicious as the creatures she ruled, and there could be no reprieve when she decided to take Bella's life. Bella wondered why she had not done so already, but whatever the reason for the delay, she was grateful. Another minute probably didn't count for much, but every breath Bella took bought her a chance to get away.

"How did you get through the door into my world if the *Fiosaiche* is in charge? Doesn't she have it all locked up tight?"

Ishbel smirked. "The witch is no' as clever as she thinks she is. In the ancient days the loch was a door used by the monsters. It was sealed, but I found it again, with the help of the hag. I made her feel sorry for me, *poor* Ishbel, and she told me what I wanted to know, how to open the stones and how to cast spells, how to creep into dreams. Nothing is beyond me now."

Bella shrugged off the boasting. "So there must be a similar door into Loch Ness," she murmured. "It would explain—"

"I dinna care for Loch Ness. *My* creature has been visiting Loch Fasail regularly, feeding on sheep and anything else that wanders too close. And I sent one of my father's men through the door, too, on his horse. To kill you, Arabella Ryan. I'm sure ye have no' forgotten that. Maclean interfered, playing the big hero, but he canna stop me this time."

Bella stilled. She had been twisting her fingers nervously in the bundle of cloth in her coat pocket, feeling the old leather strips and the silver disks, without remembering what it was.

The bridle.

When Brian called out to her, she had been polishing the thing and by chance had shoved it into her pocket.

Ye must watch for when the each-uisge *is changing its form. That is when it is vulnerable. That is when it can be captured. Ye must have the magic bridle at hand. Dinna worry, I will see to it that you have such a thing before the time comes.*

Or perhaps it was more than chance.

Slip the bridle on, but remember, the creature will no' be easily restrained, and if it knows what ye are about then it will kill you.

Bella did not want to die. She tightened her grip on the bridle in her pocket and wondered if she would have the chance to use it. The mental strength to use it.

She could die, or she could be alive when Maclean came for her.

And he would come for her, she knew that. He loved her as much as she loved him, and he would find her.

Maclean's head brushed the dank ceiling of the tunnel, and he ducked lower, ignoring the crunch and crackle of crawling things dying under his feet. The labyrinths were just as deeply appalling as he remembered. Worse. Because he knew Bella was here, too.

Bella should not be part of this; she would not survive it. She didn't deserve it. He wanted to wish he had never met her, never drawn her into his nightmare, but he couldn't. She had made him mortal again, she had changed him from a dark and bitter creature into a man with hope.

Without her he was nothing, and would be nothing again.

"Bella," he groaned, "where are ye?"

Another turn in the tunnel. The ceiling seemed even lower, so that he was bent almost double as he moved forward. But there was no use turning back; he knew he had to go forward no matter what obstacles he encountered.

Water dripped.

Maclean wiped a hand across his face and felt the smear of blood and grime. The wound where his head had struck the stone had stopped bleeding now, but he still had a headache and it didn't help him to think clearly. Something scuttled into the shadows, watching him with luminous eyes, but he ignored it and pushed on.

After a wee while he realized that there was a pale glow up ahead, as if dawn were breaking through a long dark night. Maclean fixed his eyes on it and moved forward.

Bella gave Ishbel a sideways glance and tried not to let her growing anxiety show. The woman was annoyed. Bella had found a way to get under her skin. Despite Ishbel's threats and sly innuendos, Bella hadn't allowed herself to show any feeling. She shrugged her shoulder when Ishbel told her she would be torn to pieces by the loch monster, and, when Ishbel lingered on the details, replied that she wouldn't make much of a meal for something so big. She smiled vaguely when Ishbel swore to make her suffer more than any mortal woman had ever suffered. She sang a Dido song under her breath and pretended to inspect her nails when Ishbel raised her arms and cried out, and her creature answered her with a truly hideous howling.

Somehow she had to get Ishbel angry enough to transform into the *each-uisge*. Then she could use the bridle and save herself.

"My darling, my beloved," Ishbel was crooning. She cast Bella a vicious look. "It took me centuries to tame him, to make him mine, and now I will reward him with your flesh and blood, and we will travel through the door in the loch together and teach your world the power of the old magic."

"My world will laugh at you," Bella said. "We don't believe in magic anymore."

"You will be dead soon."

"You don't like to get your own hands dirty, then?" Bella asked. "You like to stand back and order your creature to do it for you?"

"You are beneath me," Ishbel said coldly.

"And maybe you're all talk," Bella retorted. "Maybe the best you can do is steal Gregor's sheep. Was it you who ate them? The terrible *each-uisge* chasing harmless sheep about. I'm shaking in my boots—"

Ishbel seemed to swell. "You insult me," she said, and her voice was different, odd. Her body shimmered, moving, realigning itself.

Bella's fingers tightened on the bridle in her pocket.

"You will see. I will kill you and eat you mysel'," Ishbel roared, and her head was stretching, changing into an animal's head, while her body rose and broadened. Bella recognized the pony. Ishbel was turning into the *each-uisge*, and in a moment the transformation would be complete.

It would be too late.

Bella dragged the bridle from her pocket, fumbling, twisting the leather strips into the correct position. They were tangled and for a moment she thought she wouldn't be able to open them in time, but then the silver disks fell into place, the bridle opened, and she was rushing forward, her heart hammering.

Ishbel was arching above her, and Bella could see the equine snout and those wicked green eyes. The silver disks flashed and Ishbel flinched, but it was too late. Bella slipped the bridle over Ishbel's head as if it had been made to fit, and as Ishbel opened her jaws, Bella pushed the bit between her sharp teeth. And pulled the bridle tight.

Ishbel screamed, a terrible sound that was neither woman nor mare but something of both. She spun away, stumbling back and forth, her head weaving as she tried to rid herself of the bridle. Her shape shivered grotesquely, one moment horse and the next woman, and sometimes both.

Bella staggered back, gasping, too shocked to speak.

"Bella!"

There was a lone figure standing far down the beach. A big man in a plaid with his legs bare, his dark hair loose to his shoulders, and his broadsword held ready before him.

"Maclean," she breathed, and she was smiling. She couldn't help it. "Maclean!" she shouted, waving her arms.

The thing that was neither Ishbel nor *each-uisge* twisted and writhed, churning the sand. It screamed again, and now the monster in the black ocean heard. There was a great splash as it lifted itself up out of the water and replied with a groaning howl. Then it sprang forward.

Maclean was running toward her.

He knows, Bella thought, as her horrified gaze drifted to the water's edge. *He knows that the loch monster is coming for me. And he knows that he'll never reach me in time.*

Thirty-two

The loch monster was coming. As he ran, Maclean could see its head cresting the surface of the water, those savage eyes fixed on the shore where Bella stood. She had done something to Ishbel to incapacitate her, but he didn't know what, and he didn't care. All his attention was focused now on the loch monster and the need to stop it. He knew what it was capable of doing to Bella.

He knew that he would die for her, if he had to.

The monster reached the shallows and lumbered forward. The black shiny body was clumsy out of water but no less deadly. Water sprayed from its flipperlike legs as it picked up speed and the ground shook. The long snake neck weaved about, and it gave a moaning cry. And Bella didn't move. She stood before it, frozen, her head tilted back as it loomed above her.

Maclean pushed his strength, increasing his speed along the wet sand. He was closing in. His heart pounded, his breath was a ragged gasp, and he raised his *claidheamh mor*.

The monster lifted its head and howled again, the sound echoing all around them. Ishbel screamed in response, unable to escape whatever it was Bella had fixed about her face. The loch monster paused, as if preparing itself, and then it dove, straight at Bella.

Maclean took one last stride, and with a roar swung his broadsword down in a powerful and savage blow. The blade connected with the monster's neck, and he felt it jar on the hard scales and then bite. The monster, sensing his arrival, was too late to save itself completely, but was able to pull away from the full deadly power of his strike.

It had saved itself from being decapitated, but it was wounded.

With a low growl it lumbered to one side, turning awkwardly for another attack. Maclean pushed Bella behind him, and turned to face it.

"Dear God." He heard her whisper, and risked a glance. Her face was white, her dark hair tangled, and her eyes enormous. But she was alive and it was his intention to keep her that way.

"Run," he told her hoarsely. "Bella, run."

"There's nowhere to run," she said. "And anyway, you're here."

He swore, but it was in Gaelic and she couldn't understand. The monster was watching him with its large eyes, and now it feinted an attack, trying to force him forward, and Maclean realized it was far more intelligent than he had imagined. It feinted again, and this time he swung his sword, keeping the creature at bay.

He began to back farther up the beach, Bella still behind him, away from the monster's home—the water—away from where it was most comfortable.

The monster seemed to know what he was doing and roared its disapproval.

"What is the matter with Ishbel?"

He felt her cold hand at his back, clinging to his shirt. "The bridle," she said, her voice breaking. "The magic bridle."

Maclean didn't have time to consider what she meant. The loch beastie charged forth again, lunging at him ferociously. He thrust at it with his sword, trying to spear it in the head, but it withdrew at the last moment, swinging to one side with surprising nimbleness. He was caught off balance. He saw the wicked eye on him, the cruel triumph in it, and then it dove down on him again before he could adjust his position to protect himself.

He felt the impact, like a giant's fist pounding his shoulder. Luckily the monster had not been able to rake him with its teeth; the blow had been from its powerful neck, but it was enough. Maclean fell and struck the sand heavily. The broadsword was jarred from his grip.

Bella cried out something, but his skull was ringing with agony. When he landed on the sand he'd hit his head in the very same place as before, when he'd fallen on the rocks near the castle ruins, and the pain was so bad he was unable to function. His stomach lurched, the cavern spun dizzily. He could not remember where he was and why.

There was someone tugging at him, hurting him, and

he growled, trying to shove them away. "Leave me be. . . ."

"Maclean!" She was gasping, dragging at his arms, pulling him along the sand a few steps and then a few more. "Maclean, get up, get up. *Please*, get up!"

Her urgency pierced the fog. Maclean groaned and rolled onto his belly, pushing himself up on all fours. She was still hauling at him, trying to get him to his feet, but he shook her off and staggered upright alone. He lifted his head, although it hurt so much he thought he would faint, and that was when he saw it. The monster. It was moving, heaving itself over the sand toward him. Faster than he would have believed possible for such an enormous beast.

"My sword, Bella," he said in a strangely even voice, as if his belly were not clenching in nausea and terror, and his head were not exploding with pain.

The monster's neck stretched out and up, ready for the final diving blow. The killing blow.

Bella put the *claidheamh mor* into his hands, her fingers cold and shaking, and he gripped the handle hard and hefted the blade at an angle, the point up. The monster's head came down, jaws wide, and he thrust the blade deep. Into its throat.

For a moment it didn't seem to realize what had happened to it. It pressed hard onto his blade, impaling itself even further and knocking him down so that he fell to one knee, trembling with the effort not to be crushed. And then the monster wrenched away, head weaving back and forth, roaring and groaning, the sword still lodged deep in its throat. The ground shook with its fury and distress. It rose up and pounded down on the sand.

The sword dislodged and fell from its jaws, but Maclean did not try to retrieve it. He was beyond such effort, his body weak and aching, his head throbbing. He sat down on the sand, Bella huddled beside him, as the monster tumbled heavily to one side. It dragged itself up again, moving toward the *each-uisge* that was Ishbel.

Gently, almost tenderly, it took her in its jaws, and then hauled its big body into the shallows, finding new strength once it reached deep water. For a moment they were visible, Ishbel's long fair hair floating in darkness, and then they sank beneath the inky waves.

Slowly Maclean became aware that Bella's arms were tight around him, her cheek pressed so hard to his it was almost painful. But he didn't care; she was warm and soft and there was no one else in this world or any other he'd rather be with.

"I love you, Maclean," Bella was saying, as if they were the last words she ever expected to speak.

He groaned and turned to kiss her lips, and then he fell back onto the sand and lay unmoving.

Bella wailed, frantically pressing her hands to him, searching for the fatal wound she seemed so certain he had, wiping away the blood that trickled from the cut on his head.

"He's alive."

Bella looked up, her arm across Maclean's body as if she would shield him from further attack. The woman standing before her was slight, but she wore a silver cloak, had auburn hair that was brilliant in the gloomy cavern, and her eyes were like blue ice. Goose bumps lifted all over Bella's body, and she knew she was meeting the *Fiosaiche* at last.

"Maclean will recover," the sorceress said in her low, commanding voice. "He has done what had to be done."

"I'm glad you're pleased." Bella heard the anger in her own voice and could not stop it.

The *Fiosaiche* smiled as if Bella's emotion amused her. "I am."

There was something truly awful in her smile. And her eyes . . . there were things in her eyes . . . Bella looked away with a shudder. "Can we go home now?" she asked in a much smaller, far more respectful voice. "Please."

The *Fiosaiche* sighed. "Of course. But you will have to decide, Arabella Ryan, where home is."

"Why does everyone have to call me by my full name?" Bella complained miserably. She gave the sorceress a brief glance—it was all she could manage. "What do you mean, I will have to decide where home is?"

"You will see."

"Please will someone tell me straight out what is going on!"

The sorceress smiled. "You cannot know everything, Arabella Ryan, it is not your place to know all I know. You must be patient. You must wait."

"Bella?" Maclean was staring at her. He started to sit up and she helped him, glaring at the *Fiosaiche* as if daring her to stop her.

"It is time, Maclean," the sorceress said firmly. "You

have done all I wished and more. You are the man I always thought you to be. Now you must go."

"To the world of the dead?" he asked bleakly, his fingers tightening on Bella's.

"No, you are not ready to die. You must go back to your own time and prove to me my faith in you was well placed."

"Home?" he whispered, and his face shone with joy. And then he remembered. "Can I no' stay here, with Bella?"

For a moment Bella allowed herself to imagine it, Maclean and herself, together, living a sort of eighteenth century life in twenty-first century Scotland. And then she remembered that even if it was possible to do that, they could not. The loch was going to change, Gregor was building a road.

"Maclean," she said sadly, "there's something I haven't told you." Briefly she explained what Gregor planned.

He sat in silence as he listened to her, but she could tell how much her words upset him. When she was done, he took her in his arms and buried his face in her hair.

"I'm so, so sorry," she whispered. "But even if the road wasn't going to happen, you'd have to go back to the past. That's your destiny, Maclean. That's where you belong. We both know that—we've always known it."

He touched her cheek and his eyes were fierce. "And what of you?"

"I must write my book. If . . . if you don't manage to save your people, then at least I'll have set history straight. You'll be remembered just as you always should have been."

"You will do that for me, Arabella?" he said, suddenly humble.

"Yes, of course." She was surprised he would think otherwise.

There was an expression in his eyes. Love. Regret. Sorrow. Her heart squeezed.

Take me with you. The words were burning her tongue, but Bella swallowed them back down. It was impossible. Maclean belonged to the past and that was where his life was, while she had her own life, here. Their parting was inevitable and she must accept it, but the thought of being alone, without Maclean, made her feel so very empty.

"I am not my own man, Bella, not really. I'm the Chief of the Macleans of Fasail, and I canna put my own feelings above them, not again."

"I know. You don't have to explain."

He leaned to rest his brow against hers. "I love ye, Bella. You're the woman of my heart, of my body, of my soul. I ne'er thought to meet such a one as you. I canna believe I am letting you go."

A tear escaped and trickled down her cheek. "I love you, too, Maclean," she whispered. "I never knew what that was until you came. You've changed me, made me stronger."

"You always were strong, my love. Promise me you will smile that beautiful smile and no' be too serious, when I am gone."

"Oh, Maclean." She wiped her cheeks with the heels of her hands.

He tilted up her chin and kissed her. "I'll never forget you . . . us," he murmured, nuzzling her cheek, her neck, his mouth warm against her cool skin. "Mabbe when you look up into the night sky you will think of me looking up, too. Aye, the same sky for both of us."

"It is time."

Bella's heart began to pound as she sensed the sorceress growing impatient. Maclean stood up.

I love him.

How would she live the rest of her life without him? The pain was like a great wave, no less agonizing because she had always known they would have to part eventually. No fairy-tale ending.

There was a light in the cavern, pouring forth from the *Fiosaiche*'s outstretched fingers, and growing brighter. It was a strange, pure color, unlike anything Bella had ever seen before. She shielded her eyes.

"Are you ready?" The sorceress's voice was strangely gentle.

"I am." Maclean sounded both stoic and resigned.

"Then walk into the light. Say what you must, but do not wait too long, Maclean. I haven't all day. I have the between-worlds to see to and the doors to close."

Maclean frowned. "I have a favor to ask you, Sorceress. The old woman who is the doorkeeper at the *Cailleach* Stones, Ishbel tricked her, aye, but she helped me to protect Bella. She opened the way to the labyrinths to me. I ask that you treat her kindly."

The *Fiosaiche* smiled. Her face seemed to ripple, and Bella stared as for a moment the skull-like face and stringy white hair of the hag of her dreams was superimposed upon the sorceress's serene features. In another moment she was gone, and the *Fiosaiche* said, "Ishbel thought she was very clever, but I always knew what she was up to. Part of the task I set you was to defeat her, Maclean, and at the same time be willing to give up your new life to save Arabella Ryan's. But I knew you needed some help—you couldn't do it all on your own—so I chose to turn myself into the hag."

"But why?" he burst out, clearly confused by her deception.

"If you knew it was me, then you would have asked for too much, you would have asked too many questions, you might even have wanted me to do your work for you. The hag gave you just enough to help you along the road I had chosen. And you did well, Maclean. I am very pleased. Now . . . say your goodbyes."

Maclean caught Bella into his arms and held her painfully tight.

"Bella," he breathed.

Bella didn't realize she was shaking her head until Maclean reached out to touch her cheek, running his knuckles over her soft skin. "I love ye," he said. "I always will. My heart will always be here." He touched her breast. "With yours."

The tears were hot on her cheeks, but she didn't try to hide them or stop them.

"I'll write your book, Maclean," she promised. "I'll make people see you as you should be seen. As a wonderful chief and a great man."

He smiled. "I'm no' a great man, but mabbe a man who cared for his people and kept them safe in terrible times. Aye, that should be my epitaph, Bella. I kept my clan safe through terrible times. Will you say that about me?"

"I promise."

He nodded, then bent his head and kissed her mouth with great tenderness. "That must last me for a verra long time," he said with a bleak smile. "Goodbye, Arabella Ryan."

She watched him walk away, into the light. It hurt her eyes, but she would not close them, not until he had finally vanished from sight.

"Arabella Ryan."

After a time Bella realized the light was gone and the *Fiosaiche* was still standing on the sand with her silver cloak wrapped around her, her auburn hair stirred by a nonexistent breeze. Bella stared back, hating the woman, even though she knew she had no right to. The *Fiosaiche* had saved Maclean, and now he was where he had wanted to be.

"You must go back to your time, too," the sorceress said sternly. "Let me—"

"I don't understand," Bella cut in. "How can you change time like this? It's impossible! There are too many threads woven into it, too many factors to take into account. Change one thing and millions of others are automatically changed, too."

"Just because it seems impossible to you doesn't mean I can't do it, Arabella Ryan."

"Tell me. I want to know."

"I will tell you this . . . the change will not happen quickly, it takes time, like a ripple moving outward. History is a slow, unwieldy machine. You will not know in your time for a year or more whether Maclean has succeeded."

"But I have to know!"

The *Fiosaiche* smiled.

The sands were shivering, as if from an earthquake, and then the cavern seemed to grow smaller, until it was just a pinpoint in the distance. Bella was moving, traveling so fast she was dizzy. The air rushed by her, and there was darkness and there were voices wailing and crying out. Narrow black tunnels and things she had never seen before nor wanted to again. But before she could scream, it was over. The movement, the rush of air stopped, and there was only silence. Bella opened her eyes and found she was lying on the damp grass near the *Cailleach* Stones, the weak sunlight shining in her face and Brian bending over her.

Thirty-three

"I thought you were dead," he kept saying. "I don't understand. I thought you were dead."

"Brian, go to sleep." Her soothing tone was growing edgy. "You'll feel better in the morning. We can talk then."

They had made their way slowly, wearily back from the stones to the cottage. Bella was sure her shoulder was injured, but when Brian examined it he found only heavy bruising. The loch monster had broken the skin, she'd seen the blood, but somehow the wound had mended. Maybe she had the *Fiosaiche* to thank for that.

Wearing her blue robe and slippers, and giving Brian a don't-you-dare-say-anything look, Bella heated soup and rolls, and they ate them with sips of the whiskey Maclean had brought back from Inverness and never had time to drink.

Now pleasantly light-headed, Bella was insisting Brian go to bed. He looked white-faced and exhausted and still very confused.

"But how could he come through time, Bella?"

"After he died he was in the between-worlds and then the *Fiosaiche* put him to sleep until the right moment came for him to . . . eh, redeem himself. To become the man he should always have been. You see, he made a mistake, and because of that history took a wrong turn. He's earned himself another chance. That's where he is now, back in the eighteenth century, putting things right."

Brian stared at her as if she were speaking gibberish.

"I'm still going to write the book," Bella went on, more to herself than to Brian. "I need to write it. Even if he does change history, and I suppose that means everything else will change—the legend and the stories about him and the massacre. At least, I imagine that's what will happen. Somehow. But I still need to write the book, just in case."

"So, if he changes history, will you and I still exist?"

"I suppose so. I tried to ask the *Fiosaiche*, but . . ." She shrugged. "I get the feeling it isn't like an episode of *Star Trek*."

"Will Ishbel still be that . . . that thing?"

"Not if everything works out this time."

"She was so beautiful," Brian whispered. "Just like a woman should be. Perfect."

Bella laughed. *Perfect?* Trust Brian to fall under the evil spell of a water-horse! At least his taste in women was one thing she could be sure would never change.

"The *Fiosaiche* said I wasn't supposed to know everything, that it wasn't my place. Perhaps we mortals aren't capable of understanding some things—perhaps if we did, we'd go crazy."

Eventually Brian did go to bed, leaving Bella alone in the kitchen. She sat by the Aga, exhausted and yet not wanting to sleep. Maclean was gone. Was he living right now in some world that existed right alongside hers? Or was he dead and dust, his life long over? She preferred to think of him alive, in Castle Drumaird, ruling his clan wisely and well. He would not fail this time, but she had promised him she'd write her book and so she would.

Tomorrow she'd begin work. Tomorrow. . . . But for now . . . she wanted to remember every moment, linger on every word, every touch and kiss they had ever exchanged. Bella didn't want to believe that such important things would fade from her memory, but common sense told her they would. And she couldn't bear that.

Because memories were all she had left.

The women were gathering in the great hall of Castle Drumaird. Maclean could hear the noise they made as he strode into the cavernous room and walked toward his chair. When they caught sight of him, there was a hush, which quickly turned into anxious whispers. Once seated, he looked up and saw his mother, her eyes so like his own. He could see her gathering her courage, searching for the words that would bridge so many years of mistrust and pain between them.

She began her speech, just as he remembered it.

"Our menfolk have barely come home from Culloden Moor, Morven, and we do no' yet know what will happen to us because of the Rebellion. There are whispers that the English have sent ships to our coast carrying men who are ready to burn out traitors. Ye should be traveling to Inverness to ask pardon. Ye should be vowing your allegiance to King George. But now ye wish to take us with ye into further danger. I say *no*, Morven."

When he did not reply, she took a breath and carried on.

"Ishbel vowed to pay ye back. She swore it, we all heard her. Dinna go after her. There is something wrong about this matter. For your own sake, Morven, dinna go after Ishbel. Dinna do this thing. I know matters have no' always been well between us, but listen to me. Stay home here, and keep us safe."

Maclean sat forward. "Mother, I thank you for your concern, but I have no intention of following Ishbel."

There was a shocked silence. The women gaped at him, their faces almost comical.

"Ye will accede to our wishes?" his mother whispered. "Ye will no' go after Ishbel?"

"No, I will no' go after Ishbel. She is gone, she doesna want me, and to force her to my will would diminish us both. My duty is to stay here with my people. If Culloden Moor taught me one thing, then it was that this is where I belong."

A tear ran down her cheek.

"You have great wisdom, Mother. Do not fear to speak to me again on any matter, for I will always listen."

"Listen to a woman?" his mother cried out in her surprise. "Your father would never listen to me. He said there was little to distinguish women and sheep when they bleated."

Maclean stood up, and there was instant silence again. They stared at him as if he were a god, and although before that had always seemed to him the correct attitude, now he knew he was no deity. The idea of being invincible and always correct made his lips twitch. Bella had set him right and he would not forget.

"I am not my father," he reminded them quietly. "You should not confuse the two." His mouth quirked into a smile. "Besides, my temper is much better than his."

Relief made them loud in their laughter.

The ache inside him sharpened. *Bella.* He had sacrificed himself and his happiness for the sake of his people, and that was as it had to be, he knew that, but would this be enough? The English troops were still at Mhairi hunting rebels, Ishbel was still alive, and her father was weak and easily led. Maclean knew he had been at Culloden Moor, even if he had not fought, and that put everyone at risk.

He was in danger, his clan was in danger. Life had never been more uncertain. He should be glad that Bella was safe in her own time, where such things were only lines one read in a history book.

But he missed her as sharply as if she were a vital part of himself, and he knew he always would. Without her he was an empty shell of a man.

"Maclean?"

The voice was coming from above him, and he looked up. An eagle was perched on the rafters above him, gazing down with golden eyes. He blinked, suddenly dizzy. Did no one else see it? But when he looked about him, it was as if time had stopped for all the others in the hall. Only he and the eagle were allowed to move and speak.

"Maclean," the eagle said, "all will be well. In

Bella's time it is *Samhain*, the night when the doors between all the worlds are open and the spirits walk free. I think you deserve your happiness. I am a great believer in the power of true love. Now listen to me, Maclean, one last time. I have something to tell you. . . ."

"Congratulations!" Elaine's voice over the phone was warm and excited. "I've just read the new manuscript. You've outdone yourself, Bella, it's absolutely marvelous. *The Black Maclean: Bravery in Terrible Times*."

"You like it, then?"

"I more than like it. I love it! Maclean sounds like a real hero, and I'm sure he'll appeal to the same readers who enjoyed *Martin's Journey*." She hesitated. "We should talk about publicity."

Bella had done a couple of radio interviews for *Martin's Journey*, and they no longer bothered her. She was stronger, more confident, and she knew she would never be afraid again. Not many people, she reminded herself, had faced a loch monster and escaped alive.

The lease on the cottage had not been extended—Gregor didn't feel it was fair for her to stay when the bulldozers were coming in. So Bella had gone to Edinburgh and found an apartment there. Brian had been to visit her a few times. They didn't speak of the day at Loch Fasail, Bella because she did not want to share her precious memories with anyone and Brian because they frightened him too much.

Bella wondered if he was wanting a reconciliation, but she knew she wasn't interested. Apart from the fact she had well and truly moved on from Brian, she knew she could never love again. She was still in love with

Maclean. He was *the* love of her life and no other man would ever come close.

She had finished the Black Maclean book in six weeks, writing day and night. When it was done she had been so exhausted that she slept for forty-eight hours. Now she just felt flat. Empty. And sad.

"Let's talk about that later," she said now to Elaine on the phone. "There's plenty of time."

"Bella . . ."

"I know, I know. I'm not bailing on you, I promise."

Elaine gave an exaggerated sigh. "Very well. Take a break. I'll send the manuscript over to the publisher and then get back to you."

"Thanks, Elaine."

Bella put the phone down.

While she was writing she had managed to set aside the bleak fact that she would never see Maclean again. He had come alive in her book and she had felt close to him once more, almost as if he were there in the room with her. But now that the book was finished, she had to face the truth.

It seemed a long time ago that she had sat in the kitchen of Drumaird Cottage and wondered whether the core of loneliness inside her would ever be filled. And then Maclean had come and suddenly she was no longer just Bella, she was the other half of someone else. How could she go back to being simply Bella again?

She could survive, of course she could. She was strong. But the reason to go on seemed diminished.

Oh, Maclean.

Her throat tightened and she swallowed down the

tears, refusing to weep. She had cried enough tears to fill a loch. But the ache remained, threatening to paralyze her.

Impatient with herself, Bella strode out of her apartment and into the chill Edinburgh day. Late afternoon was already casting its shadow over the gray buildings and spires of the city. She walked toward Charlotte Street, her head down, ignoring passersby, ignoring the traffic. She didn't really care where she went, but the simple act of walking helped her to overcome the misery that sometimes came upon her like a suffocating wave. Perhaps she'd make her way down historic Princes Street to the gardens. It would be cold and austere. Perfect for her current mood.

"Arabella."

The voice was a murmur on the breeze, very soft, but Bella heard it.

"Arabella Ryan."

Now it was a woman's voice, commanding. And very familiar.

Shocked, Bella lifted her head, staring wildly about her. But there was no one standing close by. She was alone on the windswept and suddenly almost empty street.

"Arabella!"

Louder, shriller.

Bella looked up into the air, just as a golden eagle swept down from the sky, flashing by her so closely that the tip of its wing brushed her cheek.

She cried out, staggering back.

The eagle flapped away over the Old Town, rising above the tall buildings and gliding by the towers of St.

Cuthbert's Church, in the direction of the sprawling Castle. In a moment it was a mere speck in the sky. Bella did not move, standing and watching it go. The eagle was heading northwest, into the bleak and lonely Highlands. Loch Fasail was in that direction.

The eagle was going home.

Thirty-four

It was Samhain. Hallowe'en. Bella had not known the date's significance when she set off in her car to drive the six hours it took to reach Loch Fasail from Edinburgh. Lately everyday details just passed her by, but she heard them talking about it on the car radio, joking about ghosties and ghoulies and things that go bump. Outside the warm safety of her vehicle, the darkness had closed in early. The long twilights were finally behind them.

She drove through the rush of Edinburgh and passed by sparser towns and villages. The chatter and noise of modern civilization faded, as she entered the solitary world of the glens and the mountains. The loneliness should have made her heart heavy, but instead it seemed to have a cleansing effect. She turned off the radio and listened to the silence.

Bella was coming home, and she dared not think beyond that.

The journey from Ardloch was the most difficult part. The road seemed darker and narrower than she remembered, and there were fresh potholes, probably made by the heavy machinery. As she reached the final rise above Loch Fasail, she slowed and looked out over the place that was engraved on her heart. There was the grim ruin of Castle Drumaird against the night sky, and the cottage huddled below it. The car rolled forward and her headlights swept across the moorland. Suddenly one of Gregor's sheep appeared, making her jump. The animal turned and ran off. Smiling at herself, the intensity of the moment broken, Bella drove to the empty cottage.

She could see now, in the headlights, the torn earth where the bulldozers had been working. Some of the machines were still here, ready to resume their work in daylight. She could hardly bear to look at what they had done. At least most of the destruction was on the other side of the loch and not here, where she and Maclean had once walked together.

The cottage key was hidden in the same place as always, and Bella let herself inside. Everything seemed so quiet and eerie, and though Bella found the flashlight in the kitchen drawer, its feeble light did little to reassure her. The cottage was cold and depressing. There was nothing for her here. Even the ghosts of Maclean and Bella were gone. They existed only in her head now.

Maybe it had been a mistake coming back.

Bella wandered outside again and stood, blindly staring out over the still waters of the loch.

There were colors in the water, she realized. Green and yellow, with a touch of blue. Startled, it was a moment before she realized what she was seeing was a reflection, and looked up. The northern lights, the aurora borealis, swept along the horizon, the strange and remarkable colors strobing the sky. So beautiful. Another of the wonders of these empty northern lands.

Mabbe when you look up into the night sky you will think of me looking up, too. Aye, the same sky for both of us.

Was Maclean looking at these lights even now, wondering at their ethereal beauty and thinking of her?

"He's gone," Bella told herself. "He really is gone, and I can never see him again. . . ."

Bella began to walk along the loch in the direction of the *Cailleach* Stones. She would sit on the wall there until dawn, and then she'd drive home to Edinburgh. She wouldn't come back again. Being here was like picking at a wound, never quite letting it heal. Best to let it be, best to try and put it behind her. It was her only chance of survival. . . .

Her steps slowed.

There was someone already sitting in her spot on the wall.

For a moment she couldn't breathe, memories of Ishbel and her creature filling her head. But this was a person with broad shoulders and a long back, and the tilt of his head was so familiar she felt dizzy.

She forced herself to take another step, and another, stumbling on the uneven ground. He looked up; he'd seen her.

"Och, Bella, I've been waiting for ye."

"Maclean? Maclean, is it really you?"

"Aye, 'tis me." He was smiling, she could hear it in

the husky warmth of his voice. "I came through the door, Bella."

Tears burned her eyes, her mouth trembled, but it was anger that filled her. Hot, searing, unstoppable anger.

"Just like that? Why did you wait so long? I have been *sick* with missing you."

He stood up, at a loss, hesitating to touch her. "Bella—"

"I can't bear it, Maclean. I can't let you do this to me."

"Do what, Bella?"

"Come and go as if you were visiting a distant relative. If you don't mean to stay, then don't do this to me. Don't do this to me."

Her voice wavered to a stop and she began to cry, deep wrenching sobs that broke his heart.

Maclean wrapped his arms around her. He had dreamed of her for so long, but this was no dream. Bella was soft and real, and she smelled like Bella, like blossom, sweet and feminine. He kissed her deeply, and his body was hard from missing her so. He knew he was being rough with her, but he couldn't help it. And maybe this was not the time for gentleness.

"My love, my darling Bella, it is *Samhain*. The door is open on this night to the spirits of the between-worlds, and all who seek to pass through. I am a mortal man now, Bella, and 'tis dangerous for me, but I had to come. I have taken this journey for *you*."

"For me?" she whispered.

"I canna live my life without you. I need you beside me."

Bella lifted her head. "You want to take me back to 1746? But . . . is that possible, Maclean?"

He heard the aching need in her voice, the need he understood all too well.

"Aye, it is possible. The *Fiosaiche* showed me how, but I would no' care if she refused me. I canna . . . I *willna* live my life without you."

It was the second time he had said that. She took a shaky breath and smiled, stroking his rough cheek with trembling fingers. "I think you're wrong about your *Fiosaiche*. She's a bit of a romantic. She was the one who enticed me here tonight."

He turned his head and kissed her palm, and then he kissed her lips. The heat of her mouth made him dizzy, and despite the long and difficult journey he had made to reach her, his body demanded he take her once more. What if she didn't want to come with him? What if this time would truly be their last?

With a groan he drew her down to the ground and, removing his plaid, spread it for them. He filled his hands with her lush curves, murmuring his love, stroking her with his tongue. Bella clung and cried out and, when he slid inside her welcoming body, drew his head to hers and kissed him with long, deep kisses.

"I dreamed this, once," she whispered. "I dreamed of us lying together and the sky full of strange color."

Maclean smiled against her lips. "Then mabbe it was always meant to be," he said. "Mabbe you were dreaming of your future . . . or your past."

Afterward, they lay with their arms about each other, not feeling the cold with his plaid wrapped about them.

"I have spoken to the women," he said, his voice serious. "I have promised not to follow Ishbel, as I should have done the first time. But it is no' safe in Loch Fasail,

Bella. I dinna know if I will be arrested, or what will happen to me if I am. So far the English have stayed away, but I dinna trust Auchry."

"I don't care about Auchry, or the English."

"I am telling you so you have no illusions. If you come with me, then you come to a place where life is uncertain. We may only have a week together, we may have years. I canna promise—"

"I don't care," she repeated, and propped herself up on one elbow, staring down into his face. Her hair tickled him as it fell forward, and she tucked it behind her ear. "I want to come back with you. I belong with you. I realize, Maclean, that I've always belonged in the past. All my life I've felt like a square peg in a round hole, but until now I never knew why. I understand the dangers I'll face. I've seen through others' eyes what life is like in the eighteenth century and I have no illusions. It doesn't matter, I will relish it. I'll live every moment and be thankful that I have the chance to live it with you. And if something happens, if you're arrested, then I'll see that your people are safe. I'll care for them, Maclean, until you come home again."

He cupped her cheek in his big hand, the calluses rough against her soft skin.

"Then you'll be the wife of my hand as well as my heart."

"Can I . . . can we do that?"

"Of course." He sat up, drawing her with him. He shook out his plaid and put it back on, stretching his muscles and then turning to her with a grin.

Bella put her hands on her hips. "Maclean, how will you explain me to your people?"

"I won't." He raised an arrogant eyebrow. "I am the Black Maclean, and I dinna have to explain mysel' to anybody, remember? But dinna worry. You are my sweetheart, my love, and the Macleans of Fasail will love you, too. How could they no'?"

She laughed and shook her head at him, and he bent to kiss her again with all the longing and love in him.

"Ah, Arabella," he said, "I am a verra, verra happy man."

"Is it far?" she asked, glancing at the stones, thinking of the doorway.

"Aye, 'tis quite a way and some of it is no' verra nice, but I will protect you."

There was a strange wavering darkness between the two uprights. A shadow. Last time she had entered the between-worlds it was against her will, through the doorway in the loch, and she'd nearly died. Could she really risk it again?

Bella turned her gaze back to Maclean and realized he was holding out his hand to her.

"You dinna have to come," he said quietly, his pale eyes fixed on hers, his handsome face somber. "I would no' blame you."

Bella slid her fingers into his, her barely tamed Highlander. "I want to," she said firmly.

Maclean smiled and then he drew her toward the doorway to the between-worlds. "Let's go home," he told her, his voice echoing slightly, and then there was a rumbling sound, like a heavy portal closing, and nothing.

Loch Fasail lay as desolate as the meaning of its name, apart from a great eagle that rose suddenly from the roof of the cottage and went sailing into the sky. Briefly the dark winged shape was silhouetted against the colors of the aurora borealis, and then she, too, was gone.

Epilogue

The Fiosaiche strode through her cathedral.
Morven Maclean had been given his second chance,
time had been rearranged, and despite what Arabella
Ryan believed, it was not difficult. A stitch, a tuck, and
the thing was done. Unless you knew the seam was
there, you'd never even notice it. And Arabella and
Morven were together and happy, just as she had always planned for them to be.

"It's not as if I'm doing any harm," she said to herself, her voice an echo in the cool shadows of the great
church. "Ishbel was wrong. The Lords of the Universe
wouldn't mind, even if they knew about my interference."

She almost believed it.

The air held a tantalizing memory of flowers and incense, and there was no more sound except the swish of
her new cloak—deep red and bright as the flame of her
hair—and the soft breathing of her sleeping warriors.

Her favorites.

Each awaiting his turn.

With a smile of anticipation, the sorceress turned through an archway decorated with twining stone vines and carvings of odd little creatures. This was just one of many chapels, each one occupied. A beam of something like sunlight shone through the tiny round window high above, illuminating the face of the sleeping man who lay like an effigy on top of his own tomb.

For a moment the sorceress studied him.

Brown hair with a touch of gold, long and falling untidily across his forehead. A strong masculine face with the mouth now relaxed rather than curved in its usual cynical curl. Hazel eyes hidden beneath closed eyelids and almost feminine lashes. Handsome, yes. In his day he was renowned for capturing the hearts of the women who crossed his path.

The sorceress recalled the words spoken of him by his friends: dashing and reckless, brave and true. They were words any man would be proud to own. And yet on his headstone was something very different:

NATHANIEL RAVEN
HERE LIES THE INFAMOUS RAVEN
WHO PUT FEAR INTO THE HEARTS
OF ALL WHO TRAVELED
THE HIGHWAYS OF CORNWALL,
AND WHO WAS SHOT DEAD,
IN THE YEAR OF OUR LORD 1814

So what had gone wrong?

How had Nathaniel Raven, gentleman, ended so ignominiously, shot down in the act of highway robbery, dying on a lonely stretch of road in Cornwall without anyone to mourn his passing?

Briefly she touched his cheek, her fingers light, but even that soft touch made him stir. As if he felt the power in her fingers, as if he knew his time had come. He would need help, but the sorceress had found a suitable mortal. It might be tricky and they all might fail, but that was not up to her.

"It is time, sweet Raven," the sorceress whispered.

She lifted her arms and began to chant the ancient incantation of waking, until the sound of her voice echoed like thunder in the chapel, and the very air crackled and sparked.

And the Raven opened his eyes.

Glossary of Gaelic Words
Used in the Story

Fiosaiche (sorceress or witch)—FISS-ich-uh

each-uisge (water-horse)—Yach-oosh-ka

claidheamh mor (broadsword)—Cl-aiv-mor

Loch Fasail (desolate lake)—Loch FAH-sal

Cailleach (woman)—Cal-yach

arisaid (plaid)—AH-rissej

trews (trousers)—trooz

Turn the page
for a sneak peek
at the next book in

Sara Mackenzie's

Immortal Warriors series,

Secrets of the Highwayman

Coming October 2006

Melanie Jones slowed the Aston Martin, creeping along the narrow lane. The vehicle almost brushed the hedges growing on either side, reducing her vision to the depth of the headlights forward or the taillights backward. She felt like she was in a tunnel, with only a strip of dark, star-strewn sky above. Was she even going the right way? The last sign was miles back and she hadn't seen another one since.

She'd never felt so completely alone.

Maybe she should turn back. There'd been a pub at the crossroads and the thought had entered her mind to stop and stay there for the night, but then she'd decided it would be best to just get to her destination, and then she could wake up tomorrow morning at Ravenswood, ready to begin work.

Now she regretted she had been so dedicated.

She longed for her neat, familiar office with an actual physical ache. Melanie Jones was a solicitor with the firm of Foyle, Haddock and Williams, which had a reputation for getting things done in an orderly fashion. Everything in its place, no surprises, everything . . . comfortable.

People said that about her. You knew where you were with Melanie Jones. Others, less kind, called her a control freak. Melanie preferred to think that she lived her life just as she wanted it, the rough edges smoothed off, every possible deviation noted and sidelined. Her childhood had been a nightmare of uncertainties, and when she left home, she promised herself she would never have to worry about the inconsistencies of life again.

And now here she was, deep in Cornwall, driving a car she loathed because her Ford Escort was being repaired and her boss had insisted she take his Aston Martin. Sensible Melanie, driving a car made famous by James Bond, into the dark depths of Cornwall.

The car crept forward and the hedges abruptly gave way to a gray stone wall on one side and a dense wood on the other. She hit a pothole, and as her headlights tilted, there was a brief view over the wall and across a field, and then the road widened enough to make her feel less claustrophobic.

Maybe it would be all right after all. She'd keep going until she found a signpost and then she'd decide whether to carry on or turn back to the pub. Maybe there'd be another pub close by. With luck, the worst was behind her and Ravenswood was just around the next corner.

Melanie sped up in anticipation, just as something big and black ran in front of her car.

She slammed on the brakes and was jolted violently

forward, bruising her ribs against the steering wheel. The car engine stalled and for a moment Melanie sat, stunned, wondering what had run in front of her and whether she had hit it. She blinked to clear her vision, ignored her throbbing ribs, and peered through the windshield.

A dog. A hound. Bigger by far than a Great Dane and coal black. It sat on its haunches in the middle of the lane, facing the car, ears pricked, perfectly still. It was looking right back at her, the gleam of the headlights reflecting in its oily, dark eyes.

Melanie couldn't move.

There was something strange about the hound, something frightening. Its size was intimidating, but there was a stillness to it. And the way it stared back into her eyes, as if it were aware of her as a person. Melanie became conscious of the utter silence all around them.

Maybe I'm imagining it.

She blinked again, but the hound was still there.

Waiting.

The thought popped into her head. It *did* look as if it were waiting for something. She cast a nervous glance sideways at the woods. The trees were close together, twisted, bending like old widows gossiping, forming a wall of blackness. Anything could be in there, watching her, preparing to pounce.

One thing was for certain, she needed to get out of there.

Melanie gave the car horn a long blast. In the eerie silence, the sound was very loud, but the black hound didn't even flinch. Her heart thumping, her hands shaking, she sounded it again. Still the thing wouldn't move.

"All right then, if that's the way you want it." She fumbled with the ignition key. The powerful motor started. The black hound didn't take its eyes off her as she began to inch forward toward it. The car moved closer and the animal still didn't move. The big black head was higher than the hood of the car, high enough that the gleaming eyes were on the same level as her own.

This was worse than before, when at least there had been some distance between her and the hound. Now it loomed over her.

"Good God, what now?"

The car bumper must be almost knocking against the animal's body. She braked with a gasp.

"Will you please go away!"

A whistle came from the woods.

The black hound's head snapped around, and then it was on its feet. With one gigantic leap it cleared the lane and vanished into the thick wall of trees. And just like that it was gone.

Melanie ran a shaking hand through her short blonde hair.

So it must have been a real dog, she told herself with relief. Only a real dog responds to a whistle . . . doesn't it? For a moment she had been wondering if the hound was something else. Something like Conan Doyle's creation. Hadn't she read somewhere that he'd taken *The Hound of the Baskervilles* from west country folklore? The ghostly, demonic black hound that ran across the moors in the night, seeking . . .

"Seeking what?" Melanie muttered. "London solicitors traveling in Aston Martins on business to out-of-the-way places? It's probably someone's pet."

With her hands still shaking, she drove forward again, this time picking up speed. There was a sense of relief in leaving behind her the spot where she had seen the hound, and the woods didn't follow the lane for very long. They tapered off, and she was glad to see them go. Less atmospheric wilderness was just fine with her. Soon she was in open meadows, with only a stone wall continuing to keep her company on one side of the lane.

No houses, no lights. And no road signs. She'd have to turn back after all, Melanie told herself. The idea wasn't a comfortable one, it would mean returning to the spot she had just left. Even the thought of a good night's sleep and proper directions wasn't enough to raise any enthusiasm for that.

"Then I'll keep going. There must be something up ahead."

Clearly the caretaker at Ravenswood hadn't been up to the task of giving sound directions. Eddie, was that his name? He'd sounded about a hundred years old on the crackly phone line, as old as Miss Pengorren when she died in the London nursing home and left her personal affairs in the hands of Foyle, Haddock and Williams. Melanie, as their junior representative, was here to unravel those affairs.

Anyone else would have jumped at the chance for a week in Cornwall, but Melanie wasn't looking forward to it at all. Her life was just as she wanted it, and now she was being sent into unknown territory where anything might happen. How could she maintain her timetable? Well, she'd just have to try. And it was a brilliant opportunity to impress. From the day Melanie joined the prestigious firm she planned to make her future there. The traditional, slightly old-fashioned practice and unexciting clientele suited her perfectly. Nothing much happened, each day was similar to the next, no *surprises*—

A flicker of movement at the edge of her vision jolted her from her reverie. She turned to look, the horrible thought flashing through her mind that it was the black hound back again.

But no. It was a man. A man riding a horse beside her car. He was on the other side of the stone wall, in the field, and all the color had been leached out of him, as if he were drenched in moonlight. Except there was no moon; the night was particularly dark.

Shock made her cold as her eyes took in the details, while her brain floundered to make sense of them. The rider was bent low over his horse's neck and he wore a cloak that flew out behind him like wings, a tricorn hat and a mask covering half of his face. As Melanie stared he gave her a quick sideways glance and kicked his heels into his horse's sides. It was almost as if he were enjoying himself. As if they were having a race.

The car shuddered and Melanie swiveled, fixing her eyes unblinkingly on the road ahead. This couldn't be happening. First, the black hound like something from a horror movie, and now this.

She glanced at the man, hoping he was gone, and instead found he was almost level with her car. Something else caught her attention, and she realized it was the black hound. It was loping along behind the man and horse.

The whistle from the woods. It must have been . . .

this was its master . . . they were connected, the two of them.

Melanie moaned and did the only thing she could. She put her foot down hard on the accelerator. The motor roared, and she shot forward. She couldn't hear anything but the sound of the car, but she had a shaky feeling that there wasn't anything else to hear. No hooves striking the ground, no snap and flap of the rider's cloak, no breathing of man and beast. Nothing. Her companions were completely silent, as if they didn't really exist.

Incredibly, he was edging in front of her.

Panicking, she glanced at him again and realized he was looking back at her. His eyes through the slits in the mask were brilliant, warm, dangerous, and he grinned as if he were enjoying himself. Melanie found that her own heart was racing, but whether from sheer terror or a strange, unfamiliar excitement she didn't know. Whatever it was she felt incredibly *alive*.

The road was far too narrow and the surface too rough for her to be driving this fast, but recklessly Melanie accelerated again, speeding forward, trying to stay ahead of him.

The rider spurred his horse and, stooping even lower over its neck, prepared to give chase. A few strides and he was near her again, and then he was in front. She could see the back of his head beneath the tricorn hat and the ponytail he'd made of his dark hair. Beneath the cloak he was wearing an old-fashioned jacket and breeches. And then, with a final burst of strength and power, he outpaced her. He made it look breathtakingly easy instead of completely impossible.

She thought he'd ridden off then, leaving her behind,

but instead she watched in horrified fascination as he eased up on the reins until he was level with her again. He looked directly into her eyes, and that's when he did it. Winked.

Melanie gasped.

His teeth flashed white. He lifted one gloved hand and blew her an extravagant kiss.

Melanie slammed on the brakes, but even as her instincts reacted, her brain was telling her the man and horse were already gone. The road was empty.

For the second time tonight she sat in silence, heart pounding, hands clenched on the wheel. She tried to see to where he had disappeared, peering into the darkness, but there was nothing. All about her was absolutely *nothing*.

He must have ridden across the field on the other side, she thought desperately. He must have escaped that way. But she knew he hadn't. One moment he'd been here, beside her, grinning into her eyes like a madman, and the next . . . he was gone.

Melanie started the car again, and as she did, she saw there was a signpost next to the bumper. The paint was fresh and new and easy to read, and it was pointing ahead.

RAVENSWOOD 2 MILES.